The Blue Rose

THE BLUE ROSE

Anthony Eglin

Thomas Dunne Books
St. Martin's Minotaur
New York

THOMAS DUNNE BOOKS.
An imprint of St. Martin's Press.

Excerpts on pp. 27–8 are from *The Ultimate Rose Book* © Stirling Macoboy,
published by Harry N. Abrams, Inc., New York.

www.minotaurbooks.com

Library of Congress Cataloging-in-Publication Data

Eglin, Anthony.
   The blue rose / Anthony Eglin.—1st U.S. ed.
      p. cm.
   ISBN 0-312-32870-2
   EAN 978-0312-32870-2
   1. Rose culture—Fiction. 2. Gardeners—Fiction. 3. Gardening—
Fiction. 4. England—Fiction. I. Title.

PS3605.G53B55 2004
813'.6—dc22   2004056210

First published in Great Britain by Constable,
an imprint of Constable & Robinson Ltd

10 9 8 7 6 5 4 3 2

Chapter One

Life begins the day you start a garden.
                                    Chinese proverb

She woke to a murder of crows.

The noisy fluttering and cawing came from an entire family of them, as they took off from the top of a towering cedar in the meadow behind the wall.

Kate Sheppard yawned, stretched and sat up on the rickety old white bench. How long had she been napping, she wondered. Rubbing her eyes, she gazed up at the birds, now black specks disappearing in the hazy distance.

A murder of crows. Who thought that one up?

A parliament of owls; a mustering of storks . . . an exaltation of larks.

An exaltation of larks. That, she decided, was her favourite.

Why on earth did she retain such useless trivia? She was getting as bad as Alex, her husband – he was a veritable repository of frivolous facts, figures and minutiae, always bringing them up at dinner parties.

Kate yawned again. It was unusually warm for the time of year. She felt like taking another forty winks. Glancing down between the slats of the seat, she noted flakes of white paint on the ground. Another item for the 'to do' list. She reached into the canvas bag beside her and pulled out a small notebook with a pen clipped to it. *Repair and paint white bench by Japanese maple,* she wrote under the last line of the neatly printed list of items on the second-to-last page of the book. Since they had bought the old house the list had become something of a joke. Every day it got longer but few lines were ever crossed out. Alex was convinced they would be octogenarians before her zillion projects were completed.

Kate could recall in precise detail the events of that morning when she and Alex had stumbled on The Parsonage, a small nineteenth-century country house on the edge of the village of Steeple Tarrant in Wiltshire. With its high-walled garden that covered more than two acres, it had made a powerful impression on both of them. She still didn't know what it was that made her ask Alex to stop the car and back up as they were leaving the village early that Sunday back in March. She hadn't seen the discreet For Sale sign when they first drove by, but there it was. With nobody in sight and few cars on the road at that time of day, they had both taken turns peering over the high wall. With scarves up to their chins, shivering in the hoar-frosted silence of the sleeping village, they had stared in disbelief at a real-life version of the sketches Alex had been drawing over the past months. Sketches of their ideal country home. To see so many details replicated had been positively spooky.

A surrounding wall of russet-coloured brick some eight feet tall concealed the honey-gold stone structure from the street. Two weathered stone pillars, each with a lichen-crusted stone ball on top, flanked the driveway. Intricately scrolled iron gates – their once shiny black paint now chipped and dulled – rested permanently in the open position, the lower rails on each side anchored in a dense tangle of dark-leaf periwinkle that fringed the sandy drive. Set high in the left-hand pillar was a tarnished bronze plaque. Engraved on it in Roman type were the words, OLD STEEPLE TARRANT PARSONAGE. The villagers, they found out later, simply called it The Parsonage.

Alex, an architect, was smitten by the house, blathering on with phrases like 'sympathetic alterations', 'integrity' and 'reflective of the period'. Kate had instantly fallen in love with the garden. The house was nice, but it was the enchanting old garden that made her heart race. It was exactly what she'd always dreamed of owning.

On that bleak morning the only colours in evidence had been various shades of green, where the sheltered sides of evergreen shrubs, box and yew hedging, the leathery leaves of evergreen clematis and jasmine had outwitted the uncharitable frost. Save for them, she might have been looking at an old silver-print photo. In spite of its neglected state, there was no mistaking the garden's ambitious design. With its mature trees and shrubs, mellow brick and stonework, thick yew hedging, different levels and shifting viewpoints, it had obviously once been a garden of considerable importance. Such gardens take many years in the making.

Immediately below her, matted tangles of climbing rose canes hugged the inside of the wall. At their base, some of the main canes were thicker than Kate's arm. Farther along, the wall was given over to espaliered fruit trees. A wide border that ribboned the garden's perimeter was scattered with twiggy mounds and dark clumps of dead vegetation. Rose bushes, dotted here and there, resembled stark miniature trees. Closer to the house were several lattice structures and a long pergola festooned with silhouetted vines.

At that telling moment, Kate knew that The Parsonage would be their home.

Two months and a few days later the house was indeed theirs. Despite Kate's taking the week off, moving and settling in took longer than anticipated. Any worries they might have had earlier, about their furniture fitting in, were unfounded. With few exceptions, all the pieces from their two-storey house in Bath – most of them antique – slipped into place as if they'd been there for years. A spell of unusually showery weather hadn't prevented Kate from making several exploratory trips around the garden.

Now – three weeks after they'd moved in – the moment she had been waiting for had finally arrived. They were going to begin the daunting task of restoring the garden to its former glory. No more just looking and making notes – they were going to map the garden, begin cutting back, raking and shovelling, and start the lengthy clean-up job. Finally they'd get a true idea of just what they were dealing with. The night before, Alex had agreed – after some coaxing and a couple of glasses of wine – that, as long as the weather held up, they would devote the entire day to the garden.

They had awakened to blue skies. A day alive with the earthy smells and sounds of summer. A perfect June day for exploring the garden and starting to catalogue its over-grown contents. She'd already made a note in her book to ask her friend, Vicky, to help identify the many roses scattered throughout the garden. A few still had their original markers, but most of the roses were unknown, the markers having long since been buried or displaced. Vicky Jamieson was one of the owners of a successful nursery called Holly Hill in the neighbouring county of Berkshire. Way back, Vicky had helped establish the garden at the Sheppards' home in Bath, and since that time had become their gardening guru and closest friend.

Over breakfast they divided the property into eight distinct sections, each named and numbered on a plan drawn by Alex. Kate would start by conducting a recce of the entire garden, making notes as she went along. Alex, the self-professed 'black thumb' in the family, would start on a general clean-up.

'And whatever you do, Alex,' she had said with a smile and wag of the finger, as they were about to leave the house, 'don't cut anything or pull anything up!'

Legs stretched out, hands clasped behind her head, Kate lolled on the bench, waiting for Alex to show up. After two hours of wandering around the garden, she was enjoying the break, drinking in the surrounding loveliness. The last

several days had been warm, and a myriad of roses, perennials, shrubs and vines had exploded in a breathtaking
spectacle of beauty. Their brilliant petals and seductive
perfumes were the signposts pointing the way to pollen
and nectar for bees, butterflies, and all the flying creatures
responsible for most of the pollination essential to a
garden's survival.

She was aware of a sudden shifting of light. The scene
grew dappled as the sun dodged in and out of the fleecy
clouds moving in. It was definitely getting cooler. She'd
noticed lately that the garden was beginning to exert a
subtle influence on her. It had a pleasurable way of
intensifying her emotions, a bewildering sway over her
that she found impossible to explain. When she had insisted
to Alex that there was something very special – even spirit-
ual – about The Parsonage he had simply shrugged and
wisecracked something about Shirley MacLaine.

Where was he, anyway? Perhaps she should go and see
how he was doing.

As if on cue she heard a noise down the path. She turned
to look.

In a leather-gloved hand Alex carried a machete.
Loppers and a coil of rope dangled from his belt. He was
wearing an Aussie-style straw hat with the cord dangling
under his chin. Asp, their little Sealyham terrier, bobbed
along behind nipping at his heels.

She threw her head back and laughed. 'The Temple of
Doom's that way,' she said, pointing up the path.

He smiled. 'Well, Kate, you've got to admit, it is a
bloody jungle we're dealing with!'

'Well, nobody can accuse you of not being prepared.'

'A lot of good it does me,' he sighed. 'It'll take a bloody
lifetime to sort out this garden of yours. I've been working
half the morning on one measly corner, and it still looks
like I've done bugger all.'

She patted the bench next to her. 'Dump that stuff and
come over here, darling.'

Discarding his tools, Alex sat down heavily, took off his
hat and wiped his brow.

'Careful,' said Kate, as the bench wobbled. 'It's a bit shaky.'

He smiled. 'It's like me, it needs some love and attention.'

'Later,' she purred, kissing him on the cheek.

They talked for several minutes. Finally, Alex got up, plonked the hat on his head, and started to gather his tools. Taking his wristwatch from his pocket, he glanced at it. 'Almost eleven. How does lunch about noon sound?'

Kate hesitated. 'How about one o'clock?'

'I suppose I can hold out till then. You might want to keep an eye out for circling buzzards, though.'

Smiling, she eyed the red handle of the pruning shears protruding from his back pocket. 'Remember, don't prune anything or pull anything out, unless you're absolutely positive it's a weed. Promise?'

'Don't worry, I won't. You go and talk to the roses,' he said, pecking her on the cheek. 'See you at the house,' he added, walking off up the path.

'Don't joke, now,' she shouted after him. 'Prince Charles talks to his flowers all the time, you know!'

Smiling to herself, she watched him disappear round the curve of the path. The way he walked, with a sense of purpose and a rolling of the shoulders, had always reminded her of John Wayne. She thought back to the first time they'd met; she'd found it very hard to fathom him out. She recalled being more intrigued than smitten. At first, he gave the impression of being almost saturnine, yet there was something decidedly manly in his face and his demeanour. She had soon discovered that the sober countenance was deceptive, as if he cultivated it solely for the purpose of masking a gentleness and good humour that characterized his true nature. When she had managed to coax a smile out of him and make him laugh, he turned into another person completely. Gone was the stern gaze and distant manner, his face lit up like a flash of light on a crystal. Their marriage was now in its ninth year. She was very lucky, she reminded herself. She loved him, very much.

*   *   *

Dismissing her parting salvo with the flick of a wrist, Alex kept walking. Kate and her gardening! What on earth did she see in it all? How could she possibly derive such sheer pleasure and fulfilment from planting a puny sprig of vegetation and waiting an eternity for it to grow – then, after its pitifully short life, stand by and watch it perish? And those roses she loved so much – to him, they were downright ugly. Granted, the flowers themselves were beautiful and most of them smelled nice. But the plants themselves? As far as he was concerned, they were little more than hideous thorny sticks.

He glanced back at her. Despite her lack of make-up, frayed jeans and faded Les Mis T-shirt, she looked positively fashionable. Her hair was ash blonde and shoulder length. She was slender but not quite tall enough to be termed willowy. Except for her eyes, her features were unremarkable. But the eyes were inescapable, wide-spaced and aqueous grey-green, making it hard to look away.

He had now reached the long border where he'd been working earlier. He'd far rather be doing something else – playing tennis, or perhaps tinkering with his old Alfa Romeo Spider Veloce – but he had promised the day to Kate. He paused for a moment, sighed, then got back to work.

After an hour and a half of raking layers of rotting leaves and debris from the border, hacking away dead limbs from shrubs and trees, and cutting back wayward canes on ramblers – Kate had approved his doing that – he decided it was time for a breather. In any case, the wind was picking up and it was starting to look like rain. He eyed the border. The results of his work were noticeable. Things looked much tidier. Kate would be pleased with the improvement. He was about to turn and walk back to where he'd left his tools when he stopped.

The area where he'd finished working dead-ended in a brick wall several feet taller than he was. To his left, the wall took a sharp curve and disappeared. Since he'd only walked through the garden two or three times it was understandable that he hadn't noticed it before. Might as well do a little exploring, he thought to himself.

He followed the old brick wall, occasionally placing his palm on its gritty surface to steady himself. Now he could see that it fell back, to create a crescent some thirty feet deep and sixty long – a hidden bed invisible to anyone on the path. Despite the shade cast by the curving wall, and the shrubs and small trees along the flat side of the crescent, enough light and sunshine penetrated the foliage for the flowers in front of the wall to grow into a colourful jumble. Most of them appeared to be roses. Roses with plump nodding blooms of dusky pink, coral, carmine, damask and ivory. They reminded him of an old Flemish painting – the kind painted on a dark background.

Alex stood, motionless, for what must have been at least a minute, fascinated by the composition: the luminescence, the gradations of shadow, the muted colours and textures.

As he turned to go back to the path he caught a glimpse of a foreign colour, way in the back. No more than a flash, it was nevertheless electrifying.

He stopped.

It had disappeared.

He swayed to the left, then slowly to the right, and – there it was again.

A trick of the light, surely. That colour. . .

He eased his way in through the shrubs to take a closer look. Something scratched at his arm – he brushed away the thorn stuck into his skin. Pushing the arching cane aside, he halted, then stepped back a pace. What on earth. . .?

That couldn't be right, could it?

Goose pimples tingled across his neck and scalp. Even with his scant knowledge of plants Alex knew he was looking at something very peculiar – bizarre, in fact.

He moved forward and reached out his hand to touch it.

'Jesus Christ,' he whispered. *'Is this real?'*

Chapter Two

*Great discoveries do not inevitably result from research
and design. Sometimes they are luck . . . stumbled upon.
That is the romance of the game . . . the dramatic suspense.
On any dewy morning a miracle may occur.*

Eugene Boerner, pre-eminent hybridizer,
Jackson and Perkins

'I think the sun's got to you,' Kate panted, as she hurried
to keep up with Alex. They were now running along the
path. What on earth was making him act so un-Alex-like?
He was now gripping her hand so fiercely that her fingers
were becoming numb. Thorns and branches ripped at her
shirt. She was about to yell at him, when suddenly he
stopped.

She almost ran into him.

'Alex, what on earth are you doing?' she said breath-
lessly. 'Have you gone bonkers?'

He was facing her now. His face had a strange look. She
had never, ever, seen him this agitated.

He took her other hand.

'Alex,' she began.

'Wait,' he said, holding up a hand. 'Eyes closed,
please.'

She sighed. 'All right.'

She closed her eyes and let him lead her no more than
a dozen paces. 'Alex, this is silly. . .' she started to protest,
when they stopped. He let go of her hand and stepped
behind her. She could now feel his hands on her shoulders,
his breath on her cheek.

'Eyes still closed?' he asked.

'Yes.'

'Open them now,' he whispered.

She did.

At first, what she saw made no sense. For a second, she thought her eyes were still adjusting to the light. Behind her, Alex was squeezing her shoulders.

'I wasn't hallucinating after all,' he murmured.

'It can't be – it's not possible,' she breathed.

'It is,' Alex said.

Standing shoulder height in front of them was a rose bush, thick with thorns and silky dark green leaves. It was covered with blooms the size of tennis balls – dozens of them. They were plump and perfectly formed.

They were blue.

A brilliant blue. Not lavender or mauve, but an electric sapphire blue.

Kate edged closer and knelt until her face was inches from one of the blooms. She gripped it lightly and gently tugged one of the petals.

'Oh – my – dear – God!' she said, quietly. 'It is real!'

Moving in closer she inhaled its fragrance. It was soft and velvety. More like jasmine than rose – but more complex, more intoxicating. It was too much: not only a blue rose, but one with a seductive perfume too.

'Alex,' Kate said, getting up, still staring hypnotically at the rose, 'this is not one of your silly pranks, is it?'

She barely heard his answer. 'Not this time.'

'You know, this is supposed to be genetically impossible. That's why there's never been a blue rose. Ever.'

Alex didn't answer. He was busy inspecting the thorns on the claret-coloured canes.

'I wonder how old it is?' Kate muttered. 'How long it's been growing here?'

'Looks pretty old to me, but then, what the hell do I know?' He stood up. 'God! Those thorns are like bloody needles.'

'Alex, listen to me. I don't think you realize the

significance of this. We're looking at a horticultural miracle.'

For a moment they stood in silence, their eyes fixed on the rose bush.

Alex took a sideways glance at Kate. 'What do you think we should do, then?'

'I'm really not sure.'

'Maybe we should ask Vicky to have a look at it. She'd know. Why don't we go up and call her at the nursery?'

Her eyes still glued on the rose, Kate paused before replying. 'You're right. Vicky would almost die if we were to tell her about this, but let's not rush our fences. I think we should sleep on it first.'

'Whatever you say.'

'Alex, if this is for real – and it certainly looks like it – I have a hunch that it could be worth an awful lot of money. But if word gets out we could have a major problem on our hands.'

'Why?'

'Can't you picture it? Everybody and his brother will be hammering on our door wanting to see it.'

'Then we'll just have to keep it a secret until we find out more about it.'

'Exactly.'

Neither of them spoke for a long moment.

Finally, Alex put his arm around Kate's waist and squeezed. 'Well, I think this is really exciting. Tell you what, let's go and have lunch. Then, afterwards, I'll come back down and take some photos. Not that anybody will believe them. Blue roses are only a click of the mouse with Photoshop.'

'True. But you're right, we should take some anyway.' Kate took his hand as she watched Asp sniffing the ground by the rose.

Alex smiled. 'I think we'd better get Asp out of there or he's going to be peeing away our fortune.'

'Come on, Asp,' she chuckled.

They took one more look at the mesmerizing sapphire blooms and then started back toward the house.

'One good thing,' said Alex, as they headed up the path, 'it's perfectly safe where it is and we've got all the time in the world to think about it.'

Kate simply nodded.

He put his arm around her shoulders. 'Anyway, what makes a blue rose so valuable? It's only a horse of a different colour, isn't it?'

'No, it's not, believe me. I read an article about it. Scientists have spent years trying to create a blue rose, without success. The explanation was far too technical for me, but the gist of it was that they couldn't isolate the gene from another blue flower – I believe it was a petunia – and pass it on to a rose.'

'They're called blue genes, I suppose.'

'Very funny.'

A squirrel skipped across the path in front of them, hotly pursued by a yapping Asp.

'I bet the Internet will turn up some information,' said Alex.

'You're probably right. I'll check the library, too.'

'I wonder how much it's worth?'

'To a company selling roses, a great deal, I would imagine.'

'Hmm.' Alex squeezed her shoulder. 'Maybe fixing up the house is going to happen sooner than we expected.'

'Could be,' Kate said. 'We'll soon find out.'

Chapter Three

Won't you come into the garden? I would like my roses to see you.

Richard Sheridan

Kate had a hard time sleeping. She woke Alex several times as she tossed and turned, visions of the blue rose invading her mind. At some point during her many waking moments she recalled an article that she'd read some time ago about roses. It was devoted entirely to propagating and hybridizing, written by one of Britain's foremost experts. The more she thought about it, the more convinced she was that their next move – rather than talk to the people at Kew Gardens or the National Rose Society, as Alex had suggested – should be to engage the services of an individual expert. In doing so, there would be far less chance of word leaking out. The professor who wrote the article could be the very person they were looking for. Hopefully he could be persuaded to examine the rose, authenticate it, and, more important, give them advice on what they should do.

As the first glimmer of daybreak outlined the windows, she got out of bed and went down to the kitchen to make tea. There was no need to turn on the lights. The recently lime-washed walls were already bathed in the dawn light. With a steaming hot mug of tea in her hand, she went out to the living room and began rummaging through a stack of old gardening magazines till she found the one she was looking for. Then, with the magazine rolled under her arm

17

and her mug of tea, she walked out into the garden and headed for the crescent to take another look at the rose.

The songbirds were in full chorus as she stood facing the rose, her hands clasped around the mug for warmth. It seemed even more seductive, certainly more real, in the cool grey morning light. How on earth had it happened? It must have something to do with the house's previous owners. Hadn't they created the garden? Surely they must have known about the rose. During the negotiations for the sale of the house, neither she nor Alex had met the former owner. All they knew was that she was an elderly widow, a Mrs Cooke. Perhaps she rarely ventured into the garden or was an invalid. But that wouldn't necessarily explain it either. She or her deceased husband obviously enjoyed the garden. Judging by the size of it, the bush had certainly been growing in the same spot for more than just a couple of years. One of them should have known about it. On the other hand, the entire garden had become so overgrown that the chance of stumbling on the rose would have been unlikely. On top of that, the rose was extremely well hidden. After all, she and Alex hadn't spotted it during their several walks through the garden. There was another thing, too. She and Alex had no idea how long it bloomed. If it was like most of the old garden rose varieties it would only put out roses once a year, the flowers sometimes lasting for as little as three to four weeks. After that, nobody would know it was a blue rose bush. Despite all this, she had an odd feeling that *somebody* must have known about it.

She turned her back on the rose and walked along the path to the white bench. It wobbled and creaked as she sat down. Placing her mug of tea beside her, she opened the magazine and began reading.

'Kate!'

She sat up, startled. It was Alex, calling from the house. Glancing at her watch, she was astounded to see that she had been in the garden for over half an hour. She picked up her mug, swishing the dregs of cold tea alongside a clump of hardy geraniums, and walked up the path toward the house.

'I've got a meeting this morning with that fussy Hendrickson woman,' Alex said, putting his teacup down, dabbing his mouth with a paper napkin. 'We're going to revise the upstairs plan for the twentieth time. Never known anybody so indecisive as that blasted woman! God knows why she wants three loos – *three* mind you – upstairs. Her bladder must be completely shot!'

'At least her bank account isn't shot. She's paying her bills, isn't she?' Kate asked.

'Guess so,' Alex said, smoothing his hair.

The evening before they had checked out 'blue roses' on the Internet and had quickly found out that no such rose existed, and that scientists were working hard to make the dream of a true blue rose a reality. None of the few sites on the subject had offered any speculation as to the value of the very first blue rose.

Alex picked up his canvas briefcase and lifted his leather jacket off the back of the chair. 'Any more thoughts about the rose, Kate?'

'Yes, I do, as a matter of fact,' she said. 'I've got an interesting idea.'

'Whenever you say, "I've got an interesting idea," I get nervous. All right, what is it?'

'There's no need to look at me like that. Don't worry, you don't have to do anything. It's just that I was thinking about what we discussed yesterday – having an individual, an expert, look at it. Last night, I thought of exactly who that might be.' She held up the magazine, page open to the article. It included a picture of a man with a mop of white hair. 'Dr Lawrence Kingston,' she announced.

'A rose expert, I take it?'

'And then some. According to the article, he's the foremost specialist in the world in the business of agro ecology, plant-pollinator relationships, genetics, all that kind of stuff. For years, he was a professor and head research botanist at Edinburgh University.'

Alex studied the page more closely. 'He looks quite rakish. Love the bow tie.'

'Well, if anybody's going to know how a blue rose ended up in our garden, he certainly should,' Kate said, closing the magazine and placing it on the table.

'And how much it's worth, hopefully.'

'I'm sure he'll have some thoughts on that, too. The big question is whether he can be persuaded to come down and take a look at it.'

'Wouldn't he leap at the chance?'

'There's no question he will – if we tell him it's blue. But I don't think we should tell him that on the phone.'

'Why is that?'

'Because, right off, he's going to think we're a couple of crackpots. Besides, we can't risk his leaking the word out before he's seen the rose – before we get to find out what kind of person he is. Supposing he was – well, less than honest.'

'I see your point. Anyway, if anyone can persuade him, you can, Kate.'

Kate kissed him on the cheek. 'I'll give the magazine a call today, see if I can reach the professor. I'll check out the library, too. See what they have on the subject. See you tonight, darling.'

'Good luck with the professor, then,' Alex said, with a wink, as he walked out the door.

From the kitchen window Kate watched Alex get into the Alfa and drive off. Asp gave up his usual yapping pursuit of the car and turned back toward the house – but not before lifting a leg on one of Kate's recently planted euphorbias.

The front of Kate's shop in Bath was painted a shade of green so dark that on a cloudy day it appeared black. In rich contrast, raised serif letters in burnished gold stretched the width of the façade. They read: SHEPPARD'S PIE

ANTIQUES. The name had been Alex's idea. She liked it so much that immediately after they were married she adopted it. It was one of a cluster of antiques shops located in the heart of the city. Kate's neighbour on one side was a dealer who specialized in antique clocks. On the other side was a shop with whimsical window displays featuring old dolls and collectible toys. Kate's shop featured English and French country furniture and *objets d'art*. While Alex would often make unkind remarks about the craftsmanship and exorbitant prices of some of her more rustic pine purchases, he did admit that she was a good dealer. She had a good nose for finding quality items and an excellent eye for bargains. With her amiable personality, good looks and quick mind for business it was no surprise that the shop had shown a respectable, if inconsistent, profit in each of its nine years of operation. Once in a while she couldn't resist ribbing Alex, getting back at him for some of his rude comments about the quality of her purchases. Occasionally she would drop a comment: 'You know that hand-painted pine chest – the one you said looked like it was made of firewood and painted with a toothbrush – well, I just sold it for fifteen hundred pounds.'

It was nine thirty on Friday morning. With no customers in the shop, Kate picked up the phone and dialled the number of *English Gardening* magazine.

'Hello, *English Gardening*.' The woman's voice was cheerful and not at all businesslike. 'This is Molly Chapman, how may I help you?'

'My name's Kate, Kate Sheppard. I'm interested in contacting Dr Lawrence Kingston. He wrote a story on roses in your May issue, last year.'

'Kingston?' She paused briefly. 'Oh, yes, I'm well aware of him – the chap with the mop of silver hair. A real character, that one. Former professor of botany – among other things.'

Kate frowned for a moment. A real character? Other things? What did that mean?

'That's him,' she said. 'Could you give me an address or phone number where he can be reached?'

'I'm sorry, we're not permitted to divulge information of a personal nature concerning any of our staff or contributing writers. I'm sure you understand. What I *can* do, though, is attempt to contact him and pass on a message along with your phone number. We do that quite frequently for our readers.'

'That would be super. Yes. As I mentioned, the name's Kate Sheppard.' She spelled it out and gave her phone number.

'Is there any message? The reason you want him to call you?'

Kate wasn't prepared for that question. 'No – *yes*,' she stammered. She had no time to think. 'It's about – about a rose bush we have in our garden that's got three different colour roses on it,' she blurted.

'That sounds a trifle unusual.'

'That's what we thought. It's *quite* colourful,' Kate fibbed. 'We were hoping Dr Kingston might have an explanation.'

'I'm sure he will. Good luck, Kate, I'll pass on your message.'

Kate slowly put down the phone, and wiped a hand across her brow. 'You've done it now, old girl,' she muttered.

Not more than thirty minutes later, Kate was at the desk totalling the previous month's sales when the phone rang. She picked it up after the first ring.

'Sheppard's Pie Antiques, how may I help you?' she said in a breezy voice.

'Are you Kate Sheppard?'

'Yes.'

'This is Lawrence Kingston. I'm responding to your call to Molly Chapman at *English Gardening*.' His voice was deep and mellifluous, each word carefully but unaffectedly articulated. It fairly boomed out with an authority that took Kate off guard.

'Oh. Yes. Thank you so much for calling. Awfully kind of you.' She hoped she didn't sound as nervous as she felt. After all, she had indirectly told him a white lie – in this case, a three-coloured lie. Somehow, she would have to explain that. She swallowed and continued. 'Well, we – my husband and I, that is – would like to ask your advice. I read your article on roses, which was excellent, by the way. That's what prompted my call –'

Kingston politely interrupted. 'I see. So, young lady, what's all this twaddle about a three-coloured rose?'

Kate felt her cheeks begin to flush. She was glad that he couldn't see her face. 'Well, in all honesty, doctor,' she said, hoping that the salutation was correct, 'it's not a three-coloured rose – it's only one colour,' she gulped. Although she had rehearsed what she was going to say she knew she wasn't getting off to a very good start. She prayed he wouldn't just hang up on her. 'Actually, we'd like to show it to you. It's quite extraordinary, believe me.'

'So far, you're not making much sense, young woman. Has this *really* got to do with roses?'

'Yes – *yes*, it has. But not – not an *ordinary* rose,' she stammered. 'It's most certainly not one that's in any of the books. When you see it, you'll know why.'

'Do you know how many calls like this I get every month? Exasperating, so-called gardeners wanting to know what kind of roses they have growing at the bottom of their precious little gardens alongside their gnomes.'

Kate was taken aback by his churlish comment. 'We're not like that, at all. We have over two hundred roses in a very large garden in Wiltshire and I'm serious about gardening. And we *don't* have any gnomes,' she added huffily. To her surprise, she heard Kingston chuckle.

'I apologize,' he said, his voice now more cordial. 'Sometimes I get a touch too testy. Tell me more about this mysterious rose of yours then.'

'It *is* mysterious. *Very* mysterious, I might add.' Kate took a deep breath. 'I must ask you, first, to treat what I'm about to tell you, as *very* confidential. I must have your word on it.'

'I don't see any reason why not,' Kingston complied. 'Now you *have* got me intrigued.'

'Thank you, doctor. Here's what has happened. Yesterday, we found a very unusual rose in our garden at the house we bought recently. As I've already tried to convince you, it's so unusual – and don't laugh when I say this – it borders on the supernatural.'

She paused, trying to visualize Kingston's expression, wondering whether she was overdoing it. He said nothing, so she pressed on.

'I can assure you, it's a rose that's never, *ever*, been seen before. And we're not quite sure what we should do. About keeping it a secret – or letting pandemonium loose on the gardening world. I thought perhaps – well, maybe you could take a look at it and then help us decide how we should proceed. We don't mind paying for your time, of course.'

'I do hope this is not some kind of prank? And I *certainly* hope it's not one of those frightful lavender-coloured jobs.'

'No. Please believe me. It's not – on both accounts.'

'Then, what makes this particular rose so remarkable, might I ask?'

'I'd prefer not to have to tell you on the phone. I'd rather you saw it for yourself.'

Kate heard Kingston inhale deeply, followed by an indecisive, 'Hmmm.'

Kate adopted a change of tone, trying to walk the line between being too reticent and too forceful. 'Please believe me. If you can come down and take a look at it, I swear you won't be disappointed. In fact, if you can *honestly* tell me that your time has been wasted, my husband and I will pay you five hundred pounds and that will be the end of it. What do you think?'

'Well, Mrs Sheppard, you certainly present an intriguing proposition. I assume that this rose bush is in a place where it can't be seen? I mean by the public.'

'Right. It's in a walled garden. Well hidden.'

'Where is it? In Wiltshire, you say?'

'Yes, in Wiltshire, near Marlborough.'

'Who else knows about it?'

'As far as we know, only the two of us – and now, you,

of course.' Kate was starting to feel like a prime suspect being pumped by Chief Inspector Morse. 'We're being very careful to keep this a well-guarded secret. You'll see why. I'm not exaggerating when I say it could be the botanical discovery of the century. Maybe of many, many centuries.'

'Very well, Mrs Sheppard, you've convinced me. When I have a day free I'll come down and take a look at your rose.'

'Could you come on Saturday?' she said, knowing that she was pushing her luck. 'I'd like Alex – that's my husband – to be here.'

Kingston asked her to wait while he consulted his diary. 'Saturday – let me see – I think I can, as a matter of fact,' he replied. They agreed on a time. 'Give me your name again – and your address. Better give me a phone number, too.'

Kate provided Kingston with the information. Learning that he would be driving down from London, she gave him directions. Then she bade him goodbye and put the phone down.

'Whew,' she whistled. It had gone even better than she'd hoped. A smile broke across her face as she picked up the phone again to call Alex and give him the good news.

Chapter Four

I long to see the blue flower.
I can't get rid of the idea, it haunts me.
I never felt like this before.
It's as if I dreamed it years ago
Or had a vision of it in another world,
For who would be so concerned
About a flower in this world?

                                                    Novalis

'Hello, darling,' Kate said, looking up as Alex walked into the kitchen, throwing his jacket and briefcase on a chair. He looked tired. He was home later than usual – nearly eight o'clock. Fridays were often like that now.

'Hello, Kate.' He walked over and gave her a quick kiss.

She saw him glance at the oversized book open on the table in front of her.

'New recipe?' He closed his eyes and inhaled loudly through his nose. 'Let me guess – we're having caviar and blinis, seared foie gras with truffles, and pheasant under glass?'

'Not even close. It's something far better.'

'Better?'

'Yes, I found some information I think you'll find very interesting – about our new rose.'

'Really?'

'Yes, I got it at the library.' Kate riffled through the pages of the big book to the chapter where she had placed a marker. Though Alex was looking at it upside down, she knew it wouldn't be difficult for him to read the bold title: *The Ultimate Rose Book*.

'You'd better be sitting down.'

Alex raised his eyebrows but said nothing. He pulled up a chair and sat down facing her.

She glanced up at him. 'Listen to this. "The early Dutch discoverers of Australia were greeted with derision back home when they reported black swans in New Holland. Had they found *blue roses*, however, they would have not only been believed, but thought to have discovered a new Eden. It is odd, how humans have always dreamed of blue roses. In all the years when there were no yellow roses, or flame ones, no one seemed to miss them. Blue roses were the dream."' She paused to take a breath, glancing up to catch Alex's rapt gaze. She looked down again, tracing a finger across the page. 'Then it goes on about *The Arabian Nights* and a magician who turns roses blue. And a blue rose that is featured in one of Rimsky-Korsakov's ballets – and so on.' She continued reading for a few moments, but not aloud – then resumed reciting from the book. 'Yes, here we are, "*delphinidin*, the pigment that makes flowers blue, is absent from the rose, and indeed all its relatives in the Rosaceae" – et cetera, et cetera. . .' She picked up again, a paragraph later. '"Of course, there's always the million-to-one chance that a mutation will produce a *delphinidin*-bearing rose, just as a chance mutation some seventy years ago gave the rose the scarlet pigment *pelargonidin*." Then it talks about cornflowers – the same *cyanidin* pigment that makes the rose red – here we go – "the conditions within the flower are controlled by the DNA in the rose's chromosomes; interfering with them has not been something that, short of magic, we have been able to do." This is the part you'll like, Alex. "It will be a colossally expensive operation, but the financial rewards of success will be very great. The rose is the world's favourite flower; millions are sold each day in flower shops and when (and if) the blue rose arrives, the florists will be able to ask their own price for it. No doubt its creator will have patented their invention and will reap a huge, well-earned reward in royalties."' She looked up at him, trying not to look too smug. 'How about that?'

'Whew!' Alex whistled.

'Then it goes on to mention the inevitability of lawsuits related to patents, and so forth.'

'My God,' Alex breathed. 'We could become filthy rich.'

'Highly possible,' Kate replied, closing the book with a thump. 'I have a good feeling about our Dr Kingston. He'll know what to do. I'm sure of it.'

'What time is he coming tomorrow?'

'About noon.'

'Then I've got time to get in a good thirteen hours' sleep. A very early night,' Alex said, yawning. 'Which I seriously need.'

'No caviar before dinner, then?' Kate asked.

Alex's head whirled around. 'You don't, really – do you?'

'Well, I thought a little celebration might be in order.'

Kate stood and went to the refrigerator.

'*Voilà!*' She held up a small jar.

'I suppose I *could* be convinced to go to bed a little later,' Alex said.

'A wise decision,' Kate said, setting the jar down on the table. She turned back and took out a bottle of chilled champagne and the plate of chopped eggs, onion, sour cream and crackers she had prepared previously. 'Once dinner's over, I suppose I *could* be convinced to join you.'

Alex grinned, breaking into song: 'Caviar comes from the virgin sturgeon. The virgin sturgeon's a very fine fish. The virgin sturgeon needs no urgin', that's why caviar is my dish.'

'You're too much,' Kate giggled.

Saturday was hazy but clear with cirrus clouds drifting overhead. Kate was watering the hydrangeas in the terra-cotta pots edging the courtyard when she heard the car approaching. As she turned, a racing green Triumph TR4 with the top down rumbled into view.

'Ah,' she said to herself, setting down the watering can. 'Dr Kingston, I presume.'

Asp raced toward the car, yapping excitedly.

The Triumph crunched to a stop on the gravel alongside Alex's Alfa Romeo. She watched with amusement as Kingston extricated his lanky frame from the car's cramped confines. The picture hadn't really done him justice. He was more rugged than it had suggested.

A tangle of ivory-coloured hair unravelled over his collar. In contrast, dark bushy eyebrows jutted out over deep-set blue eyes. Though tall and lean, he still gave the impression of being physically powerful. There was a litheness about him that suggested an iron discipline concerning those habits and diets that cultivate paunches, spare tyres and jowls. To Kate, he appeared the very antithesis of the archetypal scholar. He was wearing an old suede jacket, a cream button-down Oxford shirt, and dark olive corduroy trousers. A bulky camera case hung from shoulder straps by his side. He took off his checked cap and tossed it like a frisbee into the car.

'Mrs Sheppard?' he inquired, as he approached her.

'Yes. Please call me Kate, Dr Kingston.'

Asp was sniffing at Kingston's trouser cuffs.

'Oh, and this is Asp.'

'Curious name.'

'My husband's idea of a joke. It stands for All Spare Parts.'

Kingston chuckled. 'Cute little fellow,' he said, bending down to pat the dog's head. 'And please call me Lawrence – all right?'

'I will,' she said, shaking his hand.

In his large grip her hand disappeared up to her wrist. When he smiled at her she noticed a ripple of creases fanning out at the corner of each eye.

'Welcome to The Parsonage,' Kate said, retrieving her hand. 'Alex and I really appreciate your coming down. I can assure you, you won't be disappointed.' She smiled.

'And thanks for bringing nice weather with you, too. It's been awfully soggy down here the last few days.' She gestured towards the house. 'Let's go inside. I'm sure you could do with a cup of coffee or perhaps a drink after such a long drive.'

Kingston nodded. 'Coffee would be nice. Thank you.'

He followed her into the house, stooping to clear the door beam. 'Lovely house. Mid-nineteenth century, isn't it?'

'1835, we've been told.'

'Most charming.'

'Alex is fixing something in the kitchen,' she said. 'He's really looking forward to meeting you.' She turned to Kingston and smiled. 'In all fairness,' she said, 'I should tell you that he's anointed himself the "black thumb" of the family. He's quite happy to leave most of the gardening to me.'

'I'll take that into account, Kate,' he said, following her into the kitchen.

After introducing Kingston to Alex and putting on the kettle, Kate showed Kingston into the living room.

They sat facing each other in the warm sunlight coming through the open windows.

'So, what makes this rose of yours so special?' Kingston inquired, relaxing into the upholstered wing chair.

She looked directly at him, her face expressionless, anticipating his reaction. 'It's blue,' she said, softly.

Kingston dropped his head down and shook it slowly from side to side. 'Oh, no – I was afraid of that. A purplish blue, I suppose. Mauve, eh?'

'No, it's *blue* – royal blue. Sapphire.'

'Are you serious? I take that back – of course you are,' he stammered.

Kate waited, suppressing her amusement, watching him regain his composure. For the next ten minutes she told him all about their recent purchase of the house and their discovery.

'And that brings us to you, Lawrence. But first let me get

the coffee. Then we'll go outside and you can see the rose. You're in for *quite* a shock.'

Kate and Alex stood silently, several paces back from the rose bush, as Kingston started his examination. They watched as he peered through a bone-handled magnifying glass, gently prodding and poking at various parts of the rose with stainless steel tweezers. Kate could not help but think of Sherlock Holmes. She pursed her lips tightly, barely managing to suppress the urge to giggle. A quick glance at Alex, who was grinning from ear to ear at the spectacle of the doctor's surgeon-like examination, didn't help matters.

After a while Kingston stepped back a few paces and stood, studiously tapping the magnifying glass on the palm of his left hand as he continued to stare intently at the rose bush. Placing the glass back into the pocket of his shabby jacket, he slowly stroked his chin, all the time gazing at the unearthly rose as if mesmerized by its enigmatic beauty.

Finally, he spoke.

'Extraordinary – most extraordinary,' he mumbled.

'How do you think it happened?' Kate asked, timidly.

'There's really no saying,' Kingston replied, methodically circling the rose. 'It appears to be an aberration of nature, which we've always been led to believe is genetically impossible.'

Alex was grinning. 'Then we get to keep the five hundred pounds?'

Kate could have kicked him.

Kingston simply cracked a weak smile and nodded.

Kate flashed Alex a disapproving look. 'How valuable do you think it is?' she asked.

'If it can be propagated – extremely so,' Kingston replied, tugging on his earlobe, lost in thought. 'Let me take a few snapshots,' he said, finally.

Kate and Alex waited patiently while Kingston used an entire roll of film, shooting the rose from every conceivable angle and focal length. 'That should do it,' he said, putting the camera back in its case.

'So, what do you think, Lawrence?' asked Alex.

Kingston looked at Alex and then across to Kate. It was evident that he was still preoccupied with the rose, groping for a suitable response. 'Well, first of all, there appears to be no question that the rose is genuine. And I've no doubt that it will be considered one of the greatest horticultural discoveries of all time.' His gaze drifted back to the rose, locking on to it. 'As to its value, it's anybody's guess. Let's just say that there are many individuals and companies that would go to extreme lengths to obtain the patent rights to a blue rose. The rewards could be staggering. But more important, is how the two of you handle this from now on. It's going to require considerable thought and a great deal of caution.'

'Where do we go from here?' asked Alex.

'That's going to require a lot of discussion. This is only the beginning of a long drawn-out process, I'm afraid.'

Kingston turned back to them. To Kate's surprise he was smiling. 'Not every day one runs into a blue rose,' he said. 'Bit of a jolt, I must say.'

'Well, why don't we take you for a walk through the garden and then we'll go back to the house,' said Kate. 'You're probably ready for some lunch, I would imagine?'

'Excellent. That would be very nice. We have much to discuss,' he replied.

Back in the house, Kate set off for the kitchen while Alex and Kingston went to chat in the living room. Earlier, Alex had decided to mark the occasion and celebrate the impending change in their fortunes by breaking out the good stuff – a bottle of Bordeaux that a client had given him several years ago.

Kingston's eyebrows rose when he saw the label. 'A Château Lafleur-Pétrus,' he exclaimed. 'You must have quite a cellar, Alex.'

'Yes, well–'

'What year is it?'

Alex picked up the bottle and studied the label. '1982,' he said.

'Good Lord!' Kingston exclaimed. 'That's an absolutely excellent year for a Pomerol – one of the best in the last three decades. And very drinkable, now. 1990 was excellent too, but still a little young to open yet.'

'Drinkable?'

'I should have said, ready to drink. The best Bordeaux wines take many years to develop in the bottle, and shouldn't be drunk until they have matured. '82 is plenty old enough, though.'

Alex picked up a corkscrew. 'Shall we?'

Kingston placed his hand on the bottle. 'An '82 – surely you're going to decant it, old chap. Where's your decanter?'

'Ah – we don't have one,' Alex replied.

Kingston's jaw dropped. 'Really?'

'Really,' Alex said, wondering just how humiliating his admission was sounding.

'In that case,' Kingston sniffed, 'you might want to open it now, and let it sit for a while.'

Alex nodded. He just prayed that he didn't break the cork on this one. He was good at doing that.

A timer went off in the kitchen. 'Alex!' Kate called. 'Could you give me a hand here?'

'Will you excuse me, Lawrence,' Alex said. 'I'll bring the wineglasses back with me.'

The kitchen was filled with the piquant aroma of herbs and hot pastry. Kate was chopping parsley with a wicked-looking cleaver.

'How's it doing?' Alex asked, closing his eyes and inhaling deeply.

'Couple more minutes and it'll all be ready,' she said. 'If you could get those plates out of the oven, and keep stirring the sauce, that would be great.'

Alex had always admired how simple Kate made things look in a kitchen. Everything was always under control. There was never a sense of urgency or impending disaster.

If he were in charge, the sink would be piled with pots and dishes, saucepans would be boiling over and throughout the house would be a strong smell of something burning.

'What are you two talking about?' asked Kate.

'Wine – mostly.'

'Does he know anything about wines?'

Alex rolled his eyes. 'Are you kidding? When I told him we didn't have a decanter I might as well have been telling him we didn't have a teapot. The man's an expert on everything. Next thing you know he'll be telling me how to redesign the house.'

'Now, now,' Kate said, smiling. 'I have a feeling Lawrence Kingston is going to be very helpful to us, so let's be nice to him.'

They emerged from the kitchen to find Kingston wearing horn-rimmed glasses, examining the archway that separated the dining room from the living room.

'Marvellous old house,' he said, running his hand along one of the beams framing the archway. 'Splendid architectural details.'

'Yes,' Alex said. 'That's one of the things we both love about The Parsonage. That, and the garden – which is more Kate's thing, of course.'

'Yes, the garden,' Kingston said, lost in thought, standing back from the archway. 'These beams were a later addition, I think.'

'Why, yes,' said Alex, surprised that Kingston could see the difference between the detailing, 'they are. The original house dates back to the 1830s – these were probably added much, much later.'

'You should get rid of them,' Kingston said. He ran his hand along one of the beams again. 'They're not very sympathetic.'

'They're load-bearing beams,' Alex pointed out.

'Really?' Kingston asked thoughtfully. 'I should think it would be worth getting an architect in here to confirm that.'

Kate stifled a giggle.

'I am an architect,' Alex said.

'Oh.' Kingston peered down at Alex over the top of his spectacles. 'Really?'

Considering that he had just gazed upon civilization's first blue rose ever, Kingston displayed a remarkably nonchalant attitude throughout the lunch. For fifteen minutes or so there was further discussion of the rose, but soon Kingston steered the conversation deftly back to The Parsonage. He was clearly taken with its mellow character and with the layout and plantings of the luxurious garden. Switching subjects again, he inquired about Kate's antiques shop, listening with uncharacteristic silence as Kate talked about her business, complaining about inflated prices and the difficulties of finding good quality items to sell. For many years he had collected antiques, he said, and still attended the occasional auction and estate sale. Kate's eyes lit up when he mentioned a couple of items of furniture that no longer suited his purpose that he would be happy to consign to her.

For the most part, Alex remained silent.

'So, how did the two of you meet?' Kingston asked offhandedly, taking a sip of wine.

Alex glanced at Kate, as if to ask, should I tell him, then back to Kingston.

'It was on Kate's twenty-sixth birthday,' he said. 'At a picnic organized by one of her close friends, Annabel. It turned out to be a brilliant day – on the River Avon. I must say, when Annabel's sister, Pam, asked me if I'd go with her I wasn't too keen on the idea at first.' Alex picked up his wineglass and cupped it in his hands. He rocked it gently to and fro, looking at it as if it were a crystal ball. 'I'm not very big on crowds,' he said, gazing at the glass. 'The prospect of having to spend the best part of the day with a group of total strangers was about as appealing as being invited to an undertakers' convention.'

'Remind me not to throw any cocktail parties for you,' Kingston chuckled.

Alex eyed Kate out of the corner of his eye. 'Actually

Kate's not much better – well, maybe a little better.' He paused to take a sip of wine. 'It would be fair to say that we both have the tendency to be a trifle antisocial at times.'

'Nevertheless, you obviously decided to go,' Kingston observed.

'I did, yes. In the first place, I'd always wanted to visit Bradford-on-Avon. It has some splendid old architecture and I thought, if time permitted, I'd pop up to Lacock Abbey to see the Henry Fox Talbot museum – you know, the photography fellow. Then, the more I thought about it, the idea of a picnic by the river did have a certain appeal – so I went.' He took his eyes off Kingston and gave Kate an apologetic look, knowing that he was being far too talkative.

She flashed him a hurry-it-up look. 'Annabel told me you and Pam never made it to Lacock.'

He looked flustered.

'Did you?' she asked with a knowing smile.

'Well – no, as a matter of fact we–' Alex put a hand to his mouth and coughed. 'It simply got too late.'

The smile hadn't left Kate's face.

'Anyway – where was I?' Alex mumbled. He looked back to Kingston who seemed to be enjoying the story immensely. 'Right. I never did get much of a chance to speak to Kate, though. In fact, the only words I can remember saying when we finally met were, "Happy birthday, Kate." That was about it.'

Kingston was obviously now caught up in the story. 'Did you meet again soon after?'

'No,' said Alex. 'I was working crazy hours and weekends at my job. On top of that, two nights a week I was playing trombone in a jazz band.'

Kingston smiled benignly. 'So that was the end of Pamela, I take it? Your friendship ended?'

Kate got up from the table, picked up the bottle of Pomerol and topped up their glasses. 'Let's just say that it petered out,' she said, straight-faced.

Kingston raised his bushy eyebrows and smiled.

'Needless to say, Kate and I did meet later, which happily led to all this,' Alex said, reaching over and placing his hand on Kate's.

'I'm curious,' said Kingston, taking another ninety-degree turn in the conversation, 'who were the previous owners of The Parsonage?'

'*Owner*,' Kate answered. 'An elderly widow by the name of Mabel Cooke.'

'We never met her, though,' said Alex.

'So we don't really know whether it was the Cookes who created the garden in the first place,' said Kate. 'For all we know, it could have been the owners of The Parsonage prior to the Cookes.'

Kingston took a deliberate sip of wine. 'Well, we do know, for sure, that the garden has existed for many years and whoever had a hand in it knew what they were doing. The design and selection of plants are exceptional.'

It didn't escape Kate's attention that Kingston seemed to be consciously avoiding further conversation about the blue rose. At an appropriate lull in the conversation – when Alex left the table to open another bottle of wine, one of less distinguished parentage – she politely asked him why.

Lowering his wineglass, Kingston smiled at her. 'I thought I'd save all that for this afternoon – not spoil your lovely lunch, Kate. You're right, of course. There's a lot to talk about.' His voice had lowered and she noted that, for the first time since they'd sat down, the sparkle had gone from his eyes. 'A lot more than you might imagine,' he said.

Kate brought coffee into the living room, pouring a cup for Kingston and one for herself. Alex declined, opting to stick with the last of his wine. He was comfortably settled into an overstuffed armchair awaiting Kingston's words.

Next to Alex, Kate sat perched on the edge of the sofa like a hungry fledgling about to be fed. Already she had taken a liking to Kingston. His frank yet quiet manner had a calming effect on her. At the same time, though she knew it was childish, she found it difficult not to picture him in some bygone era: as a dashing cavalry officer, flying ace or intrepid explorer. Certain of his mannerisms were not unlike those of her father.

She glanced across at Alex, hoping that he would refrain from flippant remarks about gardening. Not that it was of any consequence, since she'd already made it clear to Kingston that Alex was not much into gardening.

Kingston settled into the upholstered wing chair, which had surreptitiously become *his* chair, and eyed them from across the room over his glasses. He was obviously comfortable to be back again in his role of professor.

'While I won't rule out, entirely, the possibility that a human being has somehow fathomed the genetic riddle of the rose – which, I might add, has remained inviolate for millions of years – I'm more inclined to believe that your rose was an aberration of nature. That a freak cross-pollination has taken place between a rose and another plant. One which was probably blue, containing *delphinidin* pigment.'

'What are the odds against that happening?' Kate interrupted.

'Gosh. The odds? In the many millions – could be billions, I suppose.' He paused, rubbing a forefinger on his chin. 'Remind me, would you – I'll come to the *delphinidin* thing in a minute.'

It appeared that Kate's interjection had broken his rhythm. He gathered his thoughts. 'Not too long ago I was reading about an Australian company, Florigene. They call themselves molecular breeders of cut flowers. Since the mid-eighties, they've been working on genetic engineering projects with flowers, principally to create new colours in petals. Their number one goal is to create a blue rose. So far – over fifteen years in fact – they've spent millions on their mission, without success.'

'Fifteen years!' Kate exclaimed.

Alex whistled. 'Millions, you said.'

'That's right,' said Kingston. 'The article stated that they

38

have produced a blue carnation, now being sold commercially. But a blue rose was proving to be a much more complex and difficult task than they'd reckoned on. Let me tell you why.' He got up from the chair.

Inhaling deeply, he proceeded to explain in painstaking detail and – with neat sketches on a large artist's pad that Alex had provided – the cycle by which flowers produce seed.

'A flower's sole purpose in life,' Kingston said, 'is seduction.' To reinforce the point, he repeated the word. 'Seduction – to lure the pollinators: the birds, bees, butterflies and insects. The bright colours and patterns of the flowers act as a magnet. Nectar, resins, oils and perfumes are the reward. But the real purpose of this transaction, the veritable essence of life, is the transfer of pollen from the stamen, the flower's male organ, to the stigma at the tip of the pistil, the plant's female organ, right here.' He stabbed a long bony finger dramatically to the place on his drawing as if it were the target of a cruise missile. 'Where germination takes place,' he said. 'This is, more often than not, done by the pollinators. Bear in mind, too, that it can also be achieved by the wind, by animals and, of course, by man. When pollen is deposited on the stigma of a flower, the flower is said to be pollinated.'

At this point Kate excused herself to let in Asp, who was barking at the front door.

'I'm not putting you to sleep, Alex, am I?' Kingston asked.

'No, not at all. It's – it's fascinating.'

Kingston smiled, helping himself to more coffee, thus avoiding the immediate need for further conversation with Alex.

Kate returned and Kingston continued where he'd left off.

'Only certain insects will pollinate certain plants,' he said. 'We know, too, that the complex genetic structure of each individual plant group prohibits pollen fertilization between unlike plant species.'

'Which means?' asked Kate.

'Meaning you can't cross a rose with a daisy. But in your case it looks as if nature has finally hiccuped. It's almost certain that a rose – probably a white one – has cross-pollinated with a blue flower of some kind.'

'A freak of nature?'

'Exactly. The only other possible explanation is that it was hybridized by a person or persons unknown.'

Kingston got up from the chair, smoothed his corduroy trousers and stood facing them. With chin raised, hands clasped behind his back, and eyes twinkling, he gave Alex and Kate a self-satisfied smile. 'Well – there you have it,' he said.

'What do you suggest we do now?' Kate asked. 'What do we do with this eighth wonder of the world, Lawrence?'

'A good question, my dear,' Kingston answered in a more sombre tone. 'There are some serious issues looming here,' he said, wagging a finger in the air. 'The first thing we need to address is how to handle the bedlam that's going to erupt when word of a blue rose gets out. Your garden will be emblazoned on the front page of every newspaper and magazine around the globe. The fields around Steeple Tarrant will turn into an international settlement for every reporter and rose fanatic on the planet. Not only that, but every single entity in the world that has anything to do with growing roses will beg, cajole – even cheat or steal to get their hands on the blue rose patent.'

'God, that sounds horrible,' Kate exclaimed.

Kingston held out his open palms. 'On the brighter side, if you play your cards right, you could soon be in the tax stratosphere of superstars and sports professionals. The fees and royalties could be monumental.'

'I suppose commercial rose growers would be the most interested,' said Kate.

'Absolutely,' said Kingston. 'There are some big rose companies out there. You can bet your life that David Austin, in this country, will be clamouring to get their hands on the world's first blue rose. In the States, there's any number of big outfits. Jackson and Perkins, in Oregon, is probably the biggest. Then there's Baker-Reynolds, also on the West Coast. In France, the big player is Meilland. In Denmark, it's Poulsen. Any of them would undoubtedly pay an astronomical price for it. To give you some idea, I read recently that the relatively new German rose Flower Carpet has sold over fourteen million plants worldwide in a short span of time – you can just imagine how many *blue* roses could be sold.'

A worried look clouded Kingston's face. 'My advice is that you start immediately counselling the various kinds of professionals – patent lawyers, accountants and such – who are going to be essential to maintain control of what could otherwise become a nightmare.' He scratched his forehead, as if trying to conjure something he had over-looked. 'Oh yes, I remember what it was – there's an extensive collection of roses out there in your garden, and it's a certainty that whoever planted and cared for them is, or was, a dyed-in-the-wool rose enthusiast. What's more, it's not totally out of the question that he, or she, might have been tinkering with hybridizing. If that's the case then there may be some records stored away somewhere. It's taken for granted that anybody making a serious attempt at hybridizing *must* keep a log of some kind. It's a long shot, but you never know.'

'The only person we *can* ask is the previous owner, Mrs Cooke,' said Kate. 'I'll call Julian, our estate agent, and see if he has her new phone number. Maybe she can shed some light on the matter.'

'I very much doubt it,' said Alex. 'If she knew she had a blue rose in the garden she would have hardly kept it a secret, would she?'

'I still can't figure out how come she, her husband, or somebody else, didn't know about it,' Kate responded. 'I agree, it's well hidden, but do you mean to tell me that all the time it's been out there *nobody* has seen it?'

'And if they had, wouldn't they have known of its rarity and tried to sell it?' Alex interjected.

Kingston raised a hand. 'You're assuming that it's been

41

blooming all these years, Kate. It's a mutant, and there's a lot we don't about this rose. Who's to say that it will behave like a normal rose? Plus, there are other factors that might explain poor or non-florescence–'

'Florescence?' Alex cut in.

'Flowering, blooming,' Kingston replied. 'Roses won't do well in a soil that's too alkaline. It's possible that there's chalk in that part of the garden. It's not in a very sunny spot, either – another factor influencing flower production. Add these together and it's not beyond the realm of possibility that it's only just started blooming. We will never know.'

'You've convinced me,' said Kate.

'Well, if you do find anything more, let me know right away,' Kingston said, walking over to the coffee table, placing his cup and saucer on the tray.

Kate sensed that, for today, at least, they had exhausted the subject of the blue rose. Alex was about to leave the room when Kingston spoke again. His words were carefully chosen and articulated. 'Kate and Alex, let me say this. I'm not sure, yet, that either of you grasp fully the significance and enormous impact that this discovery is going to have on the international world of horticulture and commerce. There's no doubt in my mind that the two of you could become exceedingly wealthy, but you'd best prepare yourselves for some surprises and some sacrifices, too. I'm sure these can be minimized if you exercise reasonable care and good judgement.' His expression became less serious. 'What we have to do is to assemble a competent team of professional people to handle the legal work, management and marketing of this awesome rose. It's going to take a lot of your time and a lot of hard work on your part.'

Kate noted that Kingston had said 'we'.

'What's the first step, then?' Alex asked.

'To find a good lawyer.'

'How do we go about that?' asked Kate. 'Blue roses are hardly a legal specialty.'

'A patents specialist is the closest I can think of,' said Alex.

Kingston nodded. 'I think you're probably right, Alex.'

'There must be some kind of referral service, I would imagine,' said Kate.

'There is,' Kingston replied. 'You need to call the Law Society. They recommended a solicitor for me a number of years ago. As a matter of fact, I think they have a website. You may want to check, Alex.'

Alex grinned. 'What were you accused of?'

Kate flashed him a disapproving look.

Kingston smiled. 'We were defending old Rascal.'

Alex frowned. 'Old Rascal?'

'Our beagle. Took a chunk out of one of the neighbourhood kids who'd been baiting him. Mother took us to court.'

'You gave him the right name,' said Kate, smiling.

'What was the outcome?' Alex asked.

'He got off with probation, thankfully. Anyway, I know the Law Society will find you just the right man.'

'Or woman,' said Kate.

'Well, of course,' Kingston quickly corrected himself.

Contorting his long limbs like a giant cricket, Kingston squirmed expertly into the cramped quarters of his highly polished TR4, slamming the door with authority. 'You know, once word gets out about this rose,' he shouted over the noise of the engine, 'your world will never be quite the same.' Then, with a wave of his gloved hand, he was gone.

As the gurgling exhaust of his sports car faded into the distance, an exhausted Alex and a thoroughly bemused Kate stared at each other for a few seconds, then started laughing, helplessly. It was an outburst of both relief and pent-up exhilaration.

Hand in hand, they walked back into the house.

Chapter Five

Any fool would trade his left toe for a blue rose – it's worth
a potential fortune. Worldwide, twenty-five billion dollars
are spent on cut flowers annually, one fifth of that on
roses.

Rayford Reddell, rose grower, author

Kate brushed some breadcrumbs off the table into the
palm of her hand. 'More tea, Alex?'

'Just a drop, thanks.'

They'd finished breakfast and Alex was engrossed in the
Sunday Telegraph.

The day before, on the Law Society's website, Alex had
obtained the phone numbers and addresses of several
lawyers they were recommending. Alex picked Christopher
Adell of the firm Sheridan, Adell and Broughton, Lincoln's
Inn Fields, London.

Kate walked over to the counter and flicked the crumbs
into the sink. Glancing up at the wall clock, she flipped the
switch on the electric kettle. 'Alex, it's almost eight. You'd
better start getting ready, you know what Mrs Hendrickson
is like.'

'Only too bloody well,' Alex mumbled, still reading.
'Frankly, I think she has a lot of gall insisting we meet at
the building site on a weekend.'

'Come on, Alex, it's only a couple of hours.' She looked
across the kitchen at him. 'You've had your nose stuck in
that page for five minutes. What's so interesting?'

'It's a story about the Eden Project down in Cornwall.'

'The humongous greenhouses?'

'Right. They're calling it one of the world's architectural marvels. We should definitely go down and take a look.'

She poured the hot water into the teapot, took it to the table, and sat down. 'We could make a weekend of it, do the lost garden at Heligan, too.'

'That would be fun.' Alex folded the paper and put it down. 'Save this would you, love, I want to check out their website later.'

'Maybe that's where the blue rose will end up,' she said, pouring tea into their cups.

'On that subject, I'll try to set up a meeting with Christopher Adell. Is Thursday or Friday okay for you?'

'Yes, that's fine.'

'And you're tracking down Mrs Cooke today?'

'Right.'

'Still strikes me as a bit of a waste of time.'

'Why do you say that?'

'Well, didn't Kingston say he was pretty much convinced that it was a fluke of nature?'

Kate smiled. 'Surely, you mean an "aberration"?'

Alex rolled his eyes. 'Okay.'

'Regardless, Alex, there's still the long shot that it wasn't.' She paused momentarily. 'If the rose does turn out to have something to do with Mrs Cooke, in fairness, don't you think she should get some of the money?'

'Kate, the rose is on our property. *We* own the property now, not Mrs Cooke. Don't worry, the rose is ours all right.'

'But it would be unfair. What if it was the other way around? I bet you'd feel differently.'

'At this point it's immaterial. I don't think we should be concerning ourselves about it right now. Let the lawyer deal with it.'

'I suppose you're right,' Kate said, with a shrug.

'I was thinking,' Alex said, doodling a lopsided rose on a corner of the newspaper. '*If* this rose is everything we think it is, then we can't go on calling it. . .' He paused and stage-whispered the next three words: '. . .*the blue rose.*

We must give it a pseudonym – a nickname of some kind.'

'Any suggestions?'

'Blue Streak? Blue Moon? How about Baby Blue?'

'I don't think we should use the word "blue".'

'Okay, then what's the bluest of all blues?' Alex asked, chin resting on his clenched fist.

'Sapphire – I suppose.'

'I like that, Kate. *Sapphire*. It has a nice feel to it and nobody will have the slightest notion of what or who we are referring to.'

'Next time we talk with Kingston, we should tell him.'

'Speaking of Kingston, do you think we should keep him in our camp for a while? Formally, I mean.'

'I think he considers himself already in. Didn't you notice yesterday, he used the word "we" more than once?'

'Maybe we should have him sign a confidentiality statement.'

'I was thinking more like putting him on some kind of retainer? We may need his services down the road.'

'It makes sense. After all, he's the only other person right now who knows about the rose – oops! I mean, Sapphire.' A perplexed look flashed across Alex's face. 'Good Lord. Was he ever alone out there with the rose? It just occurred to me – he could have taken a cutting. It would have been so easy.'

'Oh, Alex, he wouldn't do that, surely.'

'If I were a botanist suddenly confronted with the greatest horticultural discovery of the century, I might be tempted.'

Kate shook her head. 'No, he was never alone out there, I'm sure of it. Anyway, I trust him – he is a professor, after all.'

'A *professor*? I can't see why that puts him above temptation. Though I'll admit in his case it would be a stretch to think of him as being that unscrupulous. But from now on, as he said, we can't be too careful. The last thing we need is dozens of blue clones out there.'

'Talking of cuttings, we must ask Vicky to take some for us. That was one of the first things Kingston asked about. I'd attempt it myself, but I never seem to have much success with propagating roses.'

Kate walked to the door with Alex, to see him off. She took his hand, squeezing it gently, as they stood on the porch. 'Alex,' she said, avoiding his gaze, 'is it just me, or is this blue rose thing starting to take over our lives? You and I haven't talked about anything else since we found it.'

'Come on, Kate, it's only been a couple of days! In any case, it's hardly small change we're talking about. With the megabucks at stake that everybody seems so sure of, I think it's more than reasonable to expect *some* inconvenience, a few disruptions. Anyway, once the whole business is in the hands of a lawyer I'm sure our life will return to normal. Until that happens – hopefully, soon – I wouldn't worry too much about it.'

'I suppose you're right, Alex.' She looked up at him and flashed an impish smile. 'You don't think we should concoct some story for Kingston, about it suddenly dying – and that could be the end of it?'

'And never know what it's like to be disgustingly rich?' Alex pulled Kate closer and put his arm around her.

'Just kidding, of course. But, truthfully, I *am* just a little worried,' she said. There was a slight tremble in her voice.

'About what, for heaven's sake?'

'About all the things that might happen. I keep thinking of what Kingston said, "Your world will never be the same." It's – it's just that I like things the way they are – the way we'd planned. I'm just afraid this rose business could spoil it all. That would be awful, Alex.'

He held her tightly, leaned down and brushed his lips across her hair. 'Not a chance,' he said.

Alex tried the doorbell again. 'Perhaps she got the date mixed up,' he said.

47

'No, we agreed on today. I wrote it down,' Kate replied. 'She's probably in the loo or something.'

'It is the right house?'

'I'll check again.' Kate pulled a scrap of paper from her pocket. 'Three thirty, Tuesday 24th, 12 St Margaret's Mews. She said it was sheltered accommodation. This is it all right.'

Juggling their schedules, they had managed to set the meeting with Mrs Cooke for today. This worked out well because, if by chance they learned anything significant, they would be able to tell Christopher Adell. Alex had set up a meeting with him the coming Friday in London.

Alex was about to hammer on the door when an approaching image rippled in the dimpled glass pane. The front door to the neat bungalow opened. A thin, pale man stood there.

'Kate and Alex Sheppard, I take it,' he said in a flat voice.

Alex nodded affirmatively. 'And you're – Graham? Your aunt said you might be here.'

'That's me,' he answered, with an awkward half-smile.

'Pleased to meet you,' Alex said, thrusting out a hand. It was like shaking hands with a rubber glove.

Graham stepped aside. 'Come in,' he said, 'Auntie's in the living room, going over the racing form. Believe it or not, she makes quite a few bob on the ponies every week. Sorry to leave you standing on the doorstep like that. Her hearing's not too good these days – I'm just fixing one of the cupboard doors in the kitchen. I'll join you in a minute.' Graham ushered them into the living room then departed.

Inside, as expected from the pristine exterior, the house was immaculate. Cheerful, too. The walls of the small living room were a sunny cream colour, making it look larger than its small space. An Oriental carpet, which Alex guessed to be an old Heriz, almost touched the walls on all sides. He recognized some of the antique pieces as being part of Mrs Cooke's furnishings at The Parsonage when they had first seen it.

48

Mrs Cooke put down the newspaper and shooed her plump tortoiseshell cat off the sofa, deftly brushing the cushion with the back of her liver-spotted hand. She stood and walked over to greet Kate and Alex. 'It's so nice to meet you,' she said, eyes twinkling, as though she really meant it. 'For the life of me, I can't think why we never met when the house was being sold.' She waved a scarlet-nailed hand dismissively. 'You know what those agents are like. They can get awfully bossy. Never wanted me around, you know.'

She was a short, comfortably plump woman with a laugh-wrinkled, heavily powdered face framed by hair that bore a resemblance to fine grade steel wool. Her smile revealed teeth too white and evenly spaced to be her own. When Alex moved closer to shake her hand, he smelled the clean fragrance of Ivory soap.

Mrs Cooke gestured towards the multi-cushioned chintz sofa in front of the bay window. Alex nodded and sank down into the fluffy cushions. He kept sinking.

Mrs Cooke sat down facing them. 'You had no trouble finding us, then?'

'No, not at all, Mrs Cooke,' said Kate.

'Although Chippenham's changed quite a lot since I was last here,' Alex interjected. 'Seems a lot bigger. Busier – more traffic.'

Mrs Cooke fidgeted with the ostentatious rings on her pudgy hands. She wore at least half a dozen. 'Well, you know, it's market day. It's not usually this busy. I don't do much driving now, anyway. I do miss Steeple Tarrant, of course, but I must say that this is decidedly more convenient. Almost everything I need is close by. Not only that, we get round the clock security and there's a nurse on call all the time. I didn't know whether I'd like it at first, after living at The Parsonage all those years, but it really is very nice. I've made a lot of friends, too.'

She paused, as if trying to recall why they were all gathered there.

Seizing the fraction of time it took for Mrs Cooke's ample bosoms to heave, Alex commandeered the conversation. 'As Kate mentioned to you on the phone, Mrs Cooke, we're interested in identifying some of the old roses at The Parsonage and thought perhaps you might be able to help us. I believe you told her there might be some books we could look at.'

Mrs Cooke smiled. 'Yes, I did. They were Jeffrey's. He was the gardener. Oh,' she added, 'that would be my late husband.'

'We were curious. Did he create the garden?' asked Kate.

'Well, not entirely. We bought The Parsonage from a retired doctor, well over thirty years ago, now. '68, I think it was. His wife had recently passed away and he could no longer look after the place on his own. Particularly the garden – well, you know how big it is. It was all very sad, knowing everything he'd put into it and how much he loved it. But it was exactly what Jeffrey wanted. Me, too.' She chuckled. 'Jeffrey always used to say that he didn't have the time left to sit and wait for trees to grow. And he was right, I suppose. He'd just retired too. The garden in those days wasn't quite what it is today, of course, but there were lots of mature trees and shrubs. The doctor had already done a lot of the important work, the things that cost so much money nowadays. Like all the terraces, the arbours and trelliswork, the greenhouse, all the stone and brick work. I remember some of those lovely old urns and terracotta pots, they were there too – the Italian ones. And the brick walls, of course – some have stood for at least a couple of hundred years, long before the house was built. I was told that at one time it was a vegetable garden for the manor house.' She gazed out of the windows, her mind lost in the past. 'But Jeffrey made it what it is today,' she said finally. 'He changed the layout of the garden, the pathways, the beds and borders. He was always chuntering on about "changing viewpoints" and "lines of sight".'

'What about all the roses?' asked Kate.

'Oh, they're all Jeffrey's doing. They were his pride and joy.'

'He did a superb job and we're very grateful to him. Did he keep records of any kind, do you know?' Kate asked.

'The Major? Oh, heavens, yes. He was one of the most meticulous fuddy-duddies you're ever likely to meet.'

Alex, who looked as though the sofa was about swallow him up, eased himself awkwardly forward and sat on the front edge of the cushion. 'He was a military man, then?' he asked.

'He was. But, as I mentioned, retired,' Mrs Cooke replied. 'He kept very good records of everything. I'm not sure that – oh, here's Graham, at last,' she said, looking to the door.

Bouncing up from her chair with surprising agility for her age and bulk, she began to introduce her nephew. With unrestrained pride, she rattled off an abridged version of Graham's curriculum vitae, emphasizing the fact that he was now the Western Region Sales Manager for Hofmann Pharmaceuticals.

Alex was debating whether Graham had had a particularly gruelling day or was in the grip of some debilitating bug. His mousy moustache drooped sourly at the corners of his mouth and thin strands of hair were vainly combed in a losing struggle to conceal the shiny pink dome of his forehead. His rumpled Donegal tweed suit, poorly knotted tie and suede shoes struck Alex as being more suited to the racetrack than the sales office. Alex had already pegged him as one of those irksome people who, despite being in reasonable health and comfortably off, are never satisfied with their lot. He also had an unsettling habit of blinking frequently through his wire-rimmed glasses, further adding to the impression of querulousness.

Graham pulled up a chair from alongside the nearby dining table, sat down and crossed his legs. 'Well, how's life in the country? Auntie tells me you're asking about my uncle's roses? About his notebooks.' There was no friendliness in his voice.

Alex glanced at Kate. He knew that she was thinking the same thing. He'd better choose his words carefully. Certainly, Graham should be given no impression that they were there for any reason other than genuine interest in all the roses at The Parsonage, not just one. Earlier, he and Kate had debated about telling Mrs Cooke – or possibly hinting to her – that a particular rose in the garden was rare, even telling her it was blue. Kate had wanted to do that, but Alex had reminded her of Kingston's admonitions and they had quickly dismissed that idea – at least for the time being.

'Yes,' Alex said, evenly. 'There are a lot of roses we can't identify. The markers have disappeared. It would just be nice – well, helpful – if we knew what they were.'

Kate turned to Mrs Cooke. 'Did your husband spend a lot of his time tending the roses?'

'Oh, yes. Barmy about 'em he was. Out there pottering in the garden seven days a week.'

'Did he, by any chance, do any propagating? Hybridizing?' Kate inquired, taking her eyes off Mrs Cooke to glance furtively at Graham. 'Anything like that?'

'What's that got to do with identifying roses, might I ask?' Graham interrupted.

'We're just curious, that's all,' said Alex. 'Actually, Kate was thinking about trying her hand at it. We wondered whether there might be some useful information among your uncle's books.'

Graham averted his eyes. 'I haven't looked at the books for years, but I rather doubt it. They're quite old now, you know. Some are falling apart. Uncle died over seven years ago.' He spoke as if he wished the subject could be dropped.

'Would you like to borrow the books?' Mrs Cooke asked.

Alex looked at Graham out of the corner of his eye just in time to see the imperceptible shake of his head and fleeting scowl at his aunt's question.

'Oh, that would be wonderful,' Kate replied. 'If it wouldn't be too much trouble.'

'Not at all, my dear,' said Mrs Cooke, turning to her nephew. 'You still have them, I trust?'

Graham hesitated, his eyes blinking rapidly. 'Yes – yes,

they're in my storage space. I won't be able to get them for a couple of days. I'll call you when I have them.'

'That's settled, then,' said Mrs Cooke.

Saying that he had to make some phone calls, Graham got up, excused himself, and ambled to the door. By his body language and sullen expression, it was clear that he wasn't pleased about giving up his uncle's books.

'Come to think of it, now,' said Mrs Cooke after Graham had departed, 'there was another chap who used to come over to help Jeffrey.' She paused, twiddling away at her rings. 'Thomas, I think his first name was.'

Kate and Alex exchanged glances while Mrs Cooke, with the tip of her forefinger pressed to her lips, stared at the ceiling.

'Farrow,' she blurted. 'Thomas Farrow. That's who it was. They used to spend hours on end in that infernal greenhouse of Jeffrey's. Wouldn't even come up for lunch some days.' She paused, then chuckled. 'Swore the two of them had a hussy in there, I did. But it was just the roses. That's all they seemed to be interested in. Quite a charmer, that Farrow.'

'Where is he now?' Alex asked. 'Is he still alive?'

'I've no idea.'

'How did the two meet?' asked Kate.

'I think it was at the club Jeffrey belonged to. A garden club. I'm not certain, but it might have been in Marlborough. Perhaps there are newsletters or notes among those books of his that might help.'

Alex would have liked to pursue the question of Farrow's involvement but knew that they'd asked enough questions already. Soon it might dawn on Mrs Cooke that their visit had to do with more than simply identifying roses in the Parsonage garden.

Graham never did return. After a few more pleasantries Mrs Cooke accompanied Kate and Alex to the front door where they said their goodbyes.

Early the next morning Kate and Alex received a call from

Graham, saying that he was going to be in Marlborough the following day and could drop off his uncle's books on the way back. 'Just for the record, I've made a list of them,' he said. 'You'll find it in one of the boxes. Still don't know what you want with them,' he added. Kate asked whether he could drop them off before nine thirty or after six, since they would both be working that day. Graham said he would try.

The next evening, when Kate arrived home from her shop, two large cardboard boxes containing Major Cooke's books and sundry papers were sitting on the front door porch. There was no note from Graham. She carried the boxes, one by one, into the kitchen and placed them side by side on the floor. She was about to open one, out of curiosity, then decided to wait for Alex. Right then, she heard Alex's car pull up outside, with the quick toot of the Alfa's horn that always announced his arrival.

Kate poured two glasses of wine while Alex slit open the top of the first box with his Swiss Army knife.

'There's more than I thought,' said Kate. 'No wonder the boxes were so heavy.'

Kate sat cross-legged, put her glass beside her and started to take out the books, placing them in neat stacks on the floor. 'There's some really nice gardening books here, by the looks of it,' she said, holding one up and studying its cover. 'Hmm, this looks smashing, *Visions of Paradise*.' She handed it to Alex.

Slowly they examined each book, and the miscellaneous printed items.

Alex cut open the flap of the second box and took out the top book.

'This looks more interesting,' he said.

Kate looked up from a garden club newsletter she was reading to see him leafing through a slim book with a dark red cover. 'What do you make of this?' he asked, handing it to her.

'Most curious,' she said, studying a couple of the pages.

'There's another like it here,' he said, rummaging

54

through the box. 'In fact there are quite a lot of them. Journals of some sort, by the looks of it.'

'It's all gobbledygook. It doesn't make any sense,' Kate said, without looking up.

Alex was examining the second journal. 'This one's the same,' he said.

Soon the box was emptied and a stack of books with identical bindings sat in front of him.

Kate placed her book on top of the pile and counted them. 'There's eleven,' she said. 'If it's Major Cooke's writing, he certainly was a neat old codger.'

'It must be some kind of code.'

'That's what it looks like. We might be on to something, Alex.'

'Major Cooke's hybridizing records, in code?'

'I've no idea. But I know someone who would, I bet.'

'Kingston.'

'Right.'

Chapter Six

All gardeners need to know when to accept something
wonderful and unexpected, taking no credit except for
letting it be.

Allen Lacy, garden writer

Announced by a discreet brass plaque, whose blackened
lettering suggested daily polishing, the law offices of
Sheridan, Adell and Broughton were situated on a narrow
alley off tree-shaded Lincoln's Inn Fields. Miscalculating
the walking distance from The Ivy restaurant in Covent
Garden, where they had spent almost two hours over
lunch, Kate and Alex arrived ten minutes late for their
Friday appointment with solicitor Christopher Adell. The
day before, Alex had phoned Lawrence Kingston to tell
him that the meeting was going to take place.

Adell appeared much younger than Alex had reckoned
when he first talked to him on the phone. After apologies
for being late and handshakes, they were ushered into
Adell's sparsely furnished office overlooking a pleasant
courtyard. Surprisingly, there was no diploma or old etch-
ing in sight. Instead, the walls displayed black-framed
action photographs of sailing boats awash with spray and
foam. These no doubt signalled Christopher Adell's first
love. His tanned face and bleached hair tended to affirm
the supposition.

Alex spent the first ten minutes or so telling Adell about
their recent purchase of The Parsonage, their discovery of
the rose, Dr Kingston's visit and his appraisal of the
rose.

Adell listened attentively, making notes on a blue-lined pad.

'And that's about it,' said Alex, finally.

'*Extraordinary*,' said Adell, putting his fountain pen down on the desktop. 'Most extraordinary. This will have enormous impact on the world of horticulture – but then you probably don't need me tell you that.' He straightened in his chair and adjusted the double cuffs of his bold-striped shirt. 'From a legal standpoint there are a number of issues which must be addressed before we get to the question of marketing and selling the rose – I gather that is your intent, is it not?'

'Yes, it is,' Alex answered.

'No need to enumerate them now, of course, but among them are establishing and recording ownership, patent applications, royalties – that sort of stuff.'

'So, you don't think there will be a problem getting a patent for Sapphire, then?' asked Kate.

'Oh, no, not at all. As far as plants are concerned, they are available to anybody who discovers or invents a new variety and asexually reproduces it. It's a straightforward process. The qualifications are quite specific. I haven't researched the point lately, but I know, without question, your rose would qualify on more than one account.' He leaned back, hands clasped behind his head. 'As I recall, one of the criteria is novelty. To be novel – generally speaking, that is – a variety of plant must not have existed before in nature. There are some requirements concerning distinctiveness, too. Simply put, that means that the new plant must have characteristics that clearly distinguish it from existing varieties. This could be a different shape or size of fruit or flower, or, as in your case, colour.' Adell paused, eyeing them both in turn. When he next spoke, his voice was perceptibly lower. 'Getting a patent is really the least of our concerns. In terms of discovery and value, it's something like having the equivalent of a living dinosaur on your hands. There's really no precedent, of course. I'm afraid that the name of the game is going to be protection.

Not only for the rose but, more important, for the two of you, as well.'

There was a knock on the door, and a young woman appeared with a tray of tea. She walked over, placed the tray on Adell's desk, excused herself and left.

Adell slid the tray a few inches towards Kate and Alex. 'Please,' he said, 'help yourselves.'

As Kate poured tea for Alex and herself, he continued in a more upbeat tone. 'Other than what brief mention I might have made to Alex on the phone, I've told you nothing about our firm, or myself. Let me give you a little background.' Arms folded, rocking his leather chair lazily back and forth, he proceeded to talk about the firm's capabilities, their experience and seventy-year history. In closing Adell mentioned of a handful of their longstanding clients including a rose grower near Brighton, a client since the early forties.

Kate slid the tea tray to Adell. He paused to pour a cup for himself.

'Before my time, one of our senior partners worked with the chap who founded the company. Ben Compton was his name – now considered somewhat of a legend in the commercial world of British roses. No longer with us, I'm afraid. He was a real treasure. Anyway, Ben's son Charlie now runs the business. I'm now the partner responsible for their legal counsel.'

'So you know a lot about roses, then.' Alex intended it as more statement than question.

'More than your average gardener, I would say. More important, I know the workings of the business, the whole-sale as well as the retail side. How roses are grown commercially. How they're marketed and merchandized. Who the big players are – most of the small ones too.'

'Excellent,' said Alex.

Adell's phone buzzed. He picked it up and, turning away from them, listened for no more than a few seconds. 'Tell him I'll call him back within the hour. Thanks, Martha.' He placed the phone down and swivelled his chair back to face Alex and Kate. 'Speak of the devil. That was Charlie Compton – now let me see, where was I?'

'You were talking about the commercial side of roses,' Alex reminded him.

'Right. It's big business – colossal, in fact. It's the world's oldest cultivated plant and the sales keep growing every year. To give you some general idea about the numbers, last time I checked – quite a while ago – the combined sales of cut flowers and plants, worldwide, was around forty to fifty billion US dollars. There's an enormous worldwide interest in gardening these days, and roses are *the* star attraction. Jackson and Perkins, the largest volume grower in the States, sell more roses in greater quality and variety than any other brand name in the world. Last time I looked, they were closing in on growing twenty million rose bushes a year. Baker-Reynolds in Washington State is not far behind.'

Alex took a quick glance at Kate. She looked impressed. 'They're mind-boggling numbers,' he said. 'So the long-term value of a blue rose would be in the many millions. Ultimately billions?'

'A lot will depend on how the gardening public receives a blue rose, but my guess would be that, yes, it could – over the course of a few years – top the billion mark,' said Adell.

'Kingston was right, then,' Kate murmured.

The conference continued for another half-hour. By that time Adell had sketched out a tentative but well-conceived plan of action. It was his last suggestion that took Kate and Alex by surprise: that the blue rose be sold to the highest bidder at an international auction. 'How would you achieve the maximum price for a Degas or van Gogh?' Adell reasoned.

'Quite ingenious,' said Kate.

Then he added a caveat. 'If we are to proceed down this road – and that is my recommendation – it stands to reason that we will not be able to contain the secret of a blue rose for long. So a word of caution. No matter how diligent we are or what constraints we apply, word *will* get out. And when it does, it's going to spread like wildfire. It's going to happen very fast. Every rose grower on the planet is going to be on our doorstep wanting to know more, trying to circumvent the auction. From the very minute we contact the auctioneers, it won't be a secret any more. I want you to understand that.'

'You think we're opening a Pandora's Box?'

'It's impossible to say, Kate. How this is going to affect the two of you, we will never know until it actually happens.' He paused to take a sip of tea then flashed a genial smile from behind the gold rim of his teacup and shook his head. 'All I'm advising is that you will have to exercise reasonable care and good judgement, because you'll become public domain as it were. Privacy will become a thing of the past.'

Alex was reminded of Kingston's similar words of caution. He said nothing.

Adell ran his pen down his list of notes and circled one. 'The question of security,' he said, rubbing his chin. 'We'll need to undertake measures to ensure the rose's safety. Until we can move it to a properly secure location, it should be guarded around the clock. For the moment – if you are absolutely certain that only the three of you know of the rose's existence and location – we have what I'll call a temporary security measure.'

'We do?' asked Kate.

'Yes. I'm surprised you didn't think of it yourselves.'

Alex scratched his head. 'What is it?' he asked.

'You simply cut off all the blooms.'

'Well, of course. Then nobody could tell it from any of the other two hundred odd roses.'

'Not unless they really know a lot about roses and saw those perfect leaves,' said Kate.

Alex shook his head. 'That's most unlikely, I would say.'

'Anyway,' said Adell, tapping his pen of the desk, 'do it when you get back. We can talk later about a more permanent security system.'

'Will do,' said Alex.

60

Kate snapped her finger. 'I could try drying the roses,' she said.

'That's fine,' said Adell. 'But I would caution you not to show them to anybody.' He looked at his watch. 'One more thing. Before we do anything, we must establish beyond any doubt that you are the rose's rightful and sole owners. We can't proceed until we have recorded that.'

'Alex and I are a bit confused on that question,' said Kate. 'In fact, we don't see eye to eye on it.' She glanced at Alex, who made a slight gesture toward Adell as if to say, go ahead, ask him. She turned back to Adell. 'Well, Alex maintains that since the rose is on our property we are the rightful owners – possession being nine points of the law, as he says. But don't you think that, if – and I grant you it's a big "if" – it's ultimately proved that the rose was created by Major Cooke, not by some freak accident of nature, shouldn't Mrs Cooke be entitled to the money? Besides, from the staggering numbers being bandied around there'll be much more money than any of us could ever want.'

'It's going to depend on how solid a case we can present,' said Adell. 'If, as you speculate, it's proved later that Major Cooke did indeed create the rose, then Mrs Cooke could, should she so decide, contest our claim. I'm afraid that it's not possible this early in the game to give you a definitive answer, Kate. Meanwhile, let's proceed on the assumption that you are the sole owners.'

Alex smiled at Kate. 'That's fine by us,' he said.

Kate nodded in agreement.

They had much to talk about on the cab ride to Paddington station.

With a sigh of resignation, Lawrence Kingston placed the folded newspaper on the side table next to him, took off his bifocals and rubbed his tired eyes. For tonight, he had gone as far as he could with the crossword. It was the Saturday *Times* jumbo puzzle with over seventy devilishly cryptic clues to solve. After wrestling with it for two hours he'd pencilled in barely a dozen answers.

Draining the remains of his cognac, Kingston gazed pensively at the framed photo of his daughter, Julie, that occupied a prominent spot on the mantelpiece. She now lived in Seattle and he missed her deeply. She was the only woman remaining in his life and would undoubtedly continue so, for he had no further notions of any female relationships beyond the occasional dinner or theatre date. Since the death of his wife, Megan, some years earlier, he had chosen to remain single.

Most people dream of retiring to a cottage in the country after a lifetime of work in the city or suburbs, but Lawrence Kingston had chosen to move to London. The city, with its theatres, museums, concert halls, excellent restaurants and libraries, suited his aesthetic tastes. More for the challenge than the income, he accepted a modest consultation job now and again. His two-storey flat on Cadogan Square, conveniently located within walking distance of the elegant shops and amenities of Knightsbridge and Sloane Street, was ample for his needs. Packed into its high-ceilinged rooms, the furniture and trappings were decidedly masculine. Overstuffed couches and leather chairs, antique furniture, book-lined walls, tasteful art and an overabundance of artifacts and bibelots, signalled good taste and a well-travelled life. The only touch that might suggest a feminine hand at work was the large vase of white roses, lilies and freesias that always occupied the same position on top of a French sideboard. Megan had always loved flowers in the rooms of their house. To preserve the custom, Kingston paid a florist's shop on the King's Road a stiff sum to replace the arrangement every two weeks all year round. Despite this plenitude of possessions and memorabilia, there was a pleasant orderliness about the place.

That morning, he had received an express package from Alex containing an explanatory letter along with the eleven leather-bound journals thought to be those that Major Cooke and Thomas Farrow used in their greenhouse experiments. Since then he had studied them at great length and concluded that, in all likelihood, they were, indeed, records of hybridizing written in a code of some sort.

He glanced at his watch. It was almost nine thirty. Surely, by now, Alex and Kate would have returned from their meeting in London with the lawyer. He would give them one last try – he was curious to know how legal minds would assess such an earthshaking botanical discovery and what they would recommend.

After the fifth or sixth ring, he was about to place the phone back on the cradle when Alex answered.

'Sorry to call so late, Alex,' he said, 'but I thought you'd probably be late getting back from town, anyway.'

'No problem at all, Lawrence. We stopped off at the Crown for a spot of supper on the way back. Let me tell you, it was quite a long day.'

'I thought you might like to know that I've taken a thorough look at the journals.'

'That was quick.'

'Well, to be honest, there wasn't much to go on. They are well organized and whoever compiled them did an exceptionally neat and thorough job. Sorry to say, though, I'm afraid they might not be of much use.'

'That's a shame. Wait a second – Kate will probably want to hear what you have to say. Let me put her on the other phone.'

Kate came on the line.

'Hello, Kate,' said Kingston. 'I was about to tell Alex my thoughts about Major Cooke's journals.'

'I'm all ears,' said Kate.

'Well, my considered opinion is that the books are, indeed, records of hybridizing. Given everything we know, it's reasonable to conclude – though there's no name affixed to any of them – that they belonged to Major Cooke.'

'Isn't there also the off-chance that they could have been compiled by the Farrow chap?' Alex asked.

'It's immaterial. For whatever reason – as you already

know – either or both used some kind of code to indicate all the crossings, the roses they used for cross-pollination, and all the accompanying notes. Unless we can break the code, we may never know whether your rose was the result of Major Cooke's experiments or not. I'm afraid it's starting to look as if we might be up against a brick wall.'

'Oh dear,' said Kate.

'On the other hand, if we could, by some chance, prove that either of them was directly responsible for creating the blue rose, then it could also raise another issue.'

'Like what?' asked Alex.

'It would mean that you could have a tough time proving ownership. Either of their heirs – or Farrow, if he's still living – could rightfully claim the rose as theirs.'

Alex interrupted. 'But we've just gone over that with Adell. He's told us not to worry about it – at least, not for now.'

'Well, he should know, I suppose,' said Kingston.

'So there's not much more we can do at this point, then,' said Kate.

'Not necessarily.' Kingston cleared his throat. 'Here's what I think. For the time being we have to rule out making further inquiries with Mrs Cooke. I seriously doubt that there's anything more we can learn either from her or from her nephew. In any case, from what you've told me, doing so would only stir up a wasps' nest in the form of the nephew.'

'So what's the next step?' asked Kate.

'If there is a next step, it's to find out if Farrow is still alive. If he is, we'll know for sure whether he took part in the hybridizing.'

'If he did, he would obviously know the code.'

'In all probability he would, yes. By the way, do we know how old Farrow was at the time?'

'I do, actually,' said Kate. 'I called Mrs Cooke yesterday, mostly to thank her. Oddly enough, she mentioned Farrow again. He was quite amusing, apparently – clever with card tricks. Among other things, she told me that if her husband were alive today he would be in his mid-eighties. She also said that Farrow and her Jeffrey were about the same age – so there *is* a slim chance that Farrow could still be alive and kicking.'

'Ticking, would be more like it, I would think,' Alex quipped.

Kingston chuckled. 'If he is, I'm sure we can track him down. I've already started working on it, in fact. I've been doing a little poking around on the garden club thing.'

'Really?' said Kate.

'Yes. So far I've called over a dozen clubs, in Wiltshire, Hampshire and Avon – but, so far, no Thomas Farrow. I did unearth – if you'll pardon the phrase – a Thomas Farr, but he was laid to rest over thirty years ago, poor chap, so he doesn't qualify. I'll keep at it, though. I simply had no idea that there were so many damned garden clubs around.'

'It is the world's most popular hobby,' Kate commented.

'Yes, I know,' Kingston sighed. 'You've only got to watch telly to know that. Doesn't seem to matter what time of day you turn it on, it's either a gardening programme or a cooking show.' He paused, then said, 'Oh, I had another theory, too.'

'What was that?' asked Alex.

'Farrow could also have been a military man. There's nothing to suggest that, I grant you. All we know is what Mrs Cooke told you – that she thought her husband met Farrow at this garden club. But what if they knew each other prior to that, maybe during the war? If they did, then it could explain why the books are encoded. It's possible they might have been in the same unit together. It might have been a little game they played – you know, boffin-boy stuff – entering the hybrid crosses in code.'

'Particularly if they suspected they were getting close to a hybridizing breakthrough,' Alex said.

'Wow!' Kate cut in. 'That's really clutching at straws.'

'Well, it is, I know,' Kingston admitted. 'But if that were the case, we could approach one of the military branches for help in decrypting the journals. Intelligence Corps would be the most likely place to start, I would think.'

'Isn't there a faster way to track him down – through the Registrar of Births and Deaths – whatever that office is called now?' asked Alex.

'I checked that out first. I was told it could be a time-consuming process. In any case, if they established that he had died, the records would only tell us when and where. I'm hoping to find him still breathing or, if not, to locate a surviving relative who might be able to provide some answers.'

'Sounds like you've been quite busy, Lawrence,' said Kate. 'Next thing we know, you'll be opening an office in Baker Street.'

'The Baffling Case of the Blue Rose,' he laughed.

Alex interrupted, 'Well, it really is, when you think about it. It's quite a whodunit.'

'It is, I suppose,' said Kingston. 'But tell me what happened at the meeting today. I'm anxious to know what Adell said.'

For the next couple of minutes Alex filled Kingston in on the key points of their meeting. Kingston listened patiently, without interrupting.

'So what do you think of Adell's idea to auction licences to breed and market Sapphire?' asked Alex.

'Damned clever.'

'That's exactly what we thought,' Alex said. 'Pretty exciting, eh?'

'It certainly is most creative.' He paused. 'Of course, you realize that, in doing so, the entire world will know about your rose.'

'Adell warned us to expect that.'

'Well, Alex, it all sounds good. You have to tell me more, when we next get together.'

'We will,' Alex replied. 'Oh, I forgot, there was something else Adell recommended.'

'What was that?'

'Security. He wants the rose put under surveillance. He's

looking into it. In the meantime, as a temporary measure, he wants us to cut off all the blooms.'

'We thought that was clever,' said Kate.

There was a long pause before Kingston responded.

'Hmm. I'm not so sure that's a good idea. Not yet, anyway.'

'Why do you say that?' asked Alex.

'Let me give it a little more thought. We'll talk about it.'

When they'd hung up, Alex walked into the kitchen. Kate was about to turn the light off. She kept her hand on the switch, squinting at Alex, a puzzled look on her face. 'I wonder why he doesn't want the roses cut off?' she said.

'I've no idea. Blooms or no blooms, nobody's going to find the rose, anyway.'

'You're probably right,' she said with a shrug. 'Let's not worry about it. We can cut them off later. I want Vicky to see the rose in bloom first, then she can deadhead and take the cuttings at the same time.'

'I bet you one thing, though,' he said, putting his arm around her.

'What's that?'

'That good old Lawrence finds a way to invite himself down again.'

A week passed with no further word from Kingston or Adell. Life at The Parsonage had resumed a pleasant orderly rhythm. With the weather much improved, Kate was spending as much time as she could in the garden.

On this celery-crisp day, she was out cutting flowers for the house. The early morning air was pungent with rich, earthy smells. Over the past six weeks, like a mother over a newborn child, she had watched the garden coming to life. There was so much to look at.

From the black decay of last year's leaves and stubble, she marvelled at how the new growth had rapidly displaced the sight of earth. How mature everything had become, almost overnight. The clematis vines fascinated her. Like inquisitive toddlers, their capricious tendrils grasped at anything in sight. Against the wall, and in some of the larger beds, fully leafed-out shrubs were now jostling for space. The snaking canes of climbing roses and coiling vines seemed to be everywhere. Throughout the garden roses were bursting forth in a dazzling confection of colours.

If Alex was home, she would have gone up to the house and dragged him away from whatever he was doing to share this moment. Perhaps, surrounded by this irresistible beauty, inhaling the seductive scents, he would at least *begin* to understand what so enthralled her. What it was that, in the fluttering of a swallow's wings, could calm or quicken her pulse, charge her emotions and stir her innermost feelings. It was a sight to make even the most jaded gasp with wonder and admiration.

It had become her daily habit to walk down to the crescent – as she and Alex now called it – to check up on Sapphire. Following Kingston's instructions, she would do nothing for the rose unless it appeared to be undergoing stress. There had been more than sufficient rain, so watering was not required. Neither was it to be fed, he had cautioned. On this day, nearly three weeks after its discovery, Sapphire looked exceptionally healthy to Kate – almost alarmingly so. Some of the petals had faded to a pretty Wedgwood blue, but new blooms were the same startling blue as before, without blemish. The perfectly formed leaves were a holly-green colour, so shiny that she could almost see her reflection in the larger ones. Then there were the thick canes, with their impenetrable armour of menacing thorns. There were no dead leaves on the ground under the bush. Unless one knew differently, the rose could be mistaken for a good silk reproduction, the kind that must be touched to make sure that it's not real.

The cell phone in her sweater pocket rang. It was Kingston calling.

'Hello, Lawrence. Your ears must be ringing. I was just thinking of you. I'm standing here, looking at Sapphire as I speak.'

'How is she?'

'She appears to be just fine. It's weird, though, she

always looks the same. Always healthy. Never seems to drop any leaves.'

'Considering that it's a mutation of some kind, it's to be expected that it will deviate in some ways from accepted characteristics of the *Rosaceae* family.'

'My thoughts entirely, doctor,' Kate said, smiling to herself.

Kingston simply grunted.

'I was just marvelling at how unreal she looks,' she said, eyeing the rose. 'More like a fake rose. It's sort of creepy.'

'I'd really like to see it again. By the way, don't forget to remind your friend to take the cuttings. Perhaps it's time I came down for another look. We should take some more photos, too. Those I took were a trifle out of focus. Next time I'll use a tripod.'

'You know you're welcome any time,' Kate said, sitting down, cross-legged on the strip of grass by the rose bed. She knew that a short phone call with Kingston was an oxymoron.

'That's awfully kind of you, Kate, I'd love to. But the reason I'm calling is to let you and Alex know that I've managed to dig up some information on Farrow.'

'Really?'

'Yes, I ferreted out the garden club that he and Cooke belonged to.' He sounded very pleased with himself.

'That was clever of you.'

'Not really, my dear. All it took was some good old-fashioned detective spadework. The club was in Newbury. Still is. The club president vaguely recalled Major Cooke – apparently he was once on the club's board – but had no recollection of Farrow.'

'How did you find out about him, then?'

'I got the names and phone numbers of all ten of the club's officers and started calling them, one by one. On the sixth call, I got lucky. The lady I talked to was the club's recording secretary. Sounded as if she smoked three packs a day. Volunteered that she was in her eighties and remembered Farrow quite clearly. Kept calling him Tommy.' He laughed. 'The way she talked about Farrow, I think she might have had a soft spot for him.'

Kate allowed a little chuckle. 'So, you got a phone number? An address?'

'Yes, and no. She recalled Farrow's moving up some-where near Bletchley in Buckinghamshire, of all places. So I checked around the post offices in the area and came up with the address of a Jennifer Farrow. She's not listed in the phone book, so I plan to take a run up there, maybe as early as tomorrow, and find out whether she's a relative.'

'Why do you say, "of all places"?'

'Well, my dear, Bletchley was the place where all the classified code breaking was done during the war. It was all very hush-hush. Just struck me as being too much of a coincidence, that's all.'

'I must say, Lawrence, you're becoming a regular Hercule Poirot.'

'Ah! *Mon ami – nous verrons ce que nous verrons, n'est-ce pas?*'

With her scant knowledge of French, Kate knew roughly what he said and it didn't escape her notice that Kingston spoke the language like a native.

'We shall see what we shall see, Kate,' he added.

He paused momentarily. 'The actuarial life expectancy tables would indicate that by now – unfortunately for him and us – Farrow is probably six feet under and has been for a few years.'

'Pushing up daisies, not roses.'

'Very good, Kate.'

'You must let us know how you get on tomorrow.'

'Yes, I will – I hope with encouraging news. Before I go, though, there's one more thing I wanted to tell you. I took another look at the journals yesterday. I went through them with a fine-tooth comb just to make sure I hadn't overlooked anything. Do you know what I discovered?'

'What?'

'I think we're missing one book,' he said.

Chapter Seven

Words fail me to picture dreams of hope, expectations, surprises – yes, disappointment, sometimes despair, that are the lot of the hybridizer. . .

Dr J. H. Nicolas, rose hybridist

Five thousand miles from Steeple Tarrant in the town of Lakeford, Washington, on the West Coast of the United States, Ira Wolff was finishing his fourth cup of black coffee. It was a quarter to ten on Thursday, 3rd July. The polished mahogany door to his office at Baker-Reynolds was closed. He had instructed his personal assistant to route all calls to his voice mail for the remainder of the morning. Save for a top-of-the-line Hewlett-Packard computer, a white telephone, some neatly stacked folders, a binder, and a tray holding a water carafe and glass, the dark leather desk surface was empty. Clutter was not permissible in Wolff's life. He'd called the staff meeting for ten o'clock; he had fifteen uninterrupted minutes to prepare for it.

Were it not for Baker-Reynolds, the small community of Lakeford would have long ago withered like those dusty ghost towns of the West that had prospered only as long as there was gold or silver to be mined. Wolff was majority shareholder, President and Chief Executive Officer of the privately owned corporation. In the case of Lakeford, the 'gold' was in the form of another of nature's gifts – roses. And, barring catastrophe, the roses would survive, as they had for millions of years.

Founded in 1931 as a two-family partnership, B-R – as

the townsfolk called it – was among the country's largest rose growers and hybridizers. Over seven million plants were grown each year at Roseland, the forty-three hundred acre rose farm on the floor of a fertile valley close to the Idaho and Oregon borders. In the planting and harvesting seasons the operation demanded a staff of over twelve hundred. Every year, ten billion gallons of water and five hundred million gallons of fertilizer were pumped into the ground to satisfy the voracious appetite of this thorny colony. Ten months of the year, a highly trained, horticulturally-savvy force of over two dozen sales people fanned out across the US, keeping nurseries and garden centres well stocked and well informed. In the peak selling months, daily sales often climbed as high as a million dollars. Twice a year, professional photographers, commanding fees that would make trial lawyers look charitable, were flown to Lakeford from as far afield as San Francisco and New York. With macro lenses on Nikons and Hasselblads, they would capture the quintessential moments in the life of those prized blooms decreed perfect enough to star in B-R's catalogues. Over two million copies of these lavish works of art and salesmanship were mailed out, three times a year, to the swelling ranks of rose-crazed gardeners across the nation.

But B-R wasn't all business. Over the years, it had given much back to the community on which it relied – a notable example being the Lakeford Rose Garden. The three-acre landscaped park was designed to illustrate the evolution of the rose. Starting with ancient species roses, the plantings in the lush park followed the journey of the rose across the globe and through the centuries. Through Asia and China in the years before Christ; thence to the Roman Empire, the Middle Ages and the Crusades; to the celebrated collection at Malmaison, assembled by Napoleon's wife, the Empress Josephine; and on to the modern roses of the present day. The garden's more than one hundred thousand visitors each year helped boost, nicely, the local economy.

The Lakeford Clinic and Health Care Services was another of B-R's community good deeds. A day-care centre, a sport and activities centre for youth, a prenatal clinic, and a number of other charitable works were either fully or partly funded by the county's number one employer. Since Wolff's acquisition of the company, however, no further acts of social conscience were forthcoming.

Baker-Reynolds staff and the townspeople would have been outraged to the point of lynch-mob ferocity had they known exactly how Wolff had managed to gain control of what was considered by economists and financial gurus throughout the US as a model company. Wolff had made certain that the unscrupulous and manipulative pressures he had brought to bear on a certain Baker family board member would never surface. There had been rumours at the time of sale, most related to the confiscatory low price he had paid for the company. There had also been letters and phone calls of protest to the Washington State Attorney General's office. But the secrets of his threatening to disclose unspeakable sexual improprieties and trumped-up financial duplicity on Baker's part were as safe and impregnable as a Swiss bank.

The transition – which had received a modest one-column mention on the front page of the *Wall Street Journal* at the time – had been swift and uneventful. In the years since his takeover Wolff had made it his mission to perpetuate – albeit, sometimes by illusion – the company's integrity and reputation. Now, as before, to all intents and purposes, Baker-Reynolds was Lakeford. And, provided Wolff continued to conduct the business as his predecessors had, profitably for sixty years, the company and the town would be around for a long time. Roses would always be in demand. Or so it would appear.

Wolff concluded the phone call to his Chief Financial Officer. He took a quick second look over the papers on his desk. Satisfied that he was fully prepared for the meeting, he shuffled them together and placed them in the nearby leather folder. He glanced at his Breitling watch, a gift from the company. It was 9.52, eight minutes before the meeting was due to start. The memo he had circulated three days before, to all B-R corporate officers and department heads, reflected his taste for brevity. It read:

Please plan to attend a special meeting on Thursday, July 3rd, at 10.00 a.m. in the company boardroom.
Ira M. Wolff
President and Chief Executive Officer

Wolff sat in the chair, locked his hands behind his head, leaned back and stared vacantly at the ceiling. He'd put a lot of years into Baker-Reynolds. The company had been highly profitable when he acquired it and he had managed to keep it so until recently. Now though, with much fiercer domestic and global competition, he was fighting for his life again. The writing was on the wall: it looked as though nothing could forestall the company's collapse. Ironically, he'd played it straight this time, operating the company in an aggressive, yet businesslike fashion, never straying from the path of legitimacy. Despite everything he had done to bolster sales and reduce overhead, profits kept slipping inexorably downward and costs continued to spiral. Red ink was seeping insidiously through the pages of each successive monthly profit-and-loss statement. More loans were out of the question. He couldn't pay those he had. The banks were now getting testy. If the company were to go under, it could be more than just a financial disaster for him. If the State Attorney General or the FBI started to get nosy, or if a cub reporter decided to resurrect the demise of Baker-Reynolds, it would only be a matter of time before Wolff's past would start popping up all over the media.

In a lifetime of constructing creative contingency plans, this time he had none.

He wondered which part of his past they would dig up first. Probably the five years' incarceration for fraud, he assumed, along with a fine of three million dollars to be used to repay his victims. This was part of the sentence he had received eighteen years ago for an elaborate Ponzi scheme that had bilked over one hundred investors in five

74

eastern states of more than two hundred million dollars. Employing, as one legal mind stated, 'a brilliantly conceived but legally corrupt and morally diabolical scheme', Bernard Wolfenden – his real name – was found guilty of establishing phony corporations, creating fake deeds of trust, fictitious balance sheets and other documents to give investors the impression of legitimacy. Even a loan officer at a prestigious bank was on his payroll at the time.

Wolff finally took his eyes off the ceiling, glanced at his watch, and got up from the chair. It was two minutes to ten. It was inevitable, he concluded, that once the name Wolfenden was in the nation's computer search engines, other unsavoury episodes of his past would ooze to the surface – the Dallas affair, for one. The media would have a field day with that. So, above all else, he had to keep Baker-Reynolds going. He preferred not to think more about Dallas right now.

The meeting started precisely at ten. Wolff insisted on punctuality. Eighteen people were in attendance. The mega-sized boardroom table, more befitting a White House banquet, left little room for anything else in the room. The story was that old man Baker bought it at auction, had it cut in four pieces, and reassembled it in the room. Sundry awards and diplomas – many faded, all with rose motifs – added listless blotches of colour to the beige walls.

At the head of the table, Ira Wolff studied some papers with Jed Harmon, the company's Chief Financial Officer. There was a stern look on Wolff's tanned face. He was fastidiously dressed in a navy pinstripe suit with a lot of white cuff showing. His only noticeable mannerism was the constant need to brush aside the strands of grey-streaked hair that flopped continually across his glaucous eyes.

Wolff handed the file he'd been scrutinizing back to Jed Harmon and walked over to the vacant chair at one end of the table. He placed his hands on the back of the chair and surveyed the room.

'Okay, let's get comfortable. Settle down. Lillian, would you close the door, please.'

There was a jockeying of chairs – the casters gliding silently on the thick, wool carpet – a rustling of papers and the room fell silent. Wolff cleared his throat.

'Good morning, everybody. Nice to see you back in the saddle, Bill,' he said, glancing across the table at his General Sales Manager, Bill Samuelson, who had recently been on leave of absence. Wolff paused briefly, to make eye contact around the room. 'These last two weeks I've spent mostly with Jed and our auditors. As a result of those meetings, we've reached some tough conclusions that you should know about. You're not getting any sugar with this pill. These are the facts. Eighteen months ago we started to experience a drop in sales. At first the decline was modest but as we entered our peak season sales started to plunge. In the first quarter of this year they were off over twenty-nine per cent.'

He paused to let the number sink in. 'Twenty-nine per cent,' he said, slowly. He shook his head from side to side. 'Twenty-nine per cent,' he whispered, mouthing the words.

The expressions around the table were stone-faced, as Wolff continued. 'Despite taking corrective measures, the situation has worsened. Now we face two simple choices. Either, by some process, to dramatically hype sales, or –' His lips tightened. 'To start downsizing.' Brushing a lock of hair from his eyes he waited a moment for the words to sink in.

'We've analysed our operational and selling costs and are satisfied that there's little or no fat to be cut there. That leaves these options: first, to start immediately on an aggressive effort to sell the products we presently own; second, we must, and I repeat must, bring new products to market now. I'm not talking about in the next year or so – we don't have that luxury. We've got to pull a rabbit out of the hat very soon or pink slips start showing up in the pay envelopes.'

Wolff's cold eyes came to rest for a moment on Bill Samuelson, who shifted uncomfortably in his chair.

'And the first casualties will be in the sales department,' Wolff added.

Turning to Steve Weber, B-R's Director of Research and Hybridizing, he continued. 'Research and Development. We need fresh, new ideas in roses. We can't rely on regurgitating the same tired old hybrid teas and floribundas any more. We're at war with the British again – with David Austin's English roses; the Germans are pounding away at our flank with their Flower Carpet roses; the French with Meilland's Romantica series. Christ! Even the Canadians are in the battle, convincing buyers that they can grow roses around igloos.'

An ominous silence gripped the room as Wolff paused to take a sip of water.

'Everyone must put on their thinking caps and come up with creative ideas. Within the next five days there'll be another staff meeting, at which time I'll expect all department heads to present their thoughts on turning this thing around. Don't give me any Band-aid ideas. I'll say it one more time. Somehow, between us, we must come up with an earthshaking new horticultural innovation to stop this freefall. I'm not talking six months from now – not even three months from now – we need it right now. I don't care what it costs. If it's a big-time idea, I'll come up with big-time bucks to put behind it. Think hard about it. Have your families and friends think about it. Because if we don't make it happen – and, I mean soon – this company is going to go under. And we're all going with it.'

With that he turned and left the room.

Chapter Eight

Gardeners, I think, dream bigger dreams than emperors.
                                        Mary Cantwell

Thomas Farrow's cottage was in a cul-de-sac at the north end of Little Stanton village. It took Kingston two passes through the hamlet before he found it. The chattering windscreen wipers of the TR4 were no match for the gusting rain that made it difficult to see much up ahead.

Finally he glimpsed the braided cap of the thatched roof peeking out above a tall yew hedge. It was the only part of the cottage visible from the street. Climbing out of his car, Kingston gingerly made his way up a narrow flight of slippery stone steps, keeping a firm grip on his umbrella and his briefcase. He had brought four of Major Cooke's journals with him, just in case. At the top of the steps the garden opened to a wide band of lawn, edged by shrub and perennial borders. On a more agreeable day the view to the south was undoubtedly splendid. Now a menacing parade of dark thunderclouds rolled across the rain-shrouded horizon. Turning away from the dispiriting view, he was cheered at the sight of the brightly painted peacock-blue door.

He lifted the tarnished lion's-head knocker and let it drop loudly. Almost immediately the door was opened by a slender young woman, casually but fashionably dressed.

'Good afternoon, my name's Lawrence Kingston. Dr Kingston. I'm trying to locate a Mr Thomas Farrow,' he said evenly. 'I was given this address by a former acquaintance of his. I wondered whether he might still live here?'

'Oh, I'm so awfully sorry – you obviously don't know,' the young woman stammered. 'Thomas died several years ago. I'm his niece. Was he a friend of yours?'

'Not exactly. More like a friend of a friend, really.'

'Your friend wasn't aware, either, then – that Thomas had died?'

Conscious of her apprehensive expression, as she gripped the edge of the partially open door, Kingston stepped back two paces. 'No. No, he wasn't,' he said. His next words were lost, as a crack of thunder echoed across the leaden sky. He waited as it rumbled off into the distance. Then it started to bucket down. 'I'm awfully sorry to learn about your uncle,' he said.

A sudden gust of wind threatened to blow Kingston's umbrella inside out. Rain splattered noisily off the porch behind him. It suddenly occurred to him what a sorry sight he must present to this pleasant young woman.

'Please . . .' She opened the door wider and stepped back. 'Do come in. It's such a wretched day. At least you can dry off a little. I'm sure you could do with a cup of tea. My name's Jennifer, by the way.'

'Thank you, Jennifer, that's awfully kind of you. It *is* getting a bit nasty out here. Yes, tea would be lovely.'

He set his briefcase down on the tiled floor of the hallway, took off his sopping trench coat, and handed it to her. 'You're very kind.'

'I'll put the kettle on. You get yourself warmed up a bit,' she said, leaving Kingston standing with his back to the meagre fire smouldering in the hearth of the low-ceilinged living room.

When Jennifer returned with the tea, they sat down and she talked about her uncle. She said he'd passed away, suddenly, about six or seven years ago. She confirmed that he had, indeed, been passionately interested in roses and, yes, he had belonged to a garden club. She had done her best, she said, to keep up his garden in the back of the cottage but, sadly, it was nowhere near as glorious now as it had been when he was alive.

'You haven't told me your reason for coming,' she said.

'I'm trying to establish whether your uncle was a friend or acquaintance of a man named Jeffrey Cooke. Major Jeffrey Cooke. He was also keenly interested in roses. I recently found out that they belonged to the same garden club.'

'You said, "was". This Major Cooke – he's no longer alive, then?'

'I'm afraid not.'

'You still haven't told me how you think Thomas might have helped you.'

'You're right, forgive me. Well, some close friends of mine recently purchased a nice old house from Major Cooke's widow. There are lots of roses in the garden – upwards of two hundred – some quite old and rare. The garden's large, of course.'

'It sounds lovely.'

'It is. Well, Mrs Cooke lent us some of her husband's journals containing records of his hybridizing roses. We're pretty certain they're Major Cooke's notes but it's also possible that some of the entries could have been made by your uncle, because we're led to believe that from time to time they worked together on the rose breeding. We're trying to find out exactly what information is contained in the journals.'

'I don't quite understand.'

'Oh, I'm sorry,' said Kingston, placing a hand on his brow. 'I forgot to tell you, they're written in some kind of code.'

She raised her eyebrows. 'That's a bit queer, isn't it?'

'It is.'

She shook her head. 'I don't think I can be of any help, I'm afraid. I inherited all of Thomas's belongings. I know there were no notebooks or journals, anything like that, among his effects. But there are quite a lot of regular gardening-related books in the guest room. That's about all in the way of reading matter.'

'Would it be terribly rude of me to ask to see them – the books?'

Jennifer shrugged. 'I don't see why not.' She got up from her chair. 'They're in here,' she said, gesturing to a partially open door to her right.

Kingston followed her into a small bedroom. It was light and airy and smelled of freshly ironed sheets. Built into each side of the leaded casement window were two symmetrical tiers of white-painted shelves, each filled with orderly rows of tightly packed books. As Kingston walked over to examine the small library, an oval framed photo standing on the marble-topped bedside table caught his eye. 'May I look at this picture?' he asked.

'Of course,' she answered.

He walked over, picked it up and studied it.

'That's Thomas, when he was in the army,' Jennifer said. 'That one, over there on the chest, is of him and his wife, Cathy. She died several years before Thomas.'

Kingston examined the grainy black and white army photograph. It was of an unsmiling slim-faced man with a dark bushy moustache. He was in a jaunty pose, holding a pipe to his mouth. The three pips on each epaulette of his uniform indicated the rank of captain. Kingston couldn't quite make out the regimental badge in the centre of his peaked cap. 'What regiment was he in?' he asked, casually.

'You know, I'm not really sure. That was a long time ago. I don't recall Thomas ever saying much about his army days – or the war. Probably, like a lot of servicemen, he preferred to forget about those terrible times.'

Kingston placed the photograph back on the table.

'There's some more pictures in here,' she said, opening the lid of a pine blanket chest at the foot of the bed. She handed him two leather-bound photo albums. Placing one of them on the bed, he started to leaf through the other. Most of the black and white photos were typical family snapshots. Two boys, pictured at different ages, appeared in a number of the photos. 'One of these little boys is your uncle, I take it?'

'Yes, Thomas, the smaller one. His brother Adrian was two years older. He was in the RAF.'

'Handsome lads,' said Kingston, closing the first album.

Four pages into the second album, which was more up-to-date than the first, his eyes came to rest on a large sepia photo. It was an informal group photo depicting a dozen smiling men, a few in military uniform but most in civilian clothes. With Captain Farrow's bushy moustache, Kingston had no difficulty identifying him. Glancing down to the caption below, he saw Farrow's name. Kingston scanned the photo, his index finger tracing the row of names. His finger stopped. There he was, fifth from the right, Major Jeffrey Cooke. Printed under the caption were the words: *Bletchley Park, Hut 8. 1943.*

'Bletchley Park,' he murmured. He held the album in both hands and stood staring at the rivulets of rain dribbling down the windowpane in front of him. 'I was right,' he said under his breath.

'Did you find something?' Jennifer asked.

'Yes, I think so,' he said, closing the album and handing it back to Jennifer. 'Something most interesting.'

When Kingston arrived at The Parsonage later that afternoon, Kate greeted him at the front door wearing a flour-dusted apron.

'You're in luck, Lawrence,' she announced, 'I'm testing a new recipe for osso buco.'

His blue eyes opened wide. 'Splendid,' he said.

Kate was surprised to see that he was gripping a small holdall. Surely she'd made it clear that the invitation was just for dinner? It certainly wouldn't have been like Alex to suggest an overnight stay. She shrugged it off – there had to be an explanation. 'Come on in,' she said with a smile. 'You'll find Alex on the terrace. I'll come out in a minute and fix you both a drink.'

A couple of hours later at the dining table, Kate and Alex sat listening to Kingston's long-winded discourse. For the most part, they ate in silence, occasionally stealing a knowing glance or smile at each other as Kingston described every detail of his afternoon with Jennifer Farrow.

Now, over strawberries and clotted cream, he was explaining the significance of the *Bletchley Park, Hut 8* caption.

'Early in World War II, a top-secret team of British code breakers set up shop at an old Victorian manor in Buckinghamshire called Bletchley Park. Station X, it was dubbed. Their objective was to break seemingly unbreakable German military codes. If they could crack them, they would be able to target German supply shipments, eavesdrop on Luftwaffe activities, and most important, locate and destroy the U-boats that were playing havoc with Allied convoys.'

'Somebody wrote a novel about it, I believe,' Kate remarked.

Kingston nodded. '*Enigma*. Damned good one, too.' He polished off the last strawberry and took a sip of the dessert wine. 'The coded messages were transmitted daily on a code-making machine the Germans called Enigma,' he said. 'It was a devilishly clever contraption capable of scrambling messages in an astronomical number of ways. To make things even more difficult, the Jerries changed the wiring set-up for their transmitters and receivers daily. So the messages intercepted by our lads were utter gibberish.'

'The odds against anyone breaking the code must have been staggering,' said Kate.

'I'm told that, for anyone who didn't know the machine settings, the odds were a hundred and fifty million million million to one,' Kingston replied.

Kate whistled.

'I read somewhere that it supposedly pioneered the age of the computer,' said Alex.

'That was actually the contraption our chaps developed to decipher the codes sent on the Enigma. It was called

Colossus. And you're right, Alex, it's believed to be the world's first programmable electronic computer.'

'Those chaps must have been awfully clever,' said Kate.

'Sheer genius is more like it. Helped by counter-espionage and a bit of luck here and there.'

'How did they find all these geniuses at such short notice?' asked Alex.

'At the beginning it was quite a motley group. A lot of them were cryptic crossword puzzle whizzes – mostly *The Times* and the *Telegraph*, I believe. There were chess masters, mathematicians, all kinds of intellectuals. One was a rare book dealer, apparently. People with eidetic minds,' Kingston added.

Kate had never heard of the word. She reminded herself to look it up later.

'What was amazing,' Kingston continued, 'was that they were all sworn to absolute secrecy – not only at the time but for some thirty years after the end of the war. Churchill described it as "his goose that laid the golden egg but never cackled".'

'Where on earth did you learn all this, Lawrence?' asked Alex.

'At Bletchley Park. After seeing Jennifer, I stopped off there. It's a museum now, run by a charitable trust – the grounds are lovely. You should go up there sometime.'

'I think we will, when this rose business is over,' said Kate.

There was a pause in the conversation while she stacked the dessert plates and placed them to one side. She smoothed the tablecloth in front of her and looked at Kingston. 'So, Lawrence, your theory is that since we now know that Major Cooke and Captain Farrow were part of the secret team at Bletchley, it's almost certain that, one way or another, they were familiar with cryptography. Is that the right word?'

'Yes, it is. And yes, that's right, Kate,' Kingston replied. 'It's quite plausible that they would have known of the Enigma programme. Which means,' he said, picking up his glass and gently swirling the last drops of wine, 'that instead of *inventing* a code for their horticultural experiments, they simply used an existing code. Perhaps one of the more fundamental ones. Impossible for most people to decipher, but a piece of cake for any former Bletchley cryptographer.'

'Why use a code for hybridizing roses in the first place?' asked Alex. 'It all seems a bit pointless. Aren't we overreaching just a wee bit? All this cloak and dagger stuff?'

'Not necessarily,' Kingston retorted. 'Not if Cooke and Farrow sensed they were close to a breakthrough as earthshaking as a blue rose.'

Kate thought Alex's question reasonable but it was clear by Kingston's frown that he didn't agree one bit.

'Under the circumstances,' he said, straightening up in his chair and looking down his nose at Alex, 'some kind of coded entries of their cross-pollinating would be logical – even advisable, I would say. It's not at all far-fetched. Besides, they were old army chums. It was fun. Brought back memories of their old days.'

'You know something,' said Kate. 'Maybe we should quit while we're ahead. It seems to me that if we continue digging into this code business we might well end up establishing that Cooke and Farrow did, indeed, create the rose. This seems counterproductive to what Adell is doing – trying to establish us as the rightful owners.'

Alex was looking testy. 'Look, if I recall correctly, Adell's last words were that we were to proceed on the assumption that *we* are the sole owners.' He looked briefly at Kate, then rested his eyes on Kingston. 'So, for the time being, why don't we do that?'

'I think Alex is right,' said Kate, breaking the momentary silence.

Kingston simply shrugged.

Alex folded his napkin and placed it tidily in front of him. 'Going back to what you were saying, Lawrence – about the code thing. I'll buy your theory,' he said, 'but who the hell would be capable of cracking the Major's code now? This Enigma business was nearly sixty years ago. Surely most of those people are long gone by now, aren't they?'

'I'm afraid so,' said Kingston, 'but I've been doing a little digging on my own.'

'Of course you have,' Alex muttered.

Kingston ignored the jibe. 'When I was up at Bletchley I posed the question to the director, a nice lady. As I expected, nobody on the staff up there has any knowledge of the codes themselves, but she suggested that I talk to the Defence Intelligence and Security Centre people at Chicksands in Bedfordshire.' He rubbed the bridge of his nose for a moment. 'If we draw a blank there, there would appear to be no other avenues left open, I'm afraid.'

'If we know the code, does that mean we can replicate the rose? Create more of them?' Kate asked.

'In all probability, yes. But there's a small problem.'

'What's that?' Alex asked.

'The missing journal,' said Kingston.

'What about it?'

'I'd bet a tidy sum that the crossing formula necessary to do that is contained in the missing journal. That's why it's missing.'

'Somebody else knows about the blue rose?' Kate asked, frowning.

'I wouldn't rule it out entirely,' Kingston said, leaning back in his chair.

Chapter Nine

But ne'er the rose without the thorn.
Robert Herrick

Another week went by and July continued miserable. An umbrella shop couldn't have wished for a better day. Stumbling along the shiny, slick pavement of Lincoln's Inn Fields, Alex did his best to shield Kate and himself from the constantly shifting curtains of rain that whipped across the square, beating a tattoo on his black umbrella. Every once in a while he would peek around the edge of the near-horizontal brolly, getting his face drenched each time he did so. At last he saw the alley and the welcoming portal of Sheridan, Adell and Broughton's offices. In the next hour or so they would get an update on Adell's progress with the auction arrangements. It was now three weeks since their last meeting.

'Nasty day,' Chris Adell said, relieving them of their coats, umbrella, and Kate's beret.

'Phew,' Alex whistled, as his body adjusted to the comfortable warmth of the room. 'They'll be pairing off the animals soon, if this keeps up.'

Adell's secretary entered the room and placed a tray of tea and biscuits on the table. 'This'll warm you up a bit,' she said before leaving.

'Please – help yourselves,' said Adell. 'Any more developments with Sapphire?'

'Not a lot, really,' Alex replied. 'Except for Lawrence Kingston's latest theory.'

'What's that?'

Alex then described Kingston's recent trip to Bletchley and his visit with Jennifer Farrow.

'He's becoming more and more convinced now that Cooke and Farrow might have had something to do with the rose,' said Kate.

Adell laughed. 'It all sounds quite cloak and dagger – a missing journal, Bletchley Park, Enigma codes.'

'Exactly what I said,' said Alex.

'This Kingston chap sounds awfully creative. I'd like to meet him one day. Meanwhile, let me update you on the auction.' He picked up the phone and punched in a single digit. 'Martha, would you bring in the Sheppards' file, please. I forgot to ask you to pull it out earlier. Sorry.'

Adell reached into the side drawer of his desk and extracted a manila folder. 'I want to show you this.' Opening the folder he removed a brochure. 'This is a colour proof of the brochure that we've put together for the auction sale of the rose.' He handed it to Alex.

Alex held it up so that Kate could see it too. It was much larger than an average brochure, folding into three panels. The artwork was a pleasing combination of fine line drawings that resembled old engravings and computer-enhanced photography. The photo of the blue rose, spanning two of the inside panels, was beautifully executed. Not quite like the real thing, thought Kate, but most impressive.

'Nicely done,' said Alex.

'Keep it. It's for you. Look at it when you get back home and let me know if you have any suggestions or changes. It's not going to go to press for a few days so there's plenty of time for corrections.'

For the next five minutes Adell outlined the marketing plan and overall strategy for the first-ever auction of a rose.

Adell looked pleased with himself. 'So there we are,' he said, leaning back and folding his arms. 'In another couple of weeks we'll send out the announcement and Bob's your uncle.' Abruptly his smile vanished. 'By the way, word is out already, by the looks of it.'

'What do you mean?' asked Kate.

'We've already received two pre-emptive bids from growers. One of them here, in the UK, the other from Holland. You can see what I meant when I said it would be nigh on impossible to keep such a discovery under wraps.'

Kate frowned. 'But how could they know about it if the brochure isn't even printed yet?'

'We've been having conversations with Bonham's, the auctioneers, since you were here last. Naturally, we requested that they treat it with the utmost confidentiality, but you can see how impossible that soon becomes. The faxes and e-mails that have already gone back and forth. We knew all along that it would be impossible to contain such—'

There was a barely audible knock on the door and Martha took one step into the room, holding the door open behind her. She was empty-handed.

'Well, Martha?' Adell said, gesturing with his hands. 'Where's the file?'

'We don't seem to be able to find it,' she said. 'Are you sure you don't have it?'

'No. The last time I saw it was a couple of days ago. I gave it back to Betsy. I'm almost certain she put it in your tray.'

Three pairs of eyes were now fastened on Martha, who shifted uncomfortably, one hand still on the doorknob. 'Do you think it might be connected with the break-in?' she asked.

Alex gave Adell a quizzical look. 'Jesus! Somebody broke into your offices?'

'Yes – two days ago. There was no evidence of a forced entry. Just a lot of stuff disturbed, as though somebody was looking for something. Whoever it was, he or she was thorough. They tried to enter the computers too. We've been taking inventory but so far we've found nothing missing.'

'Up until now, that is,' said Alex. 'What did the police say?'

'They were as perplexed as we were. All they could do was to ask us to report any further unusual circumstances.'

Kate was clearly alarmed. 'If someone has stolen our file—'

'Look, let's not jump to any conclusions,' Adell interrupted with a growing look of annoyance. 'There's a perfectly rational answer for it, I'm sure.' He looked back to Martha, who was still standing awkwardly by the door. 'Martha, why don't you go and take another look? Ask Betsy and Christine to do a search, too.'

It was another five minutes before Martha returned. There was no sign of the file anywhere, she said.

'I'm sure it'll show up,' Adell said. 'The minute it does, I'll let you know.'

'And if it doesn't?' Alex asked.

Adell's face darkened. 'Let's cross that bridge when we come to it,' he said, getting up from his chair.

After Adell had seen Alex and Kate out he went into the outer office, where Martha and the other two secretaries were busy undertaking their search for the Sheppards' file.

'I didn't want to alarm the Sheppards,' he announced, 'but this is a serious matter. I don't care if takes all day, or all week, drop everything you're doing and find that damned file.'

It had stopped raining and was inky dark when Alex and Kate finally arrived back at The Parsonage. After a boisterous greeting from Asp, they went into the sitting room to check for phone messages, go through the day's mail and read the local newspaper. As usual, Asp jumped up on Kate's lap, wriggling himself into a comfortable position.

'No phone messages,' said Alex, picking up the *Wiltshire Gazette* and slumping on the couch.

'I'm surprised Kingston hasn't called,' said Kate, scratching the top of Asp's head.

'If he does, darling, just for my sake don't invite him

down – not yet, anyway. Much as I admire him and appreciate everything he's doing, I can only take him in small doses,' he said, without taking his eyes off the newspaper.

'More than likely he'll invite himself. I wonder what he'll have to say about the missing file?'

'Hmm,' Alex grunted, his nose buried in the paper.

She couldn't understand why he wasn't more upset about the file. On the train ride home they had talked about it and despite Alex's attempts to persuade her that, odds were, it was simply misplaced, she was more convinced than ever that it had, indeed, been stolen.

'I promise not to bring it up again, Alex,' she said, 'but that file most certainly contained an awful lot of information about us, not the least of which is our address. Anybody able to put two and two together will conclude that's where the rose is located.' She picked up Asp, put him on the floor and stood up. 'Now, whoever has the file could come snooping around. God, they could steal the rose, or take cuttings.'

Starting towards the door, she looked over her shoulder – to see whether her words had made any impression at all. 'Alex, you haven't been listening to a word I've said, have you?'

Alex lowered the newspaper and peered at Kate over the top of his glasses. 'Kate, give it a break, we don't really know, yet, if the file *was* stolen,' he said. 'It's probably sitting somewhere in his office, in full view. So, let's not jump to conclusions. Wait until we hear from Adell.'

'That's fine, but I still think a burglary–'

'Businesses get burgled every day,' Alex sighed. 'Why should it have anything to do with our file?'

'Have it your way, then. I'm going to have a nice hot bath,' she said with a shake of her head, walking out of the room. Asp padded along behind her.

Alex was checking the football results when the phone rang.

'Mr Sheppard?' The voice was unfamiliar. Alex's name

was clearly enunciated and the accent was unmistakably American.

'It is,' Alex said tentatively. Another one of those bloody telephone marketers, was his immediate thought. A time-share or a free cellular phone.

The man cleared his throat. 'I apologize for using the phone for what would normally be accomplished with a written proposal, but I prefer a more direct route.'

'Who is this?' asked Alex, making no attempt to disguise his impatience.

His question was ignored. 'I understand that you have a rose bush on your property that is bearing blue roses. Is that correct?' the man asked.

Alex almost dropped the phone. 'What?' he gasped.

'This is Alex Sheppard, is it not?'

He swallowed. 'Yes but how—'

'Please, Mr Sheppard. It's my job to know these kinds of things.'

Alex's mind was still racing. How on earth—?

'You haven't answered my question.'

'You know, I can't hear you very well, this is a bad line,' Alex said, playing for time. Wait — hadn't Adell mentioned a couple of growers? Perhaps it was one of them. No, they were English and Dutch, he clearly recalled. Besides, Adell wouldn't have given out his and Kate's name and phone number. Alex was now annoyed. 'How did you come by this information?' he demanded.

Again, his question was ignored. 'It must have been a rewarding moment — discovering a blue rose. I'm sure, by now, that you are aware of the impact such a plant will have on the world of commerce.'

'Who are you?' Alex asked.

The man laughed. It wasn't a pleasant laugh. 'It's of no consequence,' he said. 'Surely you didn't think you could keep a discovery of this magnitude secret for long, Mr Sheppard? No, that would be too naïve. Look, I'm not going to pussyfoot around. I would like to make you a proposal right now. Then you can forget this dumb auction idea.'

Alex cupped his hand over the mouthpiece of the phone. 'Jesus Christ,' he breathed. 'The man knows everything.' He removed his hand, now aware of his laboured breathing. 'I'm not interested in hearing–'

'If this rose of yours measures up to expectations, the syndicate I represent is prepared to offer you a substantial amount of money – and I mean substantial – in exchange for ownership and all patent rights. Naturally, we will want to have it examined first. If it gets a clean bill of health – if it's a genuine botanical specimen – then you'll be presented with an ironclad deal that will include a generous up-front cash advance and royalty payments on sales. It will add up to more money than you've ever dreamed of, believe me.'

'I'm sorry, whoever you are,' Alex said, 'you'll have to discuss all of this with our solicitors, Sheridan, Adell and Broughton.'

'We know who your solicitors are, Sheppard. I'm making the offer to you. It'll be a nice clean-cut deal. Within a few days, you and your wife will walk away multi-millionaires. What do you say?'

Alex quickly rejected the idea of lying about the rose. That would be foolish – the man was obviously shrewd and knew too much already. 'Let me give you Adell's phone number,' he said, politely, in an attempt to close the conversation. 'Whatever he decides is fine with me. But I should tell you that plans for the auction are proceeding. That's the best I can do – I'm sorry.'

'Let me tell you something, Sheppard.' The man's voice was now cold, bordering on hostile. 'You and your lawyer are making a big mistake with this auction.'

'And you're making a big mistake trying to threaten me. I don't like it one bit.'

The American laughed again.

Alex was now incensed. Despite what he thought was a civil and firm refusal on his part, the man showed no signs of being deterred.

When he spoke next, the man's manner was more conciliatory. 'Okay, Sheppard. It's a big decision. I understand that. To tell you the truth, I didn't expect you to give me a definitive answer on the phone. Here's what I suggest. You talk it over with Kate. Think about my proposal. I'll get back to you in a couple of days with more specifics. How does that sound?'

The mention of Kate's name threw Alex completely off balance.

'Don't call me again. Do you understand?' he stammered.

'Yes, I do understand. It's probably quite a shock to get a call like this, out of the blue – if you'll pardon the phrase – but I'm a businessman, Sheppard. And you've got something that is of great interest to me and my partners. So,' his voice hardened again, 'you and your wife consider my offer. Please.'

There was a momentary pause.

'Think it over,' he said, quietly. 'Real hard.'

Before Alex could say anything, the man hung up.

Five thousand miles away, at his townhouse in iron-gated Vista del Lago country club estate, twenty miles south of Lakeford, Ira Wolff sat in the quiet luxury of his cherry wood-panelled study working at his desk. The phone rang. Before it could ring twice, he picked it up. 'Yes?' he said. He listened, nodding his head slowly in approval. 'Excellent,' he said, finally. 'I agree, a couple of days is about right. That should give them plenty of time. Good work. Keep me posted, then.' He stared at the phone for a moment before putting it down. 'Black knight to blue queen, six,' he said quietly.

Chapter Ten

A garden really lives only insofar as it is an expression of faith, the embodiment of a hope and a song of praise.
Russell Page, international garden designer

It was a day much more befitting mid-July. A little after eight thirty, when Alex had left for work, Kate gathered up tools from the potting shed and set off into the garden. Already she could feel the sun's warmth on her bare arms.

She had tossed and turned all night, thinking the worst about the missing file and the disturbing phone call from the American stranger. She was convinced they were connected. Today, however, she would put aside all negative thoughts and enjoy her day off in the garden. Nothing strenuous – it would be spent simply pottering, enjoying.

A drowsy stillness hung over the garden, stirred every now and then by a gentle breeze that rustled only the topmost leaves of the old elms. High above, in the eggshell blue sky, the twittering of swallows and lazy cawing of rooks crystallized the sights and senses. It was so easy to shut off the outside world.

She busied herself deadheading roses, staking droopy delphiniums and foxgloves, and raking rose petals and dead leaves from under the thickly planted beds. Not for the first time, she was reminded of Frances Hodgson Burnett's story, *The Secret Garden*. Though she hadn't read it since childhood, she could still recall how the garden was first described: 'The sweetest, most mysterious place anyone could imagine.' Burnett could have been talking about the very same florid excess surrounding Kate this very minute. Even to 'the high walls which shut it in' and 'the light swaying curtains, here and there, of climbing roses that had crept from one tree to another and made lovely bridges of themselves.'

Of late, Kate found herself consciously avoiding the blue rose as much as possible. She had no rational explanation for doing so, but for some time now a nagging voice skulking deep inside her warned her to be cautious. Don't be lured by its captivating beauty and promise of vast riches, the voice kept saying. She knew that if she gave Alex even the slightest hint of her uneasiness it would only aggravate matters. She still had not been able to convince him of the downside potential of their discovery.

She stopped raking, to stare in fascination at a velvety bumblebee rolling drunkenly in the golden pollen of a peony. Quickly the bee flew off to find other temptations. Just as quickly, thoughts of the blue rose returned. The whole idea of turning it over to the lawyer had been to absolve themselves of responsibility and worry, to allow more time to themselves and enjoy their new home to the fullest. None of this was happening now. Worse, the sequence of unsettling developments was now starting to adversely affect their marriage, giving rise to ripples of dissension between her and Alex. To add further fuel to her misgivings, there was last night's phone call. Alex wouldn't admit it but she knew it had unnerved him. So much so that he had phoned Adell first thing that morning to tell him of the conversation.

The church clock striking twelve broke her train of thought. Why was she thinking about the damned rose again? She'd promised herself she wouldn't do that. She just stood there for a moment, forcing her mind to think of something else – anything. She didn't have much success. 'Oh, bugger it,' she said under her breath. It was obviously a good time to take a break. She gathered up her tools and set off for the house.

Kate kicked off her shoes, left them in the small room off

the kitchen and walked into the house. The temperature inside was pleasantly cool – not surprising, since the old exterior stone walls of The Parsonage were over one foot thick. A heavy slate roof helped further insulate the house. The limestone floor tiles felt soothing on the soles of her feet. As she filled the kettle, she thought back to their meeting with Adell. Soon, the brochure would be sent out, and everybody and their uncle would know about their rose. Word of a blue rose would travel fast. No doubt it would hit the newspapers and then television. Up until now she hadn't given that eventuality too much thought. What would happen then?

By the time the kettle had boiled, she knew what she would do. Saddling Alex with further debate about her qualms would only risk touching off more bickering. That was out of the question. The answer was simple: she would unburden herself on Kingston, good old Lawrence. She walked over to the Welsh dresser, picked up the phone, and punched in his number. While the phone was ringing, she reminded herself not to sound too worked up when she told him about what was happening. She was pleased when she heard his now familiar voice.

After exchanging pleasantries, mostly about the garden – and the weather, of course – she told him about the missing file.

'Alex spoke to Adell again this morning,' she said. 'It still hasn't shown up.'

'That is strange, I must say, but you know how lost things have a way of eventually showing up,' he said. 'There's probably a perfectly rational explanation. It got mixed in with another folder. Somebody put it in the wrong file, or took it home by mistake. Any number of possibilities.'

Kingston's words were reassuring, but she knew he could hardly say anything else. He was turning out to be an incorrigible optimist. She was glad that she'd called him, though. 'That's true, I suppose,' she said. 'But that's not the only recent development, Lawrence.'

'What else?'

She told him about the phone call from the American. 'Alex tried hard to convince me not to worry about it, that it was doubtful we'd hear from him again. But I could tell that he really didn't believe that,' she said. 'At one point, he said the man became almost threatening.'

'I don't like the sound of that at all. I think you have every reason to be concerned. But an American, you say! That is interesting. I wonder how he found out it was you who owned the rose?'

'It has to be the missing file.'

'I doubt it, Kate. There's got to be another explanation. Adell predicted this sort of thing, didn't he? It doesn't surprise me that the calls have started coming.'

'I still think it's the file. It makes sense. He finds out about the auction and then knows who's handling the whole thing – Adell's firm. And if he wants to know more about us and the rose, it's all there in Adell's files. Addresses, phone numbers, the brochure, everything. He may even know about you.' She waited for him to respond.

'Hmm,' he said, obviously choosing his words. 'If he did have the file, then he – or they, I suppose – certainly would have the inside track, so to speak. It wouldn't augur at all well.'

'What do you mean?' Kate asked. Suddenly, she felt uneasy.

As if regretting his last remark, Kingston was slow to respond. 'Well, like you say, they would know everything about you, wouldn't they?' There was another pause, then he added, 'Where you live – and most significant of all, where they can find the rose.'

'The possibility hadn't escaped me,' she said. 'It's not a pleasant thought, is it?'

'Sorry, Kate. I didn't mean to get you upset. What also concerns me is why the man wanted to remain anonymous. It goes without saying that any legitimate offer to purchase the rose would hardly be presented in such a manner. If, as you're convinced, the file was stolen then it's either an inside job or a professional one. More likely the latter, I would say.'

'It's all getting very complicated. Alex has told Adell – not that he can do much about it.'

'Well, all you can do for the moment is to sit tight and, as best you can, ignore all these goings on until the auction. Meanwhile I suggest the two of you keep a close watch on the rose and, in general, be careful.'

'We will, Lawrence. I'll tell Alex that we talked,' she said.

'Why don't you ask him to call me tonight, Kate? I'd like to ask him more about this mysterious American chap. It's all very odd, I must say.'

They talked for another minute or so before hanging up.

'Hello, Lawrence, it's Alex. Kate said you wanted to talk to me.'

'Yes, thanks for calling, Alex. I wanted to ask you about the phone call you got from this American chap. Kate was telling me about it earlier. Do you have a minute?'

'Of course.'

'You're sure he was American?'

'American or Canadian. I can never tell the difference.'

'Was there anything in the conversation to suggest that he was representing somebody else?'

'Yes. He referred to "a syndicate" at one point.' Alex paused, then said, 'Oh, and his "partners".'

'Did he mention any numbers? How much he was prepared to pay? Did that come up at all?'

'Only vaguely. I think he used a phrase like "more money than you've ever dreamed of".'

Alex combed quickly through the conversation again. 'Oh, and he did say that Kate and I would become multi-millionaires.'

'So, whoever they are, they're fully aware of the rose's value, commercially.'

'He mentioned that, too.'

'What?'

'Let me think a moment. He said words to the effect that we must be aware of the impact that the rose would have commercially. I'm pretty sure he mentioned patent rights and royalties, too.'

'That's interesting. Anything else that struck you as unusual?'

'I don't think so.'

'Well, then –'

'Oh, wait a minute. Yes, there was. He said that he knew who our lawyers were.'

'Hmm. If they've got the book on you, it's likely that Kate could be right – that they're the ones who have your file. It hasn't shown up yet, I take it?'

'No, it hasn't.'

'Well, Alex, let me mull this over and we'll talk again soon. Oh, and let me know if he calls again. Correct that – *when* he calls again.'

Three more uneventful days passed with no sign of the file and no further word from the American. The fourth day was Alex's birthday. To celebrate the occasion, Kate had planned an evening out with friends at one of Alex's favourite restaurants in Shaftesbury. It was close to six thirty and they were about to leave for the forty-minute drive.

'You did leave food and water out for Asp, didn't you?' Kate said, snapping shut her seat belt buckle.

'Yes, he's fine.'

Kate pursed her lips. 'Did I leave the hall light on? I can't remember.'

'You did.'

'And the back door's locked?'

'It is. And the portcullis is lowered and I'll let the draw-bridge down as soon as we reach the end of the drive.'

Kate smiled. 'Happy birthday, darling,' she said, for the umpteenth time that day.

As they approached the entry gate the postman walked into view.

'You're awfully late tonight, Sid,' Kate remarked, as Alex pulled the car to a stop alongside him.

''Ad some trouble with the van,' he muttered. 'Piece of junk, that one.' He handed over a small bundle of letters wrapped in junk mail flyers.

Kate put the letters on her lap while mapping out a route for Alex in the *AA Road Atlas*. Once they were under way, Kate flipped through the envelopes. 'Bill – bill – doctor's appointment – last three days of sale. Final notice?'

'Final notice?' Alex exclaimed. 'Who's that from?'

'Just kidding. Hmm, this looks interesting,' she said, slipping her fingernail under the flap of an expensive-looking envelope and opening it. She pulled out a one-page letter and started to read it. 'Very interesting,' she murmured.

Alex glanced up at the rear view mirror. 'Who's it from?' he asked.

'The letterhead reads, "Trident International" – there's a London and a San Francisco address. Let me read it to you:

'Dear Mr and Mrs Sheppard,

I was most interested to learn about your blue rose. My company represents an individual – the head of an international corporation and a learned horticulturist – who is extremely interested in purchasing such a rose. Providing the plant passes certain botanical testing for authenticity and condition – which we will pay for in advance – my client is prepared to offer you a substantial sum in exchange for the rose and all subsequent patents.

Would it be possible to arrange a meeting, at which time this proposal could be discussed in further detail and a viewing of the rose made possible?

In the interests of time, please phone me at the Hampstead telephone number listed above. A prompt response would be most appreciated.'

Kate lowered the letter to her lap. 'It's signed Kenji. Tanaka, President,' she said.

'Ye gods! Here we go again. I guess the word's really out, now.'

'Out all over the planet, by the looks of it. I wonder how *he* got our name and address. Surely he can't have access to our file, too.'

'Not if the American lifted it.'

'Hmm.'

'It's probably as Adell predicted. Someone from Bonham's leaked it. I'm sure they know everything about us by now.'

'I suppose you're right,' Kate murmured.

'Anyway, I'll fax it up to Adell tomorrow,' said Alex. 'Let him deal with Mr Tanaka.'

For the next several minutes they travelled in silence. Once again the blue rose had managed to insinuate its dark presence. Would the time ever come, she wondered, when it would not be lurking beneath the shallows of her thoughts, ready to surface like an insidious creature from an alien planet? She sat silently, trying to forget the letter, watching the countryside slip by, now and then glancing at Alex out of the corner of her eye. Physically, he'd changed little in the nine years they'd known each other. A frosting of grey in his sideburns now – a little plumper in the face, perhaps. But, despite having the appetite of a ditch digger, he still somehow managed to maintain the lean physique of his college sports photos. Of late, he'd been playing a lot of tennis. Word was that he was giving some of the younger hotshots quite a whipping.

Nearing Shaftesbury, on the A350, Kate caught sight of a road sign pointing to the village of Kingston Deverill. I wonder how *he's* doing she asked herself. She thought back to Kingston's last visit to The Parsonage. She smiled inwardly. It was no coincidence how he always managed to arrive at mealtimes – invariably staying for the rest of the day and evening, too. The limp excuse on his last visit for packing an overnight bag was that he planned to stay at the local, the George and Dragon. Of course, he ended up staying in their guest room.

That same evening, after dinner Kingston had launched into a long-winded reminiscing – mostly about his experiences in various far-flung outposts when he served as a captain in the army. Around ten thirty, Alex, who looked as though he might fall asleep any minute, finally excused himself, saying that he had to get up early the next morning. She and Kingston had continued talking, mostly about gardens. Another hour passed with Kingston showing no signs of tiredness. In need of a break, she asked if he'd like more coffee. The minute she did so, she regretted it. That'll keep him going for another couple of hours, she cursed to herself.

When she returned with the coffee, Kingston steered the conversation back to The Parsonage and Kate and Alex.

'So, how did the two of you end up at the altar?' he asked out of the blue.

Kate was determined to make her answer as brief as possible. Now *her* eyes were starting to droop. Didn't he *ever* get tired?

'Well, let me see,' she said rubbing her chin. 'Alex told you how we met – all about the picnic.'

'That's right.'

'Well, for about six months after that I dated an army lieutenant. Coldstream Guards. James, his name was. He got an overseas posting, wanted me to go with him and I said no. The relationship would have fizzled out anyway. It wasn't going anywhere, not as far as I was concerned, at least. Nice chap, though.'

Kingston chuckled. 'As they say, "Nice to the regiment, but rotten to the core."'

She laughed and took a sip of the strong lukewarm coffee. 'I must be boring you to tears, Lawrence,' she said with a faint smile. 'You must be tired.'

'No, I'm fine. You're not boring me at all. I find it all most interesting. Please, go on.'

Inwardly she groaned and managed to stifle a yawn just in time. 'After that I didn't have a regular boyfriend,' she said. 'The occasional date now and again but nothing serious. Then, by happenstance, I ran into Alex again. Of all places, at my shop in Bath.'

'That must have been a surprise.'

'It was, believe me. It was a Saturday. It was bucketing down that day.' Her eyes wandered off momentarily towards the windows, then back to Kingston. 'I was in the back of the shop moving furniture, helping a customer get a better look at a large armoire. Suddenly, there was this awful sound of shattering glass. It sounded expensive. I went to the front to investigate. I was horrified to see a man there, sprawled on the floor. He was lying in a pool of broken crystal, the remains of eight of my Edwardian goblets. The smear of ice cream he had slipped on was clearly visible – the little boy who had dropped it had disappeared with his mother.'

'He wasn't hurt or anything?'

'No, only his vanity.'

Kingston smiled. 'Poor bugger,' he chuckled.

'When he looked up and I realized it was Alex, we both burst out laughing.'

'That's hilarious, Kate.'

'It really was. I still look upon it as divine intervention.'

'Hope he offered to pay for the glasses.'

'Absolutely. He left the shop a hundred and twenty pounds poorer, but not without talking me into a date for dinner the following weekend.'

'So, when did the two of you finally get married?' Kingston asked.

'It was about three months after the glasses episode. At a civil ceremony in Bath. I'm afraid I gave Alex conniptions – I dropped the ring and it rolled into a grating. It was another twenty minutes before the ceremony was able to continue.'

The rumble and buffeting of a passing truck jolted Kate back to the present.

She shifted in her seat to face Alex.

'What are you smiling at?' he asked, glancing at her.

'Oh, nothing in particular – mostly about Kingston. I wonder how he's doing?'

'Who knows? Probably hot on the trail of the mysterious American by now.'

'His own Professor Moriarty.'

Kate placed her hand on Alex's knee. 'You know, we both kid about Kingston, but I sometimes wonder whether he knows a little more than he's telling.'

'About what?'

'That's the problem, I'm not sure. For one thing, I keep harking back to his not wanting us to take all the blooms off the rose as Adell suggested. Why would he object to that?'

'I've no idea,' said Alex, his eyes fixed on the road ahead.

'It's when he talks about things like being watchful that I begin to get nervous. Isn't that what he said?'

'Yes, I believe he did.'

'Well, what does he mean by that? That we might be under surveillance? Followed?'

'I certainly hope not. But with everything that's happening, who knows? When you think about the money involved, I suppose it's not entirely out of the question.'

'I agree, but it seems out of character. Didn't you and Lawrence conclude that the American is a businessman of some kind?'

'If you talked to him on the phone, you might not think so,' Alex countered.

'Maybe Kingston's just overreacting. Next time we talk, I'll simply ask him if he's holding anything back.'

Nothing more was said for a couple of miles.

'Roses,' Alex said, breaking the long silence.

She turned and peered at him over her sunglasses. 'What about them?'

'Are they as finicky as everybody makes out?'

'No, not really,' said Kate, wondering where he was headed. 'They've really had a lot of bad press over the years. Some modern hybrids are more susceptible to disease and insects, but as a genus the rose is a remarkably tough. Tougher than most, in fact.'

'Good,' he said.

'In fact,' Kate continued, 'all over the world roses have survived, untended, for hundreds of years. I read, not too long ago, of a bunch of rose nuts in America who go traipsing about the countryside and backwater towns taking cuttings of old roses – most of them over a hundred years old.'

'The rose nuts?'

Kate ignored the remark. 'One of the more likely hunting grounds – or unlikely, depending on your point of view – is cemeteries. Not your everyday graveyards, but ones that have been abandoned or receive little care. The Texas Rose Rustlers, I think the group is called.'

'Clever name.'

'It is, isn't it? Often they can date the rose from the year on the neighbouring headstone.'

'So is it reasonable to assume that a rose can be safely transplanted when it's in bloom?'

'It's better to do it when it's dormant. But, yes, if you're careful and know what you're doing, it's fine.'

'Well, then, let's move Sapphire to another garden. A secret location.'

Kate wound up her window and adjusted the barrette in her windblown hair. 'Not a bad idea. I'm not sure–'

'No, Kate, think about it for a moment. It may be the answer we've been looking for. If the rose is no longer in our garden, the next time these creeps contact us we can simply tell them to bugger off. Explain that we don't have it any more. There'll be no point in their snooping around our house or badgering us if they know the rose is gone. We won't even tell Adell where it's hidden. Remember he wanted to have it guarded? Now that won't be necessary. Only the two of us will know. Maybe we don't even tell Kingston. It'll take a lot of the pressure off. It's brilliant.'

'So, who's going to take care of it in this secret location?

It's got to be watered. You can't just go plop it in a field somewhere and forget about it.'

'Kate, I realize that. I'm not a complete horticultural troglodyte.'

They drove in silent thought another mile or so. Deftly slipping the responsive Alfa into third gear, Alex slowed to negotiate a sharp bend in the road. On their right a collection of small buildings surrounding an old whitewashed barn came into view. Along the side of the barn was a gold-lettered sign on black background: *Pennyroyal Nursery*.

'Yes, of course,' Kate said, suddenly. 'Holly Hill Nursery – Vicky.'

'What about her?' asked Alex.

'She might know of a good hiding place.'

'Good thinking, Kate. Why don't you call her tomorrow? I'm sure she'll be more than glad to help out – you two are like sisters.'

'I will,' said Kate. 'Then, if we can get Sapphire out of our garden, perhaps we can get our lives back to normal. Close to normal, anyway.'

Chapter Eleven

*There is no gathering the rose without being pricked by the
thorns.*

Bidapi

Kate pulled the Trooper into the parking area at Holly Hill
Nursery. She turned off the engine and, for a moment, sat
in the car savouring the sight and smells. It had been a
long time since she was last here and seeing Vicky again
was going to be fun.

Next to their own precious gardens, and perhaps those
of others, there is one other sight guaranteed to send
gardeners into the state of benign delirium she now felt –
and that is a nursery. Not a garden centre – those plant
supermarkets with car parks the size of airfields and
ghastly fluorescent lighting where, if you inquire about
Leptospermum, an acned teenager will send you off to the
local chemist's. A proper nursery is unpretentious. In a
manner of speaking it is a kind of garden but the plants are
all in containers and tubs. It's where names of trees, shrubs
and perennials are handwritten on wooden markers.
Where pyramids of compost and other organic matter
attest that here is where the propagating and nurturing is
done. It is a retreat for all the senses, not just the eye.
Where overlapping aromas – earthy, cloying, pungent and
perfumed – commingle with every step. A ready source
when you want reliable answers to serious botanical
questions. A place that you never leave empty-handed.

Holly Hill Nursery was such a place. Its discreet sign,
Holly Hill Herbs and Scented Plants, suggested specializa-

tion. But the nursery was jam-packed with all kinds of plants, alphabetically displayed. Gardeners who journeyed to Holly Hill for the first time – and they came from several surrounding counties – were rewarded with a marvellous, added treat: an old walled herb garden. Within its boundaries, box hedging corralled a superb collection of old roses, scented shrubs, climbers, plants and, of course, herbs.

Most of the plants in Kate and Alex's old garden at Bath had been purchased at Holly Hill Nursery. At one time, Vicky Jamieson was visiting their garden so frequently with deliveries and free advice that Alex had nicknamed her 'Sis'.

Kate got out of the Trooper, stretched, and started towards the entry gate. Passing through it, she immediately saw Vicky up the path, loading plants on to a trolley. 'Vicky!' she shouted.

Vicky stopped and looked in her direction. Despite the distance between them Kate could see the look of surprise register on Vicky's face.

Vicky took off her gloves and walked over to greet Kate.

'What a nice surprise,' she said, hugging Kate with unrestrained exuberance.

'Careful, old girl, you're going to crack one of my ribs,' Kate giggled.

Vicky was an inch or so shorter than Kate. She was smoothly muscled and evenly tanned from years of working outdoors. Her features were unremarkable, save for apple-red cheeks that accentuated her ice-blue eyes. Her eyes always reminded Kate of the glass marbles she had played with as a schoolgirl.

Vicky stepped back and looked at Kate admiringly. 'You're looking well, Kate. What brings you here on a Wednesday, then? Don't you still have a shop to look after?'

'Still do, yes, but I do get a day off now and then, you know.'

'How's Alex?' she asked, running her fingers through her short-cropped bleached hair.

'He's fine. He's in his element with the house. I think I've been replaced as his first love.'

Their conversation was interrupted by a question from a grey-haired man inquiring about a certain strain of hellebore. Vicky answered his question and pointed to the far corner of the nursery where he would find what he was looking for.

'Let's go over to the office, Kate. We can have a good old chat there without being bothered. There should be some cold drinks in the fridge, if you'd like one. Megan can take care of things out here for a while.'

'That would be good, because there's something rather confidential I need to ask you about.'

Vicky frowned. 'Sounds intriguing. Come on then,' she said.

Vicky kicked off her boots and leaned back in an old oak swivel chair with her feet resting on another chair. Kate sat across from her, separated by a wooden desk cluttered with papers and plant markers. She poured the Malvern mineral water into her glass.

'So how's that fabulous garden of yours?' asked Vicky. 'It must look absolutely gorgeous right now.'

'It does. You really must come over and see it.' Her eyes searched Vicky's face. 'Actually, that's one of the reasons I came down today, Vicky. To ask you something – well, really to tell you something. . .'

'You sound a bit muddled. What is this "something"?'

'Sorry, Vicky,' Kate said taking a sip of water. 'Let me start again. Alex and I have made a strange – let's say a very important discovery in our garden.' She looked Vicky straight in the eyes, ready to register her reaction when she told Vicky what it was.

'Well, don't keep me in suspense,' Vicky said. 'What is it?'

'It's a blue rose.'

'You're having me on,' said Vicky. Then she put her head back and laughed.

'It's not a joke, Vicky. I'm serious. We've got this blue rose in the garden. We discovered it several weeks ago.'

'Blue – meaning purple? *Kind* of bluish?'

'No, it's a *blue* rose – *really* blue. Sapphire – that kind of blue.'

'There's no such thing, Kate. Nobody's ever been able to breed one.'

'Well, we have. Or, I should say – somebody has.'

'Jesus! You aren't kidding, are you?'

'No, I'm not. Do you want to see it?'

Vicky's eyebrows shot up. 'Do I want to see it? You must be bonkers. Of course I do. If it's what you're saying, this is an enormous discovery, Kate. When can I come over?'

'Hold on a sec, there's more.' She took a quick sip of water. 'First, you can't tell a soul about this. I mean it, Vicky. Strange things have been happening. Strange enough, in fact, that Alex and I have decided that we must get the rose out of our garden – and soon. Move it into hiding where nobody can find it – or steal it, for that matter. We were wondering if you would help?'

'You don't need to ask, Kate. You know I will.'

'You're a sweetheart. Alex and I would be rather nervous trying to transplant a rose the size of this one. I was wondering if you'd mind taking some cuttings for us too. I'm such a klutz at that sort of thing.'

'No problem, Kate. Who else knows about this, then?'

'Well, we thought it was just the four of us. The four being Alex, me, a chap named Kingston – he's a retired botany professor, interesting sort, I'll tell you all about him later – and our solicitor, Christopher Adell. But yesterday we had a letter from a Japanese man representing an international corporation who wants to buy the rose and just before that a phone call from a mysterious American who seems to know all about it, too. I know it sounds crazy but I'll give you the all the details when you come over. Can you make it tomorrow? The later in the day the better.'

'How about right after I leave here? Say six fifteen – thereabouts.'

'Perfect. I'll make an early supper?'

'Super. I'll bring a bottle of plonk.'

'As long as it's not Blue Nun,' Kate said, laughing.

At first Vicky was speechless. Like Kingston, she all but crawled around on her hands and knees to examine every inch of the rose. It was all Kate could do to drag her back to the house.

Alex opened the bottle of burgundy that Vicky had brought and poured three glasses. 'Well,' said Vicky, raising her glass, 'here's to Sapphire.' She took a modest sip and put her glass down. 'I still can't believe it,' she said, shaking her head.

'We've had time to become accustomed to it but it still gives me the creeps every time I look at it,' said Kate, with a mock shiver.

'I'm not surprised,' said Vicky. 'So tell me a bit more about this Kingston bloke. He sounds like quite a card.'

'He is,' said Alex. 'He's a Joker.'

'Oh, come on, Alex,' Kate said reprovingly, 'he's very nice – and very intelligent.'

Alex gave a little sigh. 'I suppose he has given us sound advice so far and spent quite a lot of his time trying to be helpful, but you've got to admit, Kate, he is a bit of a know-all. On more than one occasion you've even said so yourself.'

'Soonest opportunity we'll make a point of introducing you, Vicky. Then you can decide for yourself. Matter of fact, you two would have a lot in common.'

'I'd like that,' said Vicky. 'By the way, that letter and the phone call you mentioned in the garden. I hope they're talking big money. *Really* big money.'

'Yes, they are,' said Kate.

'How would you like to have your own cottage, Vicky?' Alex said with a wide smile.

'That big, eh?'

'Exactly,' said Kate. 'That's why, as I told you this afternoon, we want to move the rose out of here. Alex and I are becoming increasingly concerned that what's happened so far is only the beginning. There's a staggering amount of money involved. We're beginning to face up to the fact that things could even get a bit nasty. We have to be prepared, that's all.'

'It's not that we're paranoid,' said Alex, 'but frankly we'd both feel much safer if we get the rose out of our lives physically.'

Vicky had been toying with her wineglass as she listened. She had a thoughtful expression on her face. 'You know, I think I may have the perfect place for you.' She put the glass down and snapped her fingers. 'Yes, it would be ideal.'

'Where's that?' Alex asked.

'At my Aunt Nell's. Up in Shropshire. She lives just outside Market Drayton.'

'Certainly far enough away,' said Kate.

'Yes, and her house is quite secluded. Even better, the last time I was there, a couple of months ago, the garden was hopelessly overgrown. In places it's like a jungle. It's practically reverted to the wild. You could hide the crown jewels in there and nobody would ever find them.'

'Like they say,' said Alex, 'if you want to hide a tree – hide it in a forest. It sounds like we couldn't do better.'

'Do you think she'll mind?' Kate inquired.

'Not for one minute. She couldn't care less. Told me she rarely goes out into the garden any more. She gave up gardening years ago.'

'Threw in the trowel, eh?' Alex quipped.

Vicky chuckled. 'Nell's a treat. She's starting to get a bit frail now but you'll just love her.'

'If you think it would be all right, Vicky, could we move the rose fairly soon?'

'Whenever you say so, Kate. All I have to do is let Nell know we're coming up. It's going to take two of us, though, to transplant a rose that size. It'll require some muscle. Do you think you could come up with me, Alex?'

'Absolutely. We can go this Saturday, if that's okay with you.'

'Actually, Saturday would be perfect, I've got the day off.'

'I wish I could go with you,' Kate said, 'but I have to be at the shop on Saturday. They're delivering the things I bought at the auction last week.'

Vicky took a sip of wine and twiddled the stem of the glass on the table. 'By the way, Alex, it might be a good idea if we plan to stay overnight. Do you mind?'

'Not at all, as long as Kate doesn't mind me running off for the weekend with another woman,' he said grinning at Kate. 'But you're right, it is a pretty good hike up there.'

Vicky smiled. 'It makes sense, considering the time it'll take to plant the rose properly. Besides, I know Aunt Nell will insist on it and I wouldn't want to disappoint her. She'll really enjoy the company. She gets so few visitors these days.'

On Saturday morning, Vicky woke just before dawn. She had spent the night at The Parsonage so they could get an early start. Pulling aside the bedroom curtain, she peeked outside. There was enough light, she decided.

Before they got the blue rose out of the ground she wanted to take the cuttings. Now was as good a time as any. She put on her sweater and jeans and crept quietly downstairs, careful not to step on Asp, who was curled up at the foot of the stairs.

With sharp pruning shears, she removed a few of the blooms. Kate was going to attempt drying them. Next, she carefully snipped off twelve slender canes just below a leaflet, removing all the leaves save a couple at the top. She then dipped the lower end of each eight-inch cutting in a hormone rooting compound, after which she planted each of them in its own plastic pot filled with a specially prepared potting medium. After watering them, she enclosed each pot in a clear plastic bag to simulate a mini-greenhouse. The whole procedure took less than fifteen minutes.

She carefully placed the pots in an old wooden crate and carried it up to the garden shed where Kate had made a space for them. On the way back from Nell's tomorrow she planned to pick them up and take them to the nursery for safekeeping. Eventually she would transplant them into larger containers.

Carrying the rose blooms for Kate in a basket, she went back up to the house to make a pot of tea.

Getting Sapphire out of the ground proved more difficult than they had imagined. Vicky stressed the importance of keeping the largest possible ball of soil around the roots, to avoid root damage. The less disturbance the better, she had insisted. To minimize shock to the rose when it was uprooted, and make digging easier, Alex had thoroughly soaked the surrounding ground the night before.

To begin with, the spade sliced easily through the soft, moist earth on the surface. But the deeper Alex dug, the harder the earth became. The roots were unusually thick and deeply anchored for a rose – even an old rose. As Vicky levered up the big root ball with her shovel, Alex gradually wrapped the sheet of burlap around the ball, securing it with twine around the main cane just above the crown. At times, his face was perilously close to the dense red thorns bristling on the branching canes. Seen from inches away, they took on a vaguely menacing beauty.

They stood back for a moment, gawking at the cavernous hole that remained. Asp seized the moment to jump into it and start burrowing madly, determined to make it even deeper. Shooing him out, Alex filled it in and raked the surface smooth. With Alex and Vicky on either side, their hands under the root ball, they heaved Sapphire on to the waiting wheelbarrow. Alex figured that the sack held close to a hundred pounds of soil. With a lot of grunting, they hoisted it into the back of the van. Resting on a shallow box filled with small wood chips, it was tied on either side to the slats on the inside walls to make doubly sure there was no movement. Satisfied that Sapphire would enjoy the trip in comfort they walked up to the house to say goodbye to Kate.

'Be careful while we're gone,' Alex said, giving Kate a hug. 'If that American chap—'

'Alex, please don't worry. In another fifteen minutes, I'm going to the shop. I'll be there all day. I'm staying with Peg and Stuart tonight – then back at the shop tomorrow. I'd call that pretty safe, wouldn't you?'

After promises to phone, they debated briefly whether Asp should stay with Kate or go with Alex and Vicky. While Kate often took him to the shop, she was reluctant to take him to Peg's house overnight. Looking at him across the courtyard, sitting in the cab of the van, with his little red tongue bobbing in and out, they decided that he would enjoy the trip to Shropshire.

As they turned out of the drive on to the road, Alex adjusted the rear view mirror. In it, he could see Kate, still waving.

'We'd best take it nice and easy, Alex,' Vicky said. 'The less trauma the better. Besides, I don't think this old van is used to marathon drives.'

Alex laughed. 'Frankly I'm not sure, after all that wine last night, whether I'm up for a long drive either.'

Unnoticed by Alex, a dark-coloured BMW pulled on to the road behind them.

The journey was uneventful. They arrived at Aunt Nell's house in the late afternoon. It was located out of sight from the road, at the end of a narrow curving lane. Clumps of grass in the middle of the lane indicated that few cars had passed over it for some time. The hedge on either side was tall and overgrown. Prickly, snaking canes of dog rose and blackberry clawed against the van as they passed. Alex parked the van on a gravel patch under an old apple tree. Asp leaped out of Alex's door and was already off exploring, sniffing up and down the hedgerow, as they both got out to give Sapphire a quick check. The rose appeared to be none the worse for the journey.

As they approached Nell's modest two-storey brick Victorian house, Alex stopped to peer over a side gate. All he could see was a tangled mess of dense foliage that had once been a garden. 'You're right Vicky. They'll have a bloody hard time finding Sapphire here,' he said.

A diminutive white-haired woman stood at the open front door. 'Hello, Vicky,' she said with an affectionate smile. Then she half turned to Alex. 'You must be Alex,' she added.

With her snowy hair tied in an unruly bun, periwinkle-blue eyes, ruddy cheeks and floral print frock, she was the quintessential aunt. Right out of Central Casting, thought Alex.

'That's me,' he said, returning her smile. 'Pleasure to meet you, Aunt Nell.'

'I would imagine you both must be ready for a grown-up's drink.'

Alex knew immediately that he would get on famously with her.

A few minutes later, they sat in her small parlour in comfortable wicker chairs warmed by an aromatic wood fire crackling in the hearth. Alex had opted for scotch, not knowing that Aunt Nell poured it like lemonade. She and Vicky had settled for tea.

Aunt Nell poked a log in the inglenook fireplace, sending a shower of sparks up the chimney. 'What's all this hush-hush stuff about then, Vicky?' she asked, blithely.

'Sorry I couldn't tell you too much on the phone. The upshot is that Alex here, and his wife, Kate, discovered this rare type of rose on their property. We have it in the back of the van. There's a big chance that it could be quite valuable.'

'My heavens! All this fuss over a rose. What makes it so special?' Aunt Nell peered at Alex over the top of her bifocals.

'Only one thing, actually, Nell. The rose is an unusual colour. There's never been one like it before. Ever.'

'It's sort of a botanical aberration,' Alex said.

Nell gave him a quizzical look.

'A freak of nature,' Vicky chimed in. 'We know that people in the business are desperate to get their hands on it. In fact, the word is already out. The people advising Alex and Kate have warned them to be careful.'

'My goodness, how exciting,' said Nell, her eyes twinkling away.

'That's why we thought of your garden, Auntie. We decided, on their recommendation, to hide the rose for a while – at least until we decide what to do with it. Only the three of us, Kate and a professor, will know where the rose is hidden. By the way, we've nicknamed the rose Sapphire.'

Nell raised her eyebrows. 'A blue rose?'

'Yes, believe it or not, that's what it is,' Vicky said.

'My goodness gracious, I suppose that is a trifle unusual.'

'To say the least,' Alex added.

'You mentioned a professor, Vicky.'

'Yes, a retired professor, actually. His specialty is botany – taught at Edinburgh University. He's examined the rose and says that it's real.'

'How exciting,' Nell enthused. 'Well, it should certainly be safe here, wouldn't you think? I hardly ever go out there any more. Only to give the birds a few crumbs now and then. Don't know if you could see much when you drove in, but it's an unsightly mess. We've never been ones for gardening. Even when Ben was alive he never took much interest. Always off down to the pub the minute he got some time off. Lord knows, Vicky, I wish I could afford a gardener but, for me, that would be a total waste of money. In any case it's hard to find chaps who want to work at it these days – everybody's so lazy and unreliable. Have to watch 'em like a hawk,' she chortled.

Vicky got up and put her cup and saucer on the tray. 'We don't expect the rose to be here long. When this is all over, I'll come down and give you a hand. At least tidy the garden up a bit. You might enjoy it out there in the summer. I'm sure Alex and Kate would love to come and see you too.'

'You'll like Kate a lot,' said Alex, starting to feel the effect of the king-size scotch. 'I'll come back any time you'll have me.'

'Well, you leave Spitfire, or whatever her name is, out there as long as you please, dear. You must be jolly hungry after that long drive. Will Cornish pasties be all right? Made them this morning. You look as if you're ready for another one,' she said with a knowing grin, grabbing Alex's glass out of his hand before he had a chance to decline.

'Spitfire,' said Alex after she'd left the room. 'That's funny. It may turn out to be more appropriate than Sapphire.'

The next morning Alex was jolted out of a blissful sleep by what he first thought was a pneumatic drill. It was the old-fashioned wind-up alarm clock Nell had left by the bed. 'Just as bloody well I don't have a weak heart,' he mumbled. He got dressed and went down to the kitchen to feed Asp and see if he could find some coffee. Nell had thoughtfully left everything out for them: coffee, tea, sugar, cups, and a loaf of fresh bread. Not five minutes later, as the coffee was starting to percolate, Vicky joined him. 'That alarm clock probably woke up half the population of Market Drayton,' she said, in the midst of a lengthy yawn. 'Nell must wear ear plugs.'

Outside, it was unseasonably nippy and a thin mist robbed the garden of all colour. It looked even more of a shambles than it had yesterday. For the best part it was nothing more than an impenetrable mass of brambles, overgrown shrubs and tortured coils of rambling roses and vines. Trying to negotiate a path through it was frustrating. Only a chain saw would have made any real forward progress possible. After ten minutes, Alex and Vicky finally came across a suitable home for Sapphire: a long kidney-shaped flowerbed that had miraculously evaded the encroaching wilderness, providing a rare stretch of earth where enough sunlight penetrated for the rose to flourish. It was well out of sight.

Alex set about digging the hole while Vicky went to fetch Sapphire. Earlier, they had lifted the rose from the van into a decrepit wheelbarrow that had probably seen neither oil nor use in the last quarter century. After several unsuccessful attempts to get the wheelbarrow moving, she finally had to call Alex for help. The rose was simply too heavy for her to handle alone.

'Remember the old saying, "It's better to plant a five-quid rose in a ten-quid hole than vice versa,"' Vicky said, as she watched the pile of soil alongside Alex getting higher.

'The hole's more important than the rose, eh?'

'Right.'

'Gonna be shaking hands with an Aussie soon, if I go much deeper.'

'Tell you what, Alex. Lay the shovel across the hole and we'll measure the depth. We need plenty of extra space for the compost that's going in there.'

Vicky decided that the 'crater', as Alex called it, was wide and deep enough. She up-ended the large bag of compost and shook it into the hole. As she did so, Alex spaded it in with the earth.

'How's it going, you two?' It was Nell carrying two bottles of mineral water. 'Thought you might be thirsty with all that digging.' She handed them each a bottle.

Alex took a long swig. 'Mmm, that's good. Thanks, Nell. The hardest part's done, I think.'

'That's an awfully large hole for that bitty rose, isn't it?' Nell asked, eyeing the wheelbarrow.

'We're playing it really safe,' Vicky replied.

All this time, Alex had been fighting a losing battle to keep Asp from jumping in the hole. 'Nell,' he said, 'could you take Asp till we're finished here. I'm going to bury the little chap if I'm not careful.'

'Of course,' said Nell, picking up Asp and tucking him under her arm. 'Well, you don't need me here – I've got some ironing to do.' She turned and walked back toward the house, and Alex and Vicky turned their attention back to Sapphire.

'Let's run some water in the hole to check the drainage.' Vicky looked up at Alex and smiled. 'Then we can introduce Sapphire to her new home.'

With effort, they managed to lift the rose off the wheelbarrow. With short shuffling steps they walked it the short distance to the hole. Just as they were about to lower the heavy root ball, Vicky stumbled and lost her grip. The weight was too heavy for Alex. He couldn't hold it. The rose hit the ground with a soft thump and the thorny canes whipped around, raking Vicky's arm. A five-inch tear in the sleeve of her white shirt was instantly soaking up blood like blotting paper.

'Damn! That hurt,' she said, gritting her teeth and grasping her forearm tightly.

'We'd better get up to the house – clean that out with some hydrogen peroxide and put a bandage on it. They look like pretty deep gashes to me,' Alex said, taking her free arm and leading her back to the house.

In a matter of a few minutes, Aunt Nell, working calmly and efficiently, had treated and bandaged Vicky's arm.

'I'll leave you two together, then,' she said, getting up from the kitchen chair and walking over to the sink to rinse her hands. 'I've got to go and call my neighbour, Arthur. He's got some tomatoes for me.'

'Rotten bit of luck, that,' said Alex, after Nell had left the room. 'Don't worry, I'll finish up out there,' he said, getting up from his chair.

'No, I'm fine, Alex.'

'You sure?'

'Positive.'

He put a hand on her shoulder. 'Before all this business started, I'd always thought of roses as being beautiful and benign,' he said. 'But this one's getting to be positively dangerous.'

'Don't be silly, Alex. It was just an accident. It's not the first time I've been attacked by a rose. I'll be fine. And so will Sapphire.'

121

Chapter Twelve

The morning rose that untouch'd stands
Arm'd with her briers, how sweet she smells!
But pluck'd and strain'd through ruder hands,
Her sweets no longer with her dwells.
Sir Robert Aytoun

Kenji Tanaka – Ken, as he preferred to be called – stared out of the window of his tastefully appointed Hampstead Heath flat, lost in thought as he sipped from the cup of hot green tea. His tea ritual was one of the few Japanese customs that had endured from his childhood in San Francisco, where his maternal grandmother had raised him. Ken was fifty-two, but could pass easily for a man twenty years younger. His hair was neatly barbered, jet black and shiny. He had yet to discover – and he searched conscientiously every day – a single lurking grey hair. At a glance his Asian ancestry was not readily apparent. This was due, in good part, to a fastidiously trimmed moustache and narrow beard that circled his lower face drawing attention to his thin-lipped mouth. Everything else about him – his choice of clothes (expensive London boutiques), taste, demeanour and general lifestyle – was distinctly Western. His speech, a deceptive mix of American and cultured English, bore no trace whatsoever of Japanese, despite the fact that – thanks to his grandmother – he spoke the language fluently.

Tanaka had lived in London for nearly twenty years, enjoying a civilized and comfortable life made possible by brokering art and real estate to wealthy Japanese individuals and corporations. Despite his being a *nisei* – born in America of Japanese immigrants – he had developed, through family and friends, a network of important business contacts in Japan.

He was contemplating his good fortune, thinking about the phone conversation he'd had two weeks earlier with a business acquaintance, Roger Maltby. Roger was an executive with Bonham's, the London auctioneers in Knightsbridge. It wasn't at all unusual for Roger to give him advance notice about forthcoming auctions. But this particular auction, he had said, was not about paintings or antiques. It was a rose that was going on the block. Ken had started to laugh but quickly stopped when Roger told him the rose was blue. 'It's the world's first ever blue rose and it's going to break every auction record in the book. I'm talking huge money,' he said. And Ken Tanaka was desperately in need of money.

It was almost a year to the day since he had made a deposit into his brokerage and bank accounts. Three years ago, before the dotcom collapse, and before the Japanese art and real estate buyers had bailed out of the market, his portfolio in stocks, bonds and cash was over two million dollars. His most recent Schwab statement and his TD Waterhouse retirement account totalled little more than £25,000. Allowing for fixed monthly expenses and curtailed spending, only for day-to-day living, it would all be gone within a few months. Borrowing was out of the question, he had no tangible assets or equity of any kind. For the first time in his life he would be broke. Even now, he refused to accept that possibility. The humiliation alone would be more than he could take.

Immediately after Roger's call, Ken had combed his database and narrowed his pool of prospects. Quickly he determined that, among his wealthy client list, only three investors qualified. Each was not only easily capable of committing the vast sum that it would take to acquire the blue rose but might, for various reasons, be predisposed to the unique challenge and risk. His first offer – to a Mr Yasuda, chairman of a large industrial conglomerate –

elicited considerable interest. As luck would have it, Yasuda had a passion for horticulture. Not only that, but two of the companies in his group produced garden-related products. Mr Yasuda, as expected of somebody in his elevated position of power and wealth, possessed an exalted sense of privilege and was certainly not lacking in shrewdness. While he found the prospect of owning the world's first blue rose irresistible, Yasuda saw no need to compete with others in its acquisition. Accordingly, he authorized Ken to explore the possibility of purchasing the rose direct from the owners.

The phone was ringing. Ken put his cup down and walked over to the inlaid mahogany bureau that also served as his work desk and picked up the receiver. The caller announced himself as a Mr Moriyama, personal secretary to Mr Hiroshi Yasuda. The conversation, in Japanese, was brief.

'Yes, hello, Mr Moriyama. I didn't expect to hear from you quite yet.'

'Mr Yasuda is anxious to know whether you have had a response yet from Mr and Mrs Sheppard. Whether they are prepared to discuss the sale of the rose. It has been five days now since he gave you the instructions to proceed. He is concerned.'

Tanaka stroked his beard nervously. With Yasuda, he knew that he had to be straightforward and businesslike. Vague answers and promises were not acceptable.

'Please assure Mr Yasuda that nothing is wrong and that I understand perfectly his concern. Please inform him that I have not yet received a response to my letter. As a result, I have been trying to reach the Sheppards by phone. I have called a number of times over the last two days without success. If they continue to ignore our proposal, I must visit them personally. I will report back as soon as I have more information.'

'Very good, Mr Tanaka. I shall pass on your message. We will wait to hear from you. Thank you, and goodbye for now.'

Ken stood by the phone, tapping his manicured nails on

the polished surface of the desk. A chance like this, he knew, would never come again in his lifetime. He stood to make more from brokering the sale of the blue rose than he had made in the last ten years combined. He was prepared to do whatever it took to make the Sheppards accept Yasuda's offer. Force them, if necessary. His survival now depended on it.

He sipped the last dregs of tepid tea, brushing a stray tea-leaf from his lower lip. He must think this over carefully, prepare himself for any eventuality. He preferred not even to think about his offer being rejected. If it were, he had an alternative plan. He would devote the next few hours to reviewing that contingency making sure that all the parts were in place. But Alex and Kate Sheppard would respond favourably, he was sure. The figure that Yasuda had authorized him to offer was far higher than even he had imagined.

Kingston looked directly into the lens and waited for the camera to click. The sergeant in camouflage fatigues and black beret slanted over one eye removed the passport-type print from the camera and attached it to a plastic pass badge. Checking it briefly, he then handed it to Kingston.

'Clip this on, please, sir, and wear it at all times. One of Captain Cardwell's men will meet you outside and take you over to DSSS.' Affixing the badge, Kingston thanked the guard and stepped out in the sunshine.

He was at the Defence Intelligence and Security Centre training establishment at Chicksands in the heart of the Bedfordshire countryside. Referred to as DISC, the grounds also housed the headquarters of the Intelligence Corps. Knowing the army's proclivity for acronyms, it didn't surprise him to learn that one of the training schools within DISC was DSSS, the Defence Special Signal School. This was Captain Cardwell's department.

Following up on the Bletchley Museum director's suggestion, Kingston had established that there were only two organizations that might be capable of decoding Major Cooke's journals. One was the DSSS and the other the Government Communications Headquarters in the spa town of Cheltenham, in Gloucestershire. Intrigued with the idea of its rural setting, and as it was closer to London, Kingston had elected to start with the DSSS.

As Kingston waited for his escort he surveyed the surrounding scene. In front of him a formidable chain link barrier closed off the road. It was at least eight feet tall. He watched as a military guard went through the process of checking through a British Telecom van. Kingston counted five other camouflage-clad guards in the vicinity, each with an automatic weapon slung over his shoulder. He hadn't anticipated such stringent security. For the first time he was starting to have qualms about pursuing the whole code business. Was it a good idea, after all? Considering that these men were responsible for the nation's security, his justification for coming to Chicksands now seemed frivolous, to say the least. 'A blue rose, for Christ's sake,' he muttered to himself.

'Dr Kingston?' the soldier, a corporal, inquired, stepping out of a Land Rover.

Kingston nodded.

'Jump in, sir. Too nice a day to be doing this, eh?'

'It most certainly is,' Kingston replied.

As they drove off, Kingston glanced back at the heavily guarded entrance, and then at the scene outside. It was incongruous. They were now driving through the midst of a bucolic country estate with freshly mown lawns and tall trees.

'That's the old Priory on the right there,' the corporal remarked as they drove by a sprawling brick and stone building with tall chimneys, fronted by a row of neatly clipped yew trees. 'Built in eleven hundred and something,' he added.

'Most impressive,' was all Kingston could think of saying.

'It's the officers' mess now.'

'Lucky chaps,' said Kingston. 'Not like in my time.'

Nothing more was said for the next minute or so. Soon the car stopped outside a low brick building.

The corporal looked over his shoulder. 'Inside, follow the main corridor, dead ahead.' His words rolled out in military fashion. 'Captain Cardwell's office is the third door on the right. He's expecting you.'

Walking down the corridor, Kingston thought back to his first phone conversation with Captain Cardwell a week ago. Initially Cardwell had been reluctant to help, politely reminding Kingston that the DSSS was not in the habit of performing this type of trivial function. There would be hell to pay if a taxpayer found out, he had remonstrated. But after a persuasive appeal by Kingston, Cardwell eventually acquiesced. 'We still have a handful of officers who have many years of service,' he said. 'To set your mind at rest, I'll have one of them take a look at Major Cooke's journals.'

Kingston had couriered them to Cardwell the same day. In a follow-up phone call, Cardwell confided to Kingston that the reason for their making the exception was mostly because everybody at DSSS was proud of the magnificent work done by the cryptographers at Bletchley during the war. This was for one of their own, as it were. Secondly – but not for publication – was because he and his wife happened to be passionate gardeners. They were particularly fond of roses.

It never surprised Kingston how such a mutuality of interest in a simple flower could manage to open even the most stubbornly closed doors.

'Come in – come on in,' a voice boomed from inside Room 8 in answer to Kingston's knock on the door.

When he entered, Kingston was taken aback. He had not expected such a large man, nor one quite so athletic-looking. Somehow, he had pictured an Intelligence Corps captain to look more bookish.

After a bone-cracking handshake, the two sat facing each other across the orderly surface of Cardwell's desk. Cardwell was cordial and, as was to be expected, punctilious. Major Cooke's journals sat in a tidy stack off to one side. The high-ceilinged room with its sparse furnishings and bare windows lent a hollow sound to Cardwell's already stentorian voice. 'Well, doctor, it looks like you came to the right place,' he said. 'The only place, I believe, where you could have got your books decoded. We've got some interesting news for you.'

Kingston didn't want to appear unduly excited. 'Excellent,' he replied, leaning forward slightly in his chair.

Cardwell placed a beefy hand on the pile of journals. 'As you surmised, doctor, all the entries in these books are references to hybridizing of roses. We estimate that the books contain a total close to five thousand of Major Cooke's cross-pollination attempts. In the early books, all the crosses – as I believe they're called – are between roses exclusively.' He pulled out a book from the bottom of the pile, and opened it. 'However, in the case of the last three books, in chronological order, all the references are between roses and other kinds of flowers.' He held the open book up so that Kingston could see the translation clipped to the inside. 'On this page, for example, it's evident that he's using the same parent rose – an old French one called Madame Plantier – and attempting to cross it with several different varieties of hardy geraniums. He also refers to them sometimes as Cranesbill – is that correct?'

'Yes, that is right,' Kingston replied.

'Here, take a look,' he said, passing the book to Kingston. A moment of silence followed as Kingston read the translation, nodding his head. He handed it back.

'May I look at the last book – chronologically, that is?' Kingston asked.

'Of course.' Cardwell extracted the lowest book from the pile, briefly checked the inside page and handed it to Kingston, who started to flip through its pages.

'Were you aware that there could be a book missing?' Cardwell asked, casually.

'Yes, I was, as a matter of fact.'

'Our cryptographer spotted it, too. A gap in the dates.'

Kingston closed the book and looked up. 'I suppose there is the possibility that Cooke stopped hybridizing for a while,' he said. 'Went on holiday, maybe.'

Cardwell shook his head. 'No, it's not only the dates that don't match, nor do the hybridizing numbers. But you weren't to know that. They're out of sequence, too. Anyway, if he'd gone away, surely he would have picked up where he left off.'

'You're right.'

'That's not all.'

'What do you mean?'

A disconcerted look clouded Cardwell's face. 'There's something else you should know.'

'What's that?' Kingston asked.

'A few days after we'd decoded your journals somebody brought the missing book in and, unbeknownst to me, our chap decoded it, too.'

Chapter Thirteen

Birth, life and death – each took place on the hidden side of a leaf.

Toni Morrison

Before Alex could bring the van to a complete stop, Asp bounded out of the open window and bolted for Kate, standing at the front door. She picked him up, lifting her chin as he licked furiously at her neck.

'Come and say goodbye to Vicky,' Alex called to her as he got out of the van.

Kate walked over to see Vicky sliding over into the driver's seat. 'Aren't you coming in, Vicky?' she asked.

'No thanks, Kate. 'Fraid I'm coming down with something. I think I'm just going to go home and get some rest. On the way out, I'll stop at the shed and pick up the twelve cuttings I took yesterday. I'll drop them off at the nursery on the way home.'

'I can do that tomorrow, if you'd like.'

'It's no bother, I have to practically drive by there anyway.'

'Well, I'm sorry you're not feeling well. I'll give you a call tomorrow. Did everything go okay at your aunt's?'

'Yes. We found the perfect spot for Sapphire. Nobody will find her there. Alex enjoyed himself, too. He and Nell really hit it off. I'm sure he'll tell you all about it.'

Vicky started the engine, turned the van around and, with a wave goodbye, took off down the driveway.

Vicky parked the van by the nursery greenhouse and got

out. Stepping on to the gravel path, she felt slightly dizzy but shrugged it off as tiredness. She unlocked the padlock and opened the door. Back at the van, she took out the box containing the cuttings, and carried them inside. With a felt marker she wrote, *Don't touch, these are Vicky's* on the side of the crate. She then placed them on a high shelf in the farthest corner of the small greenhouse.

By the time she switched the lights on in the cottage it was past eight. Her mouth was dry and her limbs ached. Maybe it was the long drive and the glass of wine she'd had at lunchtime, she said to herself. Or perhaps the crab sandwich. No, it couldn't be that, she'd hardly eaten any of it.

Rummaging through the refrigerator, she found a half-full bottle of Malvern water. There was some leftover pasta and a curling slice of pizza in there, too, but the very thought of eating anything made her feel queasy. The water had lost its fizz, but she poured it into a glass and drank it anyway. She was unusually thirsty. She went to the tap and refilled the glass, swallowing it in two gulps as she stood there.

She went into the living room and plopped down on the sofa with the idea of reading the two newspapers she'd brought in with her. Why was the cottage so warm? The radiators hadn't been on for days. She took off her turtle-neck sweater, reminding herself to tell Alex that she had his. He'd left it in the van.

She was now on her fourth glass of water. And when the words on the newspaper started to blur, she knew some-thing was really wrong. She stood up, steadying herself on the arm of the sofa. Her eyes were focusing again but she felt very disoriented – as though she might pass out at any moment. Slowly she made her way to the phone and picked it up.

Alex put a hand round Kate's waist. 'Poor Vicky. I'm afraid she's really under the weather. She slept most of the way back. I promised I'd give her a call in the morning to see how she's doing.'

They walked into the living room. Alex slumped on the sofa and kicked off his loafers.

Kate put Asp down. He promptly leapt up on Alex's lap.

'Are you hungry?' she asked.

'Not really, a snack, maybe. We had a pub lunch about one o'clock. Poor thing, she hardly touched anything on her plate.'

'How about a glass of champagne?'

'Are we celebrating?'

Kate was about to answer when the doorbell rang.

'Seven thirty,' Alex said, with a frown, looking at his watch. 'Are you expecting anybody?'

'No. You stay put, I'll go and see who it is.'

'Pray that it's not our friend the doctor,' Alex called out after her.

Kate opened the heavy oak door just as the doorbell rang a second time. Standing outside on the step, thumb still on the button, was Graham Cooke.

'Graham,' she said. 'What brings you here?' He was wearing the same shabby Donegal suit as at their last meeting and held a slim leather portfolio.

'I'm sorry about just showing up like this, but I'm going away for a few days tomorrow and this couldn't wait.'

'It's not about your aunt, is it?' Kate asked, her voice overshadowed with concern.

'In a way. May I come in?' His manner was brusque and bordering on antagonistic.

'Of course,' she said, injecting as much pleasantness into her voice as she could muster. 'This way.'

As Kate led Graham into the sitting room she noticed his eyes darting around, obviously appraising the changes since his aunt's departure. 'Can I get you anything?' she asked? 'Tea? Coffee? A drink maybe?'

'No thanks, Mrs Sheppard. I won't stay for more than a moment. I don't anticipate this taking long at all.'

Alex stood up as the two of them entered. 'Graham – what brings you here?'

Graham sat down in a leather wing chair, placing the portfolio on his lap. He licked his lips, quickly wiping them dry with the palm of his hand. 'It's about the rose in your garden. The one my uncle created. The blue rose.'

Kate's gasp was not loud enough to hear.

Alex had a look of incomprehension on his face.

For several seconds there was an uneasy silence.

'Recently,' Graham continued, 'I engaged the services of a solicitor, to find out who rightfully owns the rose in question. My aunt and I feel – correctly so, as it turns out – that the rose legally belongs to us. If it were known, at the time you bought The Parsonage, that a very valuable rose existed on the property we would, of course, never have sold it to you. As you probably know by now, the value of the rose is inestimable. Hundreds – many hundreds of times that of the property.'

'You can't be serious,' Alex said, finally having found his voice. 'What do you mean by "correctly so"?'

'The overriding argument, here – and it's all been legally established – is that my aunt and I were disadvantaged by the transaction and therefore it should be voided. Meaning that title of The Parsonage reverts back to our family. Accordingly, we are entitled to possession of the rose. You simply get your money back.'

Kate's heart sank. Lose the rose *and* The Parsonage?

Alex's expression had changed to one of annoyance. 'Now just wait a minute,' he snapped. 'How do you know it was your uncle who hybridized it?'

'I have proof of that – but let me continue.' Graham opened the portfolio and withdrew an envelope. 'You might want to take a look at this. I think you'll find that it spells out our position quite clearly.' He handed the sealed envelope to Alex. 'Oh, yes. You asked for proof that my uncle propagated the rose.'

'That's right, I did,' Alex replied.

'You'll recall my uncle's journals? The ones you borrowed?'

Kate's heart sank further.

'You still have them, don't you?'

'Yes, we do,' said Alex.

Kate glanced at Alex. She could see that he was getting rankled.

'Well,' said Graham, 'if you examine the hybridizing dates – the only entries not in code – you'll discover a break in the sequence between two of the books. There's a journal missing.' He paused, then said, 'I have that journal.'

Kate leaned forward. 'And. . .'

'The crossing formula – I believe that's what you call it – for the blue rose is in that journal.'

'But if it's in code, how can you be so sure?' asked Kate.

'Look, how I found out is really none of your business. Just take my word for it that the formula to create a blue rose is in that book.'

'I'm just curious. How did you know which specific journal contained the formula?' Alex asked.

Graham heaved a sigh. His patience was clearly coming to an end. 'If you must know,' he said, 'the book in question was never with the others. According to my aunt it was in a safety deposit box along with some other valuables. After Uncle Jeffrey died, she couldn't figure out why on earth he'd put it there. When she told me about it, frankly, neither could I. Eventually, it was put in with the other books and they were all put away and forgotten about. It's a miracle, in fact, that they weren't chucked out. But when you two showed up and started asking about Uncle's roses and his records, I suddenly realized its significance. That there was a very good reason, indeed, why Uncle had locked that book away.'

Kate looked away from Graham to Alex and then to the envelope in Alex's hand.

'I suppose we might as well look at it now,' she said, in a dejected voice.

Alex opened the envelope and withdrew the one-page letter, which bore the letterhead of a Newbury law firm,

Stanhope, Stanhope and Crouch, Barristers and Solicitors. Together, they started to read it:

Dear Mr and Mrs Sheppard,

I represent Mr Graham Cooke. He is the nephew of Mrs Cooke, from whom you recently acquired the property wherein you now reside, commonly known as The Parsonage.

Mr Cooke informs me that a certain rose bush, unique in all the world, grows in a corner of the Parsonage premises; that its existence was unknown to both his aunt and you at the time of offer, acceptance, and conveyance of the property; and that, because of its uniqueness, it imparts a value to the property far exceeding your purchase price.

It thus is apparent, applying settled legal doctrine, that Mrs Cooke and yourselves entered into the transaction on the basis of a 'mutual mistake' of major proportions concerning the property's value; that, but for this mistake, the transaction would not have happened; and that the transaction therefore is voidable at the seller's instance.

My purpose in writing is to advise you that Mr Cooke, on behalf of his aunt and with her authorization, is prepared to initiate legal action to void the transaction. Before taking that extreme step, however, he proposes a compromise whereby: (1) you would retain title to The Parsonage, (2) ownership of the subject rose bush would be restored to Mrs Cooke, and (3) the rose bush would be removed from the Parsonage premises at a mutually acceptable time.

I suggest you call me at your early convenience to arrange a meeting, in my office, to consider Mr Cooke's eminently fair and reasonable proposal. Hearing nothing from you by 15th August, we will undertake legal action.

I caution you, pending resolution of this matter, not to sell, pledge, move, take cuttings from, or otherwise propagate, disturb, or tamper with the subject rose bush in any manner whatsoever.

Very truly yours,
Alexander Q. Stanhope

Still holding the letter, Alex looked up at Graham. Alex's

face was grim. 'Graham,' he said, 'I think you'd better leave. There's obviously nothing more to be said. We'll refer this to our solicitor tomorrow.'

Graham tucked the portfolio under his arm and stood, ready to leave.

'When you think about it,' he said, 'if I own the hybridizing formula and am presumably capable of reproducing the blue rose, possessing the rose itself becomes moot, doesn't it?'

'We'll see about that,' said Alex.

Graham turned and started toward the door.

'Hang on a minute,' said Kate, taking the letter from Alex and studying it. 'I'm curious.'

Graham stopped, and looked at her. 'About what?'

'This letter says, specifically, that "a certain rose bush grows in a corner of the Parsonage premises." How would you or your lawyer have known that? How can you be so sure that the rose is growing in our garden?'

'I'm sorry, I'm not answering any more questions,' he said. 'I must be going.'

Kate followed Graham to the front door. He left without saying another word.

Kate walked back into the living room, where Alex was seated on the couch rereading Stanhope's letter. As he looked up at her she threw her head back and started laughing. 'What's so bloody funny?' he asked.

'Who said bad luck is bending over to pick up a four-leaf clover and being infected by poison ivy? What a turn-up for the books!'

'I had a feeling all along that Graham was an opportunist, but why did he have to go to a lawyer, for Christ's sake? Why didn't he come to us first? What a weasel,' he said, slapping the letter with the back of his hand.

'In a way, I can see his point. It is his uncle's creation. At least, as far as we know.'

'Kate, I'm no expert on estate law but I've read any number of times that anything physically attached to a house or planted in the ground is considered part of the property when it's sold. Who created the rose is irrelevant.

The rose was planted on our land and it belongs to us. It's as easy as that.'

Kate snapped her fingers. 'That's it,' she said.

'What?'

'How Graham knew the rose was in our garden. He actually saw it.'

'What?'

'Yes. You remember he left the books on the porch, while we were gone. It would have been the easiest thing in the world for him to take his time poking round the garden. I'll bet that's just what he did.'

'You're right, Kate – the sly bugger.'

'Well, what do we do now?'

'Wait and see what Adell advises, I guess.'

Kate looked at her watch. 'It's a bit late to call him now.'

'I'll do it first thing tomorrow.' He screwed up his face in distaste. 'Losing the rose would be bad enough. But losing it to Graham – speaking for myself, that would be a really bitter pill.'

'We haven't lost it yet.'

'That's true.'

'You know, Alex, it's odd, when you think about it. Logically, one would expect Mrs Cooke to be the one to instigate such a claim. After all, it was her husband's doing–'

'– if we're to believe Graham.'

'Yes, but assuming that's the case – Graham's not even her son. I just wonder if he hasn't talked her into all this.'

'There's only one way to find out, and that is to ask her.'

'You know, I really think we should. If she's unaware of what Graham is up to – and I grant you, that's unlikely – it could change everything.'

'Kate, she must have known. It would be almost impossible for Graham to pull this kind of stunt behind her back. It's far too serious. Hiring a lawyer and everything.'

'You're right. We have to talk to her.'

'Just her.'

'Alex, I can hardly ask her to exclude Graham. But if I suggest a weekday meeting, say mid-afternoon, chances are he'll be at work. We'll just have to play it by ear.'

Alex sighed. 'I think I'll skip the champagne, Kate. A large scotch is what I need.' He massaged his forehead. 'I was thinking. Kingston's going to be really miffed when we tell him that it's all over. He was really getting into this code thing. I'll call him first thing tomorrow.'

The phone rang.

'Christ, what now?' Alex said.

'I'll get it.' Kate got up and walked over to the phone. 'Kate Sheppard speaking.'

'Hello, Kate, Lawrence here. I've got some interesting news.'

'Really? As a matter of fact, we were just talking about you. We were about to sit down and have a drink. We both need it. We've just received some rather unsettling news.'

'I'm sorry to hear that. Perhaps I should call you tomorrow.'

'No, it's fine, Lawrence.'

'All right, then. I promise to make this quick. I was calling to let you know that I did manage to get Major Cooke's journals translated. They're exactly as we suspected – records of his hybridizing. But that's not all. Guess what? Somebody else took the missing journal to the same place – Defence Intelligence and Security Centre at Chicksands – and had it translated, too. What's more, for reasons I won't go into, the Intelligence people couldn't locate their file copies of the decrypted notes of the pages in question. All they could tell me for certain was that the journal did mention a blue rose. Want to take a guess who took the journal in?'

'So it's true, then?'

'What is? What are you saying?'

'We already know who it was.'

'What do you mean, Kate?'

'The person who had the missing journal decoded.'

'How on earth would *you* know that?'

'It was Graham Cooke. He was just here and told us all about it. What's more he's threatening to repossess The Parsonage. He wants us to hand over the blue rose. He left us a very nasty letter from his solicitor. He knows all about it. Everything.'

'My God! That's absurd. He certainly didn't waste any time.'

'I know, Lawrence. It's been one hell of a shock. It hasn't all started to sink in yet. Graham just left – literally minutes ago. As I mentioned, Alex and I were just about to sit down and discuss it over a large drink.'

'I don't know quite what to say – other than I'm sorry. With everything that's happening, perhaps it's time the three of us got together again – though it sounds like this business with Graham will have to be thrashed out by the lawyers.'

'Alex is calling Adell first thing tomorrow and faxing him the lawyer's letter.'

'Good. Keep me posted. I'd like to know what Adell says.'

'We will, Lawrence. I'll ask Alex to call you later tomorrow.'

'Whenever he can. Well, goodnight, Kate. I'm sure, with Adell's help, you'll be able to sort it all out.'

'Let's hope so,' she said.

'Oh, one last thing. Our American friend. From what Alex told me, it looks like he's just a go-between. I'm not quite sure yet, but I think I may know who may be behind it, though. Give me a couple of more days to do a little more digging and I'll fill you in.'

'I'll tell Alex,' she said, wishing Kingston goodnight and hanging up.

Kate plopped down next to Alex and put her arm around his shoulder. 'Well, we know one thing,' she sighed.

'What's that, darling?'

'Graham's not lying about having had the notorious missing journal decoded.'

'How's that?'

'Kingston was saying that he just got back from meeting with some government intelligence people at a place called Chicksands. They decoded the Major's journals. They also admitted to having decoded the journal – for Graham.'

Alex's eyebrows shot up. 'Graham and Kingston went to the same place?'

'It's really not that much of a coincidence. According to Kingston it's the only branch of intelligence remaining capable of doing it.'

Alex covered his face with his hands and let out a long sigh. 'This is really getting out of hand. Next thing you know Kingston will be telling us that the American is working for the CIA. I mean, *really*.'

Kate chuckled. 'Actually, he mentioned him – the American. Lawrence said that he's pretty sure he knows who's behind it. He's doing some more checking and will let us know. Probably talking to MI5,' she said with a smirk.

'Wouldn't surprise me one bit.'

Kate got up and switched on the table lamp next to Alex. 'How about that large scotch?'

'That would be very nice.' He heaved a sigh. 'I wonder when this is all going to end? It's getting–'

The phone rang, interrupting him.

'Not yet, by the sound of it,' said Kate. 'You get this one.'

Alex got up and went to the phone.

'Alex.' It was a woman's voice, but he could hardly hear her.

'Hello,' he said. 'You'll have to speak up a bit.'

'Alex. It's Vicky.' Her voice was hoarse, little more than a whisper. 'Since you dropped me off, I've been feeling awfully sick. My temperature is sky-high, and I keep getting dizzy. I'm a little scared.'

He could hear her laboured breathing.

'I think I should see a doctor – quickly. Could you help me – please?'

'Yes, of course.' He exchanged a concerned glance with Kate. 'Hang on, Vicky – I'll be there as soon as I can.' He

140

hung up. 'That was Vicky. She's very sick. I'm going to get her to a hospital.'

He headed for the door.

'Hold on,' Kate called after him. 'I'm coming with you.'

Thirty minutes later they picked Vicky up and were on the way to the John Radcliffe Hospital in Oxford. Other hospitals were closer, but the Radcliffe, on the eastern side of the city, at Headington, was considered the best and most advanced medical facility in their part of the country.

Huddled in a tartan blanket in the back seat, her head on Kate's lap, Vicky looked gaunt and drained of colour. Her cold hand trembled uncontrollably as she gripped Kate's feebly. It all indicated much more seriousness than Kate wanted to believe.

On arrival at the hospital, an efficient triage nurse immediately directed them into one of the emergency room cubicles where they eased Vicky on to a bed. Kate held Vicky's hand while the nurse asked Vicky a series of questions. But Vicky was too out of it to be of much help.

Soon the doctor staffing the emergency room arrived. 'I'm Dr Hunter,' she said. She and the nurse talked briefly in lowered voices then, putting a blood pressure cuff on Vicky's arm, she started her examination. When she was finished, she pulled the curtain partway around the cubicle and led Kate and Alex over to the nurses' station. The doctor had a tight-lipped look. It suggested a gravity that unnerved Kate.

Out of the corner of her eye, Kate saw that the nurse had picked up the red phone on the wall and was talking to somebody.

'We're taking her up to intensive care,' Dr Hunter announced abruptly.

'What do you think it is?' Kate asked.

'Looks like a nasty virus of some kind – we'll know more when we've taken some tests.'

The nurse handed Alex a printed sheet. 'Would you

complete this, please, Mr Sheppard? You can leave it with the admissions desk at the front entrance. Don't forget to fill in your address and a phone number where we can reach you, if need be. Thanks.'

Kate turned to Dr Hunter. 'When should we call to find out how Vicky's doing?'

'Wait till tomorrow morning.' She smiled, briefly. 'I'm sure we'll have some information by then,' she added, turning away to talk with the nurse again.

In a matter of moments, the hydraulic doors opened with barely a sound as a trolley appeared guided by a muscular young man in blue hospital garb. The nurse pulled aside the curtain to Vicky's cubicle and, with help from the orderly, slid Vicky on to the trolley.

Kate stole a glance at Alex who was on the opposite side of the trolley with his hand resting on Vicky's shoulder. He looked heartbroken. Together they gave Vicky one last look. Her skin was colourless and waxen, her usually sparkling eyes vacant and resigned. To both of them, Vicky had always been a paragon of robust country life – to see her like this, like a total stranger, was alarming. Kate let go of Vicky's hand to allow the trolley to pass through the door. As she did so, Vicky looked directly into her eyes. Kate desperately wanted to lean over and throw her arms around her, to hug and reassure her, but it was too late for that. She bit her lip and looked up at the ceiling to stifle the tears that could come any moment. Just as the double doors were about to close, Vicky managed the faintest smile. Then she was gone.

Chapter Fourteen

Blue thou art, intensely blue!
Flower! whence came thy dazzling hue?
When I opened first mine eye,
Upward glancing at the sky,
Straightway from the firmament
Was the sapphire brilliance sent.

James Montgomery

The sandy gravel crunched under Kate's bedroom slippers as she wandered aimlessly along the paths of the Parsonage garden. A wool cardigan over her cotton nightgown kept the early morning chill at bay. Even the quiet and beauty of her beloved garden could not ease her aching grief. The numbing reality had finally set in. She would never see Vicky again.

Early in the morning, three days after Vicky was admitted to the hospital, the phone had woken them. Kate had somehow known it would be the hospital. She and Alex had been calling frequently, inquiring about Vicky's condition, only to learn that there was no improvement. If anything it was worsening.

The physician who had called that morning to inform them of Vicky's death, a Dr Simon Maclean, had more or less confirmed what they already expected, that Vicky's death was attributable to an unknown virus. He said that when the pathology tests were complete – within the next twenty-four hours – he hoped to be able to provide a more accurate cause of death. He thanked Kate for putting them in touch with Vicky's father, saying that the hospital had contacted him and that he was on his way down from Scotland.

Soft shadows were starting to melt in and out as the watery sunlight rose over the east wall. She inhaled deeply and looked dolefully about her. Her eyes were still red from crying. On her right, haughty spires of back-lit fox-gloves swayed ever so gently. She touched one lightly as she passed. She looked up and wiped her eyes for the hundredth time. Above her, rambling roses showered blossoms, like sea foam, out of trees. At the periphery of her vision she caught a darting flash of blue. A kingfisher, perhaps. She came to a black wrought-iron bench and sat down. Staring forlornly into space, she let go and allowed the images of Vicky to project on her mind. They were powerfully real.

Vicky's death had overshadowed everything. The funeral service, in her home town of Aberdeen, had been simple and brief. Kate finally got to meet Alex's favourite Aunt Nell, who had accompanied them on the train. Vicky's nursery partner, Jill, also made the long trip. Sitting on the hard pew in the little stone church, clutching Alex's hand, Kate had somehow managed to suppress visions of Vicky and the tears that were so near the surface. Those would come later.

Kate got up, crossed her hands in front of her, grasping her forearms and rubbing them for warmth. She ambled up the path and set her mind to focus on more hopeful thoughts, thoughts of their new home and garden, of her deepening love for Alex. Over the last several days, she'd seen yet another side of him; the caring manner in which he had responded to Vicky's plight, his calm and self-lessness in shouldering the ensuing responsibilities. They'd never shared bereavement before. She was so thankful to have someone with his level-headedness and compassion to help her through it.

Then there was The Parsonage and, of course, the question of the blue rose and the enormity of wealth that might – or now, with Graham's recent bombshell, might not – be coming their way. Over the last several days she had finally been able to overcome her initial panic at the idea of losing The Parsonage. Despite his own distrust and contempt for Graham, Alex had managed finally to persuade her to disregard Graham's callous threat. The paragraph proposing the compromise was quite specific – perfectly clear – Alex maintained. The Cookes were prepared to overlook voiding the transaction on the house as long as she and Alex agreed to turn over the rose.

It was hard to accept the fact that millions of pounds were about to slip through their fingers. While she still struggled with the idea of equating a simple flower with such a vast fortune, Alex took it all in his stride. Over the last weeks, it appeared that he was growing more and more accustomed to the idea of being super rich. Whether that would now be the case was up in the air – up to the lawyers.

But The Parsonage was another matter entirely. Whatever happened, they mustn't lose that, too. While waiting for the outcome of Graham's challenge, she could only pin her hopes on Alex's conviction that their house was not in jeopardy. 'Don't worry, Kate, the lawyers will sort it out,' he kept reassuring her.

That made her think of Adell. He had called immediately after receiving the copy of Stanhope's letter, to say that because he'd been under the weather he had only taken a cursory look at it. After Kate pressed him for his thoughts on the Cookes' claim, his answer had been ambiguous and unconvincing. He had said merely that his first-blush assessment found it frivolous but that he needed more time to evaluate it.

Adell had been more emphatic on the matter of the missing journal Graham claimed to possess, and the possibility that a formula might now exist whereby the rose could be cloned. He had gone on to allow that for it to be taken seriously the hybridizing formula could never be accepted simply on its face value. It would obviously have to be proven viable: that following its prescription would conclusively result in the creation of a blue rose. That could take three or more years to be validated. He added that as a routine procedure, he planned to make a request that the missing journal be presented for their inspection.

With Vicky's death and now the business with Graham, she'd almost forgotten about the American. She was surprised he hadn't made further contact. Then there was the man who had sent them the letter too – Tanaka. Had they heard the last from either of them? Somehow, she doubted it. 'What a bloody mess,' she said quietly, kicking the gravel at her feet.

As she walked back to the house her mood lightened. She had an idea. Before taking Nell back to Market Drayton today, they would stop off in Marlborough. That would cheer them both up. They would have a lovely lunch at the Polly Tea Rooms and she could return the library books and pick up Alex's painting that was ready at the frame shop.

At the reception after the funeral Kate and Alex had suggested that Nell come back with them before going home to Shropshire. After a phone call to her neighbour who was looking after her cat, it was settled. As a result, Nell had been their guest for the last three days. And Kate had enjoyed every single minute. She was going to be truly sorry to see Nell go.

As if someone had used an atomizer, the air became perfumed. Kate had brushed against a clump of lavender humming with bees. The scent rekindled memories of rainy days when, as a small child, she would secretly forage through the drawers of her mother's scented bedroom chests, looking for dresses and shoes to try on.

It was at times like these that Kate missed her mother desperately. Her father too, but in a different way. She had never really had the opportunity to get to know him well. While she was growing up he was always on the road, working as a district sales manager for a car-parts manufacturing company. He had died in a car accident when she was in grammar school. She would never forget coming home from school that rainy day to be told the tragic news. Her grief-stricken mother had never fully recovered from the loss. It was as if a part of her had died with him. She now lived in America, in a suburb of Boston, with her younger sister, moving there shortly after Kate and Alex married. Kate would have loved to have her mother here this very moment, so she could see the house and the garden in its present glory. Soon after they'd moved in, Kate had sent her photos of The Parsonage, but somehow none of the pictures did the place justice. She would call her later. It had been at least two weeks since they'd last spoken. The prospect cheered her.

She paused at the sight of an old rose bush in full bloom. Stooping, she read its marker: *La Reine Victoria*. The sight and scent were overpowering. 'This is really all about roses, isn't it?' she muttered under her breath. An old man's infatuation turned obsession with roses. What would the Major say, she wondered, if he knew what had happened since she and Alex had become custodians of his garden and his beloved roses? Come to think of it, why hadn't he announced to the world the miracle he'd wrought? Odd, she thought.

Her most recent tally of the roses in the garden added up to two hundred and ten different types. With few exceptions, they were old varieties: Gallicas, Damasks, Albas, Bourbons and the like. Old, meaning that the 'youngsters' in the garden were varieties dating from the nineteenth century. But the lineage of some of the senior citizens, like the Gallica roses, could be traced back through many centuries. She remembered quite clearly the day at the nursery when Vicky had told her that the oldest and the most famous of all the Gallicas was a rose called *Officinalis* – also known as the Apothecary's rose, because of its medicinal use. It was the red rose, she said, chosen by the House of Lancaster during the Wars of the Roses, which started in 1455.

'Kate! There's a phone call for you – Kate!'

Looking up toward the house she saw Alex on the veranda in his dressing gown. 'Oh, there you are,' he called down. 'It's Peg – she wants to know whether you want her to work tomorrow.'

'I'll be right up,' she replied.

Peg ran the antiques shop when Kate wasn't there. Thank goodness she'd been able to fill in these last few days.

Kate walked up to Alex and kissed him on the cheek.

'Are you all right?' he asked, brushing away the moisture from her cheek.

'Yes, I'm fine.' She gave him a melancholy smile. 'Where's Nell?'

Alex nodded in the direction of the house. 'She's in the kitchen. Lord knows what she's cooking up in there. When I last peeked in, she had practically every pot and pan we own pressed into service. The woman should run a restaurant.'

Kate managed a smile.

Yesterday evening, Alex and Kate had tried to persuade Nell to stay a couple more days but she was insistent on returning home. 'Guests are like fish,' she reminded them. 'For two or three days, everything's fine, but beyond that, the place starts to stink up a bit.'

This morning she was cooking 'a proper English breakfast', as she put it, for the three of them. The night before, she'd conjured up 'a proper English dinner', except for the Scottish trifle; and earlier, 'a real English luncheon'.

After chatting with Peg for a couple of minutes, Kate entered the kitchen to find Alex already seated at the table, staring at his steaming plate with undisguised relish. 'Gosh! What a treat,' he said, looking at Kate with eyebrows raised.

In front of him, still sizzling, was a formidable array of sausages, eggs, bacon, mushrooms, sauteed potatoes, fried tomatoes, fried bread – even fried kidneys.

'I was going to do kippers too, but I didn't, because I thought that might be a little too much,' Nell shouted from the depths of the kitchen.

'Thank God for that,' Kate stage-whispered, sitting down across from Alex, eyeing the greasy assortment of food on his plate.

Nell entered carrying Kate's breakfast and a large teapot.

'Here's some nice strong tea,' she said, joining them at the table.

'Well, I must say, Nell, you've done it again,' Kate said, raising her knife and fork. 'I can't remember when we last had such a hearty–' She was interrupted by the phone ringing.

'I'll get it,' said Alex, getting up from his chair. 'I'm expecting a call from a client, Mrs Hendrickson. I'll take it in the living room.'

'The lady of the loos,' Kate quipped.

Alex picked up the ringing phone, fully expecting a ruffled Mrs Hendrickson.

'Hello?' he said.

'Mr Sheppard?'

It certainly wasn't Mrs Hendrickson. The man's voice was cultured and completely unfamiliar to Alex.

'Yes? Who is this?'

'This is Ken Tanaka, Mr Sheppard. I'm calling about the letter I sent you.'

Damn. It was the other man after the rose. Hadn't he passed Tanaka's letter on to Adell? Yes, he had. 'Do I need this?' he muttered under his breath. 'Yes, Mr Tanaka. I recall your letter. But surely you must have heard from my solicitor by now?'

'I did, sir. My client, however, is not interested in being part of the auction. He wants–'

'Excuse me, Mr Tanaka,' Alex snapped, 'it doesn't matter to me what your client wants, we aren't selling the rose, our solicitor is. And that's my final word on the subject, I'm afraid.'

'That is unacceptable to my client.'

'Well, then – that's just too bad.'

'I don't think you understand. You're passing up an incredible opportunity – an offer in the several millions. Why don't I meet with you, to discuss it in more detail? I'll be happy to come to your house, if you prefer.'

'No, absolutely not. We've got a house guest right now – and I don't appreciate being bothered at home.'

'I will pay you well for your time.'

'Mr Tanaka, I appreciate the generous offer, but I'm afraid–'

'Would a thousand pounds for fifteen minutes of your time make you change your mind?'

'Mr Tanaka. I really must say no.'

'Unfortunately my client will not take no for an answer.' He took a deep breath. 'I won't quibble with you, sir. Two thousand.'

He could hire somebody to do Mrs Hendrickson's drawings for that amount of money. 'Stop, please, Mr Tanaka. I have to go.'

'No, please wait–'

'I have to *go*. Please discuss it with Mr Adell. Goodbye.'

He hung up before Tanaka raised the ante to the point where he would really start to listen.

He walked back into the kitchen, where Kate and Nell were chattering away.

'You'll never guess who that was,' Alex said.

'Not Kingston, was it?' asked Kate.

'No. It was our friend, Mr Tanaka.'

'The one who wrote the letter?'

'That one, yes.'

Kate frowned. 'Why was he calling?' she asked.

'He wanted to come down here and talk with you and me personally, Kate. He also offered to pay us two thousand pounds just to listen to his proposal. Can you believe it?'

Kate looked perturbed. 'What a nerve.' She put a hand across her mouth. 'He's not coming, I hope,' she said quietly.

'No, of course not. He kept insisting but I told him that it wouldn't do any good.'

'Well, let's hope that's the end of it,' said Kate.

Alex sat back down at the table. 'I wonder if Graham will have anything to say this afternoon,' he said, stabbing a congealed chipolata sausage. He sliced off a small piece, palmed it and, when Kate and Nell weren't looking, slipped it under the table where Asp was curled up by his chair.

'Very little, I would imagine.'

A few days earlier, a secretary from Stanhope's office had called requesting the return of the journals that Graham had lent them. Rather than take them all the way to Stanhope's office in Newbury, it was agreed that the journals could be dropped off at Graham's house on the outskirts of Bath. A date was established when Graham would be home to receive them and make sure that they were all in good order. Alex was delivering them that afternoon at three o'clock.

Letting out a sigh, Alex placed his knife and fork tidily on his empty plate. He looked across the table at Kate and grimaced. 'You know, Kate, the thought of having to see that twit again is really off-putting.'

'I'm sure it will be nice and brief. Just drop the books off, that's all. Anyway you'll have good old Lawrence with you.'

Alex sighed. 'Don't worry, Kate. I'm not going to punch Graham out, for God's sake.'

Alex picked up Asp and sat him in his lap. 'By the way, Kate, since you'll probably be late getting back from Nell's this evening, I told Lawrence we would all eat at the Royal Oak tonight, if that's okay with you.'

'That's fine, Alex. It'll be nice to see him again.'

'Guess I'm going to be saddled with him most of the day,' Alex said in a disgruntled tone.

'Oh, come on, Alex. Can't you be just a tad more charitable as far as Kingston's concerned?'

'It's not that I don't like him, Kate – I do. But, at times, he can be so . . . condescending, so pompous. It's almost embarrassing.' He noted that Kate was smiling. 'It's not funny, Kate.'

She reached across the table and put her hand on his. She squeezed gently. 'I have a feeling that whether we like it or not, Kingston might be around for a while longer. Just try to be a little nicer to him – a little more appreciative, that's all.'

'I'll try.'

'You have to admit,' she added, 'he has been very helpful with the rose and he is entertaining. In a funny sort of way, I grant you. I vote we keep him for a while.'

Alex sighed. 'As you said, we may not have much choice.'

'Here we are. About a hundred yards, you'll see my lane on the right,' said Nell.

Kate flicked on her signal and slowed for the turn. Unnoticed, a couple of hundred feet behind, a black Jeep also reduced speed.

'You're probably ready for a nice afternoon nap, I would imagine,' Kate remarked, glancing at Nell.

'Later maybe. First things first. I've got to go up to Arthur's house to pick up Buttons, my kitty, and the mail, and the newspapers. Through all this, Arthur's been a real dear. Think I'll cook him a really nice dinner one night this week. He loves liver and bacon.'

'I'd like to take a quick look at the rose, too, before I leave. With all the wet weather we've had lately, I'm sure it's survived perfectly well. Anyway, we're going to be moving it out soon, so you won't have to worry about it any more, Nell.'

Kate parked the Trooper by the front door and helped Nell out with her suitcase. Once inside, Nell put the kettle on. 'Bet you could do with a cuppa,' she said.

'That would be nice. While we're waiting for the kettle, perhaps I'll go and take a peek at Sapphire.' Seeing the confused expression on Nell's face, Kate hastily corrected herself. 'The rose. The blue rose, Nell.'

'Oh, of course – silly me. Yes, I'll come with you to show you where they planted it. We can go out the front. It's a little easier to get to it that way.'

Kate followed her out of the house. They walked alongside a shoulder-high picket fence for about thirty paces. Rounding the corner where the fence made a right-angled turn, they both froze. In front of them, an eight-foot stretch of the fence lay flat and splintered on the ground. Beyond the gap, wide tyre tracks and a swath of flattened vegetation ran in a straight line across the jungle-like garden to a small clearing.

Kate put a hand up to her mouth. 'My God! What's happened?'

'That's where Alex and Vicky planted the rose,' Nell said, pointing a shaking finger. 'Over there.'

Kate stumbled through the muddy tracks to where they ended. In front of her there was a hole nearly four feet wide and almost as deep.

Nell caught up with her. She gripped Kate's arm and stared in disbelief at the hole. 'Good Lord! Somebody's taken the rose. Who on earth would do that?'

'Offhand, Nell, I can think of at least three people.' She shook her head. 'This is really bad news.'

'Shouldn't we call the police?'

'Probably. But first I have to call Alex.' She took Nell's arm and they walked back to the house. Adding the police to the equation was a complication she couldn't deal with right now.

Kate put the phone down, looked at her watch, then at Nell. 'Nobody home. Alex and Kingston are probably still at Graham's. I think I'd best be leaving, Nell.'

'Won't you at least stay for tea? The kettle's boiled.'

'I'd love to, Nell, but the rose being stolen changes everything. It has me scared. I can't explain it right now but it's a lot more serious than it appears. I can't imagine what Alex is going to say.' She put her arms around Nell and hugged her. 'Next chance I get, I'll tell you all about it. Are you going to be okay?'

'Well, of course I am. Arthur's only a couple of doors away.' She smiled, making her rosy cheeks shine. 'In any case, whoever took the rose is hardly likely to come back to the scene of the crime, is he?'

'I doubt it very much, Nell.'

'You get on your way, then, dear.'

'Okay – sorry about the tea. I'll call you the minute I get home.'

She waved to Nell one last time from the Trooper. Standing at the door, waving back, Nell looked so tiny and vulnerable. Kate bit her lip lightly and drove off up the lane.

About fifty feet from Nell's house the lane curved before continuing to meet the road. As she was straightening up coming out of the bend and picking up speed, she almost ran into a black Jeep parked in the middle of the lane. It was positioned to make passing impossible. Kate slammed on the brakes. The Trooper skidded in a straight line on the loose gravel and wet leaves and came to a stop not more than six feet from the Jeep's rear bumper.

She leaned on her horn a number of times, to no avail.

'This I don't need,' she muttered. The Jeep appeared to be unoccupied. It must have broken down or run out of petrol.

The only sounds came from the noisy tappets of the idling Trooper and the gentle rustling of leaves on the trees in the surrounding woods. Her impatience was supplanted by irritation. She considered pushing it off the road but dismissed that idea, knowing she could easily damage either or both vehicles.

It looked as if she would have to back up to Nell's and call for a tow truck. Before doing that she decided to take a closer look at the Jeep. She turned off the engine and stepped out on to the muddy lane. Perhaps there was a note on the windshield. As she approached she saw that the dark tinted glass of the driver's side window was rolled half-way down. Inside, everything appeared normal. As she had expected, there was no key in the ignition. A road map, two jackets, a paperback book with a curling cover, a partially eaten apple and some magazines were spread over the back seat.

As she turned away from the door, she saw him coming for her.

He wore a black ski mask that revealed only his eyes. Before she could scream, a gloved hand was clasped roughly across her mouth. A second masked man, short

154

and chunky, appeared. A muscular arm encircled her waist. She struggled fiercely, but it was useless. Her assailants were just too strong. A strip of silver duct tape was banded tightly across her mouth. Terrified and inhaling rapidly through her nose to keep pace with her pumping lungs, she was hoisted up and shoved roughly into the back seat of the Jeep. Her head slammed into the roof. For a few seconds she thought she was going to black out. The taller man got in beside her and shoved her across the seat. The magazines and jackets crumpled beneath her as she slid across the smooth leather. He produced a length of white nylon cord and bound her wrists in front of her. Passing the cord round her waist, he knotted it behind her back so she could no longer move her hands. Satisfied that she was immobilized, he motioned for her to turn away from him. Suddenly, her world went black as he strapped blacked-out goggles on her, securing them with more duct tape around the back of her head. She winced as the tape tugged at her hair. She heard him step out of the car, slamming the door behind him. The Jeep bounced lightly as the man got into the driver's seat. He locked all the doors, started the engine, and drove slowly off. Behind, Kate heard the distinctive rattle of her Trooper's engine. The second man was following in her car. Tears rolled off her cheek and down her neck.

155

Chapter Fifteen

We are all dreaming of some magical rose garden over the horizon – instead of enjoying the roses that are blooming outside our windows today.

Dale Carnegie

Sitting by an open casement window in the sitting room, enjoying the warmth of the afternoon sun, Alex was going over Alexander Stanhope's legal ultimatum one more time. He had just finished reading it when he heard the gurgling sound of Kingston's TR4 as it crunched up the drive. He glanced at his watch. It was a few minutes before two o'clock. He smiled. Kingston was punctual, as usual. Three hours earlier, Kate had left for Shropshire to take Nell back home. This afternoon, he and Kingston were going to keep their appointment with Graham.

When he had told Kingston on the phone that he was going to visit Graham Cooke to deliver the journals, Kingston had insisted on accompanying him despite his having to drive all the way from London to do so. Alex knew full well that it was a convenient, but transparent, excuse for Kingston to camp at The Parsonage for a couple of days. Kate had welcomed the idea. More than ever, Alex was convinced that either Kingston had very few demands on his time or that he was simply an incorrigible *quidnunc* – another word he had learned from Kingston. He wouldn't admit it to Kate but he was glad in a way that Kingston was accompanying him to Graham's.

Entering the room – Alex had left the front door open for him – Kingston looked every part the English country squire: hounds-tooth check jacket, white open-necked shirt, paisley cravat, suede shoes – even a pipe, which he held in his hand. 'Splendid drive down. Couldn't have picked a more bonny day.' He ran a hand through his shock of wind-tossed silvery hair.

Alex wanted to smile but didn't as he watched Kingston stride across the room, plop down into 'his' chair and attempt to light his pipe.

'Never seen you with a pipe before, Lawrence.'

'Mostly for show, old chap. Used to smoke it quite regularly till I cracked a tooth on it. More of a placebo, now. Damned things are really more of a nuisance. Always going out. All the paraphernalia you have to carry – tobacco, matches, cleaners, what have you.'

Right off, Alex regretted mentioning the pipe. He knew how Kingston loved to dwell on minutiae and also knew that if he didn't change the subject immediately, he risked spending the next ten minutes being enlightened on the finer points of pipe smoking. He waved Stanhope's letter. 'I've memorized every single word of this bloody letter,' he said. 'Kate refuses to talk about it any more.'

'Still no word from Adell, I take it?'

'No. But if you want my opinion, I think he'll recommend some kind of compromise.'

'Such as?' Kingston lit a match and held it up to the pipe, making loud sucking noises.

'Well – probably some kind of mutual sharing of royalties. According to everybody's assessment of the rose's value, even half of its worth will certainly be in the many millions. You'd think that Graham would be chuffed to bits about a windfall like that, wouldn't you?'

'Couldn't agree with you more. But greed does funny things to people.'

'Rotten things would be more like it.' Alex placed the letter on the table next to him, got up and crossed the room to close the window, talking as he went.

'You know, Lawrence, despite all my reassurances, Kate is still paranoid about losing the house.'

'I don't know why. Stanhope's letter specifically states

that they will accept the compromise of your giving up the rose to keep the house. Unless they back out for any reason, there's no cause for her to worry. I'd just let Adell deal with it, Alex. There's no point in getting your knickers in a twist over the whole thing.'

Alex returned and sat down facing Kingston.'That's exactly what I told her.'

Kingston smiled then shook his head. 'It is preposterous when you think about it. It's a mind-boggling amount of money to give up. A bit like winning the lottery and then losing the ticket.'

'I told Kate that with the money from the rose, we could buy any property in the entire British Isles. But she's nutty about this place.'

With a look of mild disgust, Kingston took the pipe out of his mouth, tired of trying to light it, and put it in his top jacket pocket. 'I can understand her feelings, in a way,' he said.

Alex got up, put on his leather jacket and checked his trousers pocket to make sure he had the house keys.

'By the way,' said Kingston, 'I take it you haven't heard any more from the American chap?'

'No, thank goodness. As of a week ago, neither had Adell. I guess he gave up on the idea.'

'I doubt it.'

'Why do you say that?'

'Because, as Kate might have told you, I'm pretty sure I know whom he represents.'

'Yes, she said you were working on it. But how could you possibly figure that out?'

'It wasn't as impossible as it would first seem. From what you told me, he has or has access to the money – a lot of money. Next, if I recall, he said something to the effect that the rose would have "enormous impact on the world of commerce". He also mentioned "patent rights and royalties". This would all suggest that he is, more likely than not, representing a company or organization involved in the business of horticulture.'

'Even so. My God, there must be hundreds of thousands of companies in the States that could qualify.'

'Not if we're talking roses, old chap. Even worldwide, there are not that many companies able to come up with the millions that it'll take to acquire a blue rose.'

'So who is it, then?'

'From everything we know – from what you've told me and what I've been able to gather from insiders in the States – it all suggests that the person behind it is a man named Ira Wolff. He runs a big rose-growing concern in Washington State. I would have told you sooner but I've been waiting on some information from a colleague of mine on the West Coast. I got a package from him a couple of days ago and he called me yesterday to follow up. Alex, it's more complicated than you could imagine, and, from all accounts, this Wolff is utterly ruthless in the way he does business. I won't go into it right now because we have to get going. I'll save it for when we get back. It's a long story and a disturbing one, I might add.'

Alex got up. 'Lawrence, you get to sound more like bloody Hercule Poirot every day! All that's missing is the accent.'

Kingston shrugged using his hands. '*Il n'y a pas de roses sans épines, mon ami,*' he said.

'Whatever,' Alex replied, with a glance at the carriage clock on the mantel. 'I guess we'd better get going. We shouldn't keep the opportunistic sod waiting.'

Kingston got up and followed Alex to the door. 'You have the journals?' he asked.

'They're in the car.'

Buckling his seat belt, Kingston glanced at Alex. 'You know, Alex,' he said in a paternal tone, 'it might pay to be on your best behaviour with Graham when we get there. There's nothing to be gained by you venting your anger. Just keep it cordial and businesslike.'

'For Christ's sake, Lawrence, you're sounding just like Kate. That's exactly what she said.'

Alex and Kingston stood waiting on the brick porch of

Graham's red and white painted bungalow. Alex put down the cardboard box containing the journals and pressed the doorbell for the fourth time. It could be faintly heard ringing inside.

Kingston glanced at his watch. 'Ten past three. We're not that late.'

Alex resorted to hammering loudly on the door with his knuckles. Still, there was no response.

'There's nobody here – that's for sure,' Alex said, pacing up and down. 'Maybe he's forgotten we're coming.'

'I doubt it, somehow.'

Alex rapped one more time and looked at Kingston. 'What do you think we should do? We can't leave the journals on the doorstep.'

Kingston looked furtively up and down the street. 'Wait a moment,' he said, as he stepped over a narrow border of mixed annuals and walked four paces across the patch of lawn to the large bay window. With his hands held up to both sides of his face and nose pressed to the glass, he looked in. 'No signs of life inside,' he said, returning to the front door.

'Well, we can't stand here all bloody day,' Alex mumbled. 'The neighbours will start to get suspicious.'

'Let's take a peek around the back. Maybe he's in the garden.'

'Hang on a minute, Lawrence. I can't lug this box around. Let me put it in the car.' Alex crossed the grass verge, opened the boot of the Alfa, put the box of journals in and slammed the lid shut. When he got back to the path, Kingston was already half-way up the street. Running, Alex caught up with him.

'There's an alley up here – I noticed it on the way in,' Kingston said. 'I'm certain it runs along the backs of these houses. Chances are they're not numbered in the back. We'd better count them off, so we know we're at the right back gate.'

'I'm not so sure that this is such a good idea, Lawrence. Don't you think–' His words were wasted on Kingston who was already striding up the alley ten paces ahead of him. Just as Alex caught up with him they were startled by the loud bark of a large dog. Paws resting on the fence, it looked like an unwashed shag rug. As Alex and Kingston got closer the barking grew louder, reverberating off the walls of the surrounding houses. Kingston insisted that it was a giant schnauzer. Alex was not the least interested in its pedigree. 'If that hasn't alerted the neighbourhood, I don't know what the hell will,' Alex said, relieved that the beast had finally decided to give up and return to its kennel on the back porch.

Two houses up, they located Graham's. The red and white paint left no doubt. His fence was higher than those of his neighbours, and there was no latch visible on the gate. There appeared no way to gain entry. After several attempts to locate the latch, Alex was ready to admit defeat and return to the car – not so Kingston. Alex watched, mouth agape, as Kingston pulled himself clumsily over the fence and opened the gate from the inside. 'Christ! Lawrence – this is breaking and entering!' he hissed.

Kingston shrugged, hoisted up his trousers and started up the wavy brick garden path. Alex followed him, stopping half-way. He waited nervously, expecting to hear police sirens any minute as Kingston knocked on the back door.

'Well, Alex, looks like you were right, after all,' Kingston shouted, pressing his nose to the window that jutted out to the left of the back porch.

'For Christ's sake, Lawrence, keep your voice down.'

'Just let me see if I – oh, Jesus!'

'What's the matter?'

Kingston turned around, a look of alarm on his face. 'There's a body on the floor in here!'

'Don't scare me like that, Lawrence.'

'No, I'm serious. There's a man's body – come and have a look.'

Alex pushed past Kingston and peered into the poorly lit room. 'Shit,' he said, putting a hand to his forehead. 'It's Graham.'

Chapter Sixteen

In a way, nobody sees a flower really, it is so small, we haven't time – And to see takes time, like to have a friend takes time.

Georgia O'Keefe

Graham's body lay face down on the oriental carpet, his head close to the tiled hearth of the fireplace. A small table had been knocked over and a lamp, a framed photo, and miscellaneous books and magazines were strewn over the floor. Otherwise the room was undisturbed.

Kingston was on one knee, feeling for Graham's pulse. Alex hovered over him wishing they'd never come round the back in the first place.

After a few more seconds that seemed like minutes to Alex, Kingston lowered Graham's wrist to the floor and looked up to Alex. 'He's dead, I'm afraid.'

'Bloody hell!'

Kingston stood, looking down at Graham's body. For a moment he massaged his chin with thumb and forefinger, thinking. 'Alex, go and find the phone and call the police. Tell them what's happened.' It was more of an order than a request. 'While you're doing that, I'll take a quick look around to see if there's any sign of the missing journal.'

'God, Lawrence. The man's dead and you're worrying about the journal? In any case Graham's not stupid enough to have it just lying around the house. It would be locked up somewhere. You just can't go around ransacking the bloody place. We have enough explaining to do as it is.'

'Calm down, Alex,' Kingston said, his eyes searching the

room. 'You never know – and I'm not going to *ransack* the place – just have a quick look-see, that's all.'

With an angry shake of his head, Alex left to find the phone.

The Coach and Horses, five miles outside Bath, proved as pleasantly hospitable inside as it was inviting on the outside. Sitting in the cosy comfort of the saloon bar with glasses of best bitter in front of them, they were both still reeling from the grisly shock of finding Graham's body. Within minutes after Alex's emergency phone call, the police had arrived at Manor Close and cordoned off the alley. An ambulance arrived a minute later. After being questioned at length by the sergeant in charge, giving him Mrs Cooke's address, and tendering their respective addresses and phone numbers, Alex and Kingston were allowed to leave.

The wall clock behind the bar chimed six.

'Poor chap,' Kingston said, for about the third or fourth time, shaking his head and taking another draught of beer. 'I wonder how his aunt's taking it.'

'Poor Graham is right. In spite of everything, I'd never have wished that on him.'

'I wonder what happened? Beyond the obvious, of course,' Kingston said.

With his index finger, Alex traced a question mark in the thin slick of beer on the polished oak table. 'Who knows?' he mumbled.

'We were fortunate the sergeant believed our story.'

'I know. For a while there I was certain we would be thrown in the paddy wagon and taken down to the station. Kate would have loved that. Coming home to find us both in the nick!'

'You know, Alex, we may not be completely in the clear, yet.' He paused, then said, 'Well, you, that is.'

'What do you mean?'

'Well, if the police ferret out a copy of Stanhope's letter – which is highly likely – and put two and two together–'

'I'm a prime bloody suspect.'

'Of course. What better motive.'

Alex stared glumly into the foam on his beer. 'I'm wondering if the police really did believe us. I'm surprised they didn't ask us why we didn't just leave the books under the porch, which would have been the obvious thing to do.'

'Hard to say. At least we were able to show them the journals in the boot and we did tell them that they were important to Graham.' He looked at Alex squarely. 'If it turns out that Graham was murdered, they'll certainly want to question us again.' Kingston reached for his glass and took a gulp of beer. 'But let's not jump to conclusions that somebody bumped him off. Poor bugger could've simply had a heart attack.'

'There's always that possibility, I suppose.' Alex cleared his throat and paused, as if preferring not having to utter the next words. 'But let's not kid ourselves, it's far more likely that this has something to do with the rose,' he said.

'I have to agree,' said Kingston, tipping back his head and swallowing the last of his beer. 'That being the case, the most likely scenario is that someone was at the house before us and either got into a fight with Graham and accidentally killed him, or simply did him in.'

'Yes, but why – and who?'

'The only two people who come to mind are Wolff and Tanaka.'

'But we have nothing whatsoever to connect them to Graham.'

'I know. Even if they've been following your every single move there's no way that they could have learned about Graham's having the formula, is there?'

'I can't see how,' Alex replied, with a shake of the head.

There was a brief silence between them as a noisy young couple sat down at the next table.

Alex scraped his chair, making a point of turning sideways to them. 'I wonder what will happen about Graham's claim to the rose, now? Do you think Mrs Cooke will pursue it?'

'Hard to say. You're going to have to ask her, I suppose. Either that or call Stanhope. In either case, the decent thing to do is to wait a few days.'

The chatter and laughter from the bar was growing louder as more customers started to arrive.

'Kate should be home soon,' Alex said, glancing at his watch.

'You should give her a call.' Kingston tapped his glass. 'Want another?' he asked.

'No, this is it for me, thanks.' Alex yawned. 'God, I'm almost afraid to go home these days. There's no knowing who'll call next.'

Kingston shifted his position on the hard seat and crossed his legs. 'I promised I'd tell you more about this Wolff fellow, Alex.'

'The American rose grower.'

'Right.'

'Let's have it, then,' said Alex.

'Well, soon after you got that first call, I phoned an acquaintance who now lives in California. Bob Jackson's his name. He used to hold down a top management position with one of the largest garden supply companies in the States – on the West Coast. I asked Bob to do some sleuthing for me to see which companies – or individuals, for that matter – would have the wherewithal and also be the most likely to have interest, or the most to be gained, from acquiring a blue rose.

'Well, Bob did a painstaking job. Not only contacted many of his old friends in the business but told me he spent countless hours on the Internet and in the library, poring over newspaper stories and trade magazine articles.'

'And all roads led to Wolff, I take it?'

Kingston ignored the question. 'That's the good news,' he said. 'But you're not going to like what I'm about to tell you next because it's pretty heavy stuff.'

'You make it sound like a bad movie.'

'It could well be. First, let me make a quick comment about the world in which this man Wolff operates – the world of commercial horticulture. We all know it's all about nature, pretty flowers, beautiful gardens, seductive catalogues and nurseries – all that kind of stuff. But most of all, it's about money. It's a hard, tough, competitive business, where the big fish gobble up the little fish and the sharks devour the big fish. Believe me, Wolff is a shark. And right now, I wouldn't mind betting that he's circling The Parsonage waiting for the right moment to strike.'

'Oh come on, Lawrence. This isn't *Jaws*, for Christ's sake!'

'Don't dismiss this too lightly, Alex. Jackson's letter and clippings contain tangible evidence of a near pathological personality. They paint a very damning picture of our Mr Ira Wolff.'

Kingston then proceeded to recount what Jackson had told him about Wolff's history of personal failures and dubious business enterprises.

It appeared that Wolff's ascendancy in the business world of horticulture started with his acquisition of Baker-Reynolds. Jackson had been unable to find any news stories or dig up any gossip about Wolff's activities prior to that time. It was as though, until he purchased Baker-Reynolds, Wolff hadn't existed. A front-page *Wall Street Journal* story on the B-R takeover was terse and objective. Other than the fact that the journalist in question had voiced his suspicions over the absurdly low price Wolff had paid, the story contained no overtones of improbity. Clippings from other sources supported the perception that the sale was nothing other than a straightforward transaction.

Comments and opinions from individuals within the industry, however, offered an opposing viewpoint. Among the contributors to Bob's explosive package of information there was nearly a consensus that Wolff had indeed employed underhanded tactics to acquire the company. One industry insider wrote that it was the general opinion, within B-R's top management at the time, that incriminating skeletons in the partnership's family closet – some, of a highly prurient nature – led to the forced sale of the company. Another offered an opinion that to acquire the company Wolff had orchestrated a diabolical scheme – partly based on fact, partly contrived – whereby he could substantiate repeated acts of blatant insider trading, stock manipulation and other fiscal chicanery. Rumour had it that more than one board director was implicated.

Another writer recommended that a search of the records of the Washington State Attorney General's office be undertaken for the period during and after the sale of Baker-Reynolds. He maintained that the resulting evidence would prove that the sale was hotly contested, not only by suspicious B-R shareholders but also by many other concerned people close to the company and within the industry. Despite the flood of angry complaints, no legal or government action was ever taken to investigate the case or to hold up the sale. Later, there were even rumours that Wolff had bribed several officials high in the Attorney General's office.

The man's personal life read like a sensational tabloid. Wolff had been married – and divorced – four times. Each wife became more costly. In addition to a two million dollar spread on Mercer Island and several luxury automobiles, his first wife, Mary Jo, had walked away from the marriage with a cool twelve million dollars. Wife number two, who filed charges accusing Wolff of extreme physical abuse as part of her lawsuit, became fifteen million dollars richer overnight. She turned around, a month later, and married the owner of one of Seattle's most successful restaurants.

Two months later, that husband's mutilated body was fished out of Lake Washington. The case was never solved. Wives three and four further depleted Wolff's bank balance by another thirty million dollars. A graphically written, one-column clipping, taken from the *Tacoma News Tribune*, reported Wolff's involvement in an altercation in a local nightspot. After a heated exchange of words Wolff had severely beaten one of the other customers, who was incensed over Wolff's inflammatory comments about his girlfriend. There were no clippings reporting the outcome of the case.

Kingston sighed. 'Not a pretty picture, is it?'

Alex pushed away his empty beer mug. 'Jesus, what a piece of work!'

'Here's the worst part, though.'

'I wouldn't have thought it could get much worse.'

'It does. From all accounts, Wolff is in trouble right now. Short of a miracle, his company is about to go under. If it does – if it goes into bankruptcy – then a number of felony crimes perpetrated by Wolff will almost certainly be uncovered. According to Bob Jackson, Wolff could go up for a long, long time. In his words, "Wolff's in a corner and he's very dangerous. He'll stop at nothing to get what he wants to save his skin."'

'Lawrence, if you're trying to scare the shit out of me, you're succeeding.'

'I just want you to be aware of what kind of man you're dealing with, Alex. That's all. The man's pathological and unstable.'

'I won't be dealing with him, thank God. That's for certain.'

Before they left the Coach and Horses, Alex called home. There was no answer.

'She'll probably be there by the time we get back,' Alex said, as they got into the car. Within twenty minutes they were back at The Parsonage.

As Alex stepped out of the TR4 on to the gravel drive, he could hear the faint ringing of the telephone in the hallway.

'That's Kate, I bet,' he said to Kingston. He ran to the front door, unlocked it, and dashed down the hall to the phone.

'Hello,' he said, a little short of breath.

'Alex Sheppard?'

A hollow feeling gripped him. It was the American man.

'I asked you not to call again,' Alex said.

'That's hardly a polite English greeting now, is it, Mr Sheppard? Not what I would call exactly friendly.'

'I'm not feeling in a friendly mood.'

'That's most unfortunate – particularly since we have some business to take care of.'

'I have no business with you. I thought I'd made that clear before. So, if you'll excuse me–'

'You do have business with me, Sheppard,' the man countered. 'You have something we want – the rose. And we have something you want.'

'Really?' Alex shook his head. 'I don't think so. I don't think–'

'We have your wife.'

'You what?' Alex screamed.

'We have your wife. Now if you want her back–'

'Where is she? What have you done with her?'

'Just calm down.'

'What – what kind of lunatic are you? You've actually kidnapped my wife?' Alex's mind was spinning uncontrollably. Everything that Kingston had just told him came rushing back.

'Calm down and listen, Sheppard. Get a pen and paper because I want you to write this down.'

'You go to hell! I'm not going–'

'Do as I say, Sheppard, or it will just make it harder on your wife. Much harder.'

'You bastard, the minute you hang up, I'm calling the police.'

'That would be a huge mistake, believe me. You don't seem to understand – this is not a fucking game. You don't have any choice. Now write this down.'

Alex said nothing.

'Wednesday, the day after tomorrow, I want you to go to the following address in Oxford. Come alone and be there at ten o'clock in the morning, sharp. A man will meet you there. He'll have some papers for you to sign.'

'What if I refuse to sign? What are these papers, anyway?'

'Don't interrupt. Just make sure you don't screw up.'

There was a pause. 'Here's the address,' the man said.

Alex listened and wrote it down.

'I'll repeat it,' the man said. 'Just to make sure.'

He waited a few seconds, then said, 'Ten o'clock the day after tomorrow. Don't bring anybody with you or mention this to anybody. You got that?'

'Yes,' Alex replied.

'Okay, you do as I'm asking – sign those papers – and you'll get your lovely wife back. Is that clear?'

'Jesus.' Alex rubbed his head. 'You bastard! You'd better not hurt her, or–'

'Sheppard, just answer the goddamned question.'

'All right.'

'Do what I'm asking and nothing will happen to your wife. She's fine right now. One more thing. Don't be foolish and call the police. Don't talk to anyone about this. Do you hear me – nobody. That would be regrettable. And I mean very regrettable.' He paused. 'Meantime, take care of that rose! You understand?'

'You're a sick bastard. You're mad!'

Kingston had come into the room and was staring at him.

'I'll be even madder if you don't sign those papers. The sooner you do, the sooner you'll see your wife – in one piece.'

Alex heard a click and the line went dead. He stood, shaking furiously, the receiver still buzzing, gripped fiercely in his hand.

Kingston put a hand on Alex's shoulder. 'Good Lord! You look as white as a sheet, Alex. What on earth is going on? What the hell's wrong, old chap?'

Alex sat down on the sofa, bowed his head and massaged his forehead. 'It was the American. I can't believe it – the bastards have kidnapped Kate,' he said, almost whispering.

'Oh, my God – oh, no!' Kingston breathed.

Alex, staring down at the carpet, heard Kingston walk over to the sideboard. Next thing, he was handed a glass half-filled with cognac. Between sips he told Kingston exactly what the man had said.

Kingston listened, a grim look on his face.

'Alex, I think the first thing is to make sure that Wolff –

and I'm ninety-nine per cent sure, now, that's who is behind this – isn't bluffing.'

'Bluffing?' Alex exclaimed, his hands covering his face. 'That bastard on the phone wasn't bluffing, believe me.'

Kingston nodded and took a sip of the scotch he'd poured for himself. 'All I'm saying is that we should make sure. First, let's call Nell – find out when Kate left. That's a start. Then, I think we should call the police. They know how to handle these–'

'Christ, I told you, he warned me not to do that. Kate's life is at stake.' Alex leaned back, rested his head on the back of the sofa and stared up at the ceiling. 'Lawrence, half an hour ago you were telling me what a ruthless sod this Wolff is. That he's extremely dangerous. Now you want me to call the police and run the real risk of having him harm Kate? I can't risk it.' He sighed. 'I have no choice. He can have the damned rose.'

'You're forgetting. That might not be quite as simple as it sounds. What about Graham's claim and the auction? I think we'd better call Adell.'

The phone ringing startled Alex. 'Bloody hell,' he said, leaning over and picking it up. 'What next?'

'Hello, Alex,' Nell said cheerily.

'Oh, hello, Nell – we were just about to call you. Can you hold on a minute?' He cupped the mouthpiece of the phone in his hand and looked at Kingston. 'I'm not going to tell her about Kate. She'll call the police.'

Kingston nodded.

Alex put the phone to his ear. 'Sorry about that, Nell. How are you?'

'I'm fine, thanks. Kate said she was going to call me when she got home. It's been an awful long time now since she left – over five hours. I was calling to see if she got home okay. She is there, isn't she?'

Alex felt the colour drain from his face.

'She didn't feel too well when she got back,' Alex lied. 'She went upstairs to rest.' His voice sounded weak and unconvincing, even to his own ears.

'Hmm,' Nell muttered. 'That's odd. She was really upset

about the rose – scared, she said – but she didn't appear to be sick or anything. Well, I hope she gets over whatever it is. Would you ask her to call me tomorrow?'

'I will, Nell.'

'Are you all right, Alex? You don't sound like yourself.'

'I'm fine,' Alex said. 'Really.'

'I know it's upsetting, what happened to the rose, but I'm sure–'

Alex tensed. 'What did you say? What happened to the rose?'

'Didn't Kate tell you?'

Alex thought quickly. 'No, she just went straight to bed, but–'

'It's gone,' Nell said. 'Nothing but a whopping great hole in the ground. Made an awful mess they did.'

'Christ!'

'I'm sure it will work out all right, Alex. You'll get it back.'

He gripped the bridge of his nose and closed his eyes. 'We'd better,' he sighed. 'We'd better.'

'You're sure you're all right, Alex?'

'Yes, I'm fine. But I have to go, Nell.'

'Alex?'

'Yes.'

'You will ask Kate to call me?'

'Of course I will, Nell,' he stuttered. 'Goodbye.'

'Goodbye, then.'

Alex hung up and turned to Kingston.

'According to Nell, Kate was okay when she left.'

'Doesn't look good, I'll admit.'

'That's not all. The rose is gone. Somebody's taken it.'

'My God! What on earth is going on?'

'Bugger the rose. Kate's all I'm worried about.' He paused, his head in his hands, then looked up again. 'Maybe she broke down? It's a possibility.'

'If she had, surely she would have called to let you know.'

Alex swallowed hard. 'Nell said Kate left over five hours

ago. She said all that's left now is a gaping hole where Vicky and I planted the rose.'

'How much more complicated can this get? If we no longer have the rose. . .'

'How can we exchange it for Kate?'

'Exactly.'

Alex buried his face in his hands. His voice was muffled and quavering. 'I can't bear to think what that bastard might do when I tell him we no longer have the rose.'

'Will he believe you? That's another question entirely.'

Alex looked up to see Kingston pulling on his earlobe – a sure sign that his mind was in overdrive. He took a sip of the cognac.

'What about the cuttings, Alex? Were those ever taken?'

Alex sighed. 'I don't know. Why?'

'Well, if we could get our hands on them, it could change everything.'

'I remember Kate saying that she wanted Vicky to do it because she'd never had too much success at it. But that was ages ago, around the time we first met you.'

'If Vicky took cuttings – and we'll assume for the moment she did – where would she have kept them?'

'You're asking the wrong person, Lawrence. I don't think she would have left them with us. The most likely place would be the nursery.'

'Then we should call right away and find out.'

'You think that Wolff will accept the cuttings instead of the rose?'

'No, I don't for one moment think that's a possibility. The rose is still out there somewhere. And to further complicate matters, there's the crossing formula which, as far as we know, Wolff doesn't know about, yet.'

'Well, what then?'

'At some point, we'll have to tell Wolff about the cuttings. He's not that naïve. He'll know that that's the very first thing we would have done.'

'Then he'll want the rose and the cuttings before we get Kate back.'

'First things first, Alex. Let's find out whether the cuttings are at the nursery.'

'All right,' said Alex. He picked up the small address book on the table beside him, checked for Holly Hill's number, reached for the phone and dialled the number.

'Hello, is that Jill?' There was a short pause. 'Yes, it is. I'm surprised you recognized my voice. Yes, it has been. I have a question for you, Jill. It's really important.' Alex glanced at Kingston. 'I'm here with a friend of mine, Lawrence Kingston – yes.' He nodded. 'Yes, the very same,' he said. 'Jill, we're almost positive that sometime shortly before Vicky died, she took some cuttings from a rose in our garden. Kate had asked for them.' Alex shook his head. 'No, she's not here right now, she's visiting a friend for a couple of days. Anyway, we can't seem to find them. It's more likely than not that Vicky was caring for them at the nursery.'

Alex listened to what Jill had to say, then ended the conversation. 'That would be good,' he said. 'Call me back as soon as you can. You're an angel, Jill, thanks.'

Alex put the phone down and looked at Kingston. 'She vaguely remembers them. Apparently Vicky had talked to one of the staff about keeping them secure. Jill said she'd try to track them down.'

'Sounds promising.'

'What about Wolff, Lawrence? We have to tell his mouthpiece we no longer have the rose.'

'Perhaps we don't tell him – not just yet, anyway. By the way, what did he say about the papers you're supposed to sign on Wednesday?'

'Nothing – only papers. But you know damned well they have something to do with turning over the rose.'

'Of course.'

'Oh God. Poor Kate,' Alex moaned, gripping the brandy glass with both hands.

Kingston got up, stretched his legs and started to pace the room. 'One small thing in our favour,' he said. 'We've got a little time to play with until he starts asking to see the rose.'

174

'Not much, I would think. Who the hell could have taken it?'

Kingston shook his head. 'I have no idea. Any number of people knew about it, if you stop to consider. There's the Cookes, their lawyer, your lawyer, Tanaka, Wolff – anybody who works for Wolff.'

'But Wolff wouldn't have taken both the rose and Kate. It wouldn't make sense.'

'I agree,' said Kingston. 'Unless he took it as added insurance.' He leaned forward, swirling the melting ice in his glass. 'I really don't know what to think, Alex. Nothing makes sense.'

Alex downed the rest of his cognac in one gulp. His face was ashen, his eyes red and swollen. 'What an awful sodding mess,' he sighed.

Kingston stopped pacing and sat down, his eyes fixed on Alex's. 'If – and I grant you it could be a big if – they really will release Kate on Wednesday when you've signed–'

The phone started to ring, stopping Kingston midsentence.

Alex picked it up.

'Yes, this is Alex. Oh, hello, Jill. That was quick.'

Alex's face paled, like the sun going behind a cloud.

'My God! You're sure?' He waited a few seconds. 'How many were there? I see. Well, it's not the answer we were looking for, but thanks, Jill. I may come and see you later in the week. Would that be okay? Fine.'

He placed the phone down, slowly.

'What did she say?' asked Kingston.

'Apparently they all died. It seems that with Vicky's death, the funeral and everything, the drip system was never set up.'

'Jesus, what rotten luck,' said Kingston. 'Now we do have to find the missing rose.'

Chapter Seventeen

Gather therefore the rose, whilst yet is prime.
Edmund Spenser

Kate's heartbeat had finally slowed to a normal rate. She was still trembling but the initial shock of the assault had subsided. It was replaced by anger, the need to strike back, the urge to escape. Constantly moving her jaw and lips had no effect on loosening the duct tape stretched tightly across her mouth. If anything it increased the chafing. Attempting to remove the goggles strapped to her head proved equally futile.

In her maddeningly helpless state, Kate's mind replayed, over and over, the events since she had left Nell's house. Who were these men? Were they the ones who took the rose? If so, why had they taken her too? It had to be something to do with Sapphire – but what?

The screeching of tyres locked on the road, loud blaring of the Jeep's horn and swearing from the driver jolted Kate back to the present. She sensed they had narrowly avoided a collision. She nestled into the corner of the seat and closed her eyes but couldn't sleep. For the first time in her life she was experiencing terror. Not only from what had happened but the dread of what might happen. The goose-flesh of fear on her arms and neck would not go away.

At last she heard the engine die and the handbrake being yanked on. The driver got out and closed the door. She heard his retreating footsteps, then, save for the occasional pinging of the Jeep's exhaust pipe and muffler as it cooled, all was quiet. A minute or so later, she heard the two men talking nearby but couldn't make out what they were saying. Then she heard the door near to her open. A strong hand gripped her arm just above the elbow. Hauled roughly out of the car, she found her footing on the loose gravel. Birds were twittering noisily. Lots of them. In the distance there was a faint droning of a tractor or harvester. Closer by, a dog barked sporadically.

With a man on either side gripping her arms, they walked along the path. Soon, they came to a halt. She heard a key being inserted into a lock, followed by the creak of a door opening. After the sweetness of the smells outside, the pungent smoky odour inside made her stomach heave. Last night's embers must be still smouldering in the fireplace. Now, with just one of the men guiding her, they were walking on carpet. Her arm brushed against a wall – a hallway, she guessed. She stumbled as her toe bumped into something. 'Stairs,' the man said, helping her to recover. At the top of the stairs they came to a halt. She heard another key turn in a lock, then the slide of a bolt. No more than three steps into the room, they stopped again and the man released her arm. Her heart was thumping. The room was cold and smelled musty. The chafing of the cord had lacerated her wrists and the duct tape had made her face sore and itching where it was pulling against her skin. In the pitch-black darkness, she felt very frightened and vulnerable.

She felt the man behind her loosening and then removing the cord that bound her wrists. Next, he was removing the tape from the goggles. Strands of her hair were stuck to the tape. It was painfully slow. At least he didn't just rip the tape off. It gave her a glimmer of hope that from now on she might be treated with leniency.

When the goggles came off, Kate expected to be blinded by bright light. She wasn't. As the room came slowly into focus she saw why. Heavy velvet curtains covered the windows. The room was in semi-darkness. From behind, the man removed the duct tape gently from her mouth. Before she could utter a word or get a good look at him he had slipped silently from the room, closing the door behind him. The bolt slid shut.

Kate gently rubbed her sore wrists and touched her cheeks with the tips of her fingers. Her face was very tender. She breathed deeply through her mouth. Her ribcage ached as her lungs sucked in the stale air. Her eyes were now fully adjusted to the meagre light. Glancing around the shadowy room, she could make out a double bed, a large wardrobe and sundry pieces of other dark furniture. Close to her, on her right, a small table stood between two upholstered chairs. On it was a tray containing a teapot, a white mug, milk and sugar and a plate with biscuits. For a fleeting moment she felt oddly touched by the gesture, then quickly reminded herself of the gravity of her situation. The tea tasted good and she quickly devoured all eight biscuits. She walked to the window and pulled the curtain aside. Outside, it was starting to get dark and she could see little. Certainly there were no lights to indicate other houses or buildings nearby. Apparently her 'prison' had been chosen for its isolated location. For a while she sat on the bed assessing her plight. Soon, however, drowsiness overcame her. After all she had been subjected to, her body could take no more. Her eyelids drooped and she lay back on the bed. Within seconds she was asleep.

Alex let out a low moan. His temples were throbbing. He ran his tongue around his lips. They were parched and cracked like a dry riverbed. The blurry green numbers on the clock radio read 10:14.

Then it all came crashing back: the devastating call about Kate from the American, the rose being stolen, the cognac, his falling asleep on the sofa. He couldn't recall having eaten anything, just drinking more brandy. No wonder he felt so bloody awful. Pulling back the sheets, he slowly got out of bed, put on his dressing gown and slippers, and padded along the hallway and downstairs to the kitchen.

The empty bottle of Remy-Martin on the kitchen counter confirmed his worst suspicions: it had been half full yesterday.

He checked the living room – no Kingston. 'Christ, I hope he didn't attempt to drive home last night,' he muttered. Opening the front door to retrieve *The Times*, he was relieved of his concern: the TR4 was still in the drive where Kingston had parked it yesterday. He picked up the paper and went back into the house.

Consumed with anguish about Kate, he tried hard to put himself in her position, wondering where she was, how she was being treated. Mindlessly, he filled the electric kettle, flicked on the switch and walked over to the kitchen table. He sat down and stared blankly at the rolled-up newspaper. He thought back to what Kingston had said, about calling the police. He shook his head slowly. 'God, I just can't do it,' he said under his breath.

He jumped at the sound of loud knocking on the front door.

'Sod it,' he muttered. 'I must have locked him out. We do have a bloody doorbell, Kingston,' he shouted, walking to the door.

Instead of Kingston, two strangers stood facing him.

Beyond them, a nondescript beige car sat alongside the TR4. The older and taller of the two men was well turned-out, in a conservative navy suit and regimental-striped tie. He had a receding hairline, sad china-blue eyes heavily wrinkled at the corners and a trim grey moustache. Late fifties, Alex guessed. He could have passed for anybody's company director. His companion was much younger, lean, and leather-jacketed. Quite handsome in a rugged sort of way, his looks strangely enhanced by a scar that ran from his shortly cropped hairline to bisect one eyebrow. Neither of them looked threatening, Alex was relieved to note.

'Er, Mr Sheppard? Alex Sheppard?' the older man inquired.

'Yes, that's me. How can I help you?'

'We're investigating the death, yesterday, of a Mr

Graham Cooke and wondered if you could answer a few questions for us, sir.' He paused, his eyes carefully studying Alex's face, clearly gauging Alex's reaction to his question. 'I'm Detective Inspector Holland,' he said. He gestured to his partner. 'This is Detective Sergeant Taylor.'

Alex was flustered. He hesitated. 'I told your sergeant, yesterday, everything that happened,' he said.

'Yes, we've read your statement, Mr Sheppard. No need to be concerned. This is just a routine inquiry, a follow-up call – just making sure we haven't overlooked anything.'

'Did you know him, then – the deceased?' Detective Sergeant Taylor asked, in a North of England accent.

'Graham? No, not very well. I've only met him twice.' Alex felt uncomfortable talking about such a serious matter at the front door – not that there was anyone to overhear the conversation. 'It was a bit of a shock – yesterday. Why don't you come in, please,' he said, stepping aside to let them pass. 'First door on the right. Excuse the mess, my wife's away for a couple of days.'

Inspector Holland continued his polite questioning from the comfort of the sofa. 'What was your connection with Graham Cooke, then, sir?'

'Well, he is – was – the nephew of the lady who previously owned this house. We bought it from her earlier this year.'

'He wasn't what you would term a friend, then?'

'Hardly.' The minute he'd said the word he knew it had a self-incriminating edge.

Holland picked up on it instantly. 'You didn't like him?'

'No, I didn't mean that, at all. What I meant to say was that he was barely an acquaintance.'

'So you have nothing to do with his business? Pharmaceuticals sales, I believe.'

'No – oh, no.'

Occasionally, Taylor jotted down a note on his pad, always licking the point of the pencil when he did so. Alex couldn't help but reflect on how many times he'd watched this type of interview in movies and on TV.

Holland continued. 'Can you tell me why you were planning to meet Mr Cooke yesterday?'

The question took Alex by surprise.

Holland followed up quickly. 'What was the meeting about?'

'We were returning some books that Graham had lent us.'

'What kind of books?'

'They were records that belonged to Graham's uncle.'

'Records?'

Alex rubbed his brow. 'Actually, they were to do with hybridizing roses.'

'Really?'

'Yes.'

Holland didn't look convinced.

'We showed them to your sergeant at the time. I still have them in the car, if you want to take a look.'

'Roses, eh? That's a good one,' Holland said disdainfully. 'You said "we". Was that the chap Kingston, who was listed on the report?'

'Yes, a friend of mine, Lawrence Kingston,' Alex replied. 'He's a professor,' he added, in the hope that it might add more credibility.

A brief exchange between the two policemen allowed Alex a chance to recall the details of the short meeting he and Kate had had with Graham at The Parsonage earlier. They were certain to ask about that.

'I'm curious,' Alex said, when the two had finished their confab. 'How did Graham die?'

'The unofficial verdict is that it was a heart attack.'

'Christ! He was awfully young. A heart attack?'

'Well, there could be more to it. There were contusions on the body and visible evidence of a struggle of some kind. That certainly could have brought on the attack.'

Alex shook his head in disbelief. 'Good grief. That's awful.'

'Yes, sir, it is.' Holland leaned forward, as if about to get up. He stopped, and looked at Alex, resting his chin on an arched thumb and forefinger. 'Oh, there was one more thing, sir,' he said, casually. 'We found a copy of a letter addressed to you and your wife. It was on Mr Cooke's person. A letter from a solicitor – named. . .' He looked across at Taylor, who flipped back through his notebook.

'Alexander Stanhope,' said Taylor.

Holland nodded thanks to the sergeant. 'Could you tell us about that, Mr Sheppard?' he asked.

Alex paled. Already he could see the implications. 'Ah, yes. We received that letter a few days ago. Graham delivered it, personally, to my wife and me.'

'According to Mr Stanhope's statement, it appears that you and your wife stood to lose a considerable amount of money if ownership of this rose reverted to Graham and his aunt. Is that correct?'

'That's true,' Alex replied.

'A moment ago you said "roses" but it was one rose in particular, was it not?'

'It was, yes. Slip of the tongue, I guess.'

Holland shrugged, and shook his head slowly from side to side. 'I can't, for the life of me, imagine why a rose could be that valuable.' His comment was punctuated with a loud sniff. 'Takes all sorts, I suppose.' He stood, shaking his trouser legs down and twitching his tie.

Alex remained silent.

'We may have to ask you to come in to make a full statement, Mr Sheppard. I'll phone and let you know if and when that will be. You might want to tell your friend. . .' He looked at Sergeant Taylor.

'Kingston,' Taylor answered.

'Yes – Kingston. We might like a quick word with him too.'

'Actually, he's staying with me until tomorrow. He should be back any moment. Do you want to wait? I can make some tea, if you'd like.'

'No, that's fine, Mr Sheppard. We don't want to keep you any longer than is necessary. We'll be on our way. Oh, there was one more thing. In the meantime, you're not planning to leave the area, are you?'

'No.' Alex gave Holland a quizzical look. 'Look, I told you – I had absolutely nothing to do with Cooke's death. *Nothing!*'

Holland brushed his forefinger over his lower lip. 'You were planning to sign the rose over to Cooke, then?'

'We were, as a matter of fact. I know it must seem stupid – particularly in light of what has happened – to toss aside a once-in-a-lifetime chance of making an obscene amount of money, but we really don't want the rose any more. It's caused us nothing but bloody problems. It's been awful. We're only interested in keeping this property. I know it sounds hard to believe and it doesn't look good. I mean – what with Graham, the bad timing – but I can assure you I had nothing to do with it.'

'Just routine questioning, that's all. I did ask you whether you're planning any trips over the next week or so, didn't I?'

'Yes, you did, and no, I'm not.'

'Good. Good. I suggest you stay close to home until you hear from me.'

'Of course,' Alex said. On top of everything else, he was now a suspect in what could become a murder case.

Holland turned, as if ready to leave, then swivelled his head back to Alex. 'You mentioned that your wife was away. Where was she yesterday?'

'My God! Are you serious? You're not suggesting–'

Holland stopped Alex short. 'No, no. Just curious, that's all.'

'She was up in Market Drayton, staying with a friend,' Alex said. He came perilously close to blurting out that Kate had been kidnapped. If there ever was a time to bring it all out into the open, this was it. The words were about to spew forth when the recollection of Wolff's threat smothered them.

'Ask her to call us when she gets back, will you? We may need to talk to her.'

Alex nodded. 'Of course,' he said.

'Well, I think that's all for now, Mr Sheppard. If you think of anything else that might help in our investigation, we'd be most appreciative if you'd let us know.'

Taylor handed Alex his card. Alex shook hands with both of them at the front door and watched in a state of stupor as they walked to their car, got in and drove off.

Chapter Eighteen

*Who reaches with a clumsy hand for a rose must not
complain if the thorns scratch.*

Heinrich Heine

Alex was at the kitchen table staring at a bowl of uneaten
cereal when Kingston entered. Less than ten minutes had
passed since the detectives left. The unopened *Times* was
on the table.

Kingston pulled up a chair and sat facing him. 'How are
you feeling, old chap?' he asked.

'Bloody awful, Lawrence. Where have you been?'

'For my morning constitutional. Walked down to the
village. Spent twenty minutes advising a lady how to take
care of mildew on her roses. Most of the time I thought
about yesterday, though.'

'Come up with any answers?'

'No answers, I'm afraid. Have some ideas, though.' A
look of concern clouded Kingston's face. 'You look odd,
Alex. Has something happened since I left? What's been
going on?'

'Not much really. Only the CID interrogating me as a
likely murder suspect.'

'The police were here? Murder?'

'An inspector and a detective sergeant. They left only ten
minutes ago. Graham may have died of a heart attack but
they're saying it was brought on during a struggle. They
found bruises on his body.'

Kingston frowned. 'Interesting. What else did they
say?'

'They asked a lot of questions and advised me not to leave town. They even asked about Kate's whereabouts yesterday. That scared the hell out of me, Lawrence. I can't tell you how close I came to telling them about Kate being kidnapped.' He picked up the spoon by the side of his plate and started toying with the cereal. 'They'll probably call you, too.'

'Well, it's easy to see why you and Kate would be considered suspect. They know you stood to lose a hell of a lot of money – it's the perfect motive.' He started pulling on his earlobe. 'It's too much of a coincidence, though,' he muttered.

'What is?'

'For Graham's death not to be connected to the formula.'

'Christ, Lawrence. On top of everything else, now we have to find out who killed Graham? Forget it. It's *Kate* we have to worry about right now. I'm scared as hell about tomorrow.'

'Alex, I understand–'

'I know and I appreciate what you're doing, Lawrence. But let's talk about tomorrow. Everything hangs on that meeting now. It's a sure bet they're going to ask me to sign over a rose we haven't got – one that we may not even own. That's what's going to happen, isn't it?'

'I would imagine that's what Wolff has in mind, yes. I can't think of any other reason.'

'But what if he's since found out that we *don't* have it and *don't* own it?' He looked straight at Kingston. 'So what do I do then, Lawrence?'

Kingston looked down, weighing his reply. After several seconds, he looked up into Alex's tired eyes. 'I know you're not going to like this,' he said, 'but we have to tell the police. It's not too late and they can accompany you tomorrow.'

'For Christ's sake!' Alex almost shouted.

Kingston shrugged. 'Okay, then you'll just have to tell this person – whoever he is – the whole story and hope to hell he believes you, which I doubt very much.'

186

Alex sighed. 'A lot of help you are, Lawrence.'

'Well, at least you'll be talking to someone face to face, even if it is a go-between.'

'It would have to be. Somehow I don't think Wolff would show his miserable face.'

'I wonder where it is you're meeting this person. Surely Wolff wouldn't have you meet in a solicitor's office. He wouldn't expose himself like that. It would be too easy for police to follow the trail.'

'Lawrence, please don't bring up the police again. I'm not going to call them and neither are you. You know already how I feel about that.' He stood up and rubbed his chin. 'Look, I need to pull myself together, shave, and have a shower. Why don't you take a walk in the garden? Looks nice out there right now.'

'Good idea. Haven't seen it for a while.' He got up and started towards the door. At the threshold he stopped and turned. 'Alex,' he said, 'we'll find a way of getting Kate back, I know damned well we will.' Then he walked out the door.

Alex watched through the kitchen window as Kingston strode into the garden as though it was his very own. 'I only wish I could feel as confident,' he murmured to himself, turning away.

That night after a sandwich and a Mackeson's that served for dinner Alex and Kingston went over, for the umpteenth time, the events of the last few weeks, searching for the slightest clue that they may have overlooked. As the evening wore on, Alex found himself saying less and less, being satisfied simply to listen to Kingston. In doing so, he found himself subconsciously trying to pick up on anything that Kingston might say to suggest – as Kate had put it – that he knew a little more than he was telling. After a while, he gave up, dismissing the whole idea as being too fanciful. Besides, he was coming to appreciate Kingston – even to like him.

By the time they were ready to call it a night, it was

agreed that Kingston would stay on for a few more days. Alex had proposed the idea but he knew that sooner or later Kingston would have suggested it himself.

The following morning Kingston left to go up to his flat in London to pick up some clothes and other essentials. He would drive back in the evening, to be there when Alex returned from his appointment in Oxford.

It was seven thirty in the morning and Alex was about to step into the shower when the phone downstairs started ringing. He turned off the taps, slipped a towel around his waist, and hurried down the staircase. 'Why don't I just have the bloody thing disconnected?' he muttered to himself. 'These days it always means bad news, anyway.'

He picked up the phone.

'Mr Sheppard?'

Alex's mouth was suddenly dry. It was the American again. He tried to calm himself. 'What is it now?'

'I'm calling to remind you of your appointment this morning.'

'It had hardly slipped my mind, if that's what you're thinking.'

'Good. Just make sure that you go alone.'

'How is Kate? I want to know how she is.'

'Don't start that again, Sheppard. We've been over this before. As of now, your wife is fine. She's enjoying a pleasant rest. You just sign those papers this morning – then you get your wife back. In one piece,' he added.

'For Christ's sake, you really think you're going to get away with this?'

The man didn't answer right away.

Alex decided to take a gamble. 'How do you know I won't show up with the police?'

The man's voice had no emotion, no threatening tone. 'Do you love your wife?'

Alex didn't answer.

'I take it that your answer is yes.' He paused for a moment.

Alex said nothing.

'All right. I'll say this just once, Mr Sheppard. Do not mention this conversation to anyone. If there's the slightest indication that you have made contact with the police or any other law enforcement agency, you will see your wife again. You will see her but you won't recognize her. Do I make myself clear?'

'You cruel bastard.'

'Good. Well, that's settled, then.'

Alex swallowed hard, trying to suppress the bile rising in his throat. His mind was racing. It had been the plan for him to tell the man in Oxford that the rose had been stolen and that a hybridizing formula now existed, that the rose could be cloned. Should he wait or tell this man now? He took a deep breath. 'There's one small problem,' he said.

'Problem?'

'We don't have the rose,' Alex said. 'What's more, I haven't a sodding clue where it is or who took it. So let Kate go. There's no point in keeping her any more.'

The man laughed. His cynicism was undisguised.

'It's the goddamned truth,' Alex snapped.

'What do you take me for, Sheppard – a fucking hill-billy? You have the balls to tell me that somebody just walked into your garden, dug up the rose, and made off with it?'

'I'm telling you, I don't have it. I'm not lying,' he shouted.

'Bullshit! This conversation is over. You sign those papers this morning. That's all.'

'How many times do I have to tell you, I don't have the bloody rose!'

'Well, you'd better damn well get it!' the man shouted back.

Before Alex could say anything further, the line was dead.

When Alex arrived in Oxford it was beginning to drizzle. A damp greyness cloaked the city, muffling the sound of the crawling traffic and omnipresent pneumatic drilling. Umbrellas crowded the busy streets as the rush-hour jostle showed no signs of waning. Alex had left The Parsonage well before nine, allowing plenty of time to get to Oxford. Luckily, he found a two-hour parking space within easy walking distance of the address he had been given. He checked the directions again, to make sure, and replaced the paper in his pocket.

After no more than a five-minute walk he arrived at his destination, a honey-coloured old stone building on Beaumont Street, across from the new quarters of the Ashmolean Museum. Alex knew the museum well. He had visited it many times. He stood for a moment and contemplated the façade of the elegant building. How ironic, he thought. The museum was first established to house curiosities collected by seventeenth-century botanist, plant hunter and gardener, John Tradescant the Elder, and here he was about to sign away the rights to the botanical discovery of the century. He turned away and walked up the steps into the four-storey Georgian building in front of him. Running his eyes down the directory in the dimly lit lobby, he determined that Suite 36 was occupied by Alexander Lithgow, Solicitor. That figured, he thought, as he got into the self-operated lift. On the third floor, he followed the fading numbered arrows on the wall to number 36. He knocked sharply on the frosted glass window, turned the dented brass doorknob and entered.

The outer office was almost Dickensian. Stacks of books and bulging folders and papers were piled with seeming abandon on desks, in chairs and on the floor. On the wall to his left, a quartet of yellowing diplomas was displayed, unquestionably a fixture of many years. The clock on another wall showed 9.55.

A man appeared from a door in the back. For a moment Alex was taken aback. The man was not at all what Alex was expecting. He was over six feet tall, with military-style cropped hair and a square jaw. His face was evenly tanned, eyes concealed behind tinted sunglasses. He was wearing a loose-fitting black suit and a black shirt, open at the collar. In one hand he held a manila folder.

'Alexander Lithgow?' Alex inquired.

'No, he's not here right now,' the man said in a brusque manner.

For whatever reason Alex had taken him for an American but the man had an English accent. 'Who are you, then?' he asked.

'Never mind. I take it you're Alex Sheppard.'

'I am.'

The man gestured to the large partner's desk that half-filled the space. 'Sit down,' he said.

Alex dragged a wooden chair out from beside the desk, sat down and folded his arms. The man seated himself on the opposite side of the desk facing Alex. He placed the folder on the desk and opened it to reveal a thin sheaf of papers. Then he reached inside his jacket pocket, took out a pen and slid it across the desk to Alex.

Alex watched in silence.

'All right,' he said, placing his hands palm down each side of the open folder. 'This is a sales agreement. A legal document, that transfers ownership of the rose presently in your possession to another party. It's not necessary for you to read it, just sign on the line on the last page, where it's marked with an X, and write in today's date. Do the same on the two copies underneath.' He turned the folder around and slid it across to Alex.

'If I sign, when do I get Kate back?'

'Sorry. I'm not here to answer questions. My job is just to make sure you sign these papers.' He started to tap his fingers on the desktop.

Alex stared at the man for a moment, then looked down at the pen in front of him.

'Well, come on.'

'It's not going to work. You're wasting your time. I tried to tell your friend, but he wouldn't listen.'

'What do you mean?'

'We don't have the rose. It's been stolen.'

Alex expected surprise to register on the man's face, but it didn't. His look of exasperation turned into one of anger, instead. Because of the tinted glasses, Alex couldn't see the expression in his eyes but knew they were boring into his. The man's lips tightened and with an index finger resting on either side of his glasses, he adjusted them, unnecessarily.

Still nothing was said.

He pushed the folder a few inches closer to Alex. 'Just sign the papers, dammit.'

Alex picked up the pen. 'Is Ira Wolff behind all this?'

The man ignored his question.

'You know bloody well what's going on, don't you? You know all about my wife.'

The man nodded towards the folder. 'Sign it,' he snapped.

'If I do, when do I get her back?'

The man's fist moved with frightening speed as it crashed down on the top of the desk. 'Sign the fuckin' paper,' he yelled.

Alex signed and dated the original and two copies, closed the folder and shoved it roughly across the desk. It was the only thing he could do. He stood up, almost knocking over the chair. 'You bastards.' His voice was breaking, his fists clenched so tight they hurt. 'You'll never get away with this.'

The man stood and spun around the desk. Before Alex could raise his fists, the man was up against him, his two hands grasping Alex's jacket lapels. With a fierce jerk he pulled Alex close to him, so close that Alex could see his eyes reflected in the man's glasses. 'Get this straight,' he said, drawing a long breath. 'I'm not going to repeat myself. You want your wife back in one piece – you have that rose ready for delivery in forty-eight hours. You got it? Forty-eight hours, that's two days from now.' On the 'now', the man released his grip and pushed Alex away so hard that he stumbled back and crashed into the door.

'Now, get the hell out of here,' the man shouted.

Alex recovered and glared back, sizing up his chances in a fight. Deciding they were not good, he turned, opened the door and walked out, slamming it behind him as hard as he could.

Chapter Nineteen

Nature soon takes over if the gardener is absent.
Penelope Hobhouse

Gripping a large suitcase in one hand, a holdall in the other, a bulky camera case dangling from his shoulder and a wooden tennis racquet tucked under his arm, Kingston returned to The Parsonage late on Wednesday evening to find Alex more despondent than ever.

The moment Alex had opened the door, Kingston could see that the events of the past days were starting to have a marked physical effect on him. His eyes were dark-circled and lacklustre from worry and, no doubt, loss of sleep. Even his posture seemed to be bowing under the weight of his frustration and despair. His clothes reflected his resignation, too. He was wearing a badly stained Oxford University sweatshirt, blue jeans frayed to the point of exposing one of his kneecaps, and no shoes.

In the sitting room, Kingston poured himself a generous scotch, then walked over and settled his tall frame into the ample seat of *his* chair. Alex was slumped on the sofa opposite. Asp was curled up next to him. Only one lamp was lit, making the mood even more gloomy.

'So, how are you holding up, Alex?' he asked.

Alex's answer was slow in coming, his voice listless. 'Not very well,' he answered.

Kingston looked into Alex's red-rimmed eyes, then across to the side table and the amber dregs in a heavily fingerprinted crystal glass. 'You're not overdoing it on the sauce, are you, Alex?'

'No, don't worry, Lawrence, I'm not drinking myself into oblivion – if that's what you're thinking. Not yet, anyway.'

Alex looked down for a long moment, then back to Kingston. 'Wolff has given us forty-eight hours to come up with the rose or the bastards are going to hurt Kate.' He let out a long sigh. 'I don't think I can take it much more, Lawrence.'

Kingston swirled the ice in the glass held in his lap. The sound heightened the tension in the room. 'Maybe there's a way we can prove to Wolff that we don't have the rose, that you've been telling the truth.'

'How do we do that?'

Kingston took a sip of scotch. 'I don't have a quick answer but anything's worth a try right now.'

Alex got up. 'Come on, Asp, I forgot to feed you again. Sorry, old chap.' Asp followed Alex into the kitchen.

In a couple of minutes he returned and sat down opposite Kingston.

'So, tell me more about what happened in Oxford,' Kingston inquired, sipping his scotch.

'There's not much to tell. It was just as we thought. I ended up signing an agreement transferring ownership of the rose.'

'A rose you don't have.'

'Exactly.'

'You did tell them that you didn't have it – that it was questionable whether you even owned it?'

'Christ, Lawrence, of course I did. And it didn't make a bloody bit of difference. The guy went ballistic when I told him. The bastard shoved me into the door.' He rubbed his shoulder. 'It still hurts,' he said, grimacing.

'I should have come with you,' Kingston said, more just for something to say.

Alex said nothing, plainly lost in agonizing thought.

'So, this man – was he a lawyer?'

Alex sneered. 'Lawyer? He looked more like a pimp.'

'Well, whose office was it, then?'

Alex bowed his head and massaged his temples. 'Some solicitor's called Lithgow.'

'Well, you can be damned sure they borrowed the place for a couple of hours. Wolff would never leave tracks like that. Easiest thing in the world to get somebody out of their office for a few hours.'

'Lawrence, these people are evil. It wouldn't surprise me if they had Lithgow locked and bound in a closet somewhere in the back.'

A drawn-out silence suggested that Alex wanted no further discussion about the morning's encounter.

Kingston got up, stretched his legs, went over to the standard lamp by the windows and turned it on. He wanted to talk more about the rose, only in the hope that by doing so it would offer up even the slenderest clue as who might have taken it or where it may be. But he could see that Alex had had enough for one day. 'Oh, I meant to tell you,' he said, in an upbeat tone, hoping that it might help lift Alex out of his despondency. 'I got a call from Cardwell today.'

'Cardwell?'

'Yes, you know – the head cryptographer, the chap at DSSS Chicksands. He phoned to let me know that he'd made some more inquiries on the matter of Graham's journal that they decrypted. Well, it turns out that the cryptographer did make file copies of the decoded pages after all, but Graham must have quietly snaffled them while the chap's back was turned.'

'Makes sense. The crafty sod certainly wouldn't want extra copies of the formula lying around, would he? I'm surprised he was able to pull it off at all.'

'Not when you think about it. Apparently, the name Major Jeffrey Cooke still opens doors there, even fifty years later. It seems that he's in the same league as Alan Turing, Sir Harry Hinsley, and some of other top wartime Bletchley cryptoanalysts. When the people at Chicksands learned that Graham was his nephew, they were only too happy to oblige in deciphering the missing journal.'

'Well, it all becomes moot now, I suppose. I doubt very

much that we'll ever see that rose again. We might as well face up to it.'

'I wouldn't count it out altogether, Alex. Not just yet.'

'I only wish I could believe that,' Alex mumbled.

Kingston tried another tack. 'Did Adell ever get back to you – on Graham's claim?'

'Damn! I meant to call him today. I'll do it tomorrow – the answer is no.'

'About tomorrow, I take it you're not going in to the office?'

'I don't think so. But if I sit around here all day long I'll go raving mad.'

'From now on, Alex, we have to start brainstorming around the clock. We must find that damned rose. We'll start first thing tomorrow and we'll continue over lunch.'

'I don't think so,' Alex protested. 'Not lunch, that is. I really don't have the stomach for it right now.'

'Come on, Alex. You haven't eaten a decent meal in days, I'll bet. It'll do you good. It's only an hour out of the day.'

Alex shook his head. 'Lawrence, how can you be thinking of food at a time like this?'

Kingston held his hands up, palms facing Alex. 'I'm going to insist on it,' he said. 'What difference does it make *where* we are as long as we're trying to figure this bloody mess out?'

Alex sighed. 'All right, Lawrence. Only an hour, okay?'

'That's a promise?'

'I suppose so,' Alex mumbled, with a limp shrug.

'We have to keep trying, keep talking, that's all,' Kingston said in as comforting a tone as he could muster. He looked away from Alex to the leaded windows and beyond into the darkness of the gardens. He thought of the rose. Where was it, he wondered? For all they knew, it could be out of the country by now.

What an extraordinary discovery it was, and what misfortune it had brought with it. Like King Tut's curse. Had

Major Cooke anticipated this sort of thing happening? He and Farrow – if, indeed, he was involved – must have thought a lot about the impact a blue rose would have globally on horticulture. Was it possible that they had the foresight to predict that there could be a dark side to such a beautiful creation? That greedy, unethical, even corrupt individuals and interests would try to acquire it by whatever means possible? Was this why they had used codes and not told a soul – even Mrs Cooke – of what they were doing? Did they intend all along never to reveal their secret? That appeared to be the case.

'What are you thinking about, Lawrence?'

Kingston turned to see Alex standing by the sofa holding the two empty glasses, as if ready to leave. 'Oh, just about Cooke and Farrow – trying to visualize how they must have reacted when they found out they'd achieved the impossible. I would dearly love to have witnessed that. Oh, I had another thought, too, related to Mrs Cooke. I won't saddle you with it now. I'll tell you about it tomorrow.'

Alex nodded.

Kingston got up from his chair, stretched and stifled a yawn with the back of his hand then headed through the door to the hallway, where he'd left his belongings. Alex flicked off the lights in the living room and helped Kingston take his bags upstairs.

On the landing, Kingston paused at the partially open door to his room and turned to Alex. 'Thanks for asking me to stay, Alex,' he said. 'By the way – you do play tennis, don't you?'

'Yes. Not as often as I'd like, I'm afraid. But I'll bet you played with Rod Laver in your day – eh?'

'That's extraordinary – how could you have known that?'

A few minutes after eight the following morning the two of them sat down at the kitchen table with pads and pens and – not for the first time – started to recreate a step-by-step replay of every single event and conversation that had occurred since Kate and Alex's discovery of the rose. By noon two dozen sheets were filled with notes but they were no nearer to breaking the impasse.

The small French restaurant Kingston had chosen was in a back street of Cirencester. Soon after they were seated, Kingston launched into an animated conversation in French with the waiter. Most of it was lost to Alex but there was no question that Kingston knew his Provençal cuisine.

Kingston ordered a glass of wine, Alex settled for mineral water. Soon, Niçoise salads were placed in front of them and for the next ten minutes they ate and talked without further interruption.

Kingston dabbed his mouth with the cloth napkin. 'So, as I was saying, Alex, I think we should pay Mrs Cooke another visit – as soon as possible. I have a feeling it could prove productive. You have to give her back the Major's journals, anyway.'

'Our condolences, too.'

'That's right.'

'Maybe we should go this afternoon?'

'I think we should.'

'I'll call her when we get back. I would imagine she's at home most of the time.'

Kingston leaned back. 'There's another, more important reason a visit could prove worthwhile.'

'What's that?'

'Since it's likely that Mrs Cooke now has the missing journal, it would present the ideal opportunity to ask her about the Stanhope situation. To find out if she plans to go ahead with Graham's claim. There's even the long shot that we could get our hands on the missing journal.'

'Now that she knows what it is, do you really think she'll give it up? If she has it, that is.'

'I doubt it, but we have to find out, don't we? Is it possible that she didn't know what Graham was up to?'

'Unlikely, I would say,' Alex replied, 'but if she didn't know, she must do by now. You know damned well the

199

police will have been in touch with her, too. That being the case, they will have told her about Graham's claim. They will also have shown her Stanhope's letter – you can bet on it.'

'I'm sure you're right,' said Kingston, taking a sip of wine and studying the wineglass. 'There's also the chance that the journal could have wound up in Stanhope's possession.'

'That's a possibility.'

'Yes, if we can get our hands on the missing journal – just borrow it for a while – we could prove to Wolff that, even if he gets the blue rose, he'll have competition.'

'Exactly.'

They broke off their conversation while the waiter served the main course, a steaming Bouillabaisse.

Alex broke off a piece of the warm crusty baguette. 'I wonder how Wolff will react when we tell him about the formula – if we get it, that is.'

'Not too favourably, one would imagine. Though I doubt for one minute that he'll believe us.'

'I don't think I would either, frankly. All this code crap.'

'Regardless, at some point we have to tell him.'

'We have no way of contacting him, though.'

'Did the man in Oxford say when they would be back in touch with you?'

'That tight-lipped bastard? No, he didn't. Just said we had forty-eight hours, that's all.'

'Obviously they have to, Alex. Somehow I don't think they'll just turn Kate loose – just like that.'

'God only knows what they'll do. As long as she's not harmed, I don't give a damn about anything else.'

Kingston said nothing, spooning up the last of his stew. Alex frowned. 'I still wonder who would want to kill Graham.'

'Hard to say, Alex, we don't have many suspects.'

'According to you, Wolff is capable of doing something like that, isn't he?'

'I suppose we can't rule him out. But if he did, that

would undoubtedly mean that he knew about Graham having the formula. Is that possible?'

Alex shook his head. 'God knows. Anything's possible,' he mumbled. 'Look, let's not fool ourselves, we both know that Graham's death is connected somehow to the blue rose. It has to be. For it to be anything else would seem to be out of the question at this point.'

Kingston let out a sigh. 'You're probably right. As much as I want to believe otherwise, it smacks of having everything to do with the blue rose.'

Alex toyed with his empty water glass, said nothing.

Kingston gestured to the waiter. 'How about some dessert, Alex?'

'Just coffee for me, thanks.'

Another ten minutes passed before they finally left the restaurant, stepping out on to a rain-blackened pavement shiny enough to reflect their shoes. 'Well – back to the good old English summer,' Alex said, putting up his collar. 'The umbrella's in the car, naturally.'

A sullen sky and whipping rain of a gusty afternoon storm instantly extinguished all further thoughts of sunny Provence.

Three nights had passed since Kate had been imprisoned. Thinking back, she was now certain that they had put something in the tea on that first day. Waking the next morning, she had had no idea how long she had slept. It just felt like a long time. Even then her eyes were heavy-lidded and she had a dull headache. Sitting on the bed in semi-darkness, it took some time before she even realized where she was. Then it all came rushing back.

Slants of dust-speckled light entering the room through gaps in the heavy velvet curtains were just enough for her to make out the room. A few pieces of cheap furniture were placed at intervals around the high-ceilinged space. In places, seams of the faded and stained Victorian print wallpaper had separated and ripped, revealing earlier layers. In the far corner, a pedestal sink with a rust-stained porcelain bowl and oxidized brass taps stood next to a partially open door. Through it, she could see the edge of a bathtub.

She ran a hand down one arm. It was tender and she could now see the discoloration, bruising from the struggle. Turning her head, even slowly, made her wince. For several moments, she closed her eyes to shut out the dreariness and the pain.

She got up from the bed on wobbly legs and made it to the door. It was sturdy and, of course, locked. She went back to the bed, lay down and stared at the ceiling. It was blotched with brown-edged water stains and much of the paint was cracked or peeling. It reminded her of a similar ceiling, in an old seaside cottage in Cornwall that she and Alex had rented several summers back. Thinking back fondly to those wonderful days, she started to cry, quietly at first, then in heaving sobs. Her emotions had finally caught up with the enormity of her situation. Turning her damp pillow over, she eventually lapsed back into a deep sleep.

Since that awful day, she had done nothing but sleep – she only seemed to be able to manage a few hours at a time – and spend the waking hours trying to figure out who might have kidnapped her and why. She just knew the rose was behind it all. She thought constantly about Alex. He must be going out of his mind with worry by now.

The routine had been the same every day, until today – Thursday. When she had woken, she leaned over and turned on the bedside lamp. Next to it was a plate with a raisin pastry of sorts and a browning banana. By the plate was a large manila envelope. Next to that, a ballpoint pen. She got up, sat on the edge of the bed and reached for the envelope. Her name was on the label, Shepard, spelled with one p. She slipped a fingernail under the flap, opened it and withdrew its contents, a document of some kind in a folder. Paper-clipped to the folder was a covering note:

Mrs Shepard:
Please read, then sign and date the original and copies of

the enclosed agreement effecting transfer of ownership of the blue rose presently in your and your husband's possession. You will note that your husband has already signed.

After you have signed on the lines indicated, return the agreement, the copies, and this letter to the envelope and place it by the door. Do nothing more – we will know when to retrieve it.

Kate read the letter again. Close to tears, she put a hand up to her mouth. If nothing else, she now knew why she'd been abducted. The letter also confirmed her suspicion that she was being watched. The thought made her shiver. Did that mean that Alex and The Parsonage were under surveillance, too?

Placing the letter on the bed, she opened the folder containing the agreement and flipped through its pages. She stopped at the sight of Alex's signature and yesterday's date. If he had signed it, it must mean that she had to, as well. What choice did she have?

A rumble of thunder echoed in the distance. Raindrops started to patter against the windows. She placed the agreement on the table, picked up the pen and signed the original and the copies. She then put everything back in the envelope as instructed.

After devouring the pastry and half the mushy banana, Kate was still hungry. At least a pot of tea would come soon. It had every day, thus far, about this time. She went to the door and placed the envelope on the floor. Then she went over to the window and pulled back the heavy curtains. Outside, the rain had set in and the sky was the colour of pewter. The room looked even shabbier in daylight. Looking out to a gravel courtyard, she could see large bolts securing the windows from the outside. Beyond an overgrown yew hedge enclosing the forecourt, open countryside stretched to the horizon. She saw no signs of habitation in any direction.

As she stared at the dreary scene, she found herself once again thinking of the rose. The rose had brought them nothing but misery. Was it possible, having signed the agreement, that it could be all over? Suddenly she felt relief. For the first time in days, a wave of optimism. Now, perhaps, she and Alex would be free of the rose, for ever.

Chapter Twenty

It is curious, when one comes to think of it, how large a
space the rose idea occupies in the world. It has almost a
monopoly of admiration. A mysterious something in its
nature – an inner fascination, a subtle witchery, a hidden
charm which it has and other flowers have not – ensnares
and holds the love of the whole world.

Candace Wheeler

Alex and Kingston arrived at the small house on St
Margaret's Mews. Unexpectedly, Mrs Cooke opened the
door soon after the first ring of the doorbell. Once inside,
Alex placed the box of journals under the table in the
hallway. After a brief exchange of greetings and the intro-
duction of Kingston, Mrs Cooke ushered them into the
living room. This time Alex was careful to avoid the sofa.
He watched with amusement as Kingston sank slowly into
its marshmallow embrace.

'Make yourselves comfortable,' she said. 'Can I get you
something to drink?'

Alex and Kingston declined, allowing that maybe a little
later they would have some tea.

For a few minutes she talked quite openly about
Graham. Alex was quite surprised – relieved, in fact – that
she didn't appear reluctant to discuss her nephew's death.
He had fully expected her to be in a much more grief-
stricken state. Her seeming detachment led him to wonder
whether there was much love lost between her and her
nephew.

She stopped talking and looked down in her lap for a

moment. Then she looked up again, her eyes moving about the room as if trying to avoid their gaze. 'This business with the police, Alex,' she said in a quiet but level voice. 'That letter from the lawyer. I don't mind telling you, that was an awful shock.'

Alex gave Kingston a fleeting glance, then looked at Mrs Cooke. 'The police did come to see you, then?'

'Oh, yes. They were here on Wednesday for at least an hour – an inspector and a sergeant.'

'Was it Detective Inspector Holland?'

'That's right, Alex. A nice man.'

'Yes, I suppose he is. He was the one who questioned me,' said Alex. He paused for a moment. 'I'm not sure whether he believed me when I told him the only reason Lawrence and I were there that afternoon was to drop off your husband's books.' He flashed Kingston another glance. 'I don't know whether they told you or not, Mrs Cooke, but I got the distinct impression that Holland thinks Lawrence and I are somehow mixed up with Graham's death.'

'Yes, they did mention that. Needless to say, I was stunned. They acted quite surprised when they learned that I knew it was you who found Graham. That you'd already told me when you phoned. They wanted to know what you might have been doing at Graham's place. Whether there had ever been any disagreements or heated words between the three of you – you and Kate, and Graham.'

She paused for a moment, a flustered expression on her face, as if she would prefer not to be telling them this – or even talking to them at all. She ran her tongue lightly over her lips, then continued. 'Well, of course, I told them that you and Kate had bought The Parsonage and that I really didn't know you at all well, that I'd only met you the one time. They asked what we'd talked about on that occasion, so I told them it was mostly about my husband's roses – oh, and I mentioned lending you Jeffrey's gardening books. They were very interested in that, and the fact that Graham was there at the time and had dropped them off at your house.'

For a moment nobody spoke. Then Kingston cleared his throat. 'The letter,' he said. 'You said you were shocked when they showed it to you.'

'Yes. I was coming to that.' She pursed her lips and looked away from him for a second or so. 'It was a shock,' she said, her eyes reddening. 'Quite a blow.'

Kingston uncrossed his long legs and shifted his position on the sofa. 'You had no idea what Graham was up to, then? What his plan was?'

She shook her head, then said, 'I knew what Graham had in mind, but I had no idea he would go this far with his self-serving scheme. That he would go against my wishes, behind my back.'

Mrs Cooke took out the handkerchief tucked into the cuff of her sweater and proceeded to dab her eyes. Alex and Kingston waited for her to regain her composure.

She looked down in her lap, twisting the handkerchief nervously around the rings on her fingers. Then she looked up at them.

'He came to me a while ago and told me that he suspected one of Jeffrey's roses to be valuable and that he would soon have proof positive.'

'Did he say how valuable?'

'No, he didn't. I told him to forget all about it. As I just mentioned, I knew, basically, what he wanted to do – what his intent was. But I had no idea that he would actually do it. We had quite an argument about it. I'll be honest and tell you that, in the last few years, Graham has been less than truthful with me about a number of things. Most of them were trivial – about money-type things – but this one was serious. It caused a big rift between us. I was furious with him. I made it clear that I was vehemently opposed to any such action and that if he pursued it I would have nothing to do with it. Not only that, I would also do everything in my power to stop him.'

She took a breath, then continued. 'I was devastated when that policeman told me what was going on – to learn that Graham was greedy enough and malicious enough to carry out his nasty little plan. I thought that, after our last

207

set-to, he would have dropped the whole despicable idea. It really had nothing to do with him anyway. But he kept throwing it in my face, since his uncle created the rose, as the only other surviving member of the family on my husband's side, he was entitled to a share of the money. He also argued that he was the one who found out about the rose.'

'I can imagine how you must have felt,' said Kingston. 'It was a shameful thing to do.'

'Yes,' she said, nodding. 'I reminded him that when the house was being sold the man from the estate agent's office asked me whether there was anything in the garden I wanted to keep – chairs, tables, planters – things like that. I said, no, everything should stay in the garden, where it belonged. So should the rose, I told Graham. In his mind he obviously felt that he had every right to it.'

For a few seconds, she gazed into space, then back to Alex. 'He must have told his lawyer not to discuss it with me,' she said, as though the thought had just occurred to her.

'Did Graham say anything about the particular rose in question?' asked Kingston.

'Not really – except, as I said, that it was valuable.'

'I'm sure you can imagine what a nasty jolt it was, too, when Graham sprang it on Alex and Kate,' said Kingston, with a sideways glance at Alex.

'It still is – particularly for Kate,' Alex added. 'She's still worried to death about losing the house.'

'Regardless of what ultimately happens with the rose, we'd like to be able to tell her that that won't happen,' said Kingston.

'It won't, I promise you,' replied Mrs Cooke. 'The sale of the house was final.'

'She'll be very relieved to hear that,' remarked Alex.

'Has this lawyer, Stanhope, contacted you, Mrs Cooke?' asked Kingston.

'He hasn't, no. What with Graham's death and the police and everything, I haven't had time to call him, either. But if you talk to him, tell him to forget that he ever talked to

Graham. I don't want that on my conscience. No, it's over with – finished. I'm not interested in money at my age – do as you wish with the confounded rose.'

Kingston watched the relief wash over Alex's face. 'Thank you for being so candid, Mrs Cooke,' he said.

'It was rude of me and I apologize,' she said, placing a hand on her bosom. 'I completely forgot all about the tea.'

'None for me, thanks,' said Alex.

She looked at Kingston.

'No thanks, Mrs Cooke,' he said. 'I'm fine, too. In any case, we'll be leaving soon.'

He leaned forward, chin resting on his clasped hands. His expression hinted that he was about to say something serious. 'Mrs Cooke,' he said, 'the main reason we came today – in addition to offering our condolences – was to clear the air with regard to this whole rose business. To let you know exactly what's been going on over these last few weeks. Since Kate and Alex discovered the rose in your former garden, a number of disconcerting incidents have taken place – some of them very serious. I won't go into details right now, but I'm not exaggerating when I say that the rose has become somewhat of a curse.'

Mrs Cooke frowned. 'A curse?'

'I know it sounds melodramatic, but, yes, a curse. Alex and I are convinced that Graham's death, one way or another, can be attributed to the rose. Oh, and Graham was right, by the way – the rose is much more valuable than he led you to believe. Whoever eventually controls the reproduction and licensing rights will become very wealthy.'

Mrs Cooke, who had become very still, regarded him with a doubting gaze. 'Good gracious,' she said.

Kingston shrugged and continued. 'However, the question of ownership has become moot, I'm afraid, because somebody else has the rose now. It goes without saying that whoever took it is only too aware of its value.'

'You mean it's been stolen?'

'I'm afraid so,' said Kingston. 'As a precaution against that happening, we'd taken the rose out of the Parsonage garden and replanted it in a well-hidden garden in Shropshire. But it didn't make any difference. It was stolen anyway. It's certain that The Parsonage has been under surveillance. It's the only explanation.'

'My goodness, how strange,' she said.

'Strange is right,' said Alex. He could see that Mrs Cooke was grappling with the implications of what Kingston had just told her.

She twiddled her rings, then said, 'So all this business with the lawyer – it becomes irrelevant, then. Graham's scheme would have come to nothing, after all.'

'In most ways, yes,' Kingston replied.

'Most ways?'

'Perhaps Graham didn't tell you. There was no mention of it in Stanhope's letter, but it seems he had also managed to unlock your husband's hybridizing formula that created the rose in the first place. It was entered in code, in one of the journals.'

'But Graham told me he gave you all the journals, Alex.'

'All except one,' Alex replied.

She frowned and shook her head. 'This is starting to get very confusing.'

Alex nodded in agreement. 'It is, I know. Graham told us that, a long time ago, just after your husband's death, you found one of the journals in a safe deposit box. That was the one that contained the formula to replicate the rose. The one that Graham kept.'

'I see,' Mrs Cooke replied. But it was clear she didn't, fully.

Kingston gave her one of his kindly looks. 'We were wondering whether you could do something for us, Mrs Cooke. If the journal shows up among Graham's effects, we'd like to take a look at it, if that would be all right with you. It could be very helpful to us.'

'Yes, that's fine, but it'll take me some time to go through all his stuff. He was quite a hoarder, you know.'

'Whenever you get the chance,' said Alex. 'Oh, don't forget, the rest of your husband's journals are under the table in the hallway. We apologize for having kept them for so long. Thanks again for lending them to us.'

Mrs Cooke changed the subject. 'I'm sorry Kate couldn't come with you. I would have loved to see her again. You're lucky, Alex, to have such a smart and beautiful wife.'

Alex nodded. 'I am. Unfortunately she's away, visiting a friend in Shropshire for a few days. Good old Lawrence is staying with me while she's gone. Not much of a trade-off – though I must say, he's good company.'

'How are things at The Parsonage, Alex? Are you managing to get that garden knocked into shape? I was awfully embarrassed handing it over to you with it looking so bedraggled.'

'We've been working at it. Kate's out there every single moment she gets. As a matter of fact, Lawrence is helping, too. He doesn't like my mentioning it, but he was a professor of botany at Edinburgh University. He's also quite an expert on roses.'

'Just by looking through those books, I could tell that your husband was a very diligent man,' said Kingston. 'And having seen the garden I know he had a profound love for roses.' He chuckled. 'I was seduced by them years ago. I never cease to be amazed at the influence roses can have on people. The sheer power they exert.'

'You would have got on famously with Jeffrey, then. That's pretty much all he ever thought about. Spent every waking moment out in that greenhouse of his. More or less died out there, too.' She chuckled, without smiling. 'Somehow fitting, I suppose.'

'More or less?' inquired Alex.

'Yes, I found him there, late in the day. Lord knows how long he'd been lying face down on the floor. Anyway, the ambulance came and they took him to the hospital in Bath.'

Kingston shifted his position on the sofa again. 'Perhaps you'd–'

Mrs Cooke held her hand up. 'No it's quite all right. It's easy for me to talk about it now.' She frowned, and continued. 'He was in intensive care for two days. I sat at the

211

hospital all that time. Most of it in the waiting room. They wouldn't let me see him that often. Not that it really mattered – most of the time he wasn't conscious. On the morning of the third day he passed away. They said it was a nasty viral infection of some kind.' Her voice faltered as she reflected on the painful memory.

'Prior to your husband's blacking out, had he been sick at all?' Alex asked, as gently as he could.

'As far as I knew, he was as fit as the proverbial fiddle. In fact he'd just had a check-up with old Dr Hearst. Told him he was in great shape for his age and to keep on drinking whatever he was drinking. Funny old codger that Hearst. He's passed on now, too.' She bit her lip, looking first at Alex and then Kingston.

'What you've just told us could start to explain a lot of things,' said Alex.

'What things?'

'Your husband and a friend of ours. The symptoms are almost identical.'

'Your friend – did he die, too?'

'It was a she. A young woman named Vicky.' Alex stood up and began pacing 'Yes, she died, Mrs Cooke. It all happened so quickly. They didn't know exactly what killed her, either. "Unidentified viral infection" was what appeared on the death certificate. When I asked the doctor whether it could have had anything to do with Vicky being scratched by the rose, he almost laughed at me. Highly unlikely, he said – or words to that effect.' He stopped and looked at Kingston. 'What do you think, Lawrence?'

Before Kingston could answer, Mrs Cooke moistened her lips, nervously and said, 'Are you suggesting that a rose could have been responsible for my husband's death?'

'It does sound a bit far-fetched, I grant you,' said Kingston, 'but you have to remember that many plants are toxic. Even a foxglove could kill you. A potato, if you ingest enough of the green parts. Rhubarb leaves, too. This particular rose is a mutation of some kind. So it's plausible that if the plant it was crossed with had toxic parts, so could it.'

Mrs Cooke looked pale and flustered. 'Oh dear,' she said. 'Oh dear.'

'What is it, Mrs Cooke?' Alex asked. 'Are you okay?'

She got up and walked over to the sideboard, placing her hands on it, as if for support, her face to the wall. When she finally spoke – still with her back to them – it was as if the words had been waiting for a long time to be uttered. Now they came freely.

'Over the years, there were accidents in the garden,' she said. 'Oh, you know, things like Jeffrey cutting himself, a gardener falling off a ladder and ending up in hospital for a week, cuts and scratches – that sort of thing.'

Abruptly, she turned to them, her hands clasped tightly in front of her. 'But considering what you've just said, I think, perhaps, that you should know about the two deaths,' she blurted.

Alex stared at her in disbelief. 'Two deaths?'

'My God!' Kingston uttered.

Kneading her hands, she nodded. 'Yes – the first occurred some time after Jeffrey died.'

'What happened?' Alex asked, leaning forward on the edge of his chair, fearful of what she was about to say.

'Well,' said Mrs Cooke, 'we used to have a part-time gardener called Doakes – Walter Doakes. Jeffrey hired him – oh, must have been over fifteen years ago. Knew everything there was to know about gardening. A fine-looking man.' She sighed.

'A couple of years after Jeffrey died, I happened upon Doakes in the garden one afternoon. He was stretched out on a bench. At first I thought he was taking a nap. But it wasn't like him to do that, so I called his name. He just lay there, very still, his face turned away from me. Then I started to get worried. I walked over and shook his arm. His shirt was damp to the touch and cold. When he moved suddenly, it made me jump. Then he turned his face towards me and I knew he was sick. His usually ruddy face was an awful greyish colour and his skin was all sweaty. He mumbled something about a doctor, then his arm flopped down lifelessly off his lap and hit the ground.

I didn't wait any longer. I rushed up to the house and called for an ambulance. Then I got a wool blanket and a glass of water and went back down to be with him until the ambulance arrived. I forget which hospital they took him to – maybe they never told me at the time. But somebody called, two days later – his sister, I believe it was – and told me that he had died. She said they didn't know what the cause of death was. About two years ago, she died too. Liz at the post office said it was cancer. There was an obituary in the local paper. Euphemia, her name was. Euphemia Doakes.' She screwed up her face. 'Fancy calling a child Euphemia!'

'Jesus!' Alex muttered.

'It all fits,' said Kingston.

Mrs Cooke shook her head slowly. 'Poor old Doakes,' she muttered.

'You mentioned two deaths. Who was the other person? Surely you didn't mean Euphemia.' Alex tried not to show his anxiety.

'Oh, yes. It was a young boy. He was a friend of our neighbours' lad, Mark. Nicholas was his name. It was tragic. He and Mark were staying at The Parsonage while our neighbours and the other boy's parents were at some business function up north somewhere. I'd volunteered to take care of them overnight. The boys were about seven years old at the time. The two had been playing in the garden all afternoon – Cowboys and Indians, that kind of stuff. That evening, Nicholas started to complain about feeling sick. I took his temperature. It was high, but not enough to cause alarm. So I put him to bed and thought no more of it. The next morning he was much worse. I remember being frightened by his condition, poor lad. I got him dressed, told Mark to get up and get dressed too, and put them both in the car. I drove to the hospital in Bath and took him to the emergency room. They examined him right away and he was admitted. Immediately, I called Mark's mum and dad at the conference and they told Nicholas's parents what had happened. Within hours, they were at the hospital with their son.'

She let out a long sigh, as if she didn't want to continue. Alex was about to offer words of comfort when she brushed a hand lightly across one eye and said, 'I think you already know the ending to the story.'

Kingston broke the silence. 'The boy died,' he said solemnly.

'Yes, he did. And for all these years, I've had a gnawing suspicion that the deaths were linked in some way, and now, it seems, you may have stumbled on proof of it.'

'It's certainly starting to look that way,' said Alex. 'When did the young boy die? Do you remember what year it was?'

'Not exactly. It must be well over three years ago now, I would imagine. Although it could be more.'

'We should check with the hospital in Bath, Alex,' Kingston said.

Alex nodded.

Mrs Cooke looked drained and close to tears. 'I'm sorry. I suppose I should have told you all this when you bought the house. At the time, I didn't think it was important – it was all in the past.'

'It wouldn't have made any difference at the time anyway, Mrs Cooke,' Alex said, in an effort to make her feel more comfortable.

'So all of this had to do with this particular rose then? The one that my husband created.'

'That seems to be the case,' Kingston replied. 'It's certainly starting to look that way.'

Alex stood, taking her hand and holding it between his. 'Well, we've taken far too much of your time already, Mrs Cooke. Again, I can't tell you how saddened we are about Graham's passing. Promise me you'll call if you need anything.'

'I will. Thank you, Alex. You tell that Kate of yours I'd really like to see her again,' she said, letting go of his hand. She turned towards Kingston. 'It was very nice to make your acquaintance, doctor. It's such a shame the circumstances had to be so unpleasant.'

'Yes, these are, indeed, sad times,' Kingston said, his

voice heavy with solace. 'You've been more than kind and very helpful. Alex and I greatly appreciate your frankness and hospitality.' He gave her a formal handshake and a comforting smile. 'Oh, and if, by chance, you come across that journal, perhaps you'll let us know.'

'I will, doctor.'

On the front porch, Mrs Cooke took considerable time shaking hands again with them both. Clearly she would have liked them to stay longer. Finally, Alex and Kingston stepped outside and walked down the crazy-paved path to their car.

Kingston started the engine, shifted into first and let out the clutch. As they drove off, he glanced at Mrs Cooke in the rear view mirror, now a diminutive figure waving goodbye. He rolled down the window and waved back.

'I can tell you one thing,' he said, turning to Alex. 'Whoever did nick the rose is going to be in for one hell of a surprise if it nicks them.'

Chapter Twenty-one

With a garden, there is hope.
Grace Firth

Kate had hoped – anticipated, in fact – that having signed the agreement she would have been set free by now. But there was still no sign of her abductors. They had been very careful not to show their faces in all the time she had been imprisoned.

Food and other necessities were passed through the narrowly opened, quickly closed door. This happened at staggered times, often while she slept. Mercifully, they had been considerate in providing her with books, magazines and other small treats. One evening she awoke to find a small box of Black Magic chocolates by the door. She spent most of the time reading, thinking about Alex and the house or fantasizing about what she would do when the nightmare was over.

Sometimes she tricked her mind into playing out imaginary scenarios – most cast in the future, when she would be back with Alex at The Parsonage, when this wretched nightmare would be a distant memory. She always emerged from these daydreams vowing to be more attentive, more understanding, more loving when things returned to normal. She was beginning to forget what normal was like. Or whether there really was such a state.

More and more her beloved garden played a major role in these fantasies. She pictured the roses starting to fade. By now most of the old varieties doubtlessly would have finished blooming. In their place asters, Japanese anemones, chrysanthemums and other autumnal flowers would take over. Hydrangeas, too. She remembered seeing those huge mop-headed shrubs in some of the photos Mrs Cooke had shown them. It was Kate's plan to dry a lot of those when the blooms were almost spent.

She summoned a reproachful smile. Perhaps she should have listened to Alex when he had suggested destroying the blue rose. She recalled her apprehension and prophecies when they first found the rose, how it might adversely change their life, how it could imperil their marriage. Not even in her worst dreams had she envisioned anything like the present horror. While she tried hard not to dwell on her miserable situation, she could not avoid speculating on how it would play out.

She wondered how Asp was doing. Dear little Asp. She would forever cherish the memory of the day he came into their lives in Bath, over a year ago. It could easily have been yesterday. It was a Saturday, she remembered, and Alex had disappeared early that morning without waking her. When she got up and went down to the kitchen there was a note on the table: *I'll be back around noon. Stick a bottle of champers in the fridge. XXX Alex.* Shortly before twelve she heard Alex's Alfa pull into the drive and the customary toot of the horn. She looked out of the window, watching as he got out of the car and headed for the front door. He was carrying a shallow wicker basket.

Entering the kitchen, he was all smiles. 'Here, Kate,' he said, handing her the basket as if it were filled with new-laid eggs.

As she took it from him she thought she saw something move under the plaid cloth that concealed its contents. She gave Alex a quizzical look and slowly pulled the cloth aside.

Curled in a tight ball was a tiny puppy. As she gently caressed its velvety fur, it stretched, yawned, and started licking her finger. Then the tears started to roll slowly down her cheeks.

'What do you think?' Alex asked, grinning ear to ear. 'It's a boy, by the way.'

'I don't know what to say, Alex,' she said, wiping her eyes. 'He's lovely. Does he have a name?'

'Not yet.'

'What made you—'

'I thought a lot about what we discussed Wednesday evening, about selling the house and moving farther out. For some reason I couldn't imagine us living in the country without a dog. I was going to wait for your birthday but I decided not to hold off. I saw the ad two days ago and decided to go for it.' He smiled. 'If you're not sure about taking on a new responsibility, he comes with return privileges, by the way.'

'Oh, no, Alex, he's lovely. Let's keep him.'

He took the basket from Kate, put it on the floor, and picked up the puppy, holding its wet pink nose up close to his. 'We've got to think of a name for you, young feller,' he said, gently lowering the puppy to the floor. They had watched it waddle unsteadily under the table where it proceeded to make a small puddle. . .

The quick creak of the door opening brought her back to the present. She turned just in time to see a small stack of magazines being placed on the floor. As quickly as it had opened, the door closed again, and she heard the bolt slide into place. She hoped that the selection was better than the last time. Most of them had been hunting, fishing and hot-rod magazines.

She had thought long and hard about her abductors. Who were they? The only outsiders she could think of who knew about the rose were the American and Tanaka. Could it possibly be one of them? What did it matter, anyway?

She wondered if Alex had called the police. She knew that was very unlikely. Whoever had taken her would have found ways to dissuade Alex from doing so. She preferred not to think about it. She knew only too well that threatening bodily harm to the victim was the method most often used. It was very doubtful now that the police were going to come to her rescue. And, short of his somehow recovering Sapphire, she had come to the inescapable truth that Alex was powerless to help. He had signed the agreement, after all. In any case, he had no way of knowing where she was. Neither did she for that matter. It was impossible to imagine what must be going through his mind.

Thinking back to the blue rose, she recalled the cuttings Vicky had taken, but couldn't quite figure out their role in the equation. Surely the people trying to get their hands on the rose knew all about horticulture and wouldn't accept cuttings without the rose itself. She also knew enough about propagation from cuttings to know that the resulting plants ran true to form. Grown on their own roots, they would produce flowers identical to the parent. But this was no ordinary rose. It was a mutant. And who was to say that the cuttings would produce blue roses? In any case, it would be quite some time before the cuttings produced blossoms of any kind.

She had concluded by now that her only hope of escape rested with herself. And up to a couple of days ago, that eventuality had seemed remote. She now knew that these men were not amateurs. They were serious and thorough. They had rendered the farmhouse escape-proof and her room as secure as a prison cell. But two days ago she had discovered something they'd overlooked. It presented a slender chance of escape.

The muted sounds of screeching tyres and gunfire from the television downstairs filtered into the room, disturbing her train of thought. Not that she minded. The noise meant that she could safely get back to the job at hand. Her captors' reluctance to enter her room worked in her favour. Had they chosen to examine her minuscule bathroom they would undoubtedly have noticed that two-thirds of the wood moulding had been removed from the tiny fixed window above the toilet that served no function other than to provide light. She could only conclude that they'd somehow overlooked the window in their effort to make the room secure – the curtain was, after all, similar in colour to the wallpaper. There was one small problem however –

she was not quite sure whether it was big enough for her to wriggle through. It was going to be close.

With just a little more scraping, Kate would be able to pop it out.

In the beamed living room of the farmhouse, her two abductors were in shirtsleeves. Billy, the taller and younger, was stretched out on the overstuffed sofa reading a paperback. His sallow face was pockmarked, suggesting a poor diet and lax habits. Marcus – balding and dressed all in black – stood by the window, talking on a cordless phone. His speech, though American, hinted of European origins.

'No. She's fine,' said Marcus. 'Sleeps and reads around the clock.' He looked up to the ceiling, eyeing the network of hairline cracks that spidered across the yellowing plaster like an aerial road map. 'Of course we're feeding her.' He stared out of the window, listening to the caller. 'Okay, so eleven thirty it is. Right, British Airways. Don't worry, I'll be there. I'll call to check that your flight's on time.' Another short pause. 'Sheppard? No – he hasn't. Nothing unusual, except that professor guy has been staying with him. Billy's keeping an eye on them, don't worry.' Marcus yawned. 'Sure, I will. Okay. See you soon. Yes, I'll tell him.'

He turned the phone off and walked to the small TV set. He switched it on manually – they'd not been able to find a remote. Billy figured the set was so old it never had one in the first place. Marcus settled into the large upholstered armchair, put his feet on the coffee table, and stared blankly at a programme on polar bears.

Billy looked up from his paperback. 'Wolff's finally coming over, then,' he said, in a Texas drawl.

Marcus got up and walked toward the door. 'Yes, he's on his way. I'm going pick him up at Heathrow tomorrow morning. Now that the agreement's signed, Ira wants to see the rose.'

'I thought Ira told you Sheppard don't know where the rose is.'

'He did. But Ira's convinced that Sheppard's playing "find the lady". That it was really him who took it to another hiding place.'

'What if Sheppard's not lying?'

'Damned if I know. Let Ira worry about that. He tells me he's finished playing footsie with him – now it's hardball time. He's sure that Sheppard's gonna crack any day now. Meantime, Ira wants us to keep up the surveillance on Sheppard and the house. He thinks that sooner or later Sheppard'll get careless and lead us to the rose.'

'You know Marcus, this is turning out to be a full-time job. I'd figured it for ten days at the most. I'm dying of boredom in this stinking place. The shitty weather. When are we going get the hell out of here?'

'Jesus, Billy. You ask the dumbest questions. You couldn't have heard a goddamned word I've been saying. How do I know, for Chrissakes! Ask Wolff tomorrow. Ask him yourself!'

'All right. All right.'

'Oh, by the way, Ira said to thank you.'

'For what?'

'Doing a clean job of snatching the Sheppards' file. Made things a lot easier, he said. Filled in a lot of blanks.'

'Weren't exactly what I would call challenging,' Billy drawled. 'Any punk kid could have walked in there and stole the file.'

Kingston was up again at dawn. Since Kate's kidnapping he hadn't had a good night's sleep and it was beginning to take its toll. He let Asp out into the garden through the back door, then went to retrieve the morning newspaper from the front porch. Back in the house, he made a pot of tea.

He yawned and placed the folded newspaper and his favourite retractable pencil – the one with the pink eraser on the end of it – on the table beside him. He always used

222

a pencil when tackling the *Times* crossword puzzle. Corrections were all too frequent. Exactly when he had first started doing them – when he first got hooked – he couldn't say. Spending the start of the day with a cup of tea and the puzzle was a ritual. Rarely, very rarely, was the pattern broken. But for the last several days it had been. And he was becoming increasingly worried. He simply could no longer concentrate.

Every hour of every day he was alone was spent thinking of the suffering that the blue rose had inflicted on so many lives. And the harder he tried to make sense of it all, the more unfathomable the riddles became. In his now frequent dreams they twisted and writhed like slippery serpents, one minute almost in his grasp, the next, morphing into new forms, coiling into grotesque shapes, always disappearing through closed doors.

With Alex's refusal to involve the police – and he could well understand Alex's fear of doing so – the burden now fell squarely on him to find a way to secure Kate's release and put her kidnappers behind bars. Unless he found the rose, none of this would happen. Worse, what would Wolff do to Kate if he didn't? He'd rather not think about that eventuality.

He glanced up at the kitchen clock. Six forty-five. In a few hours the forty-eight hour deadline would be up and they could expect another call from Wolff's accomplice. God knows what horrors that would bring.

He reached for the folded *Times* and, without thinking, opened it to the crossword section, placing the rest of the paper aside. He stared at the tiny grid of black and white squares, pondering the thousands of them that had challenged his sense of logic and reasoning over so many years.

With a cryptic crossword, unlike a conventional crossword, one's bank of general knowledge is of little help; the solver must wrestle with construing the *clues* correctly to extract literal meaning from clever camouflage. What makes them so challenging and often frustrating, is that all the clues are couched in varying forms of disguised anagrams, cryptograms, phonetic puzzles, and cunning plays on words. Teasing out the answers is a job for an analytical, not a fact-filled mind.

He stared at the puzzle. Not reading but just staring. He thought back to the day he first saw the rose. How beautiful it was, how seductive. And now, in such a short time, what havoc it had wrought. A twisted trail of heartache and tragedy.

After all this time, after the hours of sifting through notes, creating timelines, analysing, reconstructing conversations, they were still no nearer to finding answers. He must have overlooked something – a subtle clue, a misspoken word. Or was he simply trying too hard, overlooking the obvious? Think of the enigma of the blue rose in the same way you would a cryptic clue. No, that would be absurd, he said to himself. But his mind was already in motion, stimulated and challenged by the very idea of it.

Methodically, he started with the 'players'. He got a notepad and wrote down their names – one at the top of each successive page. This, in part, was similar to the exercise he and Alex had exhausted yesterday but he was determined to try again and keep trying, if needs be. There were nine names in all: himself, Kate and Alex, Vicky, Tanaka, Adell, Mrs Cooke, Graham and Wolff. Had he overlooked anybody? Not that he could think of. The police, perhaps? No, they were too busy looking for a killer to be interested in a stolen rose. Besides, they weren't even aware that Kate was missing.

Starting from the day of Kate's first phone call, he matched each so-called player with incidents linking them to the rose. These he wrote underneath each name. It took him nearly an hour to write everything down. When the list was complete, he went over each page, retracing every incident, cross-referencing every encounter and reviewing every known conversation. It took him the best part of another hour before he had gone through all nine pages. When he crossed off the last name, he was no wiser than he was when he started. 'Damn!' he muttered.

Engrossed in the task, he had completely forgotten about Alex. Where in hell was he? He would give him another ten minutes, then go and hammer on his bedroom door.

He got up and went to the sink, filling the kettle to make a fresh pot of tea. Back at the table he skimmed through his notes one more time, finally putting them aside. He got up and climbed the stairs to wake Alex.

Ten minutes later they faced each other across the kitchen table as Alex nursed a cup of coffee.

'Sleep at all?' asked Kingston.

'Not much, no.'

'We'll see about getting you some sleeping pills today.'

'What's all this bumf, then?' Alex asked, rubbing his eyes and picking up one of the torn-off pages of Kingston's scribblings.

'That "bumf" is the result of a good two hours' worth of intense brainstorming, conceptualizing and deductive reasoning, I'll have you know.'

'Did you come up with anything?'

'I'm afraid not,' Kingston replied with a feeble shake of the head.

Alex regarded Kingston with bloodshot eyes cushioned with dark puffy bags. His skin was the colour and texture of putty. Even his usually shiny hair was lacklustre and straggly. 'We've probably got until noon. And that's it,' Alex said, with the despair of a condemned prisoner praying for an eleventh-hour reprieve from the Home Office. Absently he turned over the front section of the newspaper, pushing it, aimlessly, from side to side.

Kingston watched, not quite knowing what to say. He caught a glimpse of the newspaper headline: *Brighton Nursing Home Scandal Widens*.

'Brighton.'

'What?' said Kingston confused by Alex's odd comment.

Alex was staring out the window. 'That's right,' he muttered.

'What?'

'It was something that Adell said. The first time we met him. Maybe I didn't mention it to you at the time.'

'What, Alex? What?'

'He mentioned that their firm represented a rose grower near Brighton.'

Kingston was on his feet. 'God! This could be the break we've been hoping for, Alex. The connection is too much of a coincidence. Did he mention any names? Think hard, Alex.'

'I don't recall. I don't think so.'

'Alex, don't you see – there's more than a fifty-fifty chance that that's where the rose is right now. The connection is perfect.'

'Why do you say that?'

'Think about it.' He wagged his forefinger at Alex as he spoke. 'All along, you and Kate, and Vicky, of course – for obvious reasons – have nurtured Sapphire like a newborn baby.'

'That's true,' said Alex.

'And we know that whoever took the rose knows of her astronomical value.'

Alex nodded.

'That being the case, they, too, will make damned sure that she continues to receive the same kind of molly-coddling. They're sure as hell not going to run even the slightest risk of letting her shrivel up and die, are they?'

'No, they're not.'

'I can't imagine why I didn't think of it before. Wherever the rose is sequestered must be a location where she can get proper expert horticultural care–'

'Like a place that specializes in roses. Adell's client's place.'

'Exactly, Alex.'

Kingston paced the kitchen. 'We've got to get to Adell immediately.'

Alex frowned. 'Surely *he* wouldn't have stolen the rose, would he? A solicitor?'

'We can't be certain, but lawyers have been known to commit serious crimes – including murder, I might add. In any case, I'm not suggesting that he stole it, that he did the whole thing single-handed. But I can almost guarantee you that he is somehow involved. It all fits.'

Alex's expression quickly darkened. 'If you're right, and Adell is directly or indirectly culpable, I'll see to it that the son of a bitch is disbarred,' he said, through clenched teeth. 'What a bastard!'

'Slow down a bit, Alex. It's only a theory, you know. Let's not rush our fences.'

Kingston glanced at the clock. 'If we leave right now we could be up in town by eleven. We'll just have to chance his being there. I don't think we want to deal with this on the phone.'

'What if Wolff calls?'

'He'll have to leave a message.'

'Why don't we leave one?'

'A message?'

'On the answering machine. Record a new greetings message. Instead of saying, sorry we missed your call and wait for the beep, record a new message saying that we think we know where the rose is and that we'll call back later this afternoon. At least we'd be buying some time.'

'Clever idea, Alex. Let's just hope that we're right about Adell and his rose grower friend.'

'We'd better be. God, we'd better be.'

Adell was clearly flummoxed when Alex and Kingston showed up at his office unannounced. 'This is a surprise, Alex,' he said, taking his eyes off Alex momentarily to size up Kingston. 'What brings you two here?'

'We need to talk about something that can't wait. It's serious.' Alex turned toward Kingston. 'Oh, this is a friend of mine, Dr Lawrence Kingston.'

'Ah yes, the fellow who's been helping you with the rose,' Adell said, extending his hand. 'Pleased to meet you, doctor, at last.'

'Likewise,' said Kingston, shaking his hand.

'Well, come on in. I have a client due shortly but I can spare a few minutes.'

He ushered them into his office where they sat at Adell's desk.

'So, just what is it that can't wait?' asked Adell, sliding into his black leather chair. He looked at Alex, then back to Kingston. 'You look upset. Is something wrong, gentlemen?'

'Very wrong,' Alex replied.

'What's this all about?' Adell asked, putting on his glasses, regarding them across the large expanse of desk.

Alex looked directly at Adell. 'Well, to start with, you can forget about the auction.'

'What?'

'We no longer have the blue rose. It's been stolen.'

'Stolen! My God, this is a disaster. The auction–'

'You'll have to cancel it.'

'I can't, for Christ's sake! It's too late.' Adell put a hand to his forehead and closed his eyes for a moment. 'I don't believe it,' he sighed.

'Well, you'd better,' said Alex. 'That's not all. Lately, things have turned very nasty.'

'What do you mean by nasty?'

'You're already aware of the tragic business with Graham Cooke, so I won't go into that. But other incidents connected to the rose, incidents you're not aware of, now pose a serious threat – a threat to a number of people. To the point where their lives could be in jeopardy.'

'Serious threat to people's lives? What are you talking about, Alex?'

'I'll tell you what I'm talking about. Since this rose came into our lives, there's been nothing but trouble – serious trouble. What if I were to tell you that we know of four people who may have died because of this damned rose.'

'Died! Oh, come–'

'Yes, died,' Alex interrupted. 'They're dead. We're convinced that more will follow. Lawrence and I have been over every inch of this cursed rose business time and time again and keep coming back to the same place.' He stared at Adell without blinking. 'We come back to here,' he barked. He slapped his hand loudly on the desk. 'To your office.'

'Now wait a moment—'

Kingston didn't let him finish. 'From the very beginning, we believe word of the blue rose was leaked by you. You told somebody who stood to gain from its sale.'

Adell shifted uncomfortably in his chair, his darting eyes signalling that he was now very much on the defensive. 'Perhaps you're not familiar with the confidentiality required of me by the lawyer-client privilege,' he said, striving to gain the upper hand.

'Screw your privilege,' Alex snapped. 'It's too late for that. For God's sake, who did you tell about the rose? Who got our file? Who was it?'

'Just calm down, Alex. I don't *know* who stole your file. It's never showed up. So let's not get into a shouting match. We'll discuss this civilly, if you don't mind.'

'Go on, then,' said Alex.

Adell licked his lips nervously. 'You remember, I told you from the start that it would be impossible to prevent news of the rose from filtering down through the industry and eventually to the press. I must say, I'm very surprised that the media hasn't picked up on it yet.'

'I know full well what you predicted – but who did you tell?' asked Alex.

'Let me finish,' Adell answered, massaging his temples. He was obviously buying the time to choose his words carefully. 'I'll try to explain. Alex,' he said at last. 'it was the letter you forwarded to me that got me thinking.'

'The letter from Tanaka?' asked Alex.

'Yes, the chap who wanted the rose for his client in Japan. I was about to respond by telling him politely not to call you again, that he would have to wait for the auction and hold up his bidding card just like everybody else. Then it occurred to me. . .' He took off his glasses, put them on the desk and rubbed his eyes, 'that this might present the perfect opportunity for me to do Charlie Compton a favour. He's a client of mine. Runs a rose-growing business down in Sussex, Compton and Sons.

I told you about him when you and Kate were last here, do you remember?'

'Yes, I do,' said Alex. 'Near Brighton, you said.'

'Right. Our firm did work for his father way back, before my time. Patent stuff, mostly. The company's not big, by any means – quite small actually. Charlie's been going through a rough patch this last year or so. Between you and me, they've been having trouble lately meeting the payroll. Like a lot of industries, the big boys are getting bigger and the competition more cut-throat.' He took a breath. 'Then along comes Tanaka's letter.'

Kingston flashed Alex a sly look, at the same time giving his leg a gentle kick behind the cover of the desk.

'Go on. What happened next?' asked Alex.

Adell toyed with his glasses. 'If Tanaka was successful in bidding for the rose, I thought he would need somebody to handle the logistics of moving it: transplanting, shipping, all that kind of stuff. With the high stakes involved, that had to be undertaken by somebody who knew roses. It was out of the question for Charlie's company to consider bidding for the rose at auction, but I saw no harm in telling Tanaka to contact him. It wasn't like I was giving Charlie preferential treatment. He just couldn't be a player. But if he hooked up with Tanaka, he could be a valuable asset. My guess was that he would probably make quite a chunk of money out of such an arrangement.' He cleared his throat, nervously. 'Well, I faxed Tanaka and told him about Charlie. Suggested that the two might be able to work something out that could be mutually beneficial. Only if Tanaka was successful in acquiring the rose, of course. Naturally, I couldn't be involved in any part of it. I made that perfectly clear. That's about the sum of it, I guess,' he said, clasping his hands together.

'So, they got together?'

'Yes. Charlie called me later and told me so. That's all I know.'

'If Tanaka had our address, chances are he gave it to Compton, too.'

'Well. . .' Adell fumbled for the right words. 'I assume he

must have because – yes, I remember, now – Compton told me at the time that he wanted to meet you and Kate, Alex. He was very excited about the prospect.'

'So Compton knew early on that we owned the rose – where we lived, too – the whole story,' said Alex.

Adell ignored his comment. 'I told Charlie I'd breached ethical boundaries in telling him. That he must respect that, and not bring up the subject of the rose again. To the best of my knowledge he kept that promise.' He straightened, and put his glasses in their case, as if to indicate that the conversation was about to end. 'In any case, just because he knew about the rose hardly means he stole it.'

'Forgive me,' Kingston said, interrupting. 'Your Mr Compton seems to me to be far and away our most likely suspect. There's only one other candidate but for reasons I won't go into we're ruling him out for the moment.'

'We must to talk to Compton,' Alex snapped. 'Lives could be at stake here.'

'Even his,' said Kingston.

Adell snorted. 'Come on, aren't you exaggerating a bit?'

Alex and Kingston exchanged looks. 'I'm afraid not and I'll tell you why,' said Kingston. 'Alex and I have discovered something else about this ravishing beauty of a rose. It's hiding a dirty little secret.'

Adell looked even more confused. He chuckled, nervously. 'A dirty little secret? Like what?'

'It seems the rose is highly toxic,' Alex said. 'Deadly. I've already told you that it's been responsible for the deaths of four people we know of. There could be more, for all we know.' He waited for the stunned expression to register fully on Adell's face. 'If we don't find the rose, very soon,' he said, 'there will be more deaths.'

'If the thorns of that rose draw blood,' Kingston interjected, 'death follows within seventy-two hours.'

'How in hell did you find out that the rose was toxic?'

'It's too long a story, right now, I'm afraid. But believe

231

us, that rose can kill.' Alex replied. 'And quickly, I might add.'

Adell remained silent as he weighed Alex's words.

'You can see, now, why we must find that rose,' Kingston said in a measured voice. 'Why you must help us.'

Chapter Twenty-two

*I have never had so many good ideas day after day as when
I work in the garden.*

John Erskine

From his business class window seat in British Airways
Flight 48 from Seattle to Heathrow, Ira Wolff looked down
on the neat green patchwork of fields dotted with red-
roofed houses. Compared to the jigsaw archipelago and
conifer-clad mountainous terrain of Seattle's Puget Sound,
the scene below looked oddly quaint; like a toy shop
miniature. This was his first visit to England. Despite the
unpleasant task at hand, he was looking forward to it.

Marcus was to meet him at the terminal. They would go
directly to the farmhouse where Kate Sheppard was being
held.

Taking her had been one of his last options. It was not at
all what he had wanted. But weighing the risk against the
enormous reward, he had no choice. He had to constantly
remind himself that his job, his company, his very existence were on the line. Extreme measures were sometimes
unavoidable. A few more days, he reassured himself. Just
a few more days and his problems would be over.

At the cabin attendant's request, he put his seat in the
upright position and placed his reading glasses and book
in his briefcase. Wisps of clouds flashed past the window;
the Boeing 747-400 was about to land.

As planned Marcus met Wolff as he cleared customs.
The drive to the farmhouse near Steeple Tarrant took about

an hour and a half. The day was pleasantly cool, a welcome change from Lakeford's blistering summer heat.

'Jake tells me Sheppard's still saying he don't know where the rose is. He gave Sheppard the forty-eight hours like you said,' Marcus said, casually.

Jake Doyle was one of several men on Wolff's private payroll. He was the man whom Wolff had picked to contact Alex Sheppard. He had been in England from day one, with Marcus and Billy. It was he who had hired the Londoner – a small-time criminal – who had met Alex in Oxford to get the agreement signed.

'When I get through with him he will,' Wolff said, stifling a yawn.

'Billy's been keeping a close watch on him. He's holed up at the house with that friend of his.'

'Good. I just hope that by now he's realized he's in a no-win situation. I don't want to have to paint an ugly picture of what might happen to his wife if he doesn't come to his senses. Tell the truth, I'm getting tired of Alex Sheppard. How is his wife, anyway? Is she still behaving herself?'

'Up till now she's been quiet as a mouse – real co-operative, in fact. Billy had one too many beers the other night and wanted to bring her downstairs but I put a quick stop to that.'

'Good.' Wolff shook his head. 'What's wrong with that moron? Get rid of him after this is over – he's depriving a village somewhere of an idiot.'

For several miles, Wolff was content to admire the countryside. Winding up the window to lessen the noise, he turned to tell Marcus about his plan of action for the next forty-eight hours.

It took Alex and Kingston almost three hours to get back to The Parsonage. The traffic getting out of London was horrendous. There was one message on the answering machine. Alex pushed the play button. It was the American. 'The meter's run out, Sheppard. I'm giving you one last nickel. I'll call you again at six this evening but that's it. If you won't tell us where the rose is at that time, then the fun and games start with your wife.' Pause. 'That'll be a cryin' shame. I hear she's real pretty. Six o'clock, you got it?'

At a minute after six, the phone rang. Hand trembling, Alex picked it up. Kingston was close by his side.

'Alex Sheppard,' he said.

'Do you have something to tell me, Sheppard?'

Alex took a deep breath. Kingston had cautioned him to keep his cool and stick to the point. 'I do, yes.'

'About time, for Christ's sake. Okay, where's the rose?'

'If I tell you, when do I get Kate back?'

'First things first. Where's the rose?'

'Sorry, I must know about Kate.'

'Listen, Sheppard, I'm not going to keep on playing these dumb-assed word games with you.' His voice was dispassionate and calm. 'You tell me right now where that rose is. If it's where you say it is and it's the real thing, then we'll hand over your wife. Got it?'

Alex cupped his hand over the mouthpiece and whispered to Kingston. 'I'm going to have to tell him where it is. He won't let Kate go until they've seen it.'

Kingston nodded, okay.

'Sheppard, you still there?'

'Yes, I am.'

'Then say something.'

'Get something to write on, because I'm going to give you an address in Sussex where you can meet me the day after tomorrow. Be there at noon. When you go there – or whoever goes there – make sure you bring Kate. When I get Kate, you'll get the rose. Is that straightforward enough for you?'

'You'd better not be jerking me around, Sheppard, because my time and patience are wearing dangerously thin.' Alex could hear him breathing during the brief pause that followed.

'You ready?'

'Okay. Just remember you're dealing with your wife's life. Make any foolish moves or bring the police into this and you'll be attending a funeral in the next couple days. Understand what I'm saying?'

'Yes.'

'All right, where is this place?'

Alex gave him Compton's address.

'Sunday it is, then. Before noon,' the American said.

'Right. But one more thing. If the thought of arriving early crosses your mind, forget it. It won't do you any good. You won't find the rose and we'll already be there, anyway.'

'We?'

'I'll have a friend with me, that's all.'

'That friend better not be anyone vaguely resembling a cop or you'll spend the rest of your life regretting it.'

'Don't worry, he isn't.'

'Good. Sunday at noon, then, Sheppard. And don't screw up.'

'I'll be there.'

'You better be.' He hung up without another word.

Saturday morning arrived clear and breezy at The Parsonage. Peg had stopped by to pick up Asp around nine. When Alex had opened the door, she let out a gasp, but quickly recovered. Alex knew exactly what was going through her mind and was prepared for the reaction. After listening to him explain that he had had a severe case of food poisoning and had been under the weather for about a week, it seemed she believed his story. Then he had had to deal with the matter of Kate's absence. This time he could tell that she wasn't quite buying his trumped-up story about Kate's insisting on being by her ailing aunt's side for a few more days but mercifully she didn't question him. He felt guilty about having to tell such blatant lies.

Back outside, he introduced Peg to Kingston who was already waiting by the Alfa, overnight bag by his side and professional camera case dangling from his shoulder. Peg put Asp in the back seat of her Volvo, hugged Alex one more time and got behind the wheel. A quick wave and a blown kiss and she was off.

Alex opened the boot and put their bags in, laying his leather jacket on top. 'Okay,' he said, slamming the lid down. 'Let's get going.'

'And let's hope to God that we're right about Sapphire being there,' Kingston rejoined, getting in the car.

'Don't say that, Lawrence.'

'She's there all right, Alex. I'm certain of it,' he said.

Alex got into the Alfa and started the engine. He waited while Kingston groped for the seat belt and struggled to get comfortable in the cramped quarters. Breathing heavily, Kingston finally managed to snap the buckle closed. 'Just as bloody well I'm not claustrophobic,' he grunted. 'Driving my TR4's like being in a Roller compared to this Italian sardine tin.'

Alex ignored the remark and concentrated on negotiating the narrow winding lanes out of Steeple Tarrant. Soon they were humming along the A345 to hook up with the motorway.

More for idle conversation than anything else, Alex speculated about what would happen to the rose, once it was all over. Kingston, from the beginning, had been committed to the idea of the rose being handed over for research. He was steadfast and vociferous on the matter. Launching into one of his endless discourses, he reminded Alex that plants of all kinds, even toxic ones, were playing an ever larger role in treating various diseases and infirmities. 'Digitoxin, used medicinally to treat heart arrhythmias and congestive heart failure, is extracted from the foxglove plant,' he said. 'Feverfew, the pretty, miniature, daisy-like plant, helps relieve migraines, arthritic pains and nausea; and *Taxus baccata*, the English yew, yields taxol, a promising chemical in the fight against cancer.' Kingston chuckled. 'It would certainly be ironic if the blue rose, deadly as it is, were to yield a miracle drug.'

'Considering all the other bizarre circumstances surrounding Sapphire,' Alex said, 'I wouldn't be the least surprised if it did.'

'One way or another, Alex, we have to make sure that whatever happens to the rose – regardless of who ends up owning it – it is made available for research.'

'You might have a job persuading Wolff.'

'I know.' He waited for a moment until they had passed a long ten-wheeled lorry, then continued. 'It's a fitting paradox that a great number of plants that can take lives are also capable of saving lives. Alex, I have a compelling belief about this rose. Beyond its colour and toxicity, I'm convinced that it could hold the key to unlocking genetic information that botanists and biochemists have been trying to fathom for centuries.'

He gazed thoughtfully out of the window for a while, then turned and looked at Alex, smiling. 'There's another plant I forgot about, Alex. Good old henbane, *Hyoscyamus niger*. It's used for a sedative and sometimes as an analgesic – effective in treating Parkinson's disease. Quite deadly, though,' he chuckled. 'Want proof? In the early nineteen-hundreds Dr Crippen used it to kill his wife.'

'Charming.'

'Interesting case. He was arrested aboard ship. First time a criminal had ever been apprehended using radio airwaves. Scotland Yard was tipped off by the ship's captain, whose suspicions were aroused when he saw two men kissing.'

'Really!'

'Turned out one of them was Crippen's mistress, disguised as a man.'

'You making all this up?'

'No, old chap. Ethel, I think her name was.'

For a few miles they drove in silence, Kingston studying the map.

'By the way, I didn't tell you about my little ruse, did I?' said Kingston, looking up from the map.

'Ruse?'

'Yes, I think you'll like it,' he said. 'It's quite ingenious.'

'Lawrence, I've already got the jitters about this whole Compton's thing. Suppose we get down there and find that Compton knows bugger all about the rose having been stolen – that there is no rose there. Why couldn't we have just phoned him first?'

'We've been through that, Alex. You don't think for one minute that he's going to admit to anything on the phone? It is stolen property you know. Anyway, about my idea.'

'If this is one of your "creative ideas", I'm not sure I want to hear it. This is not some kind of bloody commando operation! You don't have camouflage outfits in that bag of yours, do you?'

Kingston looked mildly offended. 'There's no need to get stroppy, you know – it's quite simple – a little devious perhaps, but not harmfully so. Here's how it works. . .'

Chapter Twenty-three

The rose that lives its little hour is prized beyond the sculptured flower.

William Cullen Bryant

The loud slamming of a door woke Kate with a start. Shouting followed, voices raised in anger. An argument was going on downstairs. She slipped out of bed and groped her way around it, following the duvet, as her eyes adjusted to the darkness. Reaching the door, she placed an ear against the cold oak panel. She heard nothing. The argument must have ended. The only sound was the monotonous croaking of the frogs outside.

She was part way back towards the bed when she heard one of the men speak again. His voice was not quite loud enough for her to make out the words. She stood very still. In the past, if she had heard them at all, their voices were always muffled, impossible to understand. Tonight was different. They must be in the hallway. She tiptoed back to the door, placing her ear against it.

'For Christ's sake, shut up! I don't want to hear any more about it.' The voice was certainly American, though Kate detected an underlying accent. It sounded vaguely Italian.

'I'll give it a couple more days and I'm getting the fuck out of here.'

'Tell that to Wolff.' The Italian voice again.

A period of silence followed. Then she heard a creak on the staircase.

'Where do you think you're going?'

'Jesus! Relax, Marcus. I was only going up to see how the little lady's doing.' His accent was very American, lazy-sounding, as if he could have been slightly drunk.

A shiver ran through her. She didn't like the sound of it.

'Get down here, you stupid son of a bitch,' the man with the Italian accent shouted. He seemed to be the one in charge.

She pressed her ear even harder against the door. The stair creaked a couple more times. She hoped the other man was backing down and not coming up the stairs.

'I decide who goes up there and when.' His voice was angry and loud. 'Me. Do you understand?'

If the other man answered, she didn't hear it.

She thought they'd probably gone into one of the downstairs rooms when she heard them again.

'How many fuckin' times do we have to go over this, Billy? How many goddamned times do I have to repeat myself? All I know is that Ira has finally made a deal with this Sheppard guy. He's not really—' She couldn't catch the next words. She figured that one of them was now in the hallway and the other was somewhere else because she was only hearing one side of the conversation.

'Don't keep asking me the same dumb question. I don't fuckin' know!' He punched the words out. 'They're meeting at a place called Compton's on Sunday. That's all he told me. That's all. He wants me to—' She lost the end of the sentence.

A brief silence followed. Then the argument resumed, but less contentiously. It was now much harder to hear what they were saying. Kate could only pick up snatches of their conversation.

'I don't know, Ira didn't say.'

Another silence.

'Well, you tell Ira I'm getting pissed off. I'm just—'

A door slammed.

'Okay – go ahead, then – you talk to him, you dumb shit. You've probably woken him up by now, anyway.'

The exchange suddenly gave way to the faint sound of music.

Then she heard a woman's voice.

She realized someone had turned on a radio or the TV.

A door closed again. Then it went quiet.

She kept her ear pressed to the door for a few minutes more, in case they started talking again. But they didn't.

The faintest sound of gunfire and explosions reached her room. They were obviously watching television.

She listened for another minute, then went back to bed. What a stroke of luck it had been, her eavesdropping at just that very moment. She lay there going back over what she'd heard. Who was this man Ira, she wondered? Was he Wolff or was Wolff another man? And what kind of deal had he made with Alex? The only possible deal she could think of was that Alex had somehow tracked down the blue rose, got it back, and was exchanging it for her release. That seemed a lot to ask. If Alex hadn't got the rose back, then what was he trading?

She closed her eyes. Not to sleep, though. There would be no sleep tonight. What and where was Compton's, she wondered? How long was it to Sunday? The questions swirled in her mind but for now she had to put them aside. She had to stay focused. She guessed daybreak was probably only another six hours or so away. By then she should have the window out.

A businesslike Rottweiler, gurgling ominously and baring shiny drooling teeth, greeted Alex and Kingston at the entrance to Compton and Sons. They stood respectfully in the dubious safety of the other side of the wooden gate, neither prepared to test the beast's resolve.

'Hang on a minute,' a voice said from behind a nearby shed. 'Let me get Tyson. He's really a pussycat when he gets to know you.'

'Which with any luck will be never,' Alex said under his breath.

The words came from a husky young man with a florid face and lank, shoulder-length hair. He was wearing an old leather jerkin, ripped blue jeans and mud-spattered, black Wellington boots. He grabbed the dog's metal-studded collar and yanked him to a sitting position. 'Can I help you blokes? You can come in – he's all right,' he said, nodding at the dog.

Kingston slid the rusty bolt on the gate and opened it just wide enough to slip through. Alex stayed put. Kingston walked up to the young man and started to offer his hand. Upon noticing the brown muck that covered the man's hands and forearms, he quickly withdrew it. Restrained, just out of striking distance, Tyson rumbled menacingly.

'Good morning. My name's Lawrence Kingston. That's my photographer, Alex Sheppard,' Kingston said, gesturing to the gate.

Alex nodded dutifully, the Nikon 35mm with 80-200mm zoom lens dangling convincingly on his chest. He felt ill at ease with the deception, just as he had when Kingston had first proposed the charade, or 'ruse', as he'd called it, on the drive down. He wondered why he'd ever agreed to do it. 'This had better bloody work, Lawrence,' he muttered under his breath.

'Pleased to meet you,' the young man replied. 'I'm Reggie.'

'I've been assigned to do a magazine story on England's famous rose growers,' Kingston said, ladling on the Oxford accent. 'We've been up to Albrighton and talked with David Austin – splendid fellow – and we're seeing Peter Beales next week. We'd like to include a bit on Compton and Sons. Frightfully good publicity, you know.'

Tyson barked noisily. Alex jumped.

'It would be, I'm sure. I'm afraid CC ain't here right now, though.' He gave the dog a threatening look and yanked its collar. 'That would be Charlie Compton, the owner. Tell you what – why don't you go over to the office there and talk to Emma – that's his secretary. She does the books and that sort of thing. Tell her you just had a natter with Reggie.'

'I'll do that,' said Kingston, thanking him.

Alex remained behind the safety of the gate, making sure the dog was well out of striking range before he deigned to enter.

Kingston waved at Alex to come in. 'For God's sake, Alex, it's only a dog.'

'A labrador's a dog, Lawrence,' said Alex, joining Kingston. 'A spaniel, a retriever, a corgi, a chihuahua – they're dogs. That bloody thing over there's a killer if I ever saw one.'

As Reggie led him away, Tyson's panting head was turned back, his bloodshot eyes locked on Alex and Kingston. Alex turned away from the sight with a shudder as he and Kingston headed across the gravel yard toward the office.

'You've got some bloody nerve,' said Alex. 'I just hope to God they don't find out right off the bat that we're a couple of impostors.'

'Stop worrying, Alex. I'll tell them the truth when the time's right.'

Emma was pert and petite. Seen close up, it was apparent that a good share of her spare time and spare change were spent on Estée Lauder, Clairol and the Body Shop.

She welcomed Alex and Kingston as though they'd just been washed up on her desert island, clearly overjoyed to have not just one but two men to flirt with. With a tooth-paste smile, and a wiggle to straighten out her tight skirt, she stood up from her cluttered desk to greet them. She had kind eyes, Alex thought. For some reason, though, they looked older than the rest of her.

Kingston oozed charm and good breeding. Emma listened, wide-eyed, as he explained the reason for their unheralded visit. 'Ooh! CC will definitely want to talk with you. He's been on holiday in Florida for ten days. Sup-posed to get back tonight. We could do with the publicity.

My goodness, *Gardens Illustrated*, of all things,' she cooed. 'Do you have a card I could leave for him?'

Kingston managed to wink at Alex while Emma was not looking. 'Here,' he said, handing her two cards. 'I know it's awfully short notice and all that but we'd like to interview him tomorrow, if possible.' My God, Alex said to himself, in awe of Kingston's thoroughness, he's even printed up phony cards.

'I would imagine he'll be a bit tired after a long flight, but I'm sure he'll want to see you – he's a big fan of your magazine.' Emma turned to face the wall. 'See,' she said, pointing with a cerise-tipped finger to a neat row of magazines on a nearby bookshelf. 'Been getting it since it first came out. Really look forward to it, I do. Matter of fact, your editor sat next to CC at a Royal Horticultural Club do, only just recently. A very nice lady, he said she was.'

'She is,' Kingston replied.

'You know her, then?' She put her finger to her lips. 'Can't think of her name. Her picture's always in the front of the magazine.'

Kingston looked casually about the room.

A hollow feeling suddenly materialized in the region of Alex's midriff.

'Know her quite well, actually,' Kingston said, with an ingratiating smile. 'Rosie Atkins.'

'That's her,' Emma said snapping her fingers.

Alex was dumbfounded. He looked at Kingston's smug expression and shook his head. The nagging thoughts he'd had about their plan misfiring had now evaporated.

'Look around all you want, boys. And if the workmen can't answer your questions, you just come back and I'll give it a go. Failing that, CC'll be here tomorrow. I know he'd just love to meet you.'

Before they left, Emma sketched out a crude diagram of the grounds, handing it to Kingston. 'You will come back before you leave, won't you? I'll make some tea,' she said, with a tilt of her head, pursing her coral lips. Assuring her that they would, they thanked her and, with a renewed sense of purpose and confidence, walked out into the gravel yard. Alex was relieved to see that Tyson was nowhere in sight.

After studying Emma's map, they followed the perimeter cyclone fence for nearly a quarter of a mile to the far corner of the growing grounds. Twenty raised beds planted with evenly spaced rose bushes stretched out in front of them, reaching all the way to the other side of the field. Kingston estimated that there were between two and three thousand of them. Some bore many blossoms, others none. Galvanized metal markers identified sections with numerals – no rose names. Taking separate rows, they strolled up and down the grassy paths searching for Sapphire.

'I doubt very much that she's here,' Kingston said. 'These all look like hybrid tea roses. She would stick out like a sore thumb in the middle of this lot.'

'That's not a very well-chosen simile, Lawrence.'

'Unintentional, old chap.'

Satisfied that Sapphire was not lurking among the HTs, as Kingston called them, they turned their attention to an area which Emma had marked on the map as Section Number 2. It was a smaller version of the main field but planted with roses in a much earlier stage of growth. A quick glance told them that Sapphire was not there, either.

'Let's look in the greenhouses,' Kingston said. 'I can't think why they would want to put her under glass – but you never know.' After ten minutes of searching, they emerged from the third and last greenhouse. Still no sign of Sapphire. They walked past three dilapidated old barns, peering curiously inside the first one through the partially open door. The only meagre light inside filtered through cracks between some of the old timbers. As Kingston pulled the creaking door wider, a shaft of sunlight slanted through the opening, illuminating a veil of hovering mosquitoes. As their eyes adjusted to the dimness, they saw that it had once been a stable for horses or livestock. Now it was evidently just used for storage. 'She certainly won't be in there,' Kingston said, closing the rickety door. They wandered aimlessly around the office area and a corner of the yard used for composting. Kingston perused the map one more time, then shook his head. 'If Emma's sketch is accurate, we've covered every damned inch of the place.'

With nowhere left to search, they sat on a crude bench caked with dried bird droppings. A flatbed truck was parked behind it, against a tall hedge.

'So much for my brilliant powers of deduction,' Kingston shrugged, looking downcast.

Alex, fidgeting with the strap of the camera case, remained silent.

Kingston had rolled Emma's map into a tight tube and was tapping it nervously on his knee. 'I'd have bet the farm that that damned rose was here. I could feel it in my bones.'

'Looks like your bones were wrong,' Alex said. 'This is an absolute disaster.' All he could think of was what would happen tomorrow when Wolff's men arrived to find no rose. They were startled by a furious outburst of snarling and barking. The din came from behind the barns.

'Tyson's about to go in for the kill, by the sound of it,' Alex muttered. They were both staring abjectly at the ground when Reggie appeared from behind one of the barns trundling a squeaky wheelbarrow filled with compost. He stopped in front of them, rubbing his beefy hands down the side of his jeans. 'Old Tyson gets right pissed off when those cats bug him. One of these days one of 'em's gonna get too close and kiss its ninth life tata!'

'Where is he?' Alex asked, subconsciously measuring the distance to the Alfa.

'Up there behind them old sheds, mate. We keep him there when there's blokes like you around. Most of the time – and at night – he gets the run of the place.' He grasped the handles of the wheelbarrow and started to walk away. 'Ain't had a burglary yet,' he added with a cocky laugh.

Kingston stood up from the bench, letting Emma's map

flutter to the ground. 'Sheds,' he said to Alex. 'Emma didn't put any sheds on the map.' He pulled on his earlobe – a sure sign that he was on to something. 'Come on,' he said, picking up the piece of paper.

Alex followed Kingston at a jog across the yard, between the narrow gap separating the old blackened barns. Reaching the end, they came up against a high chain-link fence. On the other side was a paddock about thirty feet wide and running the full length of the sheds in the back. Weeds and tufts of grass covered most of the fenced-in area.

'Well – I'll – be – damned!' Kingston said, articulating each word. 'There she is. Incredible!' He was pointing to a wooden planter box in the corner of the paddock next to the padlocked gates. It was large, close to three feet high and about the same measurement in width and depth.

'There's still quite a few blooms on her,' said Alex.

'Those will be new.' Kingston shook his head. 'Even more amazing. Not only blue but *remontant.*'

'*Remontant?*'

'It means repeat flowering. Most old roses flower only once a season. I'd assumed that would be true of Sapphire.'

Even from where they stood, staring open-mouthed through the chain-link fence, the rose exuded an ethereal aura. But there was something distinctly unsettling about its perfection. The brilliance of its sapphire blossoms stood out, as if luminous, against the dark foliage and blur of scarlet thorns. Now, with the full knowledge of its savage and lethal secret, it seemed imbued with heightened provocation – a beauty even more awesome, more unworldly than before. Alex shivered and looked away.

When he turned to face the paddock again, he gasped and took two steps backwards. Tyson was hurtling towards them with the force of a runaway locomotive. Together, they jumped back reflexively as the Rottweiler crashed into the fence, shoulder high, in front of them. Alex swore later that he saw the chain links move nine inches, the impact was so great. The fence flexed, as if about to give way, then catapulted the hapless Tyson through the air. Hitting the ground in a rolling black and brown dust-ball he finally came to a whimpering rest, about twenty feet from Alex and Kingston.

'Serves you bloody right,' Alex muttered.

'Let's take a couple of pictures, Alex.'

Alex nodded, still trying to take it all in. A few minutes ago, sitting on the bench, he had experienced a gut-wrenching sense of fear when it appeared that they were not going to find the rose after all. His thoughts had instantly turned to Kate, and the gnawing dread of what Wolff's men might do if they arrived to find that there was no blue rose at Compton's. Now, suddenly, it was all reversed – Kingston's hunch had paid off. Euphoria like nothing he had ever known surged through him. It took him a few seconds to realize that he was trembling.

'Alex,' Kingston prompted.

Alex, still thinking about Kate, didn't respond. He simply took out the camera and removed the lens cap. Then, using the telephoto lens, he took several shots of the rose and a couple of Tyson for good measure. The dog obligingly bared his shiny teeth. Then Alex put the Nikon carefully back into the case.

Pressing down the Velcro tabs on the case, Alex thought about Emma and how she would react when confronted with his and Kingston's deception and the disclosure about the rose's homicidal past. He pictured her, teapot in hand, as Kingston stripped away his mask, telling her in all seriousness that the rose out in the paddock was not only blue but had also killed four people. She'd think that they had both just escaped from the loony bin. He started to chuckle.

'What do you find so bloody amusing?' Kingston asked, turning away from the fence, starting to walk towards the office.

'I was trying to picture Emma's face when you tell her that the rose is a serial killer,' Alex said, following him. 'Would you like me to take a snapshot of her reaction?'

'Don't be facetious. We're not going to tell her. At least, not yet.'

'Lawrence, you can't be serious. We must at least warn her not to let anybody touch it.'

'Not for the moment, Alex.'

'Why not, for God's sake? That damned rose is a time bomb!'

'I hear what you're saying, but let me explain. First, we know that Compton's not coming back from his holiday until tonight. Between now and then it's unlikely that anybody will go near it. Plus, it's a weekend, too. If it weren't safely under lock and key, I might feel differently. But if we tell Emma, the first thing she'll certainly do is tell Compton all about it later tonight or first thing tomorrow. I want to save that little surprise for us. Plus, she might call the police. We are, after all, impostors.'

Alex shrugged. 'You make a good point.'

'Let's go and have a cup of Emma's tea before we leave.' He looked across at Alex. 'Don't you feel a trifle better now, Alex? Now that we've found the rose?'

Alex didn't reply. The look on his face said it all.

It was four thirty in the afternoon when they finally left Compton's. They were headed for Lewes where Kingston had booked rooms at the Cross Keys, a three star hotel in the centre of town.

Alex took his eyes off the road for a moment to glance at Kingston, who was studying an Egon Ronay guidebook. 'Lawrence,' he said, 'I take back everything I said the other day – you know, about your crossword puzzle theory, not believing you.' He looked back at the road. 'You were right after all. It was damned clever of you. And – well what I'm trying to say is, thanks.'

'No need to thank me, old chap. Not right now anyway. Maybe tomorrow when you've got your arms around Kate, eh?'

'God, I hope so,' Alex sighed.

Fifteen minutes later, they pulled into the hotel car park. Alex yanked the handbrake on and was about to get out of the car. He turned to Kingston, frowning. 'By the way, I forgot to ask you – how the hell did you know the name of the editor of *Gardens Illustrated*? For one horrible moment, I really thought we'd been rumbled.'

'It was the truth, old chap. I've known her for a long while. As a matter of fact, I had lunch with her a couple of months ago.'

Alex shook his head. 'I might have guessed,' he said.

Chapter Twenty-four

Roses fall, but the thorns remain.
Dutch proverb

The window was almost square and barely a dozen inches across. Using a small nail file, Kate had scraped and gouged away at the moulding to the point where most of it was stripped away. Luckily the wood was rotten in one corner, which had given her a head start. She had done most of the scraping in the early hours of the morning, careful to make as little noise as possible, flushing the debris down the toilet.

The window looked out on a barren patch of ground behind the house. Farther on, perhaps thirty paces away, edged by weeds and farm debris, stood an old wooden outbuilding. Just inside the open entry, Kate had earlier spotted an old bicycle leaning against a stack of wood. From the bathroom, looking through the dusty cobwebbed window, she hadn't been able to tell whether the tyres had air in them or not. She prayed they did.

Kate sat on the toilet staring at the ceiling in the half dark. She had no idea of the time but guessed that at least four hours had passed since the television had been turned off downstairs. She had arbitrarily established that as somewhere between eleven and midnight. Assuming that to be reasonably accurate, she guessed the present time at between three and four in the morning. She decided not to wait any longer.

She slipped her nail file under the corner of the pane of glass and gently levered on it. She hoped that when it popped out it wouldn't crack or shatter. That could be disastrous.

She pulled again, the palm of her other hand flat against the glass. It didn't crack. But it didn't budge, either.

As hard as Kate tried, the pane of glass wouldn't come out. The edges were free of the moulding on all sides but many years of weathering and aging had apparently glued the glass to the putty on the outside.

'Damn it,' she whispered. 'Damned glass.'

She scraped some more, stopping occasionally to listen for sounds in the house. Slipping the nail file under the corner where the rot gave her the most purchase she pulled back again. She realized that her fingers were perilously close to the edge of the glass. One slip and she could suffer a nasty gash. She had a temporary vision of her kidnappers following her bloody trail.

She paused, took a deep breath and pulled again, this time in a quick jerking motion. She thought she could see the pane bending.

'Damn you! Come out,' she breathed. Still it stubbornly refused to budge. She had no choice but to break it, she decided. But she had nothing hard enough to hit it with. Even if she did, the sound of a windowpane shattering would wake the entire house.

Biting her lower lip, she slipped the tip of the file under the glass, this time only by barely an inch, to get maximum leverage. She squeezed her eyes shut, pulling with two hands on the slender file. Suddenly, with a crack, a corner of the pane broke off. The triangular piece of glass fell quietly on to the worn shag rug she had placed under the window for this purpose. She stopped for several seconds, straining once more for telltale sounds in the quiet of the house. She heard nothing. A draught of air blowing through the small opening caressed her face. It took another minute before she could jiggle the remaining glass free. Finally it came out in one piece. She placed it against the wall, inhaling the crisp early morning air. It had the distinct aroma of manure. But to her it was like expensive perfume.

She stepped on to the toilet and put one knee on the sill. As she was about to pull herself up to squeeze through, she detected a fleeting movement outside against the out-building. She strained in the darkness to see what it could be. A cool breeze now blew her hair lightly across her eyes. She saw nothing. Probably just the wind disturbing some-thing, she reassured herself. A wind chime tinkled on the other side of the house. Otherwise it was quiet. 'Here goes. It'll be a tight squeeze,' she said under her breath. She hoisted herself up – and suddenly froze.

Across the yard she saw the tiny glowing dot of a cigarette burning. For a matter of seconds it grew brighter, illuminating the man's face as he inhaled.

Alex had a restless night. When he awoke he was still fully dressed, the duvet crumpled around him. The copy of *Country Life* which he had been reading last night was still open by his pillow. He remembered picking it up and leafing through it for no other reason than to take his mind off the day at Compton's, finding the rose, and all the things that could possibly go wrong tomorrow.

The Cross Keys must have changed hands since the review Kingston had recited in the car. It fell pitifully short of the glowing description in the guidebook. The lingering aftermath of last night's indigestible dinner was still mak-ing itself heard sporadically from somewhere deep in his stomach. 'Three stars, indeed,' he said under his breath, listening to the dying strains of Paul Simon's 'Graceland' on the plastic clock radio. He closed his eyes, shifting on the mattress with more bumps in it than a sack of golf balls, listening to a lady with a Scottish accent giving the weather report for the south of England. It would be foggy in the early morning, she said, with sunny periods, turning to partly cloudy and breezy, with chances of scattered rain. 'In other words, another typical English summer day,' he groaned. He showered in the meagre cubicle that should have won an interior design award for most economical use of space. To add further to his discomfort, the chattering and gurgling pipes offered only two choices of water temperature: scalding hot or frigid. Abandoning further thoughts of ablutions, he dressed in a black turtleneck, tan corduroy trousers and a fleece-lined windbreaker. Remembering the 'breezy' part in the forecast, he stuffed a scarf in his jacket pocket for good measure. He looked himself up and down in a mirror screwed to the back of the wardrobe door. He was suitably dressed for anything the day might offer, he decided. He preferred not to examine his puffy eyes too closely.

Wolff woke to the acrid smell of stale wood smoke. It was one of the first things he'd noticed on his arrival at the farmhouse yesterday. More than one hundred years' worth of errant smoke had permeated every post, beam, plank and board of the old house.

He had to get some fresh air. What time was it anyway? He switched on the wobbly table lamp fashioned from a wine bottle and squinted at his watch. It was not quite five. At least he had managed to get some sleep. He dressed, put on a Seattle Mariners baseball cap, picked up his Marlboros and left the stuffy room, quietly closing the door behind him.

In the pre-dawn darkness, a breeze tousled the leaves of a graceful birch by the front door, making the sound of wavelets rippling on a pebble shore. Shielding his lighter from the wind, he lit a cigarette. Now and then, when the breeze slackened, he caught a whiff of fertilizer and other farm-like smells. He stood for a minute or so, enjoying the solitude. His eyes had now adjusted to the darkness and he could make out the shapes and silhouettes around him. For no reason, he walked to the side of the house. He started to think about the coming day and what it would be like when he finally got to see the rose that was to be his salvation. The dark mass of an outbuilding of some kind – a barn, probably – loomed to his left. The rustling of a nocturnal creature in the brush ahead of him momentarily interrupted his thoughts.

The wind had picked up. Between the corridor formed by the house and the barn it was kicking up dust and dry leaves in ankle-high eddies. Somewhere a door or window rattled on loose hinges. As he walked between the buildings, Wolff had to tilt his head down to prevent the dust from getting in his eyes. He ducked into the barn. Out of the wind, standing there, smoking the last of his cigarette, he noticed with indifference the curtains flapping in an open window on the first floor. Then he started back to the house. It took him three steps before he registered the implication of the open window.

Running into the house, he suddenly realized that he didn't know which room Marcus, Billy or Kate occupied. He started banging on every door he could find, shouting Marcus's name. Finally, Billy appeared in the hallway, pulling on jeans.

'Billy, which room is the Sheppard woman in?'

'The one on this side,' he said, pointing. 'Upstairs,' he added, still half asleep and confused.

'Shit! Just what I thought – the goddamned window's wide open.'

Marcus appeared at Wolff's side. 'What the fuck's goin' on?' he mumbled, rubbing his eyes.

'It looks like the Sheppard woman's escaped,' Wolff snapped. 'You told me there was no way she could get out of that fucking room. Christ knows how much of a head start she's got. Marcus, you get the Jeep and drive up to the main road. Chances are she's on foot, so check out the fields as you go. If you don't find her, go straight to The Parsonage. I've got a feeling that's where she'll be headed. But she's obviously not gonna stay there for long, so you'd better hustle. On the way, check out every goddamned phone box you can find, too. First thing she's gonna do is call the police.' He turned back to Billy. 'Come with me. We're gonna have to close up shop and get the hell out of here.

Chapter Twenty-five

To me the meanest flower that blows can give
thoughts that do often lie too deep for tears.
                                    William Wordsworth

Kate had stayed out of sight on the toilet seat for what seemed forever. Now and again she slowly raised her head to the corner of the window, risking a darting glimpse to see if the smoking man was still there. Who on earth was he? He had to be one of the two men who had kidnapped her. But what in hell's name was he doing out there, taking a smoke, at this ungodly hour? She glanced out for the fourth – or was it the fifth – time. She let out a little sigh of relief. He was gone. But he must have seen the open window. How could he have missed it? The flapping curtains, alone, were reason enough. She cursed herself for not having taken them down. Should she risk going now, or not? Probably they would be at her door any minute. But if one of them came back outside, she would jump right into his arms. Stay or go? Then she heard the shouting in the house.

Go, she decided.

She pulled herself up and with effort got her head and shoulders through the small opening. To her horror she suddenly found herself wedged in, arms pinned helplessly to her side. She was stuck half-way in and half-way out. Then she heard somebody downstairs shouting, 'Marcus! Marcus!' That did it. With every muscle straining she wriggled and kicked her way slowly forward. At last she was through, dangling almost upside down from the opening. In a desperate move she managed to grab hold of the sill and swing her body around. She looked down for a split second, then dropped to the ground into a patch of weeds that softened her fall. In a crouch, she scurried across the yard to the barn. Now she heard more frenzied shouts coming from the house. Pulling out the rusting, mud-spattered Raleigh bicycle, she was heartened to see that its front tyre had plenty of air and that the rear, while spongy, would likely hold up. Because the saddle was set for a man, she had to pedal in the standing position. She wobbled the first few feet across the bumpy dirt yard, quickly gathering speed once she reached the gravel drive.

Though still not daybreak, a sliver of moon peeping from time to time from behind the low clouds offered enough light to guide her way. Soon she reached the road. It had no signpost. Without thinking, she turned left, downhill. She had to put as much distance between her and the farmhouse as quickly as she could.

Crouched low over the handlebars, she freewheeled flat out down the steep incline, the rushing wind loud in her ears. She pedalled hard for another five minutes or so. She was thinking, so far so good, when she detected another sound over the wind, a low droning, growing ever louder. Taking a risky backward glance, she caught sight of the dancing headlights of a fast approaching car, about a quarter of a mile away. She had to get off the road.

Nearing the bottom of the hill, she saw the dark silhouettes of a cluster of buildings, probably a farm. She squeezed gently on the brakes. A screeching of metal on metal pierced the chill morning air as the shuddering old Raleigh slowed sufficiently to allow her to swing in a clumsy arc off the road on to a dirt path. She leaped off the bike, threw it against the nearby hedge and crouched beside it, her heart beating rapidly, eyes fixed on the road. In a matter of seconds the car flashed past, accelerating up the hill. It was travelling so fast – a momentary blur – that she couldn't tell what kind of car it was but she had no doubt that it belonged to her captors. Hearing the engine fade in the distance, she breathed more easily.

She left her bike by the hedge and walked down a rutted path in search of a house where she could use the phone to call the police and Alex. After scouting the area for several minutes, she determined that there was no farm-house, that the silhouettes she'd seen were sheds housing farming equipment, barns and various outbuildings. Aware that she'd wasted valuable time, she went back, retrieved her bike, and walked it up to the road.

For twenty minutes or so she pedalled hard along the empty country road. The ride was difficult and more tiring without a saddle to sit on. Every now and then she would have to stop and take a rest. She guessed that she was now at least five miles from the farmhouse, still with no sight of a telephone. Sooner or later, she knew she would happen on a village. There she would definitely find a phone box or get to use a phone in one of the shops. She just prayed that it would be soon, her legs were aching like hell.

It was now daylight, the pale beginning of what looked like a gloomy day. But that made no difference to the songbirds, they were up and chirping away as usual. Though she had now lost the cover of darkness, the sound helped keep her spirits up.

Rounding a curve in the road, she came to a T-junction. She stopped briefly to study the black and white signpost. Going three miles to the right would take her first to the village of Little Charwell and two and a half miles farther, to Steeple Tarrant. It all made sense to her, now. The farmhouse had been chosen not only for its isolation but also for its proximity to The Parsonage, convenient for surveillance. She was not headed for home, though. That would be the first place they would look for her. Once she had called the police and Alex, she was headed for Peg's house. Peg and her husband lived in a village five miles beyond Steeple Tarrant.

On a long uphill slope, she started to realize how exhausted she was. The adrenalin that had given her the energy and strength to make such good time was ebbing.

Her entire body ached. She was sticky with perspiration, beginning to feel the effects of not having slept for over twenty-four hours. And she still had quite a way to go. She was starting to wonder whether she had the strength to make it all the way to Peg's.

Within ten minutes she reached the village of Little Charwell. On the edge of the village, fifty feet ahead of her, an old church came into view. The gold hands on its black-faced clock showed just past seven. Where was every-body? Even at this time of morning she should encounter a few people – villagers, delivery men, dog walkers – but so far she hadn't seen a soul. Perhaps it was Sunday.

Pedalling slowly into the village, she passed the White Swan pub and a bakery, both closed. On the other side of the road a small dog yapped at her from behind an iron garden gate. Now she was in the centre of the village and finally there it was, up ahead, outside a newsagent's shop – the welcome sight of a red phone box.

She cycled up to it, walked the Raleigh the last few paces across a grass verge and leaned the bike against the phone box. Once inside, with the heavy door closed behind her, for the first time since she'd left the farmhouse she felt a brief sense of safety. As she rummaged in her pocket for the coins, she looked at herself in the small mirror over the phone. She had expected worse. Her hair was damp and bedraggled and her eyes a little bloodshot, but otherwise she looked none the worse for her ordeal.

Her hand was on the phone, ready to take it out of the cradle, when she caught sight of a man outside, reflected in the mirror. He was dressed all in black and was wearing dark glasses. He had crossed the street and was now running straight toward the phone box. She gasped and took her hand off the phone and clasped it across her mouth. She could feel the beat of her heart quicken. Sud-denly the door was yanked open. Now, she could see him clearly through the small glass panes in the door. He was holding the door in the open position.

'Okay, bitch,' he rasped. 'Come on out.'

She knew immediately by the accent that it was one of the men from the farmhouse.

She stepped outside and the door closed behind her. Now he was facing her, a short stocky man with dark stubble surrounding his thin-lipped mouth. The hood of his black sweater was pulled over his head and tightly around his face, revealing little of his swarthy features. His hands were by his side, and in one of them he held a black pistol with a silencer on it. He moved it back and forth slightly, to make sure she noticed it.

Before she knew it he was at her side, gripping her arm so hard that it hurt. She felt the gun pressed into the small of her back. His mouth was inches from her ear. 'You make a fuckin' sound and you're dead, lady,' he breathed. 'Nod if you understand.'

Kate nodded.

'Okay. Now walk nice and easy with me to the car over there.'

Reaching the Jeep, he opened the passenger door and, with a shove in her back, Kate slid into the seat.

With the pistol in his right hand rested in his lap, and pointed directly at Kate, the man drove slowly out of the village.

Kate leaned back on the headrest and closed her eyes. She desperately wanted to cry, but wasn't going to give him that satisfaction.

Chapter Twenty-six

'Tis the last rose of summer,
Left blooming alone;
All her lovely companions
Are faded and gone.
                    Thomas Moore

Entering the hotel's breakfast room – actually the dining room with different tablecloths – Alex spied Kingston seated at a corner table reading the newspaper. Alex pulled up a chair and sat down opposite him. Kingston was tapping his lower lip with the end of a pencil, eyes glued to the crossword puzzle. He had yet to acknowledge Alex's arrival.

'Bloody clever, that clue,' Kingston muttered to no one in particular as he pencilled in the answer.

'What clue?' Alex asked.

He looked up, as if surprised to see Alex seated in front of him. 'Oh, good morning, Alex. Sorry – this one's a bit of a struggle,' he said, putting the paper aside.

'Let's not forget to call Compton,' said Alex.

'I tried about fifteen minutes ago. No answer at his home number, and the machine's on at the office. Probably sleeping in late, if he just got back from the States.'

'I suppose it is a bit early. Let's try again just before we leave.'

'If we can't reach him, we'll just go up there. According to Emma he's bound to show up sooner or later.'

Alex nodded. 'Let's hope this is the very last time we see that accursed rose. One way or another we must bring the whole business to an end today. Finished. Once and for all.'

Kingston folded the newspaper and picked up the breakfast menu. Looking over the top of it, he peered at Alex.

Alex was conscious of Kingston studying him. 'What is it?' he asked.

'Looks like you didn't get much sleep last night.'

'I didn't.'

'Must say, it took me a long time to nod off. Kept thinking of that damned rose. I don't think the lumpy mattress helped, either.'

Alex glanced at the menu for a few seconds, put it down and looked at Kingston. 'I couldn't get my mind off how many things could go wrong today. I must have played every possible scenario. Not once but over and over.'

Kingston's voice took on an avuncular tone. 'Look, Alex. We have absolutely no reason to believe that Kate isn't okay and there's no doubt in my mind that we'll have her back, safe and sound, before the day's over.'

'I admire your confidence, Lawrence.'

'From what he said on the phone, I think we can be certain of one thing, and that is that Wolff *will* bring her. Then, second, we *know* the rose is there, so where's the problem? He gets the rose, we get Kate.'

Alex made an attempt at a smile. 'I suppose you're right. I can't help thinking the worst, sometimes.'

The waitress arrived with a steaming carafe, poured them both coffee, and left with their orders.

Kingston took a sip and put the cup down. 'Last night, while I was tossing and turning, I got to thinking about our conversation at the pub – about who could have killed Graham. I think I may have come up with an answer.'

'Really?'

'Well, it's hypothetical of course.'

'So, who did it, then?'

'I think it was Tanaka.'

'How so?'

'What bothered me all along was that for Tanaka to be

implicated he would have had to know about the journal and the formula. You and I had thought that was doubtful, remember?'

Alex nodded.

For a few seconds, Kingston stroked his chin thoughtfully, his eyes fixed on Alex. Then he spoke. 'Here's what I think happened.' He held up a finger and wagged it. 'Follow me carefully.'

Alex nodded again. He was visualizing a deerstalker hat pulled down on Kingston's head and a curlicue pipe in his hand. 'All right,' he said.

Kingston lifted his chin. 'Okay. When you faxed Stanhope's letter to Adell he dismissed it as frivolous. I believe that was the word Kate told me he used. But at the same time – correct me if I'm wrong – you also told him about the existence of the missing journal and the crossing formula Graham claimed to have; that it was highly likely that the blue rose could be replicated.'

'That's right, I did.'

'Well, stop and think for a moment what that meant to Adell. The auction is fast approaching and now, out of the blue – pardon the expression – he learns that the rose is no longer exclusive. That, in time, there could be thousands of blue roses on the market. It would really put the lid on things as far as the auction is concerned. So he had to do something to neutralize the situation, quickly. Don't forget that Adell has a big financial stake in the auction and he can see those fat commissions evaporating.'

'You're right. I keep forgetting how much Adell was going to make on the sale.'

'Exactly. It had to be a huge amount of money.' He scratched his temple. 'So where was I? Oh, yes. So Graham suddenly coming on the scene with the formula has an adverse cause and effect to whoever owns the real blue rose – or, putting it bluntly, it certainly reduces the rose's value dramatically. The rose and the formula are sort of self-cancelling, if you see what I mean.'

'I do, yes. So far, so good.'

'Okeydokey. So Adell decides the only way out of the fix

264

is to tell Tanaka that the rose's value is substantially less and ownership no longer exclusive because it can be cloned – right?'

Come on, Lawrence, get to the point for God's sake, Alex thought. He frowned, then said, 'I think I see where you're going with all this. He tells Tanaka – and Tanaka's no fool. He realizes, instantly, that he must now own not only the rose but the hybridizing code too. Having one is no good without owning the other. Which is exactly what Adell hoped for.'

Kingston smiled. 'Clever of you. But that's not all.'

'Really?'

'No, there's more. And this is pivotal. Our Mr Tanaka is very cunning. Owning either one is still acceptable – if the other is destroyed. And that's what, I think, Tanaka decided to do. Probably he contacted Graham, telling him that he was interested in buying the formula. Then, he shows up at Graham's house hoping to make a deal, in all probability demanding to see the missing journal containing the hybridizing code. From here on, exactly what happened is anybody's guess. But from what we know, there was a struggle and Graham ended up dead. Thinking that he had killed Graham, Tanaka most likely got the hell out of there.'

'Good heavens, did you figure that out last night?'

Kingston shrugged, then smiled. 'It's only a hypothesis, you know.'

Whether Kingston purposely avoided further conversation about Sapphire, Alex could not be sure. He seemed to be content to talk about other matters throughout breakfast. Most of what he said was lost on Alex, whose mind was preoccupied with thoughts of Kate and what they might encounter at Compton's. He let Kingston drone on about the importance of research in botany as he concentrated on scraping the last drops of juice from his grapefruit.

Noting Alex's indifference, Kingston took a final sip of coffee and turned to look out at the darkening sky.

'Well, it looks like summer's over. Ready to go?'

'I suppose so.'

'Let's get on with it then,' he said, tucking *The Times* under his arm.

Alex shook his head. Kingston behaved more as though they were off for nine holes of golf rather than to persuade a total stranger – a rose grower, of all people – that he and his client had to give up a billion dollar, death-dealing rose, all in the name of humanity and science. Not to mention confronting a psychopathic and dangerous American, who would stop at nothing to get his hands on the same rose. Alex couldn't help but admire Kingston.

One last attempt to reach Compton from a phone in the lobby proved unsuccessful.

They left the comforting warmth of the hotel and stepped into the cool breezy silence of the morning. The sky was a seamless canopy of grey. A street-cleaning vehicle droned its way up the High Street. Otherwise, it was too early for the first rumble of traffic that would later clog Lewes' steep and ancient streets. They crossed the narrow road to the hotel car park, where Kingston slipped a metal token into the machine at the gate and the red-and-white striped barrier creaked upwards. Kingston struggled into the Alfa and closed the door. Once comfortable, he looked at Alex. 'Baldie, was that the watchman's name?'

'That's right,' Alex replied.

Emma had told them to watch out for the day watchman – Archibald, Baldie for short. She'd promised to leave a note for him, to let him know that Alex and Kingston would be there Sunday morning.

The sound of the Alfa's high-strung engine reverberated between the walls of the old Georgian buildings as they motored up the narrow street. Alex sighed, a long sigh of relief. Finally, they were on their way.

Alex brought the Alfa to a skidding stop on the gravel, facing Compton's rustic front gate. He glanced at his watch. It was nine forty-five. The trip had taken them longer than he had estimated. Kingston was about to get out of the car but Alex insisted they wait for a few moments. On the drive from Lewes, Alex had told Kingston that he was not going to take one step out of the car until he was absolutely, positively certain that Tyson was chained up or had been given the day off. He'd been bitten as a young boy, he said, and had a scar to prove it.

To satisfy Alex, they waited for a couple of minutes. The only sounds came from the far-off lowing of cows and the uninterrupted birdsong. The sombre sky appeared even more menacing. Alex wondered what had happened to the promised 'sunny intervals'.

'Let's go, then,' Kingston said, getting out of the car, swinging the long wooden gate open, following its path along the arc that the bolt had gouged out of the dirt. Alex drove through and pulled into the same spot as the day before. Two other cars were parked nearby, a mud-daubed Land Rover and a shiny black new BMW. Kingston closed the gate behind him.

'Ten to one that's Compton's Land Rover,' said Alex, eyeing the cars. 'I somehow don't picture him as the BMW type.'

'Who belongs to the BMW, then?'

Kingston nodded. 'We'll find out, won't we?'

Alex took the camera case out of the Alfa and slammed the door closed. 'You really think we're going to need this?'

'You may want a couple of pictures for your scrapbook,' Kingston replied. 'Let's see if Compton's in the office.'

'More likely at the house, I would think, after a long flight. Didn't Emma say it was close by?'

'Yes, she did.' Alex frowned. 'I should have parked the car facing the other direction, just in case we have to make a quick getaway. Maybe we should have left the gate open.'

'No, you never leave gates open in the country. The watchman chap, Archibald, would close it anyway.'

'Talking of Baldie, that must be him.' Alex was nodding towards the old barns, forty feet away. An elderly man was approaching. He wore a crumpled Barbour coat that reached to his shins. On either side of his checked cap, puffs of white hair protruded like candyfloss. He was wiry, with a face resembling a worn leather glove, and walked with a slight limp. As he came closer, they could see he had a shotgun under one arm.

'That's all we need,' Alex whispered. 'An armed guard.'

'You don't need to whisper. Emma said he's deaf.'

'You must be Archibald,' Alex shouted.

'That's me. You don't have to shout. I'm not deaf, you know.'

Alex glared at Kingston.

Baldie gestured towards Alex's camera case. 'You must be them fellers from London?' His accent had a rural singsong charm.

'Yes, we are,' said Alex, trying to sound as urbane as the three words would allow.

'Emma said you'd be here to meet the boss. That's his car over there,' he said, pointing to the Land Rover. 'But I ain't seen him around yet.' He tapped a bony finger on his temple, as if to jog his memory. 'That's what it was. Emma told me to tell you she took the dog with her – so no one's going to bother you.'

'What are you doing with the gun?' Alex asked, now more at ease knowing that Tyson was no longer a threat.

Baldie put a cupped hand to his ear. 'Eh? What was that?'

'The gun. What's with the gun?' Alex mouthed the words as he said them.

'Gonna see if I can get me a brace of rabbits up in the spinney in back of the village. You like a couple, too?'

'That would be very nice,' Kingston answered. 'We'll check the office then.'

'You do that,' said Baldie. He gave them a half-hearted wave and started toward the gate.

Alex and Kingston walked over to the office and knocked on the door. They waited for a moment, then Alex turned the doorknob. It was locked. Kingston put cupped hands up to his temples and peered into the window.

'Nobody home,' he said. 'Let's go and have a look at Sapphire.'

A ground fog had moved in, cloaking the area in a fine mist. Alex shivered, glad that he'd brought the scarf. Not surprisingly, the gate in the fence that circled the paddock was secured with a new padlock. Alex was relieved that they wouldn't have to go in for a closer inspection after all. Kingston motioned to him with a beckoning movement. 'Pass me the camera case, would you, Alex,' he said.

Alex handed it to him, watching with curiosity as Kingston opened one of the outside pockets, fished around and produced a Swiss Army knife. He held it aloft for a moment and winked at Alex. 'One of the world's greatest inventions, me boy!' he said, starting to probe the lock with the tiniest screwdriver Alex had ever seen. 'Good – it's not a tumbler type padlock. Shouldn't be much of a problem,' Kingston muttered as he probed with the miniature tool. Alex heard a click and the lock fell open. Smiling smugly, Kingston replaced the little screwdriver back in its ingenious housing inside the corkscrew tool, folded up the knife and put it back in the camera case.

'I would never have guessed that burglary was among your many talents, Lawrence,' Alex said. 'You never cease to amaze me.'

The gate swung noiselessly and easily on its galvanized hinges and they entered Sapphire's sanctum. A rabbit scurried along one side of the fence looking for a way of escape. The sudden movement made Alex flinch.

They had now reached the planter box. Alex lowered the camera bag gently to the ground. Kingston walked slowly around the box, studying the rose from all angles, occasionally bending down for closer inspection. Seemingly satisfied with what he saw, he stood back and folded his arms. 'Doesn't seem credible, does it, Alex? That something so innocent-looking could be capable of such evil. I'm not sure why we need them, but we might as well take a couple of pictures while we're waiting.'

'The light's very bad,' said Alex, 'but what the heck.' Taking out the Nikon, he put it up to his eye, framed the rose in the viewfinder and adjusted the focus. Just as he was about to take the shot, Kingston walked into the frame, bent down and picked something up from inside the planter box. 'You're in the picture – what's that?' Alex asked.

'A marker of some kind.' He held it at arm's length attempting to read it.

'What are you two up to?' a loud and commanding voice barked.

Alex spun round, lowering the camera, to see two men walking toward them across the paddock.

The shorter of the two had slick black hair, a well-groomed beard and wore a long trench coat. As they came closer Alex could see that his features were slightly Asian. 'I bet you anything that's Tanaka,' Alex whispered to Kingston.

Kingston nodded imperceptibly.

The other man was balding with greying sideburns and ruddy cheeks. He wore a sleeveless leather jacket over a khaki rib-knit sweater and corduroy trousers that were tucked into his boots.

'I'm Charlie Compton,' he said in a measured tone. 'You must be the two chaps that Emma mentioned – from the magazine.'

'Yes, we are,' Kingston said, stepping forward. 'She mentioned us, then? About wanting to interview you?'

'She did,' said Compton.

'Well, I'm afraid that's not the case.'

Compton looked perplexed. 'What do you mean?'

'I'm sorry to say, none of it is true. We told her that as a cover, to gain access to your property to search for this rose,' Kingston said, nodding in the direction of the rose-bush. 'By the way, I'm Dr Kingston and my friend here is Alex Sheppard.'

'Search my property?' Compton folded his arms across his chest and glared at them. 'You've got a hell of a bloody nerve! That's all I can say.'

'I apologize for the deception,' said Kingston. 'But there was no other way.'

'This had better be good,' Compton grunted.

'Don't worry, it will be,' said Kingston. He paused. 'Actually, that's not entirely true,' he added. 'You're not going to like what I'm about to tell you.' He glanced at Tanaka. 'Particularly you. You are Kenji Tanaka, aren't you?'

Tanaka's eyes narrowed. 'It's none of your business who I am.' He turned to Compton. 'These two have no business here, they're trespassing. I think you should tell them to leave.'

Kingston ignored Tanaka's remark. 'Compton, you should know that this rose is stolen property. It was taken from the garden of a friend of ours in Market Drayton over a week ago.' He nodded at Tanaka. 'Taken by him.'

'You're lying,' Tanaka snapped. 'I purchased this rose for a client of mine. Legitimately. Mr Compton—'

Kingston didn't let Tanaka finish. 'This rose belongs to Alex Sheppard, and you damn well know it.'

Clearly upset and lost for words, Compton scowled at Tanaka, then at Kingston.

'It's all true,' said Kingston, quietly.

Tanaka, his face screwed up in frustration, searched Compton's eyes. 'Surely, you're not buying this,' he said. 'It's obvious what they're trying to pull. Can't you see that they want the rose for themselves?'

Compton looked at Tanaka again. 'Come to think of it, Ken, you never did mention who you bought the rose from,' he said.

Tanaka didn't answer. Not a muscle moved on his face. His dark eyes went slowly from Kingston, to Alex, then back to Compton. His voice was unexpectedly calm. 'I bought that rose over there from a man named Graham Cooke. It was his uncle who hybridized it, in fact. Isn't that correct, Sheppard?' He paused, now looking at Alex. 'You *know* it is, don't you?' he snapped.

Alex looked quickly at Kingston out of the corner of his eye. 'We believe that might be the case, but—'

Tanaka cut in before Alex could finish. 'You see,

Compton, he admits it. This has nothing to do with them whatsoever.'

Compton looked more confused than ever.

Tanaka's tone became angry, his voice louder. 'Look, we have a lot of work to do, Compton. I'm starting to get impatient. Just tell these two to get the hell out of here, before it gets nasty.'

Compton said nothing, nervously rubbing his chin.

'Well, do *something*, man, don't just stand there,' Tanaka shouted.

The four of them stood by the rose, each waiting for the other to say something. Instead, another voice, strident and menacing, broke the eerie silence.

'Stay right where you are. All of you.'

Alex spun around. That voice. American. At first he thought he recognized it. But no, it wasn't the man who had been phoning. He'd know that voice, anywhere. A tall man wearing a dark windbreaker zipped up over a black turtleneck stood at the entrance to the paddock. He was gripping a sinister-looking small black pistol in his right hand.

'That rose doesn't belong to any of you. That rose is mine,' he said, starting to walk toward them.

Chapter Twenty-seven

Someone said that God gave us memory so that we might have roses in December.

Sir J. M. Barrie

When Marcus and Kate arrived back at the farmhouse two cars were parked in the courtyard, but there were no signs of the other men. Marcus locked her up immediately in a much smaller room than before.

Few words had passed between them since she had stepped out of the phone box. During the drive she had tried to remain calm, trying to convince him that she and Alex no longer had the rose, that it had been stolen. Then, losing patience, she had questioned him angrily, but Marcus was very short on words.

She had been lying on the bed for less than an hour when Marcus returned. Saying nothing, he escorted her downstairs. Seated in the kitchen, she was given a ham and cheese sandwich, a bottle of mineral water, and a bruised apple.

'Try to do another runner and you'll end up a cripple,' he said, leaving the room.

After ten minutes, he returned. A hollow sensation started in her stomach and rose up into her chest when Kate saw he was holding a dark-coloured scarf and a length of nylon cord in his hand. Commanding her to remain seated he knotted the scarf around her eyes and expertly tied her wrists with the cord. Leading her outside, he bundled her back into the Jeep – she recognized the same air freshener smell – and slammed the door behind her.

Soon she heard footsteps on the gravel. Two people got into the front seats. The doors slammed and the engine started. 'We're going for a long drive,' Marcus said, snapping his seat belt buckle. 'You might as well settle down.'

'This looks like it, boss,' said Marcus, slowing at the sight of the green and gold Compton's Roses sign. He pulled the Jeep over on to the grass verge a few yards before the closed gate.

'Good,' said Wolff. 'So far, Sheppard's not lying.'

Kate sat in darkness in the back seat, listening. She had concluded earlier that the American man with Marcus must be the 'Ira' they'd referred to at the farmhouse. The man who was going to 'make the deal' with Alex. Her wrists were sore from the chafing of the cord that was also tied to the inside door handle and covered with tape. It had been a long drive but thankfully – for part of it at least – she had involuntarily drifted off into an exhausted sleep.

She heard the passenger door open and slam shut as the man got out. Next, the grating of a bolt followed by the metallic squeal of a gate being opened. The Jeep eased slowly forward for several yards, then stopped. Marcus turned the engine off and got out, slamming the door hard, shaking the car.

Kate could hear Marcus and the other man talking outside but couldn't make out what they were saying. Next, the door beside her was opened, the tape was cut, and the cord attached to her wrists was untied from the door handle. It was then knotted around her waist preventing her from moving her hands. 'Get out,' Marcus said.

Kate slid across the seat and, without assistance, got out of the car. The turf was springy beneath her feet. She felt the mist dampen her cheeks. A smell of manure was heavy in the air, the nearby sound of bleating sheep, muted. With

Marcus gripping her upper arm, they started walking in silence.

After a minute or so they came to a halt.

Despite the scarf covering her ears she could hear faint voices. It sounded as though an argument was taking place. She couldn't be sure if it was just two people or whether more were involved. She strained harder but the voices were sufficiently distant to make the exchange unintelligible.

Her concentration was broken by the American man's voice. 'You stay here with her while I go and see what's going on. And for Christ's sake keep her out of sight.'

Still gripping her arm, Marcus walked her several paces until they were up against a building of some kind. The argument must be over, she could no longer hear the voices. Or perhaps it was because they were now shielded by the building. For the first time since getting out of the car she felt very cold. She shivered, wishing that she wore a heavier jacket. It had gone awfully quiet. The sheep had stopped bleating and there were no other country sounds – for that was surely where they were. Even the chirping of birds was eerily absent.

Kate heard Marcus clear his throat and spit. She was glad she couldn't see the despicable man. She thought back to the voices, the argument. It was more than likely that Alex was one of them. She was now getting increasingly concerned for his safety. These men were dangerous and set on a mission. The thought of Alex getting into any kind of confrontation with them was frightening. It comforted her to realize that Kingston would probably be with him. She doubted that Alex would have come alone.

She thought she heard a slight rustling noise behind her. It couldn't be Marcus because she knew he was off to her right. Perhaps it was a dog or a cat. She was about to dismiss it when a voice broke the silence. It was an incongruous and unexpected voice – a rural accent, spoken in a loud whisper. 'You, over there, stand very still and turn around slowly. You, miss, step back four paces.'

Kate felt a hand behind her head unknotting the scarf

and removing it. When she opened her eyes they hurt. She closed them quickly; the light was too bright. After opening and closing them a few times she was gradually able to see clearly. The black scarf was on the ground in front of her. Facing her, ten paces away, was Marcus, still wearing dark glasses despite the dismal weather. He stood motionless, a grim expression on his face, his eyes glued on whomever was standing behind her. She half turned and looked over her shoulder. Standing just a few feet away was a scruffy old man with a deeply lined face wearing a weathered raincoat and cap. He was gripping a shotgun at his waist, pointed directly at Marcus's midriff. It looked like he knew how to use it.

'What's going on here, then?' he inquired.

Kate turned fully so he could see her bound wrists. 'This man kidnapped me,' she said, nodding toward Marcus. 'We have to call the police.'

'Jesus! What in hell has he done to you?'

Kate moved behind him. 'Be careful, he may have a gun.'

The old man brandished the shotgun at Marcus. 'You move a finger and you'll be full of bloody holes, mate.'

'There's another man here with him,' said Kate. 'I think he might have gone looking for my husband.'

He squinted at Kate. 'We'd better get you out of 'ere.'

'I have to find my husband.'

'First things first, young lady. In my right pocket there's a knife. Press the thumb button to open it, and we'll get your hands free.'

Kate got the folding knife and after struggling for a few seconds she opened the sharp blade and handed it to the old man. Resting the shotgun on his hip with one hand, still keeping his eyes on Marcus, he took the knife and deftly severed the cord. The skin on her wrists was red and lacerated where the cord had cut in.

'All right, miss,' he said, covering Marcus. 'You follow this path till it meets another. Turn left and stay on the path for about a hundred yards. You'll see Mr Compton's house up on the hill. You go on up there and call the police. If he's there, tell him to come down here right smart. Oh, and tell him Baldie – that's me – said to bring his Purdey with him.'

'Purdey?'

'Shotgun.'

'What about my husband?'

'I'll take care of things here. Don't you worry.'

'You don't understand. It won't be that easy. They're professionals. Don't take even the slightest chance with them. They won't think twice about shooting you.'

'We'll see about that,' he said.

'Please, be careful.'

Kate turned and started up the path. All she could think of was Alex and whether he was here or not. He must be. She remembered distinctly when she'd eavesdropped at the farmhouse that Marcus had said Ira was meeting Alex on Sunday. But was it Sunday? Everything indicated that it was – the absence of people in the village and this place, too, whatever it was.

Making the left turn past a large barn, her question was answered. Fields stretched out for several hundred yards, on both sides of the path. Fields filled with evenly planted rows of roses. There must be thousands of them, she thought. She slowed momentarily to look around. Then the pieces started to fall into place. Of course, that was it, she said to herself. Whoever had stolen the rose had brought it here, where it would not only be well hidden but could be cared for professionally.

A jarring explosion coming from behind jolted her to a stop. It had to be Baldie. God! Had he shot Marcus? She pictured it happening, the gory mess. She found herself hoping that Marcus wasn't dead – only badly injured. She sure as hell wasn't going to turn back to find out.

Passing the cover of a large copper beech tree she saw the house. A modest whitewashed bungalow with a tiled roof. In less than a minute she was standing on the porch trying to regain her breath, waiting for somebody to answer the doorbell. She rang it again. Still there was no response. She gripped the door handle and turned it. To her surprise, the door opened. She didn't have to go far into the house to find the phone. It was facing her on a table in the hallway. She dialled 999.

Marcus walked along the dirt path alongside the large barn-like building, his body language betraying no indication of defeat. Baldie followed a few steps behind with his shotgun levelled at Marcus's back. The voices from the paddock could be heard again.

'Nice and easy, mister,' said Baldie. 'When you get to the end of the barn, turn right.'

They were approaching the entrance to the barn, an opening wide enough to allow farm vehicles to go in and out.

It all happened in less than two seconds. It was like a disappearing act: one moment Marcus was there, the next he had vanished, spinning into the opening of the barn in a low crouch.

Baldie's finger squeezed the trigger but his reflexes were not quick enough. A jarring explosion reverberated off the side of the barn and echoed around the grounds. A cloud of dirt and dust began to settle where Marcus had stood a few seconds earlier. Baldie lunged forward, reaching the entrance, but there was no sign of Marcus. He took four steps into the barn then stopped, listening for any kind of sound. All he heard was the wind soughing through the cracks in the old timber walls. He was loath to go in farther because he knew how dark it was. The barn was used exclusively for storage; mostly equipment, machinery, bagged soil amendments and fertilizers. 'Bastard,' he muttered.

Now his eyes had adjusted to the dim light. He stood very still, eyes searching the area for any signs of movement. There was none. Then he remembered what the young woman had said: 'He may have a gun' and 'They won't think twice about shooting you.' Suddenly he realized what an easy target he made. He had to find some cover. Against the wall on his left was an old workbench.

A handful of tools and mechanical parts were spread out on its scarred surface. Next to the bench was a small tractor. He'd seen it in use many times around the growing grounds. 'That'll do,' he said to himself. He sidestepped over to the tractor and was about to crouch down behind it . . . then, a blinding flash and everything went dark.

Marcus stood over Baldie's prostrate body, the carpenter's mallet still in his hand. He rolled Baldie over with his foot and bent down to check the pulse in his neck. Satisfied that he was still alive but unconscious, Marcus got up and saw just what he was looking for. It was on the bench, a roll of silver duct tape. He dragged Baldie's body up against one of the upright posts supporting the roof and lifted him to a sitting position. He placed two strips of tape over Baldie's mouth, then proceeded to band his entire upper body, arms and all, to the post.

Marcus dusted himself off and walked out of the barn. He thought of going up to the house to look for the Sheppard woman but decided that by now she had had plenty of time to call the police. She might even have roused other people to come looking for him. He had better go and find Wolff and tell him what had happened. That was going to be an ugly scene.

All eyes were now on the tall American holding the gun.

'Which one of you is Alex Sheppard?' he asked, halting a dozen feet away from them.

'I am – and who are you?' Alex answered, glancing nervously from the gun to the man's face.

'First things first,' he said, walking over to the rose. For a long moment he stood studying it, then slowly circled the container, never once taking his eyes off the rose. Then he turned and approached Alex, stopping a dozen paces from him, the gun at his side.

'You're Ira Wolff, aren't you?' said Alex.

The man ignored him. 'In a couple of days that rose is leaving here,' he announced in a commanding voice. 'All the export documentation and shipping arrangements have already been made.'

'That's fine by me,' Alex interrupted. 'But where's Kate?'

'That rose is going nowhere,' Compton butted in.

'I want to see her, dammit!' Alex shouted. 'That was the deal. That's what your man and I agreed on – Kate in exchange for the blue rose. Where the hell is she, you bastard!'

'Shut up,' Wolff barked. 'You, too,' he said, glaring at Compton. He turned back to Alex. 'You, Sheppard, have caused me a lot of grief. This whole business could have been wrapped up a long while ago, but you had to screw it up by playing hide-and-seek with the rose. You should have stayed at home in your nice house and done what I asked you. I'm sure your wife would have found that a much more pleasant experience than the one you have put her through.'

'What I have put her through – me?' Alex yelled. Suddenly, he lunged at Wolff. 'You son of a bitch–'

Kingston grabbed him just in time. 'Careful, Alex, for God's sake.'

'That was extremely foolish, Sheppard,' Wolff said, raising the gun. 'Try that one more time and I won't be quite so charitable. From now on, keep your mouth shut.' He looked at Kingston. 'And just who are you?'

'I'm Dr Lawrence Kingston.'

'Ah, yes – the professor. I know all about you.' He waved the gun at Compton. 'And what about these two?'

'I just happen to own the place. The name's Compton – Charlie Compton. And this is a client of mine, Ken Tanaka – who, I might add, claims to own the rose you are all arguing about.'

'Is that so,' said Wolff, his lips tightening. 'We'll see–'

An ear-splitting blast shattered the foggy silence, drowning out his words. All heads turned in the direction of the barn waiting for the echo to fade.

'What the hell's that about?' Compton yelled, starting to

walk in the direction of the barn. 'I'm going to see what's going on. That must have been Baldie.'

Wolff raised the gun and aimed it directly at Compton. 'You stay right where you are, mister. You're not going anywhere,' he snapped.

Compton paused for a moment, as if weighing his chances in challenging Wolff, then turned and walked back.

Compton shifted on his feet, growing impatience showing on his face. 'Would somebody kindly tell me what the fuck is going on here? This is starting to get very serious, and I don't like it one bit.'

'Why don't you tell him, Wolff?' said Alex.

'I warned you, Sheppard. Keep your mouth shut,' Wolff snarled.

'Where's Kate, you stinking bastard? What have you done with her?' Alex demanded.

Wolff ignored the outburst, returning his attention to Compton instead. 'I don't know what kind of game you two are up to and frankly, I don't give a shit. That rose now belongs to me.' He nodded briefly to Alex. 'Ask Sheppard. He and his wife have signed it over. So if you two have any other ideas you'd better forget 'em right now.'

For the first time since Wolff's appearance, Tanaka spoke. 'All of you are trespassing. This is private property,' he said, walking closer to the rose. 'And I'm sorry to tell you, Mr Wolff, whatever your name is, that this rose has been already purchased – by a client of mine. I've just explained it all to these two,' he said, pointing to Alex and Kingston. 'Your piece of paper is worthless. So I suggest that you leave right now and take Mr Sheppard and his friend with you. Then you can argue this among yourselves.'

'You're lying, Tanaka, you bastard! None of it's true,' Alex shouted.

Wolff threw his head back and laughed. He walked over and prodded Tanaka's ribs with the pistol. 'Get away from that rose before I do something I'll regret,' he snarled.

Tanaka stared at him, fuming.

Compton's patience was clearly running out. 'Look, I've asked once already. Would somebody tell me exactly what the hell is happening here? Who does this goddamned rose really belong to?' He wiped the perspiration that had beaded on his forehead. 'And I wish you'd put that bloody gun away,' he muttered angrily, nodding at Wolff.

Kingston stepped forward, motioning for Compton to be quiet. 'Pay attention, all of you. And don't interrupt – please.'

Wolff was having none of it. 'You listen to me, you interfering fool. There's nothing more to talk about. Just shut your damned mouth and–'

'Wolff.' Kingston spat out the name, contemptuously. 'You're the one who's the fool. Listen to me, dammit!'

'You'd better make it quick,' Wolff growled.

'Don't worry, I will,' said Kingston.

All eyes were fixed on him, as they waited for the roar of a low-flying military jet to subside. Then he spoke. 'We all know that this rose is truly a miracle. As a scientist for well over forty years, I know just about everything there is to know about plant molecular biology and genetic engineering – and this rose is a one-in-a-billion fluke. And you're all convinced that by owning it, you'll become exceedingly wealthy.' To everybody's surprise, he started to chuckle.

'What do you find so goddamned funny?' Wolff asked.

'The irony of it.'

'Of what, for Christ's sake?' Wolff demanded.

'There's a minor problem,' said Kingston.

'What's that?' asked Compton.

'The problem is that there's something diabolical about this rose. Something very dangerous.' He eyed them each in turn. 'Wolff – Compton – and you, Tanaka,' he said. 'You have to believe what I'm about to tell you. It doesn't matter now who owns it. It's irrelevant – because the rose carries a deadly poison in its thorns. Even the slightest scratch can result in death. A quick and nasty death, I might add. Alex saw it happen, at first hand. He lost a dear friend because of this monstrous plant. She was not yet thirty years old. That's not all. Three other people have lost their lives because of this bloody rose. Believe me, you don't want anything to do with it.'

'Bollocks!' Compton snorted. 'A load of codswallop if I ever heard it. Thirty years I've been growing roses. In all that time, I've never heard of such a thing as a poisonous rose.'

'Me neither,' said Wolff. 'You expect us to believe all this bullshit?'

'Look, Wolff,' Kingston said, exasperation now showing in his voice, 'I'll say it one more time. This rose can never be sold. It's extremely dangerous. It must be confiscated and quarantined immediately.'

Tanaka interrupted. 'It's all lies,' he snarled. 'Just like the lie you used to get in here.'

'I only wish that were so,' said Kingston in a calm voice. 'You're in a no-win situation, I'm afraid, and there's nothing you can do about it.'

Tanaka was about to explode again when Kingston cut him off. 'When we leave here, it's our intention to go straight to the local county health authority and inform them that you are harbouring a highly toxic and dangerous plant. You know that's automatically going to involve the police.'

'What proof do you have of all this?' asked Compton.

'Lots,' Alex replied. 'And we can get it easily enough.' He looked at Wolff. 'Give it up, Wolff. It's worthless.'

'Shut up!' Wolff snapped.

'Where's Kate? Did you bring her with you? That was the deal.'

Wolff didn't answer.

Alex kept his eyes locked on Wolff's. 'Where is she?'

Wolff's eyes narrowed, his answer was slow in coming. In the pause that followed, Alex caught sight of the figure of a man over Wolff's shoulder. He was hurrying across the paddock towards them. He was stocky, dressed in black, and wore dark glasses. The others had noticed him too.

For a moment, Wolff and the man spoke in hushed voices, the man doing most of the talking and shrugging frequently. It became clear that Wolff was furious at what he was hearing. At one point he clenched a fist and stamped his foot hard enough on the ground to raise a veil of dust.

'I'm leaving,' said Compton, interrupting them. 'You want to talk to me I'll be in my office. You lot can stay here and argue all day long as far as I'm concerned.' He motioned to Tanaka. 'Come on, Ken, let's go,' he said.

Wolff spun around. 'You two just stay right where you are. You're not going anywhere until I say so.'

'You didn't answer my question, Wolff,' Alex said as calmly as he could. 'Tell me where she is, and we'll leave, if that's what you want.'

For a moment, Wolff said nothing. He stood with his feet apart, caressing the left sleeve of his jacket with the barrel of the gun. Ignoring Alex's pleading, he turned to face Kingston. 'Poisonous or not, I'm shipping that rose out of here.'

'The hell you are,' Tanaka said. 'This is my rose.'

Wolff's face darkened. He muttered something to Marcus, who stepped forward with alarming speed and grabbed Tanaka around the waist, hoisted him off his feet and with a fearsome display of strength, threw him to the ground like a sack of potatoes. With a grunt, Marcus strode over and placed a boot on the neck of the groaning and prostrate Tanaka.

Wolff walked over and stood with his back to the rose. 'No more talk. Compton, you go over there by the rose and stay put. You make any attempt to leave and Marcus will take care of you. Understand?'

Compton glared at Wolff, said nothing and walked over to the planter box.

Wolff looked at his watch. 'I have to leave, but you make damned sure that rose stays right where it is, Compton.' He gestured with his gun to Tanaka. 'Let him go, Marcus.'

Marcus took his boot off Tanaka's neck and they all

watched silently as he slowly got to his feet, clutching his throat and spattered in mud.

'Get over there with Compton until I decide what to do with you.'

With a scowl, Tanaka turned and walked over to join Compton.

'Now for you two,' said Wolff, turning back to Alex and Kingston.

'You're making a huge mistake, Wolff,' said Kingston. 'You haven't believed a bloody word I've said, have you? You want proof? Okay, let's all go to Compton's office and I'll call the John Radcliffe Hospital in Oxford, where a young woman who handled the rose died. Then we'll call a Mrs Cooke, whose husband dropped dead in his greenhouse after hybridizing it. She'll tell you about two other deaths she knows were caused by the rose, one of them a little boy, dammit!' He turned and started across the paddock toward the gate. 'Come on, if you don't believe me,' he barked, over his shoulder. 'It's your choice. Either that or I'm calling the police.'

Alex picked up the camera case at his feet and started to follow Kingston.

Wolff's voice rang out. 'Sheppard, stay right where you are. You, Kingston, stop! Turn around.'

Kingston was now half-way across the paddock. He looked over his shoulder. 'You're going to shoot me in front of a witness? I doubt it. You're not that stupid, Wolff.' He turned and continued toward the paddock gate.

Alex's eyes were riveted on Kingston's back. 'Lawrence,' he shouted. 'Don't—'

A shot rang out.

Kingston crumpled to the ground. He wasn't moving. Alex stared in sickened disbelief.

Chapter Twenty-eight

When the rose perishes, the hard thorn is left behind.
                                                    Ovid

Kate stood on the painted wood porch of Compton's bungalow, both hands gripping the wooden handrail of the
balustrade that ran across the front of the house. She was
trying to make up her mind what she should do next. Stay
put until the police arrived, or go back to find out what
was going on. Since it was Sunday – she was convinced
now that it was – and also in the depths of the country, it
could be some time before the police showed up. She still
didn't know for sure whether Alex was here. And what,
she wondered, had happened to the caretaker and Marcus?
She hoped she was wrong in thinking that the old man
would be no match for Marcus. Then there was the shotgun blast – had he shot Marcus? And what about the other
man – the American? Where was he and what was he
doing?

She stared out over the grounds considering her next
move. It didn't seem a good idea to stay at the house,
waiting for the police to arrive. Now Marcus knew where
she was, that might be the worst thing she could do. No,
she was going back to find out what was happening. She
would just have to be very, very careful.

As she let go of the handrail, small flakes of white paint
came off on her hands, which were sticky with perspiration. She brushed them off on her jeans and ran down the
four steps to the path. Quickly she retraced her steps and
was soon back at the barn where she'd last seen Baldie

marching Marcus off to God knows where. She wasn't sure which way to go. Where was everybody? The only sound came from the wind and the leaves falling on the corrugated roof of the barn. Knowing that she had called the police, had they all taken off? Then she heard men's voices. She couldn't make out what was being said. She had to get closer.

She took a few tentative steps watching for any movement in her peripheral vision. She was beginning to wonder whether she should have stayed at the house.

The voices stopped.

Kate did, too.

The jarring crack that followed hurt her eardrums. The sound of the single gunshot echoed off the buildings. Ears ringing, she turned and ran to the barn wall, crouching sideways against it as if it would protect her. She waited like that for half a minute or so, but no shots followed. The shot had come from beyond the end of the barn. It certainly wasn't Baldie's shotgun.

Edging forward, telling herself to remain calm, she reached the end of the barn. Flattening herself against the rough wood siding, she paused, expecting the voices to resume any moment, but there was silence. The temptation, despite the risk, was too great. She had to step out of the cover of the barn to see what was going on. She only needed to walk a few steps.

What Kate saw sent a ripple of panic through her. She almost screamed but at the last second clasped her hand tightly across her mouth.

Not much farther than a stone's throw away, Kingston was curled up on the ground. Clearly he had been shot and was injured. Alex was bending over him. Twenty feet or so beyond them, a tall man in a windbreaker, holding a gun by his side, appeared agitated and was talking to Marcus. Behind them stood two other men. Petrified, she stood with her hand still raised to her mouth, unable to move or speak.

'Kate!'

Alex had seen her. 'Kate,' he screamed. 'Get out of here. Run!'

She hesitated for a second. Then, out of the corner of her eye, she saw Marcus leap forward. God! He was coming after her. She spun round and started running down the path past the barn.

Then she heard the gunman's voice bark out. The words echoed in her ears. 'Go get her, Marcus. Go get the bitch!'

Kate couldn't run any faster. She knew that her chances of outstripping Marcus were slim. If she stayed out in the open he would soon be breathing down her neck. He probably had a gun, too. Up ahead she saw the opening to the barn. She stopped in her tracks, skidding on the dirt path, almost losing her balance. The entrance: it was her only chance. She knew it was risky, aware that she could easily be cornered in there. She took a quick glance behind – still no Marcus – and stumbled into the barn.

Coming from daylight into the semi-darkness of the cavernous barn, she was running almost blind for the first several yards. She never saw Baldie, strapped to the post. She staggered right by him, part running, part walking, stumbling over debris as her eyes adjusted to the dim light. Her ankle struck something hard and metallic and she fell to the ground. Her eyes filled with tears of pain. Grimacing in agony, she got up, hobbled a few yards and started running again.

She could see better now. Sufficient light was coming into the barn through cracks and knotholes in the siding. She was scrambling through a narrow dirt corridor with stalls on each side, apparently once used for stabling. She stopped and listened. The muffled sound of Marcus's stumbling feet was getting closer. She leapt forward, running as fast as she could along the path, praying that it wouldn't lead to a dead end.

Suddenly the path widened and she was in a large rectangular area that looked like a hayloft. Frantically she looked around. She was trapped. Then she spotted a flight of stairs built against the wall. Without hesitating she ran up it into the loft. In the half-light she could see cartons, plastic bags and barrels stored across the width of the shed. Some were stacked high above her head. Nearby, old galvanized irrigation pipes, rolls of wire fencing, tools and lumber were stored along the wall. Gasping for breath, she hesitated on the landing, gripping the railing, uncertain whether to venture farther into the darkness.

Marcus's words made her spin round.

'You might as well come out now,' he taunted. 'Don't make me come up and get you.'

She still couldn't see him but knew he was right below her somewhere.

'All right, bitch!' he shouted.

Then she saw him racing for the steps, a gun in his right hand. She catapulted into the darkness of the loft.

Hurtling blindly across the loose planks, banging into objects in her path, Kate encountered a dark looming mass. She had stumbled against a tall stack of plastic bags. By the smell, they contained fertilizer or manure. They were piled on a platform extending the length of the barn. Kate jumped up on the platform and ducked around behind the bags. She was up against the barn's inner wall. She crouched in the dark, pulse racing, unsure whether to stay put or move farther along the wall. The stench from the manure was starting to make her retch.

There was a sharp crack, then an almost simultaneous thud, as something smacked into one of the bags next to her. Christ! A bullet. She stifled a gasp. A tabby cat, hissing and yowling, leaped from the bags right in front of her and skittered across the shed to safety.

A mixture of tears and sweat was coursing down Kate's face. The blouse under her jacket was soaked and clinging to her skin.

There was the tread of a cautious footstep on the floor-boards – and then another. He was now very close.

The footsteps stopped.

'You'd better come out. That bullet was not meant to hit you.' A pause followed. 'The next will – believe me.'

His words raised the fine hairs on her arms. Her heart was thumping.

A floorboard creaked as he shifted his weight from one foot to the other, edging toward her. Then the creaking stopped.

She had to move. With her back flattened against the rough timbers of the wall, Kate crab-walked along the narrow gap between the stacks of plastic bags and the wall, praying that the floorboards wouldn't give her away. Splinters of wood pulled at her jacket.

She heard a shuffling noise.

Then stillness again.

She stopped and held her breath. The cat meowed plaintively in the distance.

Inch by inch, she edged along the wall. In front of her, the bags were now stacked much higher – almost up to the crossbeams of the roof. At last, she reached the end of the loft. It had dead-ended. She was trapped.

A crashing sound made her recoil.

Another crash followed.

Then another.

Oh, God! He was heaving the bags off the platform. In only seconds, he would reach her. 'Come on, lady.'

'Jesus,' she breathed.

'You wanna play games? Fine by me.'

Her stomach convulsed.

'Come on,' he taunted.

He was standing directly below her, she reckoned. This was it. It was her only chance. And she would only get one shot at it. She braced her back against the pile of heavy plastic bags, and then put one foot up on the plank wall in front of her. She took a deep breath, then pushed off with all the force she could summon. The bags didn't budge. She grimaced. She needed more leverage. Manoeuvring her spine as high up as possible on the bags, she was about to push, when he spoke again. This time his tone was deliberate and mocking. 'Last chance, babe. Come out or start saying your prayers.'

That did it. Kate shoved, taxing every muscle in her

straining body, every inch of nerve and sinew, mobilized in one superhuman effort. Suddenly the bags gave way. Unable to check her momentum, Kate went over with the bags, tumbling helplessly off the platform.

Shaken but unhurt, she managed to stand up on the slippery bags. There was no sign of Marcus. She looked down at the lumpy pile. My God, she realized, he could be right underneath her. She had to move fast. She'd hardly taken a step when his hand lunged out from under the heavy bags and grabbed her ankle.

'Gotcha! You bitch!' he shouted.

Kate screamed. He was gripping the ankle she had bloodied earlier. Looking down, she saw that he was still partially buried under bags but his hold on her ankle was giving him the anchorage he needed to pull himself out from underneath.

He jerked hard. She tottered awkwardly, then lost her balance, falling, face down, shielding her head with her crossed arms and hit the floor hard. She winced as needle-like slivers of wood pierced her palms.

His relentless grip on her injured ankle was making it numb. In a matter of seconds he would be free.

Chapter Twenty-nine

Sweet rose, whose hue, angry and brave,
Bids the rash gazer wipe his eye:
Thy root is ever in its grave
And thou must die.

George Herbert

Kate dug her fingernails into the floorboards and pulled. She couldn't break his hold. She screamed, redoubling her effort, but it was no use. She had nothing to hold on to and simply hadn't the strength to break free of his grip. She began to cry tears of pain and frustration. Trying to blink them away, her eyes came to rest on a broken posthole digger and a garden fork. They were among a jumble of old implements stacked against the wall. Close to her, less than an arm's length away, was a shovel. The long wooden handle was weathered and grey. Despite age and rusting, it looked sturdy. She reached for it, fingertips barely touching.

Marcus jerked her backward. Turning her head, she could see that his upper body was now almost free of the bags. She could make out the tendons stretching in his neck. She looked at him with revulsion. His dark, ferret-like eyes bore into hers like black marbles, relentless and vengeful. She lunged forward, straining for the shovel. She barely managed to grasp the bottom of the handle before he jerked again. Kate turned, pulled herself up to a kneeling position, raised the shovel above her head, and swung it down with all the strength she could muster. She closed her eyes just before it crashed down on his head. A hard, metallic sound echoed around the barn. It made her stomach turn. She tensed, expecting him to scream. But no sound came, as he lay slumped, eyes closed, his cheek distorted grotesquely on one of the bags. She turned away from the sight.

Her leg now free, she scrambled to her feet and started to stagger towards the steps. As she did, her foot struck something small and metallic that slid along the wooden planks in front of her.

The gun.

My God! He'd dropped it!

She stooped and picked it up. Gripping it in her right hand, she turned and ran.

She could see a patch of daylight ahead: the entrance. What would confront her when she returned to the paddock, she wondered? She was fearful but determined to find out. She was almost out of the barn when she heard a strange noise. She stopped and looked to her left. Alongside a small tractor, Baldie – still strapped to the post – was furiously thumping the ground with his feet. He stopped when he saw he had her attention.

Kate put the gun in her pocket and ran over to him. Remembering Baldie's knife, she reached in his pocket, unfolded it and cut through the duct tape. She let him pull the tape off his mouth.

Cursing profusely, he told her how Marcus had outsmarted him. His shotgun was nowhere to be seen – Marcus had undoubtedly taken it. In turn, she explained briefly everything that had happened to her, finally telling him that the police were on their way.

Together they headed toward the paddock.

The fog was thicker than ever, swirling in grey curtains, beading the grass with moisture and deadening sound. From behind the cover of the barn, Kate brushed the damp sheen off her eyebrows and lashes and stared into the paddock. Barely visible, though no more than thirty feet from her, the tall man in the windbreaker she'd seen earlier was pacing back and forth as if waiting for somebody or for something to happen. He was still holding the gun.

Immediately behind him, looking out of place in the empty paddock, was a large shrub in a wooden container. Two men still stood by it. In her panic she must have missed it before. It took a few seconds to register on her. It was the blue rose.

A few paces off to the left of the rose, she could make out the blurry figures of Alex and Kingston sitting on the grass-tufted dirt.

All this time Baldie, standing behind her, hadn't said a word.

'They're waiting for Marcus,' Kate whispered over her shoulder.

'Is that your husband over there?'

'Yes. And our friend, Lawrence, with him. Look,' she said, 'I've got Marcus's gun,' and she took it out of her pocket.

'It's too risky, going out there,' he said, shaking his head. 'That bloke looks like a nasty piece of work.'

'He is. He shot Lawrence.'

The faint sound of a siren interrupted them. As they listened, it came closer.

'Thank God,' said Kate.

Baldie gripped her arm. 'Wait! Looks like he's about to do a runner. Quick, gimme the gun.' Without thinking Kate handed it to him. The minute she did so, she knew it was a mistake.

Baldie took careful aim at Wolff, but sufficiently over his head so as not to hit him, then fired. 'Drop the gun and stay where you are,' he shouted over the din.

Wolff, who had already started running, stumbled, then stopped, dropping into a crouch. With his gun raised straight-arm at eye level he panned it slowly from left to right, his eyes searching for signs of sound or movement. Kate froze, knowing that a mere flinch from her or Baldie could be catastrophic.

The sirens were loud now. Kate bit the inside of her cheek, determined to remain motionless, her eyes riveted on the gunman. It would only be moments before it would all be over, but in those few nail-biting seconds she knew anything could happen. What did happen was the last thing she expected.

Out of the grey drizzle a body hurtled horizontally through the air aimed directly at the gunman. It was Alex!

The man collapsed under the jarring impetus of Alex's perfectly executed rugby tackle. Kate closed her eyes for an instant, opening them just in time to see the man's body twist grotesquely and smash into the planter box.

It was as if she were watching a slow motion black-and-white movie. A sickening crack followed as the bone of his forearm snapped on the sharp edge of the planter box. His pistol went spinning through the air.

Unable to break his fall, the man had plunged face-sideways into the rose.

She gasped and looked away for a moment as his scream echoed around the paddock. Turning back, she saw the man writhing on the ground, one bloody hand splayed across his face. Alex had picked himself up and now stood over the injured man, panting heavily.

'Alex! Alex!' she shouted, running toward him through the mist.

Turning, he staggered a dozen steps, and wrapped his arms around her in a bear hug. Kate was shaking convulsively. 'Oh, thank God, Alex. Thank God it's over,' she breathed in his ear.

Alex was kissing her, on her lips, her cheeks, her eyes, her hair. 'You're safe now, darling. Nothing else matters – nothing else.'

She was about say something when Alex put two fingers gently on her closed lips.

'Shhh,' he murmured over the wail of the sirens.

For a short time they stayed locked together listening to doors slamming and shouting from the parking area.

She jerked her head in the direction of the man on the ground, not wanting to look at the grisly sight again. 'Who is he, Alex?' she asked.

'His name's Wolff. Ira Wolff.'

'His men kidnapped me.'

'We know, Kate.'

'Marcus, the one who chased me, is up in the barn. I think I might have killed him.'

'If you did, he bloody well deserved it. Let the police worry about him.'

'My God! What a nightmare.'

'It's ended, Kate. Finally.'

He held her away from him and leaned forward to kiss her forehead. 'Wait here, Kate, while I get that gun.' He let her go and walked over to where Wolff's gun lay on the dirt, and picked it up. Going back to Kate he passed close to Wolff, who was now half sitting, propped up on his good elbow. His face was a mask of dirt and blood oozing from a latticework of deep gashes. He held a blood-streaked hand splayed over his cheek and ear. The other hand dangled uselessly from his broken arm. He looked up at Alex through venomous, blood-caked eyes. His voice was laced with hate. 'I'm not through with you yet,' he growled. He coughed, wincing with pain. 'You'll be hearing from me, you bastard.'

Alex said nothing. He just stared down, slowly shaking his head. Finally, he turned away and said quietly, 'I doubt it. I doubt it very much.'

He walked over to Kate and took her hand in his. She put her head on his shoulder. Her eyes were pooled with tears, making white lines in the grime on her cheeks. She realized she was still trembling. Neither spoke. Her head remained buried in Alex's shoulder until the shaking stopped. Then they kissed.

'Is Lawrence all right?' she asked.

'Yes, he's fine. He was very lucky – it's only a flesh wound.'

'There were two other men here.'

Alex looked around the paddock. 'I guess they took off when Kingston was shot. Can't say as I blame them.'

'Who were they?'

'One was Charlie Compton. He owns this place. The other was our friend Tanaka, the one who wrote us the letter. I'll explain it all later, Kate.'

They walked over to Kingston. All this time he had been anchored to the ground nursing his wound, helplessly watching the horrendous spectacle that had just taken place.

Kate knelt beside him. He was still grasping his thigh. The scarf Alex had used as a bandage and Kingston's trouser leg were both dark with blood. His face was ashen. She looked into his eyes. Despite his discomfort, they still had sparkle in them.

'Looks a lot worse than it probably is,' he grunted. 'Bloody painful, though.' He managed a smile, nodding toward the barn. 'What the hell happened in there?'

'An awful lot, Lawrence. But we've got to get you to a hospital – I think there's an ambulance here.'

'What about Wolff?'

'Not too good, I'm afraid. He's a bloody mess – but I think he'll survive, they're only scratches.'

'Somehow, I don't think so,' Kingston said, shaking his head from side to side. 'Alex and I have an awful lot to tell you, Kate.'

Baldie, two policemen and two ambulance attendants carrying a stretcher were walking towards them. Then a third policeman, with a hammerlock on Marcus, came into view. Marcus's head was bloodied and he appeared to have trouble walking properly.

Kate gently patted Kingston's arm. 'And I've got quite a story to tell the two of you – believe me.'

Chapter Thirty

Shed no tears! O shed no tears!
The flower will bloom another year.
Weep no more! O weep no more!
Young buds sleep in the root's white core.

John Keats

'Well, Kate, we might as well polish this off,' said Alex, picking up the bottle of Veuve Clicquot and pouring the last of the champagne into their glasses.

It was an agreeable Sunday afternoon at The Parsonage, the sun going in and out, but enough to keep it pleasantly warm. They were relaxing in white wicker chairs on the flagstone terrace, at a round table draped with a Provençal print tablecloth. On the table, in addition to the now empty bottle of champagne and two almost empty bottles of wine, were the remains of lunch. It was a week to the day after the showdown in Sussex.

Kingston had left half an hour earlier to drive back to London. After his wound had been treated at the Victoria Hospital in Lewes, Kate and Alex had insisted – over Kingston's thinly disguised protestations – that he come back with them and stay at The Parsonage for a few days to recover. On the drive home, Alex had to suffer the discomfort and indignity of the Alfa's jump seat.

Towards the end of lunch Kate had expressed concern about the quantity of wine Kingston had consumed and had invited him to stay overnight.

'The offer's tempting, old girl, but I really must get back. You know I have an awful lot of catching up to do.

Besides,' he grinned, 'there is a limit to how many times one's underwear can be washed.'

In the hours and days after the Sunday in Sussex a clearer picture of what happened that morning had emerged. Surprisingly, it had all taken place in less than an hour. Nine people were involved. Of the nine, one had since died.

Two days after returning home, Alex had phoned the hospital in Lewes to inquire about Wolff's condition. The hospital spokesperson informed him that Wolff had succumbed to the massive infection resulting from his wounds. Describing Vicky's symptoms and death and pointing out the similarity with Wolff's, Alex urged the Lewes doctors to confer with those at the John Radcliffe Hospital. He was assured that the hospital staff would follow up on the matter and keep him informed of their findings.

They had heard from Charlie Compton, too. He had phoned Alex to report that the local environmental health officer had visited the site and that the Department of Health had taken custody of the rose. The official informed Compton that the rose would 'remain in the department's custody until further notice'. That was the government's official position.

Alex was curious to know what had happened after the two of them took off, when Wolff shot Kingston. Compton said that the minute he got to the office he phoned the police, telling them that all hell was breaking loose and that someone had been shot. He also told them about the shotgun blast, earlier. The police told him that they'd already received a similar call from a woman and that a car and ambulance were on their way. The policeman had been emphatic about his not going back outside, particularly with his shotgun, as he had wanted to. He told Compton under no circumstances should he intervene and that he should stay put until they arrived.

As for Tanaka, Compton said that the last he saw of him, he was running towards his car. He hadn't heard from him since. He also learned that the police had later picked up Tanaka's BMW, which turned out to be hired.

Questioned on the theft of the rose, Compton told Alex that he had no inkling Tanaka was involved in anything unlawful. He assumed, from the beginning, that what Adell and Tanaka had both told him was true: that Tanaka represented a wealthy Japanese industrialist who wanted to purchase the rose. And it was, of course. But Compton had no idea that it was Tanaka – or somebody in his pay – who had nicked the rose out of Nell's garden.

Not surprisingly, when news of the blue rose's discovery and the incidents and deaths linked to it hit the streets, an avalanche of press coverage followed. The story was splashed across the front page of just about every newspaper and magazine in Britain. The international press was quick to follow. Garden publications, of course, clamoured for stories and photos and several major American publications, including *Newsweek* and *Time*, dispatched reporters to cover Wiltshire's now notorious blue rose. Even pictures of the farmhouse where Kate had been incarcerated appeared in the press. She had filed a police report of her kidnapping and her time held captive, and had helped the police locate the farmhouse.

Then there was the matter of Graham's death. Soon after they had returned from Sussex, Alex had received a not-unexpected phone call from Inspector Holland, requesting a follow-up meeting. Naturally, Holland had seen all the press coverage. The get-together at The Parsonage with Kate, Alex and Kingston lasted over an hour. It was more cordial than the one to which Alex had been subjected the first time.

Holland informed them – as he had earlier told Alex – that at first it was thought that Graham had died from a heart attack caused during a struggle. But further examination by the pathologists had revealed that his skull was fractured. Blunt force trauma, Holland said. Confirming Kingston's suspicions about Tanaka's involvement, Holland volunteered that they had witnesses who had seen two men – one of them Asian – enter Cooke's house about half an hour before Alex and Kingston discovered the body. Alex, of course, was no longer a suspect.

Alex leaned across the table and put his hand on Kate's. 'It's going to seem awfully quiet around here for a while,' he said.

'Thank God for that,' said Kate, with a winsome smile. 'By the way, I gave Peg a sterling silver frame the other day for taking such good care of the shop and for looking after Asp while you were gone. She sold quite a lot of stuff, actually.'

'That was nice of you.'

Their talk turned to more prosaic matters, mostly concerning the house, Kate's shop and the amount of catching up facing Alex at his office. At a pause in the conversation Kate looked at him for a long moment, but said nothing.

'You look a little sad, darling. What are you thinking about?'

She tilted her head back and looked up into the coppery leaves of the Japanese maple that hung over the edge of the terrace. 'I was thinking about Vicky.'

Alex said nothing, not wanting to disturb her thoughts.

'All because of that rose,' she sighed. 'All because of that damned rose.'

'How were we to know, Kate?'

'I know.' She took a deep breath and exhaled slowly. 'I have to stop by and see Jill at the nursery.' She hesitated. 'You said you talked to her.'

'Yes, briefly, when Lawrence and I were trying to find out whether you or Vicky had taken cuttings. And if you had, what had happened to them. I told you about it. Since they had all died and had already been disposed of I didn't think it necessary to report it. But thinking back on it, I suppose I should have at least told the Health Department.' He shrugged. 'Of course, Jill never knew what they were.'

'Thank God she didn't handle them.'

'I should say. You know, in a way, it's just as well that

they died. They were a time bomb sitting on the shelf of that greenhouse. Ten baby blue killers.'

A startled look crossed Kate's face. 'Ten?'

'That's what Jill said.'

'You're certain?'

'I'm positive. She said all ten died from lack of watering.'

'Oh dear,' Kate said, biting her lip.

'What's the matter?'

'It may not be over yet, Alex.'

'Why?'

'Because Vicky took twelve cuttings.'

'You could be mistaken, couldn't you?'

'No. She took them early the morning you and Vicky dug up the rose. She put them in our garden shed until the two of you returned. When you did, she picked them up and took them to the nursery on her way home. At least, that was her plan. I remember offering to bring them in the next day because she wasn't feeling well, but she insisted it wasn't a problem.'

'Are you absolutely sure? It *was* quite a while ago,' said Alex.

'No, I'm sure of it. Vicky made a remark to the effect that she stopped at twelve because one more would have been unlucky. I thought at the time that a dozen was quite a lot.'

They exchanged awkward glances. Neither spoke.

Kate looked at her watch and got up. 'Just to be absolutely sure, let me call Jill.'

She turned and walked into the house.

Five minutes later she returned and sat down to face Alex, an enigmatic look on her face.

'Well?' he said.

'You were right. Jill swears there were only ten and that nobody else on the staff had access to them – only her.'

Alex frowned. 'Wow!'

Kate's expression was a mixture of resignation and disbelief. 'That means that two cuttings are missing.'

'Now what?'

'We have to tell the police, I guess.'

'The Health Department, too,' Alex added.

Nothing was said for several moments while they pondered the implications.

'Who could have taken them?' asked Kate.

'God knows.'

'Despite Jill's certainty, it could have been somebody at the nursery.'

'Not likely – Jill said she's the only one with a key to the greenhouse.'

'I suppose it could be any number of people. But how on earth would they have known the cuttings were there? And another thing, when did they have the opportunity?'

'Let me think a moment.' Alex folded his napkin neatly and placed it on the table, smoothing it out with his palm. 'We know full well that both Wolff and Tanaka would anticipate that we would take cuttings as a means of insurance.'

'Plus, we know that they were both watching us all the time.'

'Yes, but didn't you say that Vicky took those cuttings at crack of dawn?'

'I know, but they could have been watching the next day when she picked them up from the shed.'

'But from that point on, they were under lock and key.'

Kate shook her head. 'I don't know. It's just too much. Looks like the damned rose is going to have the last say after all.'

Alex was rubbing his chin, deep in thought. 'You know, there is another possibility.'

'What's that?'

'Well, we've been going on the assumption that the two cuttings were stolen sometime after Vicky picked them up, from the nursery. But isn't it more likely that they were taken from the shed while Vicky and I were gone?'

Kate nodded. 'Yes, I suppose it is.'

'Remember, Vicky was very ill when she picked them up. I doubt she would have bothered to count them. Why would she?'

'It makes sense,' said Kate.

'Question is, who filched them?'

'I suppose we'll never know for sure.'

'Somehow, I don't think it was Wolff. If it were, chances are that he would have mentioned it sooner or later. No, I think it was more than likely Tanaka.'

'But it's still a guess,' said Kate.

'Yes, but a calculated one. We know he had people watching us, and it's more than likely that they saw us dig up the rose and then followed us up to Aunt Nell's, which would explain how Tanaka knew where the rose was hidden.'

'I think you're right, Alex. We were all gone most of that weekend. I was at the shop all day that Saturday and stayed overnight at Peg's. You and Vicky were up in Shropshire. It would've been all too easy for somebody to take a couple of cuttings out of the shed.'

'I bet that's exactly what happened.'

A brief moment of silence was punctuated by the faint chime of the hall clock striking the hour.

'Then there's two more killers out there,' Kate said, in a near whisper.

A long shadow fell across the table as the sun vanished behind angry gathering clouds. A sudden and noisy fluttering. Then strident cawing, as the murder of crows took off from the stately cedar at the edge of their vision. Kate and Alex watched silently as they vanished into the grey distance.